CAMPUS LEGEND

JENNIFER SUCEVIC

Campus Legend

Copyright© 2022 by Jennifer Sucevic

This is a work of fiction. Names, characters, businesses, palaces, events, locales, and incidents are either the products of the author's imagination or used in a fictitious manner. Any resemblance to actual persons, living or dead, or actual events is purely coincidental.

Cover Design by Mary Ruth Baloy at MR Creations

Editing by Evelyn Summers of Pinpoint editing

Subscribe to my newsletter https://www.subscribepage.com/l5v9e4

LOLA

"**H**ey," Carmen calls out as she rushes past with a tray loaded down with food, "you've got a new table in the back."

I give her a nod and continue preparing a bill for a customer. "Thanks for the heads up."

"No problem." She throws a sassy smile over her shoulder. "He's hot with a capital H." To emphasize the comment, she uses one hand to hold up the large, circular tray while fanning herself with the other.

I lift a brow.

Here's the thing you need to know about my cousin—while I love her to death, she isn't overly picky when it comes to men...as proven by a long string of ex-boyfriends that goes way back to high school. There are so many, they could start their own club if they wanted.

So...do I expect her assessment of the situation will turn out to be accurate?

Nope. Not even a little.

As soon as I'm finished, I tear off the piece of paper from my notepad and beeline toward the couple before laying the check face down on the table.

"Thanks for coming in," I tell them. "Have a great night."

They smile in return, telling me to do the same. They're regulars at Taco Loco. Even though I only work part time, I see them here at least once a week. The guy is usually a good tipper. The girl...not so much. I'm lucky if she leaves ten percent.

Here's hoping that he'll be the one taking care of the check today.

I glance at my watch and huff out a breath. Only three more hours until my shift ends for the night. As much as I'd love to fall face first into bed and sleep for a solid seven hours, that's not going to happen. I have a ton of homework to plow through and a marketing test to study for.

Whoever said there's no rest for the weary was spot on. I'm only twenty-two years old and already mentally and physically exhausted.

The grind, unfortunately, is all too real.

And from what I've discovered, it never ends.

Just as I swing around, ready to head to the table in my section that was seated a few minutes ago, my gaze lands on the trio occupying the booth and my feet grind to a halt.

Oh, fuck no.

For a second or two, I remain frozen in place before slowly retreating, not wanting them to catch sight of me. I almost roll my eyes at such an absurd thought. Like they would glance up long enough to notice their waitress?

Unlikely.

The guy and two girls are much too wrapped up in one another to pay attention to the people around them. I quickly scan the crowded area before beelining to the kitchen, where I find Carmen loading entrees onto her serving tray from the long stretch of stainless steel counter.

"How would you like to do a favor for your favorite cousin?"

"I have a favorite cousin?" she asks, grabbing plates and strategically placing them on the massive platter. "Wait a minute—is Valeria here? I must have missed her."

"Ha-ha, very funny." When she grins, I say, "I need you to take the table that was just seated. I'll love you forever if you do."

"Don't you already love me?"

"We're talking forever," I say, impatient to secure her agreement. "Promise."

"Which table? The one with the hot guy?" She glances at me with a furrowed brow. "Why? What's the problem?"

I jerk my shoulders and try to keep my response casual. "Who said anything about a problem?"

With her attention focused on me, she searches my face with more care. "Do you know them or something?"

"Ummm…" I wave a hand. "Not really. I've met the guy a couple times." There's a pause before I reluctantly admit, "We don't exactly get along."

"What? I can't imagine that happening." She feigns shock by widening her eyes. "You've got such a sunny disposition and are so easy to get along with. Who wouldn't like you?"

With a scowl, I give her the finger. José, one of the line chefs, smirks before setting another plate under the lamps.

"As much as I wouldn't mind waiting on that hottie, I can't. I've got three tables left and then I'm out of here." She gives her booty a little shake. "We're heading to a couple of clubs downtown. You should join us."

"Can't. I'm here until close and then I have a ton of homework to finish up."

"Sucks to be you, girl."

Sometimes, it really does.

My teeth scrape across my lower lip. If there's one thing I loathe, it's asking for help. I'd much rather suck it up and do what needs to be done, no matter how painful, challenging, or time consuming. That being said, when it comes to dealing with Asher Stevens, I'm willing to make an exception.

I steeple my hands together. "Please? Just this one table. I'm sure they'll be quick."

Hopefully.

If they can stop making googly eyes at each other long enough to order their food and eat.

Her expression softens as she shakes her head. "Sorry, I really need to get home and shower before I head out tonight. If I didn't already have plans, I'd stay. I could use the extra money."

Damn.

Once she loads up the rest of the food, she swings away without another word.

It's just my luck to get stuck dealing with that guy after an already long day. I don't have much in the way of patience left. Although, that doesn't seem to matter when it comes to Asher. All I have to do is look sideways at him and my irritation skyrockets through the roof.

With no other options available, I straighten my shoulders.

Maybe I'm worrying over nothing.

So what if we've had two explosive run-ins?

That doesn't necessarily mean he'll recognize me. Asher is a major player on campus. Every time I catch sight of the guy, there are different girls hanging all over him. Western is a large Division I college and there's a ton of athletes who go on to play professional sports, but only a select few are treated with his celebrity status.

It's a little sickening.

All right, maybe more than a little.

I spend the next thirty seconds giving myself a silent pep talk before forcing my feet into movement. The smile pasted across my face feels brittle as I stalk through the dining room before grinding to a halt in front of their table.

Just like when I caught sight of them a few minutes ago, they're all wrapped up in each other. It takes effort to swallow down the acidic taste of bile rising in my throat. If I'm not careful, I'll spew chunks everywhere.

It's doubtful that would be appreciated.

Which makes it tempting.

"Hello," I mutter. "My name is Lola and I'll be waiting on you today. Can I start you off with something to drink?"

The girls barely glance at me. They're way too busy pawing the six-foot, golden-haired man sprawled out in the semi-circle booth between them.

Like a sandwich.

Gross.

He stares straight at me as a slow smile spreads across his handsome face. It's obvious that he remembers our encounters.

He only reinforces that suspicion by saying, "If it isn't taco girl, my favorite waitress. What a surprise to find you here."

My jaw locks as I grit my teeth. Keeping the faux smile firmly in place is no easy feat, especially when all I want to do is bare my teeth and growl.

"How about we skip the pleasantries, and you tell me what you want to order?"

The last time he showed up here with a group of friends, I might have called him a dick in front of my uncle and ended up getting my ass chewed out. I have zero interest in being treated to another lecture. Plus, my *tía* and *tío* have been good to me. I don't want my behavior to be a reflection on their restaurant. Trust me, I was obsessively checking Yelp reviews after the incident occurred.

So…if that means I need to be cordial to this knuckle-dragging jerk, then that's what I'll do.

But that doesn't mean I have to like it.

Or that it'll be easy.

It doesn't go unnoticed that he has a brawny arm wrapped around each girl. With his bright blue gaze pinned to mine, he hauls them even closer. The smile turns into more of a smirk as a strange sizzle of electricity zips through my veins before settling like a heavy stone in my core.

As soon as the unwanted desire bursts to life, I ruthlessly stomp it out like it's a kitchen fire that has the potential to burn down the joint. Asher Stevens is the very last guy on the face of the earth I want to find myself attracted to.

Other women might be taken in by his handsome face, chiseled body, and athletic prowess, but not me. I see him for what he is—a muscle-bound, steroid-infused meathead who drinks like a fish, smokes weed, and screws like he's being sent to prison for life without the possibility of conjugal visits.

When you live paycheck-to-paycheck and have to continually

worry about having enough money to pay for groceries and utilities, along with all the little necessities, you don't have the luxury of getting caught up in frivolous things that don't matter. At that point, life becomes very black and white. There aren't many shades of gray.

"Now, where's the fun in that?"

Fun?

There's nothing about this situation that even resembles a good time.

I narrow my eyes before shifting my weight. Is it really too much to ask that they give me their order so I can get the hell away from this table?

The less interaction I have with him, the better off we'll all be.

What's funny is that I've waited on my fair share of conceited jerks while working here, and I've always been able to smile and take their order without incident. Even the ones who hit obnoxiously on me.

For whatever reason, this guy is the exception to the rule. It defies logic how he's managed to burrow under my skin like a nasty infection that's in need of a steroid treatment.

Possibly two rounds.

When he remains irritatingly silent, I rip my gaze from him and glance at the girls. "Would either of you like to order?"

Neither of the blondes pays attention to me. One is nibbling her way along the thick column of Asher's neck while the other strokes lethal-looking acrylics down his chest. It's almost a surprise when the T-shirt doesn't shred beneath her sharp claws.

"They'll both have your hard taco platter with sides of rice and beans. And a couple glasses of water." He squeezes them again. "Right, ladies?"

When they coo and laugh, it takes every ounce of self-restraint not to roll my eyes.

I stare at my notepad while jotting down the order. "And for you?"

A few more seconds and I can escape his insufferable presence.

"You know what I'd like? A little eye contact."

I pause, lifting my gaze to stare even though it's the last thing I want to do. "Excuse me?"

"I said, I like a little eye contact when I'm being serviced. Is that too much to ask?"

My mouth falls open. He really is an insufferable asshole.

When I snap my teeth, barely able to suppress the growl rumbling up from deep in my chest, he actually has the audacity to chuckle. I quickly glance around for my uncle. That's the last thing I need.

When my attention returns to him, he's tapping his forefinger against his lips as his gaze roves over the menu. "I'll have four hard tacos, one beef burrito—you know what—make that two beef burritos. Three chicken enchiladas, and—"

I stop scribbling and glance up from the notepad. "Seriously? Aren't you afraid you'll ruin your girlish figure?"

He pops a brow as humor sparks in his eyes. "It kind of sounds like you've been checking me out. If you're interested, I'd be more than happy to show you that there's not an ounce of fat on me."

My cheeks heat as I scowl. "Hard pass. Anything else?"

"Yeah, throw a couple chicken taquitos on there."

I write down the last of the order before swinging away in relief. I hate how the air gets clogged in my throat, making it impossible to breathe whenever I have the sad misfortune to be around him. Sure, I'll admit that Asher is good looking, but I don't have time for guys who are under the misguided assumption that they're god's gift to the female species.

Actually, I don't have time for guys.

Period.

I don't get more than two steps before I hear, "Lola?"

I stiffen and grind to a halt before reluctantly glancing over my shoulder.

"I'd like a glass of water as well."

It's so tempting to give him the middle finger. Except I've done that before, and it didn't end well for me.

I jerk my head into a tight nod and stomp away.

Since Taco Loco is close to campus and the food is delicious, not to mention reasonably priced, we get a ton of student traffic. Most of the college kids I wait on are decent. Sometimes we'll get a group of guys who are asshats, but I've never had a problem handling them. A few well-placed snarky comments usually cuts them down to size. They're like wild animals—as long as you don't show fear, they'll grudgingly respect you.

For whatever reason, waiting on this one annoys the crap out of me. Instead of dwelling on the reason for that, I shove Asher from my brain and focus on the task at hand. The faster I get their order to them, the quicker they can eat and get the hell out of here.

I fill three glasses of water and drop them off at their table. Even though Asher's penetrating gaze feels more like a physical caress, I refuse to give him the time of day before taking off to wait on other customers. As I bustle around the dining area, I can't shake the feeling that I'm being watched.

Or maybe it's just my imagination.

It's a relief when I circle back to the kitchen and find their entrees waiting on the counter under the lamps. I shake my head, slightly awed yet sickened by the sheer volume of food Asher plans on consuming. If he actually eats all of it, we'll have to call Guinness World Records. And if I'm really lucky, he'll explode, and I'll never have to tangle with him again.

Wouldn't that be nice?

It takes two trips to bring out all the food. The blondes are barely able to stop pawing at him long enough to eat their meals.

I just can't with these girls.

"Is there anything else I can get for you?" I ask, ready to sprint away.

Asher's gaze stays locked on mine. "Nope, I think we're all good."

"Great." My pulse picks up its tempo as I force my attention from him, swinging away to check my other tables.

Fifteen minutes later, the girls have eaten half their meals and Asher has amazingly managed to plow through most of his entrees. It's a relief when he catches my eye and makes the universal sign with his hand for the bill.

Yay! As soon as he walks out the door, I'll finally be able to relax.

I give him a nod before grabbing his check. Usually, I write a little note of thanks, but I can't bring myself to do that this time. I glance at their table again and watch as one of the girls nips at his lower lip while the other snuggles against the broad expanse of his chest.

Ugh.

What a chauvin—

An idea takes root as my pen flies over the paper before adding a few finishing touches. My shoulders shake with silent mirth as I lay the paper face down on the table before saying sweetly, "Thanks so much for coming in. I really hope you enjoy the rest of your evening."

Before he can reply, I take off, laughter bubbling up inside me. There's no way I'll be able to contain it for much longer.

And here I thought waiting on Asher would piss me off.

Turns out, he managed to put a smile on my face after all.

ASHER

My gaze stays pinned to the dark-haired waitress as she speed walks from our table like her ass is on fire. There was a barely suppressed smile simmering around the edges of her lips. Kind of like she had a secret.

Dare I say it's the happiest she's ever looked while staring at me?

The expression hit me like a punch to the gut.

All right…maybe it struck a little lower than that.

I've run into this girl two other times and each one has ended in fireworks. Honestly, I'm not sure what her problem is. It's like there's a giant stick wedged up her ass. Most females melt at the sight of me, tripping over themselves to catch my attention.

This one couldn't be more different.

She'd rather avoid me like a communicable disease.

I dig through my wallet for a couple of bills as I grab the check and turn it over. All the food we ordered is listed along with the prices. Instead of double checking the items, my gaze is drawn to the bottom of the paper and the illustration of a pig with a bowtie around his neck. There's a bubble above him that says 'oink.'

My eyes narrow as I stare at the farm animal.

"OMG, that's so cute," Audrey giggles.

I glance at her with a raised brow. "You think so?"

She nods as Mallory chimes in, "It's adorable."

Yeah...I don't think so. I know damn well this girl isn't commenting on the amount of food I just plowed my way through.

Nope. She's calling me a sexist pig. I'm not a total idiot. I saw the disgust swimming around in her dark depths every time she was forced to look at me. Hell, I felt it the first time I walked into the restaurant and saw her behind the hostess stand. For whatever reason, she took an instant dislike to me and now, every time we run into each other, her loathing only ratchets up in intensity, radiating off her like a living, breathing entity.

Hmmm.

What to do...

What to do...

Option one—I ignore the drawing and simply pay the bill before hustling these two females out of here.

Or...

I slip my arms from around the girls. "I'll be back in a minute. I'm going to take care of the bill."

Mallory makes a few unhappy noises before sliding from the booth. Once I'm on my feet, she rises onto the tips of her toes and presses her lips against mine. Even though the softness of her mouth should be enough to recapture my distracted attention, it does nothing for me. My mind is too full of the snarky waitress with the slim body who scowls at me like she hates my damn guts.

"Hurry back," she whispers, voice full of promise.

"Will do."

And then I'm off, gaze coasting over the dining area, searching for taco girl.

I'm not going to lie, there's enjoyment in watching her eyes flash with irritation every time the pet name rolls off my tongue. Or how color stains her cheeks as she grits her teeth, on the verge of bearing them at me like a rabid dog.

Her anger shouldn't be a turn on, but I'll be damned if it isn't.

Is it perverse of me to get a kick out of her annoyance?

Probably.

But that doesn't change the facts.

It takes a few seconds to locate her near the beverage center tucked around the corner as she fills a tray of glasses. I'm almost tempted to rub my hands together in anticipation as I carefully sneak up behind her. I might weigh over two hundred pounds, but I'm surprisingly light on my feet when I need to be.

Once I'm within striking distance, I whisper near her ear, "Exactly what are you trying to imply with your drawing?"

She yelps before swinging around to face me. When her chest bumps into mine, she attempts to retreat, putting more distance between us until her spine hits the drink station. Her fingers grip the hard surface as she flattens against it.

"What are you doing here?"

There's a breathless quality filling her voice, and my cock twitches with a shocking amount of interest.

I hold up the piece of paper. "Any reason in particular you felt the need to draw this?"

Her gaze flickers to the check and her muscles loosen. Even though she attempts to hide the smile trembling around the corners of her lips, it's not possible.

"Of course not." Innocence fills her wide eyes. "Why would there be?"

Mine narrow in response. I'm more than aware I'm being fucked with. And not in a good way either. I probably should be happy that she chose to make a rude drawing instead of spitting in my food.

Well…let's hope she didn't spit in my food.

When I raise a brow and remain silent, she shrugs. "Customers usually enjoy my little sketches."

I almost snort.

Yeah, right.

Unable to help myself, I step closer, swallowing up the distance she put between us until it becomes necessary for her to tip her chin to hold my gaze.

"Somehow, I don't think that's the reason."

Ignoring the comment, her eyes dart to the girls seated at the table before she jerks her chin toward them. "Shouldn't you get back to your friends before they wander off? I'm going to hazard a guess and assume they don't have much of an attention span."

I shake my head and make a *tsking* sound. "Wow. Shaming other females isn't cool."

A burst of color scalds her cheeks as her mouth falls open. My attention drops to the movement. It's so damn tempting to yank her into my arms and crush my lips against hers. Except that would probably get me junk punched.

Her shoulders stiffen. "That's not what I was doing."

My gaze resettles on hers. Have I ever peered into eyes so dark?

They're almost black in their intensity.

It takes effort to focus on the conversation instead of the steady rise and fall of her chest through the colorful Taco Loco T-shirt she's wearing. "You sure about that?"

Her lips smash together until they're a thin, bloodless line. Any humor dancing in her eyes has long since disappeared. In its place is anger.

Bright and shimmery.

Sharp enough to cut glass.

"Yes." She grounds out the word between clenched teeth.

I cock my head, continuing to study her as her nostrils flare. If I had any brains whatsoever, I'd cut my losses and carefully back away from this confrontation. And I'd be sure to give her a wide berth in the future. She's been nothing but prickly toward me. There are plenty of girls who clamor for my attention, but this isn't one of them. For some strange reason I don't understand, I can't bring myself to do that.

A light floral scent catches my attention, cutting through the spicy aromas that hang heavily in the air. I lean forward and inhale, trying to figure out if it's originating from her.

Her body stiffens and there's a moment of silence before she whispers, "What are you doing?"

"Nothing." I take another deep breath.

"Are you...*sniffing me?*" Her voice comes out sounding as if she's being choked.

"Of course not."

That's *exactly* what I'm doing.

Losing the internal battle being waged, I swallow up the remaining inch or two of space that separates us until the stiff little points of her breasts are pressed firmly against the steely strength of my chest. Not only am I aware that the perfumed scent has grown in intensity, but I'm also cognizant of the place we're now intimately connected.

It takes effort to pick up the threads of our previous conversation. "What offends you so much about my friends?" My voice dips until it sounds like crushed gravel. "Is it that they're free with their affection? Clearly, a little PDA doesn't bother them. Did you ever consider that people like to watch two beautiful girls who aren't afraid to express their sexuality? Here's a thought—maybe you should try not to be such a judgmental prude in the future and adopt more of a live and let live kind of mentality. It might serve you well in life. Certainly better than the stick-up-your-ass attitude you have going on."

I didn't think it was possible for her eyes to widen any more than they already had. But I was wrong. They're now on the verge of popping out of her head and rolling around on the ceramic tile floor at her feet.

She sucks in a sharp breath and jerks upright. "Excuse me? Did you really just call me judgmental?" She drills a hard finger into my chest. "How dare you say that when you don't know anything about me."

I lift a brow and push against her finger. "Maybe not, but I know enough to recognize when a chick is sexually repressed."

Another gasp escapes from her. "That's not true."

"Sure, it is." I tip my head toward Audrey and Mallory. "Here's a bit of unsolicited advice—maybe you should try loosening up and taking a page from their book. Who knows, you might actually enjoy it." I allow my gaze to crawl down the length of her. "Maybe."

When a growl vibrates from her chest, I grin. It's almost too easy to stoke the flames of her anger and rile her up. I don't remember the last time I purposefully teased a girl with the intention of pissing her off. Maybe middle school. It was somewhere around eighth grade that I realized annoying them to secure their attention was no longer necessary.

This girl is the exception to the rule.

"Not that it's any of *your* business, but I enjoy sex just as much as everyone else." She pulls back her hand just enough to drill her finger into my pec again. "What I don't like is watching groupies hang all over a guy just because he plays a sport. It's pathetic."

Is that really what she thinks the allure is?

Well…let me kindly disabuse her of the notion.

I lower my face to the side of her head until my lips can graze the outer shell of her ear. The delicate fragrance I'd caught a whiff of minutes ago now inundates my senses.

"They don't want to be with me because I play football, sweetheart. They do it because I'm hung like a bull and know how to make them scream when I eat their pussies."

I pull back just enough to see her mouth tumble open for a second time before giving her a wink and strolling away.

If my intention had been to shock her into silence, that mission has been accomplished.

3

LOLA

Two and a half hours later and I'm still steaming at what that asshole said to me.

The sheer audacity of him!

And furthermore, he has no idea what he's talking about.

I'm not repressed.

Like, at all.

Well…not really.

So what if I've never been that into sex?

Between school and work, I barely have time to breathe let alone get involved in a relationship. The ones I've taken a chance on usually end up petering out after a few weeks. Shocker—most dudes aren't interested in being third or fourth on my priority list and usually show themselves to the door before I get a chance to do it.

Once I'm done closing out all my tabs and clearing off the tables, I grab my purse and jacket from my locker in the backroom before heading out. After sitting through three classes at school and then waiting tables for five hours, I'm exhausted. The realization that I have a test to study for along with thirty pages of reading makes me want to cry.

Unfortunately, there's no time for that. I learned a long time ago that tears are pointless. It's better to focus on what needs to be accomplished and plow my way through that than complain or feel sorry for myself. If I'm lucky, I'll finish up a little early so I can crash. Then I'll wake up at the crack of dawn the next day and do it all over again.

On my way to the door, I pass Carmen's younger brother, Mateo. When his feet stutter to a stop, mine do the same. He's still in high school and is probably at the restaurant more than I am.

"Yo cuz, you'll never guess who showed his face around here the other day."

Ugh. I'm almost afraid to ask.

When I raise a brow in silent inquiry, he says, "Tony."

Tony?

I blink. No matter what name I thought might pop out of his mouth, that wasn't it. My brain somersaults, and it takes a couple of seconds before I'm able to find my words.

He drags a hand through his jet-black hair as his face sobers. "Sorry," he mumbles. "I was just as surprised when he walked through the door."

I clear my throat, striving for nonchalance even though it feels like I'm being strangled from the inside out. "What did he want?"

He jerks his shoulders. "Dunno. Just asked if you were around and wanted to know when you're working next."

My belly drops into a freefall, and I have to moisten my lips with my tongue. "Did you tell him?"

His expression darkens as his upper lip curls with disdain. "Of course not. That guy can go fuck himself."

It's only when my muscles loosen that I realize how tight they'd become in a few short seconds. "Thanks, Mateo. I appreciate it."

"No worries." A smile quirks his lips. "I got you, fam. I would never do anything to cause you problems."

I nod, grateful for this part of my family. I don't know what I would do without them. Other than my mom, they're all I have.

He drops his voice before asking, "When was the last time he reached out?"

Years.

Four, to be exact.

I haven't heard a peep from him since the child support payments stopped the day I turned eighteen. Not that he was an actual presence in my life leading up to that. The most I'd get was a card in the mail on my birthday or maybe a small gift sent to the house at Christmas.

Other than that, nada.

"Not for a while," I mutter.

His fingers rise to stroke his chin. "I wonder what he wants. Don't you think it's kind of strange that he just showed up out of the blue?"

Yeah, it is. He was nowhere to be found when I actually needed him. So…no. He doesn't get to slide into my life now that I'm an adult and graduating from college this spring.

When I remain silent, lost in the chaotic whirl of my thoughts, he says, "He spoke with *Má* for a couple of minutes. I'm pretty sure she has his number."

"Tell her to throw it into the trash where it belongs."

He gives me a sympathetic smile before opening his arms. "Need a hug?"

Under normal circumstances?

No way. I'm not a touchy-feely kind of person. I like my space.

Although, after hearing that my biological father has popped up and is now attempting to track me down?

Maybe I do.

He grins when I step into his embrace. Before I know it, his arms are locked around me in a bearhug and he's lifting me off the ground.

"Damn. You need to add a little bit of weight, cuz. You're way too skinny."

"Thanks, I'll take it under advisement," I say dryly.

"Don't you know that men like chicks with a little meat on their bones?"

When he finally sets me back on my feet, I draw away enough to glare. "Men are the least of my concerns."

"Maybe that's part of the problem," he jokes. "You know my friend Eric?" When I nod, he continues. "He was in last week and you waited on him. Anyway, he thinks you're pretty hot and wants to take you out."

I narrow my eyes as my mind conjures up a mental image. "Umm...isn't he still in high school?"

His shoulders shake as he flashes a grin. "Yup. Is that a problem? He happens to like older women."

I roll my eyes. "Is the dude even eighteen?"

"Next month."

No, thanks.

Before he can say anything more on the subject, I rise onto my tiptoes and brush a quick kiss across his cheek. "I need to get moving. I've got a ton of homework to get through tonight."

"All right."

As I walk past the hostess stand toward the entrance, he calls out, "I'll tell Eric that you're considering it."

Even though I shake my head, I don't bother with a response. I know my cousin well enough to realize that it'll fall on deaf ears. He's probably texting his friend at this very moment that I'm interested and then I'll have to deal with that situation on top of everything else.

Pushing my way through the glass door into the chilly night air, I try to shove all thoughts of Tony from my head. Most of the time, that's easy enough to do. I barely think about the guy. He took off when I was six years old.

My mind tumbles back to the day he packed up his bags. With a pounding heart, I sat silently on the bed in their room with tears filling my eyes and watched as he folded up every piece of clothing before neatly stacking it inside the suitcase. After wheeling his luggage to the front door, he hunkered down in front of me and said he'd come by as often as he could to visit, and that nothing would change.

That was a lie.

One of many.

Everything in my life changed that day.

He stopped by half a dozen times before eventually disappearing from my life. When I was a kid, I couldn't understand why he walked away. It took years to realize that my mother struggled with mental health issues. Bipolar depression, specifically. Every day was a veritable rollercoaster of emotions with high highs and low lows. Some days were good, and I could trick myself into believing everything was fine. Others were the opposite, and she wouldn't leave her bed, talk, or eat. It was like she was an empty shell of a human being. Those were the scariest times, because I was never sure if she'd snap out of it.

Before Tony took off, I was shielded from the reality of who she was. He was always there to get me up in the morning. He fed me breakfast, took me to school, picked me up at the bus stop at four o'clock, helped with the worksheets I came home with, and prepared dinners. Maybe I ate too much macaroni and hot dogs, but at least it was warm and somewhat nutritious.

After he walked out, I was left to my own devices and quickly learned how to fend for myself. Cereal became a staple not only for breakfast but dinner as well. Thankfully, I could always grab a hot lunch at school. While other kids complained about what the lunch lady was serving, I gobbled it down and couldn't get enough.

When I was seven, I figured out how to drag the step stool to the sink and wash dishes. I discovered how to gather up the dirty clothes from our rooms and throw them into the washing machine. I ran the vacuum around our tiny one story and made sure everything was tidy and the bathroom clean. When I was older, I hopped on my bike and rode to the grocery store, using my backpack to bring home food.

Over time, I came to understand that Mama's moods were cyclical. When she was involved with a man, everything was good. She was functional and able to hold it together. The longer the relationship lasted, the more cracks showed in her thin veneer until finally, she splintered apart, and they'd break up. Then she would spiral into a deep depression. This scenario played out countless times like a broken record until I could predict when her life—and mine—would fall to shit.

I shake those thoughts away and slide behind the wheel of my ancient silver Ford Fusion before shoving the key in the ignition and turning it. This is exactly why I hate thinking about Tony. All it does is dredge up crappy memories that are better left in the past.

When the small car sputters to life, I send up a silent prayer of thanks. The last thing I need is for my baby to break down. Every cent I earn from working at my uncle's restaurant gets divided between a tiny savings account I started a few years ago and paying the bills.

Mama is currently between jobs and boyfriends. The last one decided her mood swings were too much to deal with and pulled a disappearing act. They'd been together for six rocky months. After he vanished from her life, she stopped showing up for work and after a couple of weeks, they fired her.

It was during my junior year of high school that I took an AP Psychology class and recognized her symptoms. I was able to convince her to set up an appointment with a psychologist. She's tried a lot of different medications, and some have worked better than others, but nothing has been a cure-all.

There are times when I lay awake at night, wondering what she'll do when I finally move out. The idea of leaving Mom to her own devices scares the shit out of me. Obviously, I won't be able to go far, but at some point, I'll need my own space.

Hell, maybe even a boyfriend.

As much as I would have loved to move into the dorms freshman year, the scholarship I received only covered the cost of tuition and books. Hitting Tony up for money was out of the question.

When I played soccer in middle school, my coaches urged me to try out for a competitive travel team. I knew it would be expensive and worked up the courage to ask if he would be willing to cover the cost. Even part of it. He told me that he'd just bought a new house and couldn't afford it.

That was the first and last time I asked him for anything.

Unwilling to dwell on those ugly memories, I turn on the radio and crank up the music. It's just earsplitting enough to blast him from my thoughts. By the time I pull into the driveway of our tiny ranch, I've refocused my mind on the work that needs to be accomplished before I can delve between the sheets and grab a couple hours of sleep.

A small lamp illuminates the living room as I slip inside the house. Even though it's only ten o'clock, silence surrounds me, making it feel as if I'm the only one here. The locks click quietly into place as I beeline to the short hallway on the left where our bedrooms are located before tapping lightly on Mama's closed door.

When there's no response, I press my ear to the thin wood and listen for any sign of movement from within. A handful of seconds later, I turn the handle and push it open before peeking inside. I find her curled on her side and snoring lightly. My gaze combs the darkness, finding a few pill bottles on the nightstand.

It's tempting to wake her and make sure she called her therapist for an appointment, but there's no point in doing it right now. The office is closed. It'll have to be dealt with before I leave for school in the morning.

For a few silent minutes, I watch her sleep before tiptoeing from her room and heading to my own. There's barely enough space for a twin mattress and dresser. A couple years ago, I painted the walls lavender, hoping it would spruce up the area and make it more cheerful.

Once inside, I close the door and lean against the hollow wood. My backpack slips from my shoulder before landing on the floor near my feet with a soft thud. Now that I'm finally home, exhaustion crashes over me like a tidal wave. I can't remember the last time it wasn't there, threatening to suck me under. It would be all too easy to give up, drop out of college, and find a full-time job so I can stop busting my ass from sunup to sundown every single day.

But I refuse to do that.

Especially when the end goal is so close that I can practically taste it.

I just have to hang in there for a little bit longer.

4

ASHER

I push open the lecture hall doors and pause over the threshold. If the people filing in behind me are irritated that I've created a traffic jam and they have to wait, they keep their traps shut. As my gaze coasts over the sea of students, Mallory swivels in her seat before waving. It's like she's got a tracking device attached to me and knows the exact moment I step foot in the room. The two girls parked next to her mimic her exuberant movements. All three wear big, toothy grins as their hands flutter through the air.

With a nod of acknowledgment, I move down the thinly carpeted steps to the row they're parked in. Audrey slides over, quickly making room for me in the middle of the trio. I drop my backpack before settling on the chair for the next fifty minutes. These girls are the only thing that makes this lecture bearable.

"You're late," Mallory whispers. "I wasn't sure if you were even going to make it."

Dr. Nichols has a strict policy regarding tardiness. Her philosophy is that if you can't get your ass here on time, don't bother showing up at all. And hey—I'd be more than happy to oblige; except I'd fail the course and I need it to graduate.

Just as I'm about to respond, the dragon herself stomps to the podium and clears her throat. It's almost a surprise when fire doesn't shoot out of her mouth, burning us all alive. Her narrowed gaze settles on me for a long moment before sliding over the rest of the students. She stands ramrod straight before launching into a long-winded lecture about the theoretical approaches to the study of relational communications.

Three.

Two.

One.

My eyelids droop, and it becomes a fight to stay awake. As she continues to drone, I settle in my seat and carefully slip my phone from my pocket before scrolling through ESPN to check stats.

We have two more regular season games before playoffs and then, hopefully, we'll make it to the conference championship in California. This is my last year playing college ball and I want to go out with a bang. Adding one more championship ring to my collection would definitely do that. Then there'll be the NFL Combine at the beginning of March and the draft in April. I'm so damn close to making all my dreams come true. I just have to stay focused and keep my eyes on the prize.

With a loud yawn, I realize Dr. Nichols is on the verge of wrapping up class. And not a moment too soon. This lecture is boring as hell and our professor doesn't help matters. By the looks of her, she's older than dirt. Her voice has one level and that's monotone. It's like she's actually trying to lull her students to sleep.

All I have to say is thank fuck for Mallory, Aimee, and Audrey.

"I just emailed your notes and highlighted the important parts you should spend extra time reviewing," Mallory says, cutting into my thoughts.

I flash her a grin. How amazing is this girl? "Thanks, you're a real doll."

She flutters her lashes before leaning closer and stroking one hand along my bicep. "You're welcome. Want to get together later and study for the upcoming test?"

I smirk, knowing that's not what she has in mind. "If you'll remember the last time you came over to help, we didn't crack open the book once."

Obviously, I bombed that exam.

But still, we had a damn good time.

A blush hits her cheeks as her eyes light up. "We'll just have to study first and then, if you do well—"

"I can help, too," Audrey interrupts eagerly.

Grinning, I throw an arm around her shoulders before tugging her curvy little body close. "Of course you can help, sweetheart. We all know I need every bit of assistance I can get." They giggle and press closer. "You ladies ready to get the hell out of here?"

All three nod before packing up their books and computers.

With a stretch, I rise from my seat. As far as I'm concerned, graduation can't come soon enough. I'm tired of these boring-ass classes taking up my time. I just want to focus on football. It's the only thing I give a damn about.

"Mr. Stevens, I'd like a word before you leave," Dr. Nichols says, voice ringing sharply throughout the spacious room and cutting into my thoughts like a dull-edged knife.

I blink in surprise, focusing my attention on the tiny woman standing next to the podium with a thick stack of papers in her hands. "Me?"

She lifts a brow. "You are Mr. Stevens, are you not?"

Unfortunately.

Her cool gaze encompasses the girls who flank me. "You three, as well. I'd actually like to have a word with all of you."

Mallory pales, giving me a bit a side-eye before the four of us reluctantly walk down the shallow stairs to the front of the lecture hall. The rest of the students flee as if running for their very lives. I can't help but watch them vacate the area with longing.

I clear my throat and shift my weight. "I, um, wish I could, but there's someplace I need to be."

Dr. Nichols narrows her eyes. "I'm sure you can put off your gym time for ten minutes. The weights will still be there when you arrive."

My lips flatten.

Well, hell. Has this woman been stalking my schedule or something?

Because that's not creepy at all.

She quickly dismisses me, giving each girl a steely-eyed stare until all three are cowering, practically shaking in their high heel boots. "From now on, none of you will take notes for Mr. Stevens or," she sets the papers on the podium before lifting her hands to make air quotes, "assist him with homework." She glares at each one in turn until they drop their gazes, ruddy color hitting their cheeks. "Because that's exactly what's been happening this semester, isn't it?"

All three mumble their agreements.

"If I even suspect that you're completing work or taking notes for Mr. Stevens again, it will be an automatic fail for this class."

Every single one of their mouths fall open.

And not in a good way, either.

"Are there any questions?" the dragon asks.

Mallory chews her pink-slicked lip before giving her head a little shake. The other two follow her lead.

"Excellent. You're dismissed."

This is such bullshit.

Who does this woman think she is?

When I swing around, ready to stomp away, she snaps, "Not you, Mr. Stevens. I want a private word without your entourage."

Great.

With my teeth clenched tightly, I turn back to her as the three girls sprint from the lecture hall. A few seconds later, the door swings closed behind them, echoing throughout the space, leaving me alone with this woman who probably moonlights as the crypt keeper.

An uncomfortable silence falls over us as she continues to glare. "I suspect that you've spent your entire academic career skating blithely by at this university, and it stops now. At least, it does in my class. From here on out, you will be attentive, diligently take your own notes, and complete your own homework assignments. In essence, Mr. Stevens, you will become something you have never been—a model student. I'm saddened to say that this institution has failed you miserably, and I won't stand by a moment longer and allow it to continue."

I blink and try to wrap my head around everything she just dumped on me.

It almost sounds like...

Like...

I'm on my own.

What the actual fuck?

When I open my mouth to argue, one rail-thin hand slices through the air, cutting me off.

"I don't want to hear any excuses. And don't bother crying to Coach Richards about this, either." A triumphant glint sparks to life in her dull gray eyes. "Not only am I tenured, but I'll be retiring at the end of the spring semester. There is nothing the administration can do to compel me to bend the rules for the athletes at this university. For too many years, I've been forced to turn a blind eye and award students with passing grades who didn't deserve it. The integrity of this institution has unfortunately been compromised by people who, like you, don't give a damn about their education. That ends here —*now*—with me."

Any moment, this woman is going to start frothing at the mouth. I'd like to escape before that happens.

My head continues to spin as I mentally scramble to figure a way out of this mess.

Is it too late to withdraw from this class?

Fuck. I can't do that. I need it for graduation. Even if I dropped out at this point, the dragon is the only one who teaches this specific course. I'll be stuck with her in the spring, and there's no way I'll be able to endure this again.

When I remain silent, she continues. "There's one month left before the semester comes to an end."

A whole fucking month?

How the hell am I going to make it through that long on my own?

I haven't paid any attention to the lectures. I've spent a good portion of this semester scrolling through ESPN, checking out lifting regimens, and watching TikTok. There's some funny shit on there.

Mallory and the other girls take diligent notes, complete my homework, and turn in any assigned projects. All of which received As. The only thing I do is show up to class and take the actual tests and quizzes. Even though I glance over the information the night before, I usually eke out a D.

There's no way I'll pass this class on my own.

And she damn well knows it.

Dr. Nichols rifles through a bunch of papers before setting a thick stack on the podium. My gaze drops to them in curiosity before realizing it's everything I completed throughout the semester.

All right, obviously I didn't complete any of it. Not technically. I added my John Hancock to the top when necessary.

"You know, Mr. Stevens…I thought it quite odd that your homework assignments along with your project had been exceptionally well done. The details added and the fleshing out of ideas speak of a student who has a high level of mastery over the material."

She flips through a few examples before holding them up as evidence. "Wouldn't you agree with that assessment?"

I clear my throat and shift my weight. Unfortunately, I know exactly in what direction this convo is heading. I've watched enough crime dramas to recognize entrapment when I see it. "Yeah. I guess so."

"There's no *I guess so* about it, Mr. Stevens. This is exemplary work."

Again, she flicks through the stack before pulling out half a dozen exams. "And yet, all these tests tell a very different story. They suggest the person taking them has almost no grasp of the concepts." There's a pause as her cool, gray eyes sharpen. "I'm sure even you can understand how that would be confusing…right?"

Since that seems more like a rhetorical question, I remain silent. There's no point to incriminating myself any further. We both know what the truth of the matter is.

"You failed one test miserably and barely scraped by on the others.

Homework is fifty percent of your grade, which means that you're passing this class with a C-."

A bad feeling flares to life in the pit of my gut as I wait to hear how she's going to fuck my life up.

Because I can tell it's coming.

Like a runaway train barreling down the tracks.

"Instead of automatically failing you, I've decided the only fair thing to do is wipe your previous grades from the book." She angles her head. "Since you didn't actually earn them. The remainder of the semester will hinge upon what marks you receive moving forward from this day. Do you understand what I'm telling you, Mr. Stevens?"

"Yeah," I say with a grunt. "I get it."

A slow smile curls around the edges of her lips. It's probably the first one I've seen from her. It's a little frightening.

Maybe more than a little.

"Excellent."

The words escape before I can stop them. "I hope you realize that if I fail anything, I'll get benched."

Her eyes become even more wintery. Any second, my balls will freeze and fall right off.

"Then I suggest you not only study but work hard so that doesn't occur. The grade you earn in this class is now in your hands. Not mine. And not your harem's." She gathers up all the paperwork before shoving it toward me. "My advice is that you relearn all this material, because you'll see it again on the final."

When I stare at the thick pile in dismay, she snaps, "You are *now* dismissed."

My fingers bite into the stack, crumpling them as I swing around and stalk out of the lecture hall.

Fucking dragon.

When I strolled in here the first day of class and got a good look at the professor, I had a sneaking suspicion she'd find a way to make my life hell. It might have taken a few months, but I wasn't wrong.

5

———

LOLA

I slip my phone from my back pocket and glance at the screen as I hustle my way across campus. At this early hour, I'm still bleary-eyed and barely functional. I was up later than anticipated last night. A homework assignment that should have taken an hour took almost three.

I didn't fall face first into bed until after two o'clock, and then my alarm failed to go off. Or maybe I forgot to set it. At this point, I have no idea. All I'm trying to do is make it to class before it begins. Dr. Harrison is a real stickler for punctuality, and I don't want to do anything that will land me on his shit list.

Since I barely had time to throw my hair up into a ponytail, there was no way I could make a cup of coffee to go. And I'm definitely feeling the effects of it. At this point, I'd consider trading my future firstborn for an extra-large Robusta.

A frown tugs at the corners of my lips as I stare at the cell, noticing a missed call from Tony. This is the third time he's reached out.

When the Communications building comes into view, I hasten my pace. It's already after nine and I'm officially late. Just as I reach the wide stone steps, my phone rings. My attention shifts to the screen, hoping it isn't Tony again. If he keeps this up, I'll block his ass. As I slide my thumb over the screen to decline the call, I smack into a hard body and stumble back a few paces. My arms pinwheel as I lose my balance and the phone slips from my hand, dropping to the concrete with a thud.

Strong fingers wrap around my upper arms, yanking me close as we fall like a redwood. In that moment of shocked suspension, I'm tucked against a steely chest as muscular arms band around me. Instinct kicks in as I squeeze my eyes tightly closed and brace for impact. When we finally hit the ground, there's a grunt as we roll to the side. I end up sprawled on top of a hard body, only to find myself staring down into bright blue depths. It feels like my brain has been rattled as I blink and attempt to find my bearings. As soon as I do, my eyes narrow.

Could this morning get any worse?

"You."

White teeth flash in the sunlight that streams down on us. "Ahh, taco girl. My favorite repressed waitress."

I huff out an annoyed breath. Of all the people at this university I could have collided with, it had to be him. I mean, of course it did.

"I am not repressed," I grumble.

Even though he absorbed the brunt of the fall and must be in pain, he still smirks. "That's what you claimed."

My lips pull back into a snarl. I can almost feel the growl vibrating deep in my chest. Barely have I glanced at him, and tension is already filling every muscle in my body as anger bubbles up like a geyser. It's tempting to snap at him like a rabid dog.

It's aggravating.

No, *he's* aggravating. If I never ran into Asher Stevens again for my entire life, it would be much too soon. For some reason, it's like I can't get away from the guy.

As we stare, I become aware that his arms are banded around me, and our faces are scant inches apart. Minty fresh breath drifts across my lips as my body rises and falls with each of his steady inhalations. My palms settle against his broad chest as I force myself upward. His hands lock around my waist, the fingers slipping beneath the hem of my sweater, singeing my bare skin as he holds me anchored in place. Sparks of awareness surge through me at the innocuous contact.

My legs fall to the sides, and I find myself straddling lean hips. An unexpected wave of arousal crashes over me, threatening to drag me under. Say what you want about the guy, but he's all chiseled strength. When his cock jerks, I realize that it's nestled against the vee between my thighs.

Eyes widening, I freeze. Oh, god...please tell me this isn't happening.

What makes the situation even worse is the way my panties are flooding with heat. It's like my brain has gone on hiatus and I have no idea how to jump start it into action.

The smirk marring his handsome face slowly grows into a wicked smile. "Like what you're feeling?"

My mouth falls open.

Did that seriously come out of his mouth?

What am I asking?

Of course it did.

I might not know Asher Stevens well, but the guy has already proven himself to be a conceited jackass. And yet, I remain paralyzed, unable to move a muscle. My brain is firing off all sorts of urgent messages to the rest of my body, but they're not being received. When I remain immobile, his fingers tighten around my waist, pulling me to him as he rolls his hips until I'm able to feel every bit of his hard length.

My reaction is instantaneous. Heat explodes deep within my core before echoing throughout my body until it reaches my fingertips and toes. The delicious friction has my eyelids dropping, becoming half-mast as my teeth sink into my lower lip. It takes effort to bite back the groan that rises in my throat before desperately trying to find a way free.

For years, I've heard the rumors that sweep through campus regarding the size of Asher's...equipment. From what I'm able to feel, it would seem like all the gossip is true.

When he flexes his hips for a second time, I come alive and roll to the side so I can get away from him and the strange sensations he's able to rouse within me so easily.

I don't like it.

Not one bit.

All I can say is that it's been a long time since I've been with a guy. That's the only reasonable explanation for my reaction and the excitement rushing through my system, lighting me up from the inside out. It's almost a relief when my shoulder crashes into the concrete, filling me with pain, before I scramble onto my hands and knees. Even though I tell myself to avoid all eye contact, my gaze darts to his.

A smile curves his lips as his broad shoulders shake with silent laughter. That's all it takes for heat to flood my cheeks. In one swift motion, I jump to my feet and dust off my jeans. He does the same with a surprising amount of grace. Especially for someone his size.

This run-in has left me feeling out of sorts and panicky. The humiliation coursing through my system is palpable. As much as I want to pretend I feel nothing for this guy, that's clearly not the case. I'd thought it was simply annoyance, but now I realize it goes much deeper. Honestly, I couldn't be more disappointed in myself. When it comes down to it, I'm no different from all the silly groupies on this campus who throw themselves at his feet, begging for scraps of attention. If I understand anything from what just happened, it's that I need to get away from Asher and avoid him like the plague.

I spot my phone and bag on the concrete a few feet away. The backpack must have slipped from my shoulder when I smacked into this oversized neanderthal. As I pop a squat, he mimics the motion and our foreheads bump as we reach for the cell at the same time.

"Ow!" I grumble, pulling away and falling backward onto my ass. I rub my head and scowl. "Is it possible for you to stay out of my way for one minute?"

His smile never falters and for some reason, that pisses me off even more.

"I'm just trying to help."

"Well, don't," I snap. "You've done quite enough as it is."

"You do realize that you're the one who was staring at your phone and not paying attention to where you were walking, right? By the time I saw you, it was too late."

Grrr.

He's not wrong, damn him. I was staring at my cell.

Ignoring the comment, I hold out my hand. "Can I have my phone?"

His eyes glint in the morning sun streaming down on us. "Only if you tell me the magic word."

"Now."

He shakes his head. "Nope. Sorry, that's not it."

I will literally kill this guy.

With my bare hands.

"Please," I growl.

There's a pause before he carefully sets the cell on my palm. As soon as the plastic case makes contact, my fingers wrap around the slim device, and I rip it away. The only good thing about this conversation is that all the desire rushing through my veins has been snuffed out.

"You're welcome."

"Don't push it," I mutter, dropping my gaze to inspect the phone for damage.

Carefully, I brush away the debris and examine the screen. A breath of relief escapes as I scroll through a couple of apps and find everything to be in working order. For the second time in a matter of minutes, I rise to my feet before picking up my bag. Only then do I realize that there are papers scattered around us. Since my backpack is still zipped, they're not mine. When Asher leans down to gather them up, I silently do the same.

I grab the closest one and glance at the top sheet. The first thing I notice is that it's an exam for Relational Communications Theory. I took that class last year. Dr. Nichols can be a challenge, but she's an excellent professor and I learned a lot from her. The second thing is that there are a ton of red marks that make the paper look like it's been wounded and is slowly bleeding out. My gaze slides to the right-hand corner of the page and the number circled in bright red ink.

Sixty-three percent.

Shocker.

My previous embarrassment melts away as the corners of my lips lift. My gaze locks on his. "Ouch. That grade had to hurt."

As much as I'd like to say I'm surprised he's nothing more than a dumb jock, I'm not. It's precisely what I suspected all along. In all honesty, it's exactly the balm I needed to soothe my aggravation.

It's as if everything has once again been righted in the world.

The smile plastered across his face falls away as a scowl takes over. With a flick of his wrist, he rips the test from my fingers before hastily gathering up the rest. Several pieces of paper get crushed in his large hands.

Not bothering to hide my interest, I catch a glimpse of more low grades. If I needed any further confirmation regarding his mental aptitude, I have it in spades.

Almost gleefully, I needle him the same way he enjoys poking at me. "You know what's funny? I didn't think the class was hard at all. In fact, I'm pretty sure I got an A." I send him a faux pout. "Looks like you're having the opposite experience."

My reward for the comment is a glower.

There's no longer a smile in sight, and I can't help but relish it.

"Nichols is a fucking dragon," he grumbles.

"No way." I shake my head and grin. "I found her to be a real sweetheart. If you get on her good side, that is." Which clearly, he isn't.

"That woman doesn't have a good side." He glares at the tests and quizzes that fill his hands. "She's intent on making my life hell."

For a morning that started out like complete shit, it's improved dramatically. Knowing that Asher won't be able to skate by in Dr. Nichols' class with his good looks, charm, and football prowess has lightened my mood considerably.

I'm almost giddy.

Sucks to be him.

Ah, well...time to take off. I'm late as it is. I'm just about to skip away from the scene of our accident when he waves around the stack of failed tests.

"If I don't pass this class, I'll end up getting benched. And I can't afford for that to happen. Not now when we're headed into the play-offs and so close to the championship."

Oh my god, is he actually *trying* to make my morning better?

It takes every ounce of self-control to keep the laughter buried deep inside.

Asher might not realize it, but this is a little something I like to call karma. I'd tell him that, but I have the feeling I'd have to explain the concept in painstaking detail, and I don't have time for that. Plus, I'd probably need a dry erase board. My guess is that he does better with stick figure drawings.

And pre-school level picture books.

I shrug. "Hmmm, that sounds more like a *you* problem than a *me* problem." With a smile and wave of my fingers, I step around him, ready to haul ass. "Good luck!"

Instead of allowing me to pass, he slides over, blocking my escape. The smile fades as I glare. I've had more than enough of this guy for one morning. Make that a lifetime.

"Get out of my way, I'm late for class."

He ignores the directive. "Look, taco girl—"

My eyes narrow. "You know that I have a name, right?" There's a beat of silence. "And contrary to what you think, it's not the idiotic nickname you've come up with."

One thick brow slides upward as he cocks his head. "What's wrong with taco girl? I think it fits you perfectly."

All my lighthearted happiness goes up in smoke as I grit my teeth. It takes effort not to snap them like a wild animal. This is the only guy I've ever encountered who makes me lose my composure in the blink of an eye.

"Lola," I grunt. "My name is Lola."

"I'm gonna be perfectly honest—I don't give a rat's ass what your name is. What I do care about is keeping my grade above a C- so I don't get my ass benched."

I sweep my tongue across my front teeth. "Seems like that's going to be a challenge. Maybe you should head to your advisor's office and find out if there's an easier class you could transfer to that doesn't involve any real brain power. Or…you could just quit the team. Then you wouldn't have anything to worry about."

He gives me a well-honed death stare. "Yeah, that's not going to happen. Football is the most important thing in my life, and I won't let that dragon take it away from me."

"As much as I admire your fighting spirit, kindly discuss this with someone who actually gives a shit." I cup my hand around my mouth before dropping my voice. "Here's a hint—that's not me."

He tilts his head and gives me a considering look. "I could use a tutor, and since you've taken the class before and know exactly what that woman expects, you'd be the perfect one to help me through the rest of the semester."

Laughter rises in my throat as tears leak from my eyes. "You can't be serious."

I'm not sure what world he thinks we're living in, but that is *not* going to happen.

Like, ever.

His blue gaze sears mine as he warms to the idea. "I'm as serious as a heart attack, taco girl. My guess is that you don't follow football, but this season is an important one. If I'm not out on the field, it affects whether I get drafted and play in the NFL." He raises a brow. "Understand?"

"Here's what I *understand*—you have an entire semester of shitty grades. If football was so important, then you should have been working hard this entire time instead of trying to kick your ass into gear at the last minute."

His expression becomes pinched. "How was I to know that she'd put the kibosh on friends helping me with homework?"

I shake my head and scrunch my face. "What do you mean?"

When he presses his lips together, I think about the scattered papers on the ground. They hadn't all been low grades. In fact, a surprising number had been As, which doesn't make a whole lot of sense. If you put the time and effort into the assignments, then the tests should be—

Oh.

I shift, cocking a hip and shaking my head. "So…Nichols figured out that you weren't doing your own homework, huh?"

Un-freaking-believable.

Here I am, busting my ass with eighteen credits this semester so I can graduate on time and get a job. And this guy just skates on through, not even bothering to do his own homework. I didn't think it was possible to lose any more respect for him, but I just did.

He shrugs, unashamed of his cheating. Because that's exactly what it is.

"What do you want me to say? I've got a lot on my plate, especially when we're in season. And those girls were eager to offer their support."

Yeah…I'll just bet they were. Unwanted images of the females that were hanging all over him at the restaurant flood through my brain. I roll my eyes and shove them away. Now that I have the full story, I can understand why Dr. Nichols came down on him like a ton of bricks. She's not a professor to put up with shit. Not even from the athletes on campus who are treated like demigods.

Good for Dr. Nichols.

"As much as I'd love to offer my assistance, I can't."

"Can't?" He lifts a brow.

If he needs me to spell it out for him, I will. Slowly. So he can understand it.

"*Won't.*"

His tongue darts out to moisten his lips. "Come on, taco—"

When my eyes narrow, he trails off abruptly before clearing his throat.

"Lola." His voice dips, becoming deeper as he takes a step closer, once again invading my personal space and making my heart flutter. "Come on. I need help and you're in the perfect position to offer it."

"That might be so, but I don't want to. And even if I did, I don't have the time. Some of us do our own homework *and* have to bust our asses working a part-time job in order to afford school. So, no…I don't feel sorry for you one bit. Honestly, I find it refreshing that someone around here is finally holding you accountable. It doesn't sound like that's ever happened before." I raise both hands. "Welcome to the real world."

He blinks. "If it's a matter of money, I can pay you."

It's so easy for him, isn't it?

There's not enough money in the world to convince me to spend more time with him than I already have. I shake my head before slipping my phone from my front pocket and glancing at the screen. Great. Now I'm fifteen minutes late. Professor Harrison is going to have a field day when I walk through the door.

"Look," I snap, fed up with this conversation, "I need to go."

"Will you at least consider tutoring me?"

"Nope." It gives me pleasure to pop the P at the end of the word.

It's a relief when I attempt to step around him for a second time and he doesn't stop me. Without a backward glance, I hustle up the wide stone steps before flying through the glass door and into the quiet corridor.

That's twice now that I've run into Asher Stevens in a handful of days.

Which is two times too many, as far as I'm concerned.

6

ASHER

An hour and a half spent lifting in the gym has done nothing to diminish my irritation with the dragon. For a couple of minutes, I considered taking this to Coach, but I have a feeling there's nothing he'll be able to do. So, in the end, I didn't bother.

What I need to do is find a way to pass that class.

As I head out of the athletic center to my truck, a familiar ringtone knocks me from my thoughts, and I fish the cell from my pocket before answering it.

"Yeah?"

"Hey, dipshit. How goes it?"

One side of my mouth quirks as my brother's deep voice booms over the line. "It's all good. How's work?"

Jack launches into a lengthy explanation about securities and the current market. When he starts throwing in terms like 'fungible financial instruments' and 'ownership rights to holders,' my eyes glaze over.

Here's what I can tell you—I don't want to be a stockbroker.

Or whatever the hell he does.

It sounds hella boring.

After a couple of minutes of bullshitting, he asks the dreaded question. "How's school going?"

I clear my throat and strive for nonchalance. "It's good. Fine."

"Really? If that's the case, why'd you pause?"

I glance at a group of girls walking toward me in the parking lot. As soon as I make eye contact, they smile and giggle before waving. When a teammate shouts my name, I give him a chin lift in greeting and keep walking.

"I don't know what you're talking about."

"Sure, you do." Exasperation rings throughout his tone. With the 'rents living abroad, he's unfortunately become my de facto parent. "Which class is giving you problems now?"

Now.

I grit my teeth at the jab.

"And for fuck's sake, don't say all of them," my brother jokes.

Except...he's not kidding.

Not really.

Between the two of us, Jack has always excelled in school. Academics came easy to him. He didn't have a difficult time paying attention or following along. Not only was he class president, but he was also high school valedictorian. Then, he went on to graduate from Stanford summa cum laude before landing a plum job that makes a shit ton of money.

Needless to say, my folks couldn't be prouder. Jack is their golden child. The one who can do no wrong.

Me, on the other hand?

I'm more of a black sheep. For as long as I can remember, school has been a struggle. Even when I was in kindergarten, the teacher would place me on one of those weird bouncy seats because I wriggled around too much and couldn't sit still.

And from there, it never got easier.

Where Jack's teachers called my parents to offer praise, mine reached out to let them know all the ways I was fucking up.

Not paying attention—check.

Getting into trouble with my friends—double check.

A slew of missing assignments when the quarter was just about to end—triple check.

Bombing a test in spectacular fashion—quadruple check.

What made it even worse was that Jack was only two grade levels ahead of me. Each fall, I'd walk into a new classroom and the teachers would gush about my brother and what a talented student he was. It didn't take long for them to realize that I was nothing like him. We might have the same biological parents, but that's where the similarities end.

"It's a Communications class," I say grudgingly.

"Wait a minute, isn't that your major?"

"Yeah."

It's a relief when I click the locks on my truck and slide behind the wheel.

"Jeez, Ash. Maybe you need to stop partying so damn hard and buckle down for a change."

I force out an aggravated breath. That's been the standard refrain for as long as I can remember.

Just buckle down and get the work done.

Except it's never been that simple. I wish it were. My life would be a hell of a lot easier. I squeeze my eyes tight and remind myself that I just have to get through the rest of this year and then I'm done. I won't have to take another class for as long as I live. Relief rushes through me at that comforting thought.

Not wanting to discuss the issue with him, I say, "Look, I've got to get going."

His voice bursts over the line before I can hang up. "Have you talked to Mom or Dad lately?"

And have them drill me with the same questions before launching into a rendition of *why can't you be more like your brother?*

As fun as that sounds—hard pass.

"I was going to give them a call later." And by later, I mean weeks from now. Preferably after graduation.

"Yeah, right." He snorts, seeing through the lie. "Whatever you say, baby bro."

My lips tug at the corners as some of my irritation fades. It's not that I don't love Jack—or my parents—but I don't fit in with them. I never have. It's like one of those kid games where you have a grouping of four objects, and you have to pick out the one that's different from the rest.

I'm what's different.

I'm the one who doesn't belong.

Dad has a doctorate in Linguistics from the University of Chicago and works for the FBI. He's currently in the middle of a three-year stint at the Hague in the Netherlands. I spent a month there last summer, traveling around Europe. It was an amazing experience. With the draft in April and training camp starting up in July, it's doubtful I'll be able to visit after graduation this year if I get picked up by the NFL.

Mom has a doctorate in Nursing and teaches at Western. She's taken a sabbatical in order to travel abroad with Dad and is using this time to write a book on epidemiology, which is her specialization.

Jack is applying to prestigious MBA programs as we speak.

And I'm just trying to get through college.

"Well, do it. They've been asking about you," he says.

I wince at the not-so-gentle reminder. "I will."

"And for fuck's sake, get the Communications grade up. Mom and Dad will be pissed if you don't graduate in the spring. They don't give a shit about you playing in the NFL. They want you to get that degree."

A truer statement has never been spoken.

They'd be happier if I were more like Jack, and they could brag about all my academic accomplishments. Me potentially being drafted and playing a professional sport where I knock other grown-ass men to the field isn't something to gush about.

Trust me, I'm way past feeling butthurt about it.

It is what it is.

"I'm on it," I say.

"Later, asswipe."

With a shake of my head, I hit the end button and toss the phone onto the passenger seat before starting up the engine and flying out of the parking lot. It takes less than five minutes before I'm pulling up in front of the house I share with Rowan, Brayden, Easton, and Carson. Crosby's name might not be on the rental agreement, but his ass is here most of the time. Although, that hasn't been the case lately. In fact, now that all the guys are wifed up, they've been conspicuously absent.

As I shove through the front door, laughter and raised voices greet me. I glance in the living room and realize that none of the guys hanging out actually live here. Andrew, another senior football player, gives me a chin lift in greeting before refocusing his attention on the video game he's playing. There are a handful of younger guys and an equal number of girls chilling out. A few flash bright smiles and wave.

It's not even noon. What the hell are these people doing here?

Don't they have classes to attend or homes of their own?

Annoyance flares inside me as I shake my head.

Instead of joining them in the living room and getting my mind off the fire-breathing dragon of a professor intent on making my life hell, I stalk past before swinging into the hallway and slamming into my bedroom. Under normal circumstances, I'm more than happy to push off studying for a couple of hours, but that's no longer an option.

I'll admit that I don't do a lot of homework. Maybe an odd assignment here and there. In every class, I've found a few girls who are happy to offer their assistance. Is it my fault they practically insist on doing it?

Nope, don't think so.

It frees up my time so I can focus on important stuff—like practice and lifting. I've spent the last six years keeping myself in top form, knowing that the only path forward was getting drafted to the pros. You bet your damn ass I work hard in the off season with speed and agility training. Nutritional supplements and pre-workout. I lift a couple hours in the gym six days a week so that I'm a force to be reckoned with on the field.

Irritated by the way my entire day has been blown to shit, I unzip my backpack and yank out my Communications book. There's been a few times that I've flipped through the pages. It's boring as shit.

My official review—I give it zero out of five stars.

I have no idea how I'm going to plow my way through the fifteen chapters we've already covered throughout the semester. Thank fuck Mallory takes impeccable notes, or I'd be totally screwed.

I settle reluctantly on the queen-sized bed and crack open the tome. Less than twenty minutes later, my eyes have completely glazed over and it's a struggle to stay awake. And it's not even one o'clock in the afternoon.

This doesn't bode well for me.

After another five painful minutes drag by, I contemplate the merits of withdrawing from this class, even if it means taking an F. There's no way I'll pass it on my own. It's like I'm trying to translate Latin.

A soft knock has my head popping up. I don't think I've ever been more thrilled to be interrupted in my life.

Tossing aside the book, I call out, "Come on in."

The door gets pushed open before Audrey peeks her blonde head around the thick wood. "Hi."

"Hey."

Not waiting for an invitation, she steps farther inside the room before closing the door behind her and leaning against it. A sly smile simmers around the edges of her red-slicked lips. She's wearing skinny jeans and a crop top that clings to her breasts and shows off a fair amount of toned belly. Her hair has been straightened and she's wearing a face full of makeup. If I didn't know better, I'd think she was heading out for the night.

"Whatcha up to in here all by your lonesome?"

That question is enough to have me frowning. "I'm working on an assignment for Comms."

She perks up before pushing away from the door. "I can help. Nichols won't know if I fill out the sheet for you. I'll just make sure there are a lot of wrong answers thrown in there."

Hmmm. It's a tempting offer. Except...I don't want Audrey to get in any more trouble than she already has. The dragon will be watching her and the others like a hawk, just waiting to hand out Fs like gifts on Christmas morning.

No…what I need is assistance from someone who isn't currently in this section. Someone who already passed it with flying colors. Someone like the feisty female who refuses to give me the time of day.

How ironic is it that I could probably convince any female on this campus to help me with the exception of her?

I blink back to the present when Audrey settles on the bed next to me and strokes her talented fingers across my chest.

"You know that I'm a good study buddy," she whispers.

I almost snort. I've been down this road too many times with her before. The girl is good at a lot of things. Many of which have nothing to do with academics. I know exactly what will happen if I agree to her special brand of assistance.

And that won't help at all.

Even though it's tempting to push aside Comms and indulge in a little one-on-one time with the pretty blonde, passing this class isn't an option for me.

I can't afford to get benched.

Not even for a single game.

"I know you are, but this is something I have to do on my own." Those are words I never expected to pop out of my mouth. Guess what they say is true—there really is a first time for everything.

She leans closer, pressing her breasts against my arm before staring at me through heavy-lidded eyes. "Are you sure? I could always hang out for moral support."

"Maybe later, all right?"

The corners of her lips wilt as she gives me a full-on pout. "Promise?"

My brows draw together at the lispiness that bleeds through her voice which makes her sound suspiciously like a toddler. While some dudes might be into that kind of thing, I'm not one of them. Let's save the babytalk for the actual babies.

"Umm, yeah. Sure."

When a few minutes tick by and she doesn't budge from the mattress, I clear my throat. I don't want to be rude, but this shit isn't going to complete itself. And I've got practice in a couple of hours.

"Okay then…"

She nods before reluctantly rising to her feet. "I'll be waiting."

Great.

"Right in the living room," she adds.

I point a finger at her. "Got it."

"Just call me if you need anything."

"Will do."

By the time she reaches the door, I'm more than ready for her to leave. I almost groan when she hesitates, pressing one hand to her lips before lifting it in my direction.

When I remain still, unsure what she's doing, she says, "Aren't you going to catch the kiss and tuck it away for later?"

What the—

I hesitate before forcing my hand in the air before closing my fingers around absolutely nothing.

"Now tuck it away in your pocket for safekeeping," she encourages.

I pretend to stuff the kiss into the front of my jeans.

She grins before fluttering her fingers at me and finally disappearing into the hallway. As soon as she's gone, I spring from the bed and lock the door.

Sheesh.

For some reason, taco girl nudges her way into my brain, and I try to imagine her doing the same thing. Even the image is enough to make me chuckle. With a shake of my head, I return to what must be considered one of the circles of hell. And if it's not, it certainly should be.

7

LOLA

*M*y head is on a constant swivel as I pull into the parking lot closest to the athletic center. It's only nine o'clock in the morning, and already the place is jampacked.

I release a frustrated breath.

Had I been smart, I would have hauled ass out of bed an hour earlier and gotten here before the morning rush. Even if that meant working in the library for an hour or so, it would be totally worth avoiding this congestion.

Like a shark, I cruise up and down the rows before spotting a car that's leaving. I stomp on the gas, hoping to beat everyone else and get there first.

Score!

I shift the gear into park and wait for the shiny BMW to leave. As soon as they're out of the way, I pull forward. I'm halfway into the space when another vehicle slams into me from behind, jolting the car forward. My eyes widen as the seatbelt snaps, restraining my upper body from crashing into the steering wheel. My heart thunders until it feels like it'll explode from my chest. The sound of it roars in my ears, drowning out everything else.

Aw hell.

This is exactly what I don't need.

I shift into park before unclipping the belt with shaking fingers and slamming out of the door. Whoever just hit me is about to get an earful. Except, as soon as I stalk around the side, tires squeal and the vehicle takes off, speeding away.

"Hey!" I raise both arms in an *are you kidding me* gesture before grinding to a halt in the middle of the row just in time to see a dark truck with tinted-out windows swing around the corner and disappear with a roar of its engine.

Even though it's too late, I yell, "Get your ass back here!"

It's not a surprise when they don't return. For a moment, I stand frozen in place, unsure what to do. Even if I jump in my car and take off after them, there's no way I'll be able to track them down. They're long gone. And it happened so fast.

If I call the police or campus security and fill out a report, I'm not even sure what I'd say. I don't know the make or model of the truck. And it was dark in color but was it blue or black? Or dark gray?

I'm not sure.

Fuck.

"That really sucks."

Startled from my thoughts, I swing around, only to find Asher hunkered down, inspecting the damage.

My gaze fastens onto the back end of the vehicle. I was so intent on finding the culprit, this is the first time I'm taking a good look at it. I can't help but wince. Even though it didn't feel like a hard hit, the bumper is totally smashed in.

I drag a hand over my face, unable to believe this actually happened.

"Did you by any chance get the license plate or see what kind of truck hit me?"

He glances up before shaking his head. "No, sorry. I'm parked a few rows over and was just walking by. Maybe you should talk to campus police and see if there are any surveillance cameras that caught the accident."

I nod. That's a good idea. "Yeah, I'll do that."

As his gaze holds mine, unwanted electricity zips through my veins before settling at the bottom of my belly. Just as quickly as it flared to life, I quash it. I don't want to feel whatever this strange energy is that ignites whenever we're together. If I had my way, I wouldn't feel *anything* at all where this guy is concerned.

His hand rises to stroke the light shadow that covers his jaw. "I'm gonna hazard a guess and say that it needs to be towed."

"What?" My shoulders sink under the crushing weight of that statement. "Are you being serious?"

He grips the tread of the tire before giving it a good shake. My eyes widen when it wiggles, looking as if it might fall off. I don't know much about cars, but I'm pretty sure that's not supposed to happen.

This just keeps getting worse and worse.

I thread my hands through my hair before glancing up. Even though it's chilly, the sun is shining brightly in the vast stretch of cornflower blue sky. It takes everything I have inside to fight down the emotion that is welling in my throat and not burst into tears. I have no idea how much a repair like this costs, but it certainly won't be cheap.

It never is.

Most of the time, it feels like I'm on the cusp of drowning. I'm barely able to keep my head above water. And this expense will only suck me down further. It's so frustrating to bust my ass and never get ahead in life.

Asher's gaze swings to me as he straightens to his full height. "It shouldn't be a huge problem. Just more of an inconvenience. It's not like you don't have insurance," there's a pause, "right?"

My teeth rake across my lower lip.

When I remain silent, his deep voice rumbles. "Lola?"

"Don't you mean taco girl?" I say absently, unwilling to focus on the disaster in front of me or how I'll pay for it.

His lips quirk at the corners. "I wasn't looking to get junk punched this early in the morning."

I huff out a reluctant laugh before answering the question. "Yes, I have insurance. But my mom was in an accident a month ago and it was her fault. They've already raised our rates. Since there have been a few others within the past couple of years, they sent a letter warning that if there's another, they'll cancel the policy. So, I don't feel like I can report this."

The longer I study the wheel, which is now bent at an odd angle, the more I realize that Asher's assessment is correct. There's no way I can drive this home. It'll have to be towed and fixed. Which means more money I don't have flushed down the drain.

A suffocating silence falls over us as those dark thoughts circle viciously through my head before he clears his throat, drawing my attention.

"I have a buddy who's a mechanic. I'll give him a call and see if he can tow your car to his shop. At the very least, Declan can look at it and give you an estimate."

"I don't know," I mumble.

Asher Stevens is the last person on the face of this earth I want to accept assistance from. God only knows what he'll expect in return. Even the thought is enough to frighten me.

He hikes a brow and shifts his stance. "Do you have any other ideas? You can't just leave it here or the university will tow it away and then you'll have to pay to get it from impound. Trust me, it's not cheap. It happened to me in Pittsburg. Worst fucking weekend of my life."

My mouth falls open. "What?"

"Yeah, we went out to party Friday night and the next—"

"I meant about my car being impounded." When he continues to stare, I remind, "You said the university will confiscate it?"

He points to a rectangular sign behind me that clearly displays a graphic of a tow truck and the dollar amount for added emphasis.

Seriously, this just keeps getting better and better.

Even though I should thank him for his assistance, especially when every interaction we've had up until this point has ended in disaster, the words shoot out of my mouth before I can rein them back in. "Why are you being so helpful?"

Surprise flickers in his blue depths as he shrugs. "Ever consider that I'm actually a nice guy?"

With a snort, I fold my arms across my chest. "Nope, not for a single second. So, tell me…why are you doing this?"

He huffs out a breath and shifts his stance. "Like I said the other day, I need your help with Comms. You tutor me and," he points to my poor, beat-up baby, "I'll fix your car. It'll just be an exchange of services. Pure and simple."

Simple…ha!

This must be what it feels like to make a deal with the devil. I dredge my brain, searching for another way out of this mess. One that doesn't involve Asher.

Unfortunately, nothing comes to mind.

"Well? What do you say?"

There has to be something else I can do.

Maybe get another part-time job?

Except…I need to sleep. I'm barely managing with the amount I'm getting as it is.

"Fine," I mutter, disgruntled that this is what my life has come to. "I'll tutor you."

A slow grin spreads across his face, making him even more handsome than usual in the morning light that slants across him. I blink and shake away the errant thought. It's the last thing I should be dwelling on.

Especially if we're going to spend time together.

Oh god…I'm going to be stuck working with Asher Stevens.

Of my own free will.

Sort of.

Before I can second guess our agreement, he whips out his cell and arranges for his friend to pick up my car.

They BS for a couple of minutes before he hangs up. "All taken care of."

The relief that rushes through me is almost enough to weaken my knees. I hate to admit just how nice it is to have someone swoop in and deal with a problem. Even if it's as small as making a phone call.

"Do you need a ride home after class?"

Well, shit. I no longer have a vehicle at my disposal. Somehow, I need to get from campus to Taco Loco later for my shift. I guess I'll have to Uber it. And piss away even more money I don't have.

Moisture pricks the backs of my eyes, making it necessary to blink away the emotion. I refuse to cry. This isn't the end of the world. The car just needs to be drivable, not totally fixed. Hopefully, that'll lessen the repair cost. Even though Asher offered to fix the Fusion, I can't allow him to do that. At least, not totally. I'll have to cover the bulk of the expense.

When I fail to respond, he says, "Want to get together after your next class and work on Communications? Then I can drop you off at home. You live around campus, right?"

I glance away, not wanting to accept any more help from him. "I have a full day of classes. I'm available at three and then I have to work at Taco Loco." I'd been toying with the idea of dropping a few shifts so I could focus more on school this semester, since everything feels like it's been kicked into a higher gear, but I can't afford to do that now.

Most students enjoy their college years and want to stick around so they can party their asses off before getting a job with real responsibilities. That's never been the case for me. I can only hope that life will get easier once I graduate and start earning some real money. Maybe then I'll finally be able to stand still for a moment and catch my breath.

"Three o'clock doesn't work, I've got practice. And there's no way I can skip that. What time does your shift start?"

"Five."

He nods before fishing something out of his pocket and tossing it to me. My hands automatically rise to catch the small object that flies through the air. Once my fingers curl around it, I open my hand and take a peek.

Keys.

My brow furrows as I glance at him.

"You can take my truck to the restaurant, and I'll catch a ride after practice to get it. That way, we can work together after you're done."

"What? No. I can't just take off with your vehicle."

My confusion must be contagious because he cocks his head and frowns. "Why not?"

I blink. Is this guy serious?

How the hell can he hand over his truck to me like it's no big deal?

"Because…" Unsure how to answer that, my voice trails off.

He raises his brows. "Because why?"

"You don't even know me."

"Sure, I do. You're friends with Demi and you work at Taco Loco. Are you planning on hightailing it out of town or something?"

I roll my eyes. As tempting as that thought is… "Of course not."

"How many accidents have you been in?"

I point to my car. "Just one."

"And that wasn't your fault, which is exactly why that asshole took off." There's a beat of silence. "So…should I be concerned?"

"I guess not," I mutter. But still, I'm not comfortable with this arrangement. Then again, it's not like I have a ton of options. "What do you drive?"

He points a few rows over. "You see the white Escalade?"

I crane my neck and shift my body to get a better look. I wait for him to say 'I'm parked next to it.' If my eyes don't deceive me, it's an older model Chevy Blazer that isn't in any better shape than my car, which actually makes me feel better about the situation. "Um, yeah."

"That's it."

"Are you kidding me?" My eyes widen as my voice escalates. "I can't drive that!"

"Why not?"

"It's way too expensive." It probably costs more than the house we live in. And if that's not a sobering realization, I don't know what is.

"Sure, you can." He shrugs those impossibly wide shoulders. "It's only money."

Laughter gurgles up in my throat before attempting to burst free.

How do I even begin to respond to that statement?

The only people who would say something so ridiculous are the ones who actually have it.

All I can hope is that one day, I'll be one of them.

8

ASHER

I grab a towel after my shower and dry my hair before wrapping it around my hips. Every muscle I have and a few that I didn't realize were there are screaming bloody murder from being overworked on the field. If I weren't heading straight to Taco Loco, I'd sit my ass in an ice bath.

But there's no time for that, since I need to catch a ride to the restaurant. Even though I have zero interest working on this assignment, I'd be lying if I didn't admit that I'm looking forward to seeing Lola.

It's the strangest thing.

And it doesn't make the least bit of sense, but every run-in with her leaves me jonesing for another. I've never met a girl like her. One who is so blatant about her dislike for me.

I give Crosby a bit of side-eye as he yanks his boxers up and grabs a T-shirt. Now here's a guy who seems like he's in a hurry. And I can imagine why. Ever since he and Brooke McAdams made their relationship official, they've been glued to each other's hips.

It's a little nauseating.

He used to spend all his time snarling at people. Now, he's more like a tamed pussy cat.

I shake my head as my gaze flits over all the guys. Rowan is dating Coach's daughter, Demi, who also happens to be one of the star players on the women's soccer team. Brayden, Mr. Campus Heart-throb himself, is with Sydney, another feisty soccer player. She's not one to put up with his shit. It's kind of hilarious.

Easton is going out with his best friend, Sasha. A girl he's known since they were in diapers. And Carson finally decided to take his life into his own hands by dating Brayden's younger sister, Elle. I can't help but snicker, remembering how he'd been sneaking around behind his best friend's back. After Brayden found out what was going on beneath his nose, shit hit the fan. They've finally settled down, but they're not as close as they once were.

I'm the last man standing.

Or the odd man out.

I guess it's all about perspective.

Don't these boneheads realize they've got the rest of their lives to be tied down? They should be enjoying their final college year by being free as a bird and doing whatever the hell they want. Instead, they're sitting their asses at home, ordering in, and watching Netflix. For fuck's sake, just the other day, Brooke posted a pic of them wearing matching charcoal face masks.

Let that visual sink in for a minute.

Once I'm done drying off, I haul my boxers up. "Rhodes, can I bum a ride?"

Crosby glances at me before jerking his shoulders. "You heading back to the house?"

I shake my head. "Nah. Taco Loco."

"By yourself?" Before I can respond, he pops a brow. "Wait, wait. Let me guess." He pretends to ponder the situation for a moment. "Does this have anything to do with that waitress? The one who'd rather claw her own eyes out than look at you sideways?"

I can't help the slow smile that curls around the edges of my lips. "As it just so happens, I'm meeting up with her there."

He raises a well-shaped brow. Actually, upon closer inspection, it's perfectly sculpted. It makes me wonder if he let Brooke pluck it for him.

What a fucking pussy.

"Word of advice, if she gives you tacos, refrain from eating them. They're probably poisoned."

"Hardy har har. You're hilarious."

"No, really. Why are you heading over there?" He tosses his shoulder pads into his locker. "And where's your truck?"

"Lola borrowed it," I throw out casually. "I need to pick it up from her."

His eyes widen. "Lola? Wait a minute…are you actually talking about taco girl?"

"Her *name* is Lola. Don't you know it's rude to refer to someone like that?"

With a snort, Crosby shakes his head.

I can't help but grin. "Believe it or not, she agreed to tutor me."

"Huh. Will wonders never cease. And here I thought after she nearly bit your head off at that party, there was no way in hell the two of you could be in the same room together."

I shrug and spread my arms wide. "What can I say? I won her over with my good looks and charm."

"Shocking."

He picks up his athletic bag before hoisting it over his shoulder. "If you want a ride, get your ass into gear. I've got things to do."

I roll my eyes. Yeah, right. "I know exactly what you gotta do. More like whom."

He elbows me sharply in the ribs before grumbling, "Shut the fuck up."

My shoulders shake with silent laughter as we walk out of the locker room, pushing through the glass doors of the athletic center and into the cold night air. After a short walk to the parking lot, we slide into his Mustang.

A few seconds later, the engine purrs to life and we're shooting onto the tree-lined streets near the university. Taco Loco is located about ten minutes away from campus. The way Crosby drives—kind of like he's in a game of Grand Theft Auto—it's more like seven. He swings into the parking lot with a squeal of the tires and pulls up to the front door before letting the vehicle idle.

"Thanks, man." With my athletic bag and backpack in tow, I give him a wave before heading inside the restaurant.

Music hits my ears as I stroll past the hostess stand and find myself at the entrance of the dining room. My gaze coasts over the crowd, looking for one person in particular. It's just after six o'clock and almost every table is filled with either families or hungry college students looking for a meal that doesn't cost an arm and a leg.

It doesn't take long to locate her. For a few seconds, I watch her in action while she's not aware of my perusal. There's a serious expression on her face as she carries a tray loaded down with entrees. As soon as she reaches the table, her disposition transforms, and a smile curves her lips.

I rack my brain, trying to recall if she's ever looked at me that way. Normally, I'm treated to a lot of scowling. A couple times, she actually growled. And once—if I'm not mistaken—she bared her teeth.

But a smile?

Nope, don't think I've ever seen one of those directed at me. I watch as she passes out the plates and chats for a few seconds before swinging away. The girl is in a total zone. She's all business.

And from what I've been able to see—no play.

Does she ever cut loose and have fun?

Her feet slowly grind to a halt as our gazes lock and hold across the space that separates us. In that second or two, a punch of need hits me square in the gut.

Or maybe it's hunger.

Practice ran over and I'm fucking famished.

Because there's no way I'm attracted to this prickly girl. I like my chicks nice and soft with kissable lips and fuckable bodies. Can you even imagine what she would do if I attempted to kiss her?

I almost snort.

Probably rip me to shreds.

With her teeth.

Instead of ignoring me—which is exactly what I expect—she pivots, changing directions. My gaze stays pinned to her as she cuts a path through the room. She might have grudgingly agreed to work with me, but it's only because she needs her car fixed and has been left with no other options.

When she's a couple feet away, she grinds to a halt. There's a few seconds of silence as she tucks a stray lock of dark, silky hair that has escaped from her ponytail behind her ear. Is it strange that I'm tempted to knock her fingers away and do it myself?

I shake the errant thought away before it can take root and refocus on the reason I'm here.

"Hey," she says, voice a little breathless and cheeks stained with color.

I rip my gaze away and jerk my chin, glancing around the dining area. "Looks busy."

She follows my stare. "It's always slammed at dinner. You should know that. You've been here enough times."

She's right about that. Guess I never paid much attention. I'm either here with a group of friends or a couple of girls. Needless to say, they hold my interest.

My gaze returns to her dark one as I shift my weight. "Are you going to have time to get together tonight, or should I just take off?" As soon as the words escape, I wince. Giving her an out was a mistake. She'll probably jump at the chance to get rid of me.

She presses her lips together and considers the question. "I'll put you at a table out of the way and you can try and get through as much as you can on your own. In about twenty minutes, I can take a break and check over your work. After that, I'll stop over between customers. Hopefully, that'll be enough to get you through tonight." There's a pause. "Did you have a chance to start the assignment?"

"There wasn't time." And…I didn't really understand the material. It's kind of hard to get through the questions when you have no idea what the hell they're asking.

"All right." She releases a steady breath. "Guess I've got my work cut out for me, don't I?"

"Yup." That's putting it mildly.

She points to a small table wedged in the back near a hallway that leads to the bathrooms. "Why don't you work over there."

I scope out the situation. "Sounds good."

"I'll be over when I can."

"No worries."

With that, she takes off, beelining for a group of customers as I cut through the large space to the table and drop onto the chair. It feels good to take a load off as I open my backpack and grab my book before firing up my computer and pulling up the assignment.

I glanced at the questions earlier this afternoon, but since I haven't been paying attention during the lectures and have barely read over the notes, I didn't get very far. For the most part, I've enjoyed my Communications courses. I have no problem getting up in front of a class and talking. Hell, I've bullshitted my way through most of my speeches. But this theory crap?

It literally sucks the life from my soul.

It's so fucking dry.

Shoving those thoughts from my head, I crack my knuckles, ready to get serious and hammer this out. I harness all my mental capabilities and read over the question—several times since it doesn't seem to be computing—before drawing the book closer, carefully searching through the chapter for the answer. Laughter and chatter from neighboring tables draws my attention away. When a baby lets out a loud cry, I glance up. It takes a couple seconds to realize that I've become distracted. And then I can't remember what the hell I was hunting for in the first place.

I straighten and plow a hand through my hair.

Just as frustration spirals through me and I wonder if I'm doomed to repeat this course next semester, Lola stops by with a glass of water and a plate of tacos. I've never been so thrilled to see a Mexican entrée in my life.

"Thanks."

"I figured you might be hungry," she says with a shrug.

"Starving, actually," I admit.

"Hope it helps you concentrate."

Yeah...that's doubtful. Not even a plate of tasty tacos will be able to help with that.

"Thanks," I mutter, reminded of the assignment that needs to be accomplished tonight when the clock strikes midnight.

Before I can ask her to clarify the question, she rushes away, moving from table to table, bringing drinks and food, or clearing away dishes. I don't realize I've spent this entire time watching her until I glance at my plate and find it wiped clean. Not even a shred of lettuce remains.

I've never seen anyone hustle the way she does. It's like her ass is on fire as she zips through the restaurant. Even though I keep refocusing on my work, my gaze continually gets snagged by her. After another ten minutes, she drops onto the chair across from me and huffs out a breath.

"Okay. Show me what you have so far."

9

———

LOLA

*H*oly crap, it feels good to finally take a break and get off my feet. Even if it's just for a handful of minutes.

Since there isn't time to waste, I get straight to it by swiveling his laptop toward me. Asher has been sitting here for a good thirty minutes, so I'm expecting to see at least a couple of problems completed. I should have just enough time to look them over, correct some grammatical errors, and add a little more information to beef up the answers.

Instead, I barely find a few sentences. I skim the question and then his answer. My brow furrows as I blink and read it over for a second time.

This...doesn't even make sense. It's like the guy has no idea what he's talking about. For reasons I can't explain, disappointment fills me as I realize that everything I've heard about Asher is true. There's not much going on upstairs. He's all brawn and no brains.

Jeez.

And I'm supposed to tutor him?

What the hell have I gotten myself into?

When I glance up, silently debating how to handle the situation, he shifts on the red vinyl chair he's parked on. "I, ah, had to read part of the chapter and search for the answer. It took a while."

Except this response doesn't even make sense.

Or answer the question.

This is going to take longer than I anticipated, which means I'm going to have to find the time to spoon feed him.

My fingers rise to my temples where a headache brews. "All right. Show me where you found the answer and let's work from there."

He clears his throat and pulls the book closer before skimming over the page and moving on to the next. "I, um, actually haven't found it yet," he mumbles, a dull flush creeping into his cheeks.

Air leaks from my lungs as I read over the question before grabbing the book and flipping through the section until I find what I'm looking for. There's no point in wasting time. That's a precious commodity I don't have nearly enough of. And I'll be damned if I allow him to squander any of it.

When I rise to my feet, his brows jerk together. "Hey, where are you—"

I drag my chair close enough for our elbows and knees to bump and brush. If a little zip of awareness skitters across my flesh, I ignore it. "It'll be easier if we can both see the computer and book at the same time."

The muscles in his broad shoulders loosen as he nods.

Now that we're sitting practically on top of each other, the woodsy scent of his aftershave inundates my senses. Instead of focusing on the work that needs to be accomplished, it's tempting to shift and inhale a big breath of him.

I blink and shove that strange thought from my brain before refocusing my attention on the assignment. "Read over the question again." I point to the section on paradigmatic assumptions. "This is where you'll find the answer."

He leans closer and reads through part of the chapter with painstaking deliberateness.

When a few minutes slowly tick by, I tap my foot, wishing he'd hurry. "Did you find it?"

Instead of answering, he draws his lower lip between his teeth and chews on it as his brow creases. My gaze drops to the movement and an odd sensation stirs in the pit of my gut.

"Maybe."

Refocusing my attention, I repeat the question, delving deeper into what it's asking along with the key terminology and what knowledge Professor Nichols wants students to walk away with. Occasionally, I pause and check for understanding. Relief rushes through me when he's able to parrot the ideas back using his own words. As miniscule as it is, it still feels like a win.

Once I wrap up my explanation, I nudge the laptop toward him. "Now you need to take what you've read, along with what I've explained, and put it into your own words."

Again, he pins his lower lip with his teeth before jerking his head into a tight nod. As he bangs away on the keyboard, my gaze flits from the computer screen to his face. It takes about five minutes for him to tap out his thoughts. As he does, I point out necessary corrections or where information needs to be expanded.

When he finally finishes, I read it over again and nod with satisfaction. It's not perfect, but it'll have to do. "Looks good. Let's start the second problem."

He blows out a breath. "Okay."

We find the section where the answer is located, and I quickly break it down again before rising to my feet. "I want you to work on the answer while I check on my tables. After about ten minutes, I'll be back to look it over. Sound good?"

As soon as he gives me a nod, I take off.

Every time I walk through the dining room, my gaze is unconsciously pulled to Asher. Now that the dinner crowd has thinned, I'm able to stop by his table with more frequency and check his progress. It's slow but steady. He's making more headway since I took the time to go over the material in more depth.

I suppose that's something.

As I lay the bill on my last table, telling them to have a nice evening, Carmen waves me over. Her attention stays locked on the blond football player as she loiters by the beverage station. I was really hoping she wouldn't notice him. Guess I should have known better. Her gaze is like a heat seeking missile when it comes to hot guys.

I wince at that internal thought.

If I know my cousin—and I do—she'll be brimming with questions.

Ones I have no desire to answer.

As soon as I'm within striking distance, her hand snakes out and her fingers wrap around my wrist before dragging me closer. "Isn't that the guy from the other night? Why were you sitting with him?" Her eyes light up with undisguised interest. "Are you two now a thing?"

I shake my head, appalled she would think that. "Absolutely not."

The idea that I would actually date a muscle-bound jock is almost laughable.

Not in this lifetime. Or any others, for that matter. We couldn't be more different. I'm definitely not the kind of girl he likes to...*spend time* with.

She raises a brow. "Hmmm. You were awfully quick on the draw with that answer."

Unwanted heat floods my cheeks. "That's because it's the truth." When she continues to stare with an unnerving amount of scrutiny, I grudgingly admit, "I'm helping him with homework, okay? It's nothing more than that."

"Huh." Her curious gaze returns to Asher, who is still hunched over his computer.

Strangely enough, he's focused on his work. I'm not sure if that has to do with the restaurant quieting down or that I took the time to explain the concepts in more depth.

Or maybe a combination of both.

I can only begin to guess at the inner mechanisms of his brain.

I'm just relieved he's working. If I'm lucky, he'll finish the assignment before I'm done cleaning up and I can head home. I still have my own studying that needs to be completed before I can call it a night.

It's been a long day. One that started out like shit and will most likely end that way. Added to that, I'm tired, my feet hurt, and I'm concerned about how much it'll cost to fix my car.

My cousin cocks a hip as interest sparks to life in her dark eyes. "If you don't want to help him, I'd be more than happy to do it."

Not bothering to dignify that comment with a response, I roll my eyes. There's no way I'm letting Carmen within five feet of Asher. I love my cousin to death, but she's something of a maneater. She goes through guys the way most people go through underwear. Then again, these two would probably hit it off and get along like gangbusters. Which is even more of a reason to keep them apart.

Once the last customer pays their check and leaves, I grab a cloth to wipe down the tables. It takes roughly fifteen minutes to run through my closing responsibilities. After working here for years, I have it down to a science. I grab my coat and purse from the backroom before heading to the table where Asher is still typing away.

When I'm close enough, he glances up before lifting his arms over his head and stretching. It's difficult not to get distracted by the play of muscles that ripple beneath his form-fitting T-shirt.

Objectively speaking, Asher is a good-looking guy with short blond hair and piercing blue eyes that remind me of the ocean. Not that I've seen it firsthand, but from all the photographs, this is exactly what I imagine the color to look like. He stands well over six feet and is broad in the shoulders with bulging biceps. They're so big that it's doubtful I could wrap both hands around the thickest part of his arm and they'd touch.

So…yeah, on a pure superficial level, I get his appeal.

It's almost a surprise when my mouth turns cottony from the thorough inspection I've just treated him to.

It takes effort to clear away those thoughts. "Are you ready to go?"

With a nod, he shuts down his computer.

"Were you able to finish up the assignment?" Fingers crossed he says yes.

He glances away. "Almost. I still have three questions to go."

I bite back the groan that bubbles up from deep within. "When's it due?"

Please don't say tomorrow.

"Tonight at midnight."

Even worse.

My shoulders wilt under that knowledge. As much as I want to tell him to finish up the rest on his own, how can I do that after he took care of my car this morning?

"Okay. Well…" Taking him back to my house is the only viable option. Especially when I don't have transportation of my own. "I guess we can head to my place," I mumble.

"Are you sure?" His gaze narrows before searching mine. "You seem kind of beat."

Yup. Nothing new there.

"It's fine. Hopefully, it won't take long."

"I think you're being overly optimistic."

I snort out a reluctant laugh. "Probably."

With that, he rises to his feet and grabs the thick gray sweatshirt from the back of his chair before tugging it on. And then his bags get hauled over his shoulder. "Ready when you are."

I jerk my head into a nod as we make our way to the front of the restaurant. *Tío* Alejandro gives me a quick hug as we pass by the hostess station.

"See you tomorrow," he says in lightly accented English.

"Yup." Even though I wanted to scale back my hours at work, I've already picked up as many shifts as I can. It'll make studying more difficult, especially since I need to squeeze in room for Asher, but what other choice is there?

"Did you speak with Tony?" my *tío* asks.

My gaze flickers to Asher, who has paused beside me. "Nope. And I don't have any plans to either."

Emotion flickers in my uncle's dark eyes. He's always been big on family and encouraged me to have more of a relationship with my father, but he needs to understand that it's a two-way street. And I refuse to put myself out there to be hurt by a man whose love should have been unconditional from the beginning.

With a nod, he waves. "All right, *mija*. Have a good night."

Relieved that he isn't going to force the issue, my lips lift into a slight smile before we push out into the cold night air. Even though I'm wearing a coat, a chill slides through me. As I burrow into the cozy fabric, Asher throws a brawny arm around my shoulders and tugs me close.

Eyes widening, my gaze collides with his.

"What? You seemed cold."

"Thanks," I mutter, torn between escaping from his hold and burrowing against his brawny body, "but I'm good."

Even though I don't necessarily want to, I do the smart thing and pull away.

10

ASHER

It's not exactly a shocker when she ducks out of my arms. What's surprising is how much I enjoyed the feel of her tucked against me. As we cross the parking lot, the convo I'd just overheard circles through my head. It takes a handful of seconds to reach the truck. Once we do, she fishes the keys out of her bag and hands them over.

The question shoots out of my mouth before I can rein it back in. "Who's Tony?"

Even in the darkness that surrounds us, the way her muscles stiffen is obvious.

When she doesn't immediately respond, I click the locks and open the passenger side door. After she's safely secured inside, I slam it shut and hustle around the hood before settling on the leather seat and pressing the button that ignites the engine. Her silence only piques my curiosity as I shift the truck into gear and back out of the space.

Since that question has gone unanswered, I ask another. "Do you live around campus?"

Her gaze flickers to me before she shakes her head and rattles off an address. "No, but it's not too far from here."

Huh. Almost everyone I know lives on or near the university. I didn't realize she commuted. It only drives home the fact that I know very little about this girl.

Another silence descends before she admits, "Tony's my father. Or, more accurately, my sperm donor."

My attention flickers to her, taking in the seriousness of her expression before resettling on the ribbon of road stretched out beyond the windshield. The tense exchange at the restaurant now makes more sense.

"Ouch."

She jerks her shoulders. "It's the truth."

Even though she keeps her voice level, a hint of darker emotion mixed with hurt bleeds through. I know what it's like to have parental issues. As much as I love my family, we definitely have our problems. That being said, I've never referred to my father as a sperm doner. That's a level of contempt not easily attained. It's tempting to reach out and wrap my fingers around her hand and offer a small bit of comfort, but it's highly doubtful she'd be receptive to the physical contact.

My brain spins, trying to come up with something that will make the sadness lurking in her voice disappear. "I'm sorry."

It's a surprise when she adds in a softer voice, "He left when I was six and pretty much faded from my life. We haven't been in contact for years."

Wow. That really sucks.

Again, my gaze shifts to hers, attempting to get a read on her emotions. "Why do you think he's reaching out now?"

"Honestly?" Her brow furrows. "I don't know, and I really don't care."

We both fall silent as I turn off the main road and onto a side street before pulling in front of a modest ranch that sits on a tiny postage stamp of lawn. It can't be more than seven or eight hundred feet in square footage.

Lola grabs her bag from the floor of the truck before opening the door and stepping onto the curb. I do the same, exiting the vehicle and coming around to join her with my backpack slung over one shoulder. I have no idea what to say—if anything—as we make our way up the thin concrete path to the front door.

She slips a key in the lock before twisting the handle and stepping inside. My gaze flies around the living room as I trail behind her. There's a worn-looking sofa with a matching floral armchair, wood side table, and television crammed into the area. Even though it's compact in size, everything is neat and tidy.

"It'll be easier to work at the kitchen table," she says, interrupting my perusal.

With a nod, I follow her into the other room. Lola peels off her jacket and hangs it on a coatrack near the backdoor before pointing to the table shoved up against the far wall beneath a window.

"Why don't you get set up, and I'll be right back?"

"Sure." I watch as she disappears around the corner before pulling out a chair and dropping onto it. Then, I fire up my computer and grab my Comms book.

When there's a babble of soft voices, I cock my head, trying to pick up the thread of conversation. I'm curious as to who else is here. A roommate? Maybe a boyfriend?

Hmm. I don't like the idea of that.

A handful of minutes later, Lola returns. The first thing I notice is that she's changed out of the jeans and T-shirt with the Taco Loco logo stamped across it and is now wearing black yoga pants that fit her like a glove and a cropped Western sweatshirt that shows off just a bit of toned midriff. Fuzzy purple socks cover her feet, and her hair is no longer pulled up into a ponytail. Instead, the silky mass floats around her shoulders, giving her a softer, more approachable look.

The second thing that hits me is the exhaustion that fills her eyes. I caught flashes of it earlier at the restaurant when she dropped onto the seat across from me. Is it more visible now because she's at home and no longer needs to mask it? Or is it that the hour has grown late and she's unable to keep it under wraps? Whatever the reason, guilt pricks me. This is obviously a girl who is burning the candle at both ends.

I clear my throat. "You know…if this isn't a good time, we can get together tomorrow or the day after."

She steps farther into the small space before pulling out the chair from the other side of the table and dragging it next to mine. "Isn't the assignment due at midnight?" She glances at her phone. "That's in two hours."

I shrug. "It is, but I can finish it up on my own. The way you explained the other problems now makes more sense. If you could check over the questions I completed and tell me if I'm on the right track, I'll be good."

She ponders it for a second or two before shaking her head. "It's fine. Let's just knock it out right now." Her voice turns softer as she glances away. "I owe you for taking care of my car this morning, and I don't like feeling indebted to people."

The way she says it along with the implication leaves a bad taste in my mouth.

"You're not indebted," I mutter. "It's like I said before—this is an exchange of services. That's it."

Even though she's exhausted, one corner of her mouth hitches. "Exactly. And I need to provide that service."

When she settles next to me, I swing the computer toward her so she can read through the work I completed at the restaurant. As she focuses on the screen, I can't help but stare. With her this up close and personal, it would be hard not to. Her eyes are so dark, they're nearly black in their intensity, and the lashes framing them are just as inky. Her nose is slim and straight. My gaze falls to her lips. They look like a cupid's bow with a deep pink color that seems more natural than makeup. Her skin is a deep golden hue that doesn't strike me as sun kissed.

It's only when her gaze locks on mine that I realize she's been talking to me. It takes effort to shake away the mental fog that has descended and focus my attention on the words coming out of her mouth instead of the hue and poutiness of it.

"Sorry, guess I zoned out for a moment."

When her brow furrows, I realize she probably thinks I'm a total dumbass. That thought has a dull heat creeping into my cheeks. Normally, I don't give a shit what people think. I've spent my entire life being looked upon as the less intelligent Stevens brother. It's a part I eventually accepted. If I couldn't compete in the classroom, then I'd be the best on the field. But with Lola...

I don't know...it bothers me that she probably thinks I don't have two brain cells to rub together.

"I said that this looks pretty good." She points out a few sentences that need to be reworked with more in-depth information.

As she re-explains a few key concepts, I make the necessary changes, and then we get to work on the last two problems. It takes about an hour but goes much faster now that I understand what I'm doing and how to write out the responses.

After I'm finished, she reads over the last question and makes a few tweaks. "I think that should be good."

"Great." I shut down my computer before shoving it in my backpack along with my book. "I should probably take off and get out of your way."

There's a teeny tiny part inside me that hopes she'll tell me to stick around.

Stifling a yawn, she stretches her arms above her head and arches her back. "Yeah, I've got some stuff of my own to finish up. Thankfully, that didn't take as long as I thought it would. Once you caught on, we were good."

Instead of focusing on that semi compliment, my gaze drops to her breasts as they press against the fabric of her sweatshirt. Even though she's thin, they're surprisingly generous in size. I rip my attention away before she can catch me ogling her. This is a girl who would have no problem slapping me upside the head if she caught me checking out her rack.

"Do you need a ride tomorrow? I can swing by and pick you up before your first class."

She shakes her head as her arms fall back to her sides. "No, my mom isn't using her car. I'll be able to borrow that for the time being. Hopefully, mine won't be out of commission for too long."

I rise from the chair and haul my backpack onto my shoulder. "You live here with your mother?" For some odd reason, I'm relieved it's not a boyfriend.

"Yeah."

When she doesn't elaborate on the situation, I keep the conversation moving. "I'll call the shop in a day or so to see if they've had a chance to assess the damage. Then I'll let you know."

She nods before rising to her feet and walking out of the kitchen into the living room before loitering at the front door. Her hand is already resting on the handle as if she can't hustle my ass out of here fast enough. Which is probably the way she feels. All I've done is eat up her time.

My feet slow as her gaze stays pinned to mine. Another sizzle of awareness shoots through me. "Thanks again for your help. I couldn't have done it without you."

Her lips lift into a small semblance of a smile. I think it might be the first she's ever flashed at me.

"It wasn't a problem."

I almost snort, knowing that she's being polite by lying.

"We both have tight schedules, but I guess we can try to get together a few times each week until the semester ends."

"As long as we can work around practice, that would be great. How about tomorrow afternoon at one o'clock at the library?"

"Yeah, I think that's doable."

"Good." I shift my stance but don't make a move to leave. Lola isn't like anyone else I've met, and spending time with her has only piqued my interest and left me with a lot of questions bubbling beneath the surface.

It's kind of funny…most of the girls I've been with are carbon copies of all the others. There's nothing about them that surprises me or makes me want to dig deeper and figure out what makes them tick.

But that's exactly how I feel about this one.

She's like a puzzle I want to solve.

The question is—will she allow me close enough to actually do it?

11

LOLA

*L*ast night, I was up until two o'clock finishing up homework before falling face first into bed. This has—unfortunately—become a pattern. The good news is that I remembered to set my alarm for the morning and was up early enough to make a massive cup of coffee, which I'm currently nursing as I make a mental list of everything that needs to be accomplished for the day.

"Hey, Lola—wait up."

I swing around, only to find Demi jogging toward me with a bright smile. That girl has always been a morning person.

Bitch.

Even with the caffeine pumping through my system, I'm still barely cognizant.

Heads turn in her direction as she catches up with me. Demi is gorgeous with long, dark hair and a toned, athletic body from years of running around on a soccer field. It wouldn't surprise me if she ends up playing for the Women's National Soccer Team after college. She's always been a dynamo on the field. I try to catch as many games as I can, but with my schedule, it's not easy to carve out the time. Plus, as much as I hate to admit it, sitting in the stands only makes me realize how much I miss the sport. Watching everyone on the field doing something I used to love kind of sucks.

"Hey, how are you?" I ask.

"Good," she says with a slight huff. "I'm glad we ran into each other. I wanted to invite you to my birthday party on Saturday."

"This Saturday?"

"Yup," she says with a nod.

I quickly run through my schedule for the restaurant. "I should be able to make it. Even if I have to work, I can swing by afterward."

"Yay!" There's a pause as some of her happiness drains away. "All right, I need to warn you about something."

Uh-oh. I give her a bit of side-eye as we continue walking along the path that winds through campus. I'm almost afraid to ask. "What?"

"It's at the football house," she admits, scrunching her face like that might change my decision. "I know you and—"

Before she can finish that sentence, a muscular arm is thrown around my shoulders and I'm hauled against a rock-solid body. A woodsy fragrance invades my senses and my belly flutters in response.

No.

I refuse to feel this way about him.

Demi's eyes widen as her mouth forms a small O. Her surprised gaze bounces from me to Asher and back again. After our run-in at the one and only football house party I attended this year, I can understand why she's gaping at me like a fish out of water.

"Umm." She waggles a finger between us. "I thought you two couldn't stand each other. What happened?"

"We came to an understanding," I say lightly, attempting to escape his hold.

"Yup," he adds, tightening his grip and shooting me a grin, "we're totally chill. Practically besties."

Yeah...I don't think we're quite there yet, but we're certainly better than what we were. We met up the other day at the library, and I didn't even growl or glare at him once. So...that's progress made in the right direction.

I think.

Before I can respond, she says, "Really?" Her eyes narrow. "Exactly when did this happen?" There's a pause. "Maybe a better question would be *how* did this happen?"

"Well…we're adults." Mostly. I glance at Asher. "And we had an adult conversation regarding our differences."

"Wow. It's like a birthday miracle," Demi says, lips lifting with humor as she shakes her head.

"That it is." I clear my throat before pointing to the tall brick business building looming in the distance. "I should probably get moving. Just shoot me a text with all the details and I'll be there."

"Awesome. It's going to be so much fun. Rowan's insisting on a Hawaiian theme for the party. So, if you have a grass skirt, be sure to wear it."

With a wave, I slip out of Asher's hold and take off. Just as my heartrate settles, his brawny arm is thrown over my shoulders for a second time and I'm tugged against his hard body. The students passing by stare in our direction with raised brows before waving to the guy at my side. He acknowledges them like a king greeting his loyal subjects.

It's a strange sensation to have so much attention directed our way. I'm usually able to move inconspicuously around campus. Now that Western's very own football legend is by my side, that's not possible. With so many envious stares aimed at me, I don't think I've ever felt more under the microscope.

"I was actually looking for you," he says, knocking me out of the strange thoughts circling through my head.

His mouth is so close to my ear that an unwanted shiver of awareness scampers down my spine, making me even more cognizant of his towering presence.

"Oh?" I stare straight ahead, wanting to avoid eye contact. "What about?"

"I heard back from Declan. Good news—he says the damage to your car wasn't as extensive as it looked, and you should have it back by the end of next week."

My muscles tighten as I steel myself for the expense. As much as I don't want to hear the number he's going to throw out, I need to know what it is.

"How much will the repair cost?"

He shrugs. "I don't know. About three hundred, give or take a couple of dollars."

Air rushes from my lungs in shock.

No way.

Did I hear him correctly?

"Three hundred?" I thought it would end up being thousands. It almost seems too good to be true. Before I allow the relief fighting to break free to flood through my system, I say, "That's it?" The number tumbles from my lips for a second time. "Three hundred dollars? We're talking US currency?"

He slants a look at me. "Did you think I meant euros?"

My brows pinch together as memories of the damage to the backend and wheel fill my head. "It's not like I'm complaining, but I don't understand how a repair like that can be so cheap. It doesn't make sense." A thought occurs to me, and I narrow my eyes. "Are you sure this guy is reputable? I'm aware that my car is a hunk of junk, but it needs to be held together with more than duct tape and bungee cords."

A chuckle escapes from him. "Trust me, Declan is the best in the biz when it comes to collision repair. When our vehicles get fucked up, this is the guy we take them to. Maybe I should have mentioned that you're getting the friends and family discount." His twinkling gaze latches onto mine. "See how advantageous it is to be friends with me?"

I snort out a laugh.

Yeah, right.

But still…this is amazing news. For the first time in my life, something is actually working out better than I expected it to. How often does that happen?

"I'm really appreciative of your help. I wasn't sure how expensive it would be, and I can't let you pay for it all yourself. So, I already picked up extra shifts at the restaurant." The vise grip squeezing my chest loosens just a bit as I rake my teeth across my lower lip before admitting, "I don't know what I would have done if it had been more."

Probably forgone the repair. I would have been stuck sharing a car with Mom. For this week, the situation works out. She's been looking for a job and I'm hoping something will come through soon. I can't be the only one contributing to the bills that continue to mount.

"We already agreed that I'd cover the cost and you would tutor me. It's just a couple hundred." He gives me a wink. "Don't worry, I'll make sure you work it off."

I blow out a relieved breath. "Thank you."

"No worries," he says easily, tugging me closer.

That comment is so laughable that I don't dwell on our closeness or how good it feels. There has never been a time in my life when money wasn't a source of concern, stress, and worry. There are nights when I lie awake, unable to sleep, staring sightlessly at the ceiling, wondering how everything that's due at the end of the month will get paid on time. Or at all.

Unless you've lived with that kind of fear and anxiety, you have no idea how mentally draining it can be. It's obvious from Asher's blithe attitude on the matter, along with the ridiculously expensive truck he drives—because yeah, I looked it up online—that finances aren't a concern.

And you know what?

That's great for him.

It's just not where I'm at in life. Hopefully, I'll get there one day. That's the end goal. It's the reason I bust my ass and am constantly hustling.

"I was hoping we could get together tonight," he says, drawing my attention back to him.

It takes a second to refocus my thoughts on our conversation. "What time were you thinking?"

"After practice. Probably around seven. Does that work for you?"

I nod. Today, my classes end at four. I can grab something to eat and concentrate on my own coursework for a couple hours. "Yeah, that sounds good."

"Perfect. We can head to my house or the library."

"Library," I say quickly.

Definitely the library.

The moment he removes his arm from my shoulders, a sense of loss fills me. I didn't realize how much I was enjoying his masculine presence until it disappeared. With a wave, he takes off. I lift my hand to return the gesture and watch as he strides confidently through the sea of students.

People make room, clapping him on the back and calling out his name in greeting. Not that I pay the slightest bit of attention to the gossip that swirls through campus, but if everything I hear is true, he'll get drafted to the NFL this spring. A group of girls surrounds him as they continue to walk. With every step he takes, he picks up more adoring fans.

Thank god I feel absolutely nothing where Asher Stevens is concerned.

Can you imagine if I did?

A shudder of horror slides through me.

Maybe he's turning out to be different from the meathead jock I initially pegged him as, but he's still a major player.

And that, I don't have time for.

12

ASHER

*A*s soon as practice wraps up, I hustle to the library. Coach kept us over when a few players half-assed it on the field. What a bunch of dickheads. Afterward, the guys were planning to grab something to eat. Most gave me a look of disbelief when I declined the offer, telling them I was headed over to the library instead. Crosby actually laid his palm across my forehead and asked if I was sick or something.

With a roll of my eyes, I knocked his hand away.

What I failed to mention was the person I was meeting.

It's none of their damn business.

Once inside the sprawling brick building, I take the stairs two at a time, anxious to reach the third floor. As soon as I crest the landing, my gaze coasts over the tables scattered across the vast space until it lands on Lola.

Earlier this morning, her dark hair had been left all long and loose around her shoulders. Now, it's pulled up into a messy bun at the top of her head, allowing me to glimpse the long line of her neck. Her gaze stays pinned to the book in front of her as she fidgets with a pen before bringing it to her mouth. A punch of arousal hits me in the gut, imagining something much thicker nudging her pouty lips.

I shake away the mental image and force my feet into movement. Once I reach the table, I drop down onto the chair parked next to hers. As she glances up, her gaze collides with mine and she gives me a slight smile. It's doubtful I'll ever be on the receiving end of a full-blown one. Although, it's way better than the scowls she usually aims in my direction.

"Hey," she says.

"Hi." I unpack my bag so we can get straight to work. If I've learned anything about Lola, it's that she doesn't have time to sit around and shoot the shit. "Were you able to get most of your homework done?"

"I think so. At least enough for tonight." She glances at my laptop. "Do you mind if I take a look at your assignment?"

"Sure, have at it." As she swivels the computer closer, I shift and the floral scent that clings to her captures my attention. I have to fight the urge to inhale a big breath. It takes effort to clear those thoughts and force down the semi that now stirs in my sweatpants. "I had an hour between classes and was able to get a head start on it. Maybe you can check those answers first before we work on the rest."

With her attention focused elsewhere, I'm able to study her with more care. How is it that she gets prettier every time I see her?

It doesn't make sense.

"It looks good so far," she says, interrupting my perusal.

She points out a few places where the verbiage needs to be altered or a line needs to be inserted to complete the thought, but other than that, I'm actually on track for a change.

Unlike the other times we've worked together, I attempt to tackle the problems on my own before she checks them over. In my Comms class, I'm also making more of an effort to pay attention and take notes. It's a lot of work, but the flip side is that I understand the material in a way I never have before. I guess being attentive in class and completing your own homework on the daily is helpful with that.

Who knew?

Dr. Nichols asked me to stick around after the last lecture and showed me that I received a solid B on my latest homework assignment. Her eyes were narrowed as she fired off a few questions to check my understanding. She looked surprised when I was able to answer them somewhat coherently. I can't begin to tell you how good that felt.

Take that, Nichols.

Better yet, shove it where the sun doesn't shine.

So, for this week, I'm safe to play football and my ass won't be sitting with the third stringers. At the end of the day, that's all that matters.

"I really hope this compliment won't come back to bite me in the ass," she says, drawing my attention to her, "but you're actually doing a good job."

"You don't have to sound so shocked," I say with a snort.

"Can't help it." There's a pause before her voice dips as if confiding a secret. "The first time I met you, I thought you were a steroid-infused jock, coasting through school on his football prowess and good looks."

I pop a brow, latching onto the most important part of that sentence. "You think I'm good looking?"

She rolls her eyes. "You're all right…I guess."

I scoot a little closer, swallowing up some of the distance that separates us. "On a scale of one to ten, exactly how good looking would you say I am?"

She contemplates the question for a long moment. "Maybe we should discuss how conceited you are instead. On a scale of one to ten, you're definitely a ten. Maybe even an eleven. The point I'm trying to make is that you've turned out to be more than what I expected. And that usually doesn't happen."

I find her words oddly touching.

No one—including my own family—has ever said that to me. My looks and my athletic abilities are what people normally focus on. Maybe I've become used to and accepting of that as well. It's strange for a girl who I've only just started spending time with to look beyond my shiny exterior to what lies beneath.

Instead of finding me lacking, she actually sees more.

Warmth radiates throughout my chest, flooding to parts I didn't realize were there.

"Thanks," I mumble before glancing away, not wanting to meet her eyes when I make this confession. "I feel like a real asshole for admitting this, but I haven't always worked hard. In fact, what you said is pretty spot on. I coasted through both high school and college on my athletic abilities. People were always happy to do my homework, and most teachers didn't have a problem passing me through if I didn't quite make the grade. I think some of them saw it as a way to help out the team and make sure we had a winning season and won state."

What's even worse is that it didn't bother me to take advantage of the situation.

With a shake of her head, she clucks her tongue. "That is such a sad indictment on our educational system."

I shrug as a prick of shame flares to life inside me. "Yeah, I guess it is."

Especially when I see how hard she busts her ass at school and the restaurant. It's hard not to respect that kind of work ethic. The fact that she doesn't view me in the same light leaves me squirming.

She clears her throat. "Anyway, I just wanted to say that maybe you're smarter than you give yourself credit for."

There are things I'm good at—football—and things I'm not—school. That's the way it's always been. Jack was the family's academic all-star and I excelled on the field. I never thought to question it or push myself harder. It was just easier to check out mentally and focus my attention elsewhere.

"You really think so?" I ask, thrown off by the comment.

"I actually do."

The air around us seems to shift as a strange intensity takes hold and our gazes stay locked. Her eyes are so dark and rich in hue that it wouldn't take much to become trapped within their depths.

That's all it takes for the library to fade to the background as my body sways toward hers, almost as if there's a magnetic force pulling me in that direction. Instead of second guessing my actions, I give in to the rush of sensation coursing through me.

When her tongue darts out to moisten her lips, my gaze drops to the movement. I can't stop myself from thinking about how much I want to kiss this girl. Like a deer caught in the bright glare of headlights, she freezes. I angle my head to the left until my mouth can ghost over hers.

Just as I'm about to sink into the caress, a chipper voice says, "Hi, Asher."

A slight gasp escapes from Lola as she jerks away, her chair scraping against the carpet as she swivels toward the desk, avoiding all eye contact.

I glance at the girl who has sidled up to the table while I wasn't paying attention. "Hey, Mallory. How's it going?"

"Better now that I've run into you," she says with a bright smile that shows off lots of pearly white teeth.

Awkwardness descends.

Just when I'm about to tell the blonde that we're in the middle of studying, Lola jumps to her feet. "I, ah, need to take off."

"What?" My brows pinch together. "Already? I thought we were going to work for a couple of hours."

Color blooms in her face as she focuses her attention on her laptop before slamming it shut and shoving it inside her bag. "Sorry. I just remembered something I need to take care of. Maybe we can get together tomorrow. Or the day after that."

My mind spins, trying to come up with a way to detain her. "But—"

"I can help you," Mallory cuts in. "I've got plenty of time."

I don't glance at the other girl. I've spent most of the day thinking about Lola, looking forward to spending time together, and now, after about an hour, she's ditching my ass.

"We'll talk soon, okay?" she says, refusing to make eye contact as if I have the power to turn her to stone with a single glance.

I pop to my feet, trying one last time to keep her from leaving. "I don't even have your number."

Ignoring the comment, she takes off, practically racing to the staircase and rushing down the steps before disappearing from sight.

"It's like she couldn't get away from you fast enough," Mallory chirps.

My gaze reluctantly flickers to the blonde. "Yeah, I seem to have that effect on her."

Unfortunately.

13

***

LOLA

*H*oly crap.

Did that seriously just happen?

For all intents and purposes, I just locked lips with Asher Stevens.

Instead of putting a kibosh on the kiss, I'd sat there and allowed it to unfold.

The way his minty fresh breath feathered across my lips before his mouth settled on mine plays through my head on a constant loop. Even though it only lasted a second or two, it had been more than enough to make a permanent impression.

What would have happened if we hadn't been interrupted? My fingers tremble as they rise to my mouth before I shake the question from my brain.

Nope. I'm not going to dwell on it.

Maybe Asher has surprised me and isn't the total asshat I pegged him to be, but he's still a jock who walks around campus like he owns the place. That realization certainly isn't a reason to go off the rails and get crazy.

As soon as I shove through the heavy glass door of the building, the cold night air slaps at my cheeks, instantly cooling them and

88

making me feel more in control of the strange emotions careening around inside me.

I don't have time for guys. And certainly not ones like the blond football player.

I mean…come on.

He's a campus playboy who takes nothing but football seriously.

I almost snort at such a ridiculous notion.

If there's an upside to the situation, it's that I'll get home at a decent hour and can hit the sack earlier than anticipated. A prick of guilt stabs at me for bailing on him the way I did.

Until I remember the gorgeous girl standing at the table, more than eager to help him.

As soon as a flicker of jealousy ignites in the pit of my belly, I ruthlessly stomp it out until there's nothing left.

"Lola?"

My feet grind to a halt as recognition slams into me. No more than a dozen feet away from where I stand, a man rises from one of the metal benches strategically placed throughout campus.

Tony.

That's all it takes for air to get wedged in the middle of my throat as I stare at the person I called Papa once upon a time. He doesn't look all that different. His build is still slim, and, even in the darkness that surrounds us with only lamplight for illumination, I can make out the graying around his temples. The lines bracketing his eyes and mouth have deepened.

Honestly, I never thought I'd see him again. The fact that he stalked me on campus is disturbing. Why would he go to such great lengths when he spent more than a decade ignoring me?

Once the shock wears off and I've steeled every bit of emotion, I force my voice to remain calm. "What are you doing here?"

He takes a few steps in my direction, carefully closing the distance between us. "I wanted to talk with you."

I straighten my shoulders and tilt my head. "Why?"

Something unidentifiable flickers in his dark eyes before he glances away. Instead of answering the question, he points to the bench and asks one of his own. "Do you have a few minutes to sit and talk?"

With him?

No way.

Even though there's nothing humorous about the situation, laughter rises in my throat and my fingers tighten around the padded strap of my bag, as if that will protect me from the emotional damage this man is capable of inflicting. Over the years, his disinterest and neglect have eroded my self-confidence. It's always been a thought buzzing around in the back of my brain that if your own father doesn't have the time or inclination to bother with you, who will?

There are times when I wonder if that's the reason I never allow anyone too close. Not only guys, but girls as well. I've experienced enough rejection and heartache over the years. I don't need more.

"Sorry, can't. I'm busy." When I take a hasty step in retreat, panic flashes across his expression.

It's an unexpected reaction and piques my curiosity, but not enough to stick around and find out what the reason behind it is.

"Please?" He plows a hand through his thinning hair.

I remember a time when it was thick and full. As shiny and glossy as a raven's wing. Now, it looks as if it's been ravaged by the hands of time.

"I'm, ah, sorry for the lack of communication," he says before glancing away.

Lack of communication?

That's a joke, right?

How am I supposed to respond to that?

When I remain silent, lips pressed together until they feel blood-less, he shifts his stance, shoving his hands into the pockets of his leather jacket. "It was never intentional. I suppose life just got in the way."

Of seeing his daughter?

I fold my arms tightly across my chest, not bothering to dignify that excuse with a response. "What do you want, Tony?"

I can't bring myself to call this stranger *Papa*. He hasn't been one—

at least not to me—since he packed up his bags and walked out the door.

"To sit down and have a conversation. That's it."

"Sorry, we don't have anything to talk about." That being said, I swing around and turn my back to him.

I don't care if I have to take an alternate route to the parking lot. I just need to get away as quickly as possible. My heart is jackhammering against my ribcage with so much force that it's actually painful. Part of me wonders if it'll explode from my chest.

There were so many nights after he abandoned us that I cried myself to sleep because I had no idea how to handle the situation I'd been thrust into. Those were the times when I needed this man to step up and be my parent. Even if they were divorced, he could have remained in my life and offered support. Anything would have been appreciated. But there was nothing.

So...if he's delusional enough to think he can crash into my life now, he's in for a rude awakening. As far as I'm concerned, it's too little, too late.

"Kylie's kidneys are failing." His voice trembles as he blurts out the words in the quietness that surrounds us. "She needs a transplant."

For the second time in a matter of minutes, my feet stutter to a stop before I slowly turn back to face him. A sheen of moisture coats his eyes and his bottom lip quivers, even though he's trying desperately to rein in his emotions.

His words echo in my head as the realization slams into me like a sledgehammer. "That's the reason you've been trying so hard to get ahold of me."

Oh my god, I'm such an idiot. Anguish rushes through my veins, filling every conceivable space. And here I didn't think it was possible for him to wound me any more than he already had.

Joke's on me.

When he remains silent, my voice escalates. "It wasn't out of some burning need to reignite our fractured relationship, was it?" I shake my head as resentment boils up inside me. "It's because your daughter needs a transplant. And you think I can help with that."

"Kylie's your sister." Wetness fills his eyes.

I shake my head. "No, she's not. I don't know her, and I've never been a part of her life." There's a pause. "You made sure of that."

He glances away before swiping at a tear that slowly treks down his cheek.

"Please, Lola." He takes a hesitant step in my direction. "I realize that I've fucked up, but please don't make Kylie pay the price for my mistakes." His voice dips, turning desperate. "Do you want money? Is that what you need?"

My mouth tumbles open as my eyes widen. I couldn't be more stunned if he reached out and slapped me.

Money?

Is he really offering me cash for my kidney?

A growl works its way up from my throat before bursting free. "I don't want or need anything from you."

Not anymore.

Not ever.

"I'm sorry." The misery that flashes across his face does nothing for me. "I just thought—"

"You thought wrong," I bite out.

"I'm sorry. I didn't mean to offend you. We're desperate. Her health is failing and we're out of options."

He wouldn't be here, begging me for help if that weren't the case.

I'm his last resort.

An afterthought.

Which sums up our non-existent relationship perfectly.

"I'll think about it." When he opens his mouth to argue, my eyes narrow. "That's the best I can do. Feel free to take it or leave it."

His shoulders collapse as if a heavy weight is forcing them to the earth. He jerks his head into a tight nod as a flicker of hope ignites in his eyes. "All you need to do is get tested. That's it."

That's it he says.

Ha!

"When I've made a decision, I'll be in contact."

Unwilling to be in his presence for another second, I swing away.

"Lola," he calls out desperately.

I stiffen, refusing to turn and meet his gaze again. "What?"

"Just know that time is of the essence."

"Noted."

Not bothering to say goodbye, I retrace my steps to the library, planning to take a different path to the athletic center parking lot. I don't get more than six steps when strong fingers wrap around my upper arms, halting me in my tracks. There is so much emotion whipping through my body that I don't realize tears sting my eyes until I meet the gaze of the person holding me.

14

ASHER

*M*y gut clenches as I search Lola's face and find wetness shimmering in her eyes. I have no idea what happened in the ten or fifteen minutes since she took off, but I'm going to damn well find out. I glance at the older dude loitering on the walking path. As soon as we make eye contact, he swings around and hurries away. My eyes narrow before I pull her against my chest and wrap my arms protectively around her.

"Who the hell was that?"

"Tony." Her voice is barely more than a whisper.

Her father?

The one she referred to as a sperm donor?

My gaze tracks his movements until he turns the corner of a building and disappears. "Why is he here on campus?"

"I don't want to talk about it."

Unwilling to let her go, I press her thin body closer. "Whatever he said obviously upset you. You're crying."

"No, I'm not. Crying is weak and pointless."

I blink, surprised by the hardness that fills her voice. "My mistake," I say carefully.

She sucks in a shuddering breath as I stroke my fingers up and down the long line of her spine through the jacket she's wearing.

"I need to get out of here."

"All right, let's go. Want to grab something to eat?"

She pulls away enough to search my eyes. There might have been tears shining in them moments ago, but they're now long gone. "No, I'm not hungry."

"When was the last time you ate a meal?"

Her brow furrows and I can almost see her mentally sifting through her brain for an answer. "I had a bowl of cereal before I left the house this morning."

"Then we definitely need to get something in your belly. It'll probably make you feel better."

Not giving her a chance to argue, I lock my fingers around her wrist and pull her toward the parking lot. She must be in some weird state of shock, because she doesn't fight me tooth and nail like I expect. Even though there are a ton of questions buzzing around inside my head, I keep them to myself.

At least for the time being.

As soon as we reach the Escalade, I click the locks and open the passenger side door. Her gaze briefly meets mine before she slides inside the vehicle. Then I jog around the hood and settle beside her. When she continues to stare straight ahead, I reach over and grab the seatbelt before dragging it across her body and clicking it into place.

Her head swivels until our gazes collide. A mixture of surprise and confusion simmers in her dark eyes. As the moment stretches, I'm reminded of the brief kiss we shared in the library. And just how much I want to do it again. But now isn't the time. Reluctantly, I twist around and stare into the darkness beyond the windshield before pushing the button until the engine roars to life.

It takes effort to concentrate on the road instead of the girl sitting beside me. "Can I assume you don't want Mexican?"

With a snort, her lips tremble around the edges as she gives her head a slight shake.

"Figured as much. How do you feel about Italian?"

"I like it."

"Good," I say with a nod. "Me, too."

Ten minutes later, I pull into the parking lot of a popular chain restaurant close to campus. Sure, I could take her someplace more intimate and romantic, but that's not the vibe this evening. This place is casual with surprisingly delicious food. And that's what she needs.

As soon as she exits the truck, I snake my arm around her waist and steer her toward the entrance. A blast of heat hits us as we step inside the building. The girl loitering behind the hostess stand straightens as soon as she catches sight of us.

A big smile lights up her face. "Good evening. Do you have a reservation with us?"

"Nope," I say. "Is it possible to get a table for two?"

She glances at her iPad and drags a finger across the screen before peeking up at me from beneath a dark fringe of lashes. "I think we can squeeze you in," her voice dips as she leans forward, "Asher Stevens."

I give Lola a bit of side-eye before tightening my grip. Part of me is afraid she'll bolt if given half a chance. "Great."

When a starry-eyed look enters the girl's eyes, I clear my throat. "Is there something available now?" I don't mention that the restaurant is barely filled and it's after eight o'clock.

She jumps to attention as her eyes widen. "Of course! Let me check on that for you." With another bright smile aimed in my direction, she disappears into the main dining room.

"Wow," Lola whispers, "it must be difficult for you to go anywhere without adoring fans falling at your feet."

The sarcasm filling her voice is loud and clear.

"You have no idea," I say lightly.

"Oh, I think I do."

Before I can fire back with a response, the hostess returns and grabs two menus. "If you'll both follow me, I'll show you to your table."

"Awesome." I place my hand on Lola's lower back, propelling her forward.

A few people stare as we walk through the dining room. It's a relief when no one stops me, wanting to talk football.

Once we're seated at a booth in the back, the hostess lingers. "Is there anything else I can get for you?"

I shake my head, annoyed that she's hanging around when all I want to do is figure out what happened with Lola's father. She's normally so spunky, just waiting for the opportunity to sharpen her claws on me. I don't like seeing her subdued or upset.

"We're good, thanks."

"Okay. If you're sure."

"We are." My smile becomes forced. I'm uncertain how much longer I can hold it in place.

"Your server will be by momentarily."

"Great." I keep my gaze pinned to Lola, hoping the younger woman gets the subtle hint to leave.

"Have a wonderful meal!"

"We will. Thanks."

Even then, it takes another handful of seconds for her to reluctantly disappear. As soon as she does, I huff out a breath and shake my head.

A slight smile quirks the corners of her lips. "Poor Asher. So beloved."

I roll my eyes and grumble under my breath.

"I'm beginning to understand how you were able to coast through school without actually doing any work. Girls just jump to do your bidding, don't they?"

I give her a hard look. "Not all of them."

She arches a brow, holding my gaze for a heartbeat or two before dropping it to the white tablecloth. "That's probably for the best."

It's a relief when the server turns out to be a dude. The last thing I need is more women fawning over me in front of her. Normally, I eat that kind of thing up. The more the merrier has always been my motto.

But with Lola?

I don't feel that way. I wish people would just leave me alone so I could focus my attention on her without interruption.

"Can we get two waters and a bruschetta as an appetizer?" I ask.

"Of course. I'll be back in a few minutes with your drinks and to take your order."

"Thanks." My gaze stays pinned to the girl across from me.

Once our drinks and appetizer have been dropped off, and our orders placed—spaghetti bolognese for me and chicken alfredo for her—I say, "So, tell me what Tony wanted."

Any light shining in her eyes vanishes as the edges of her lips wilt.

For a long moment, her gaze flits around the restaurant. Just when I think she'll leave me hanging, she clears her throat. "He has two kids with his second wife, and one of them needs a kidney transplant."

It takes a few seconds for her words to fully sink in. When they do, I lean forward, closing as much distance between us as the table will allow. Even though I try to keep my voice level, shock colors it. "Are you telling me that he wants you to donate one of your kidneys?"

No fucking way.

Her teeth sink into her lower lip before she jerks her head into a tight nod.

"What did you tell him?" It's almost inconceivable that after not bothering with her for years, he crawled out of the woodwork for the sole purpose of asking her for an organ.

"What was I supposed to say?"

"No." A mixture of anger and outrage vibrates in my voice. "You should have straight up said no."

Her shoulders sink as she drops her eyes for a second time. "How could I do that? I told him that I'd think about it."

My jaw stiffens. It's only when my teeth begin to ache that I realize how hard I'm clenching them. The need to touch her thrums through me as I reach across the table and lay my hand over her smaller one. Her gaze drops in surprise to where we're now connected before lifting to mine. Part of me expects her to draw away and break the contact. When she doesn't, I squeeze her fingers.

Even though we don't know each other well, I want her to know that she's not alone. It takes a few heartbeats for the thick tension filling her muscles to gradually dissipate.

"You're not obligated to do anything." There's a pause. "You know that, right?"

She nibbles at her lower lip as confusion flickers across her expression. "It kind of feels like I am."

"From what you've told me, they're strangers. Have you even met this kid?"

"Kylie," she says.

"Have you even met her?" I ask again.

"No."

Another burst of anger detonates inside me, and it takes effort to tamp it down so it doesn't bubble over. That's not what she needs right now. "It's unfair that he put you in this position."

"Does it even matter?" she whispers.

It should, but I have no idea if it does.

Only wanting to offer comfort, I say, "Whatever you decide will be the right choice."

She draws in an unsteady breath before looking away. "I wish I could believe that."

When my fingers tighten around hers, our gazes lock and something undefinable passes between us. Something I've never experienced before. I'm not sure what to make of it.

All I know is that I want more.

15

LOLA

I stare sightlessly out the passenger window at the scenery that flies by in the darkness as we return to campus. Instead of filling the silence with idle chitchat, we're both quiet, each lost in our own private thoughts. Mine keep circling back to the conversation with Tony. It feels like a bomb has been dropped in the middle of my life and my ears are still ringing from the force of it. As of yet, I haven't regained my equilibrium. It's doubtful I ever will.

The warmth of his fingers covering mine is what pulls me out of those tangled thoughts. I stare at our clasped hands in confusion. It's a strange sight. Almost surreal. Two weeks ago, standard operating procedure had been to bare my teeth every time I had the sad misfortune of running into Asher. His golden boy status on campus, easy disposition, and confident charm rubbed me the wrong way and set my nerves on edge. Every time I caught sight of the guy, yet another female—or more—were clinging to his brawny form, just waiting for him to give the word so they could fall onto their backs and spread their legs wide.

It doesn't make sense that he's now holding my hand, offering both comfort and support. Not in a million years did I see this coming.

What makes even less sense is that I actually like the way his fingers feel wrapped around mine. Strangely enough, I don't feel so alone.

Or adrift.

When was the last time I opened up and let anyone into my life?

It doesn't take long to comb through my memories and arrive at an answer.

Not since I was a kid and the world crumbled around me. Suddenly, I was on my own, fending for myself, tackling adult problems. Ever since then, I've been careful to build a fortress around myself, never wanting to feel that kind of heartache again.

And yet, here Asher is, attempting to scale my walls.

Uncertainty swirls through my brain. I have no idea what any of this means.

Probably nothing.

What I've discovered is that while he is a flirt, girls literally throw themselves at his feet, begging for his attention. For some reason, I assumed he was the instigator, seeking out the limelight, encouraging it so he could lap it up with a spoon. Only now do I realize that isn't necessarily the case. I watched him firsthand with the hostess. She would have crawled over the podium that separated them had he given her an ounce of encouragement. Even when he expressed polite disinterest, she still continued to hover.

I blink out of those thoughts when he swings the Escalade into the parking lot and pulls up to Mom's faded blue Buick LaCrosse that has seen better days.

More like years.

Maybe even decades.

He releases my fingers and shifts the gear into park, allowing the truck to idle before turning toward me and holding out his hand. "Give me your phone."

I quirk a brow. "Excuse me?"

"I don't have your number, and we need to rectify that situation pronto."

"Do we?" I narrow my eyes and pretend to contemplate the request. "Do we really?"

He snorts as his lips quirk. "Absolutely."

I grumble under my breath before digging around in my bag for my phone, unlocking the home screen, and reluctantly handing it over. He quickly pulls up the messaging app and inputs his number before hitting send. There's a corresponding ding from his pocket before he returns the slim device.

"Now you can call anytime, even if it has nothing to do with tutoring." His voice dips. "Like if you just want to talk about what's going on. That's cool."

I stare at the cell in my palm, because it's so much easier than meeting his searching gaze. I blink away the emotion attempting to gather in my eyes. My guess is that it has more to do with the news my father sprung on me than Asher's unexpected offer of friendship.

At least, I hope it does.

I'm jolted out of those thoughts when his fingers settle beneath my chin. He raises it until I don't have any other choice but to meet the steadiness of his gaze in the darkness that swamps us.

"I mean it. Call if you need anything. There's no reason for you to go through this alone."

Doubt swirls through me, and it takes effort to summon my voice. "You're not the person I thought you were."

He cocks his head as if giving serious consideration to the statement. "Is that such a bad thing?"

"I'm not sure yet." His actions tonight have thrown me off balance. "It was so much easier to dislike you when I thought you were nothing more than an entitled athlete strutting around campus with an overinflated ego."

Instead of laughing, he says, "Maybe I didn't realize I was more until I saw myself through your eyes."

Any lightness filling the truck vanishes as a strange tension takes hold.

"You are, Asher. You're so much more." The words escape from my mouth before I can stuff them back inside where they can't do any damage.

I almost wince, afraid of giving away too much or trusting the wrong person and making a mistake. The last thing I can afford is to get burned.

When he draws closer, my heart beats a crazy rhythm against my ribcage. For just a moment, I consider putting the kibosh on whatever is happening between us before realizing that I don't want to. Maybe I just need to forget everything that weighs me down, pinning me to the earth. Even if it's for a few minutes.

As soon as the softness of his lips sweeps across mine, I open under their firm pressure and wait for the onslaught. Instead of delving in and taking what I'm so freely offering, his mouth drifts across mine with gentle strokes that leave me impatient for more.

Once.

Twice.

Three times his mouth grazes mine. A whimper escapes from me when he nips at my lower lip, tugging it with sharp teeth.

Oh god…

Arousal bursts to life in the pit of my belly before sinking lower as he presses kisses against the corners of my mouth. Just as a potent concoction of need and frustration bubbles up, his tongue dips inside to mingle with my own. There's nothing rushed about the movement. It's like we have all the time in the world to explore one another.

One hand rises before strong fingers wrap around my jaw as if to hold me in place. Except we both know that's not necessary. I'm here willingly.

I hate to admit just how many times he's surprised me this evening. When I expect him to do one thing, he does the opposite. It's enough to leave me feeling strangely off kilter and unsure of my own instincts.

What I like most is that all the issues circling a million miles an hour through my brain have disappeared into thin air. My car breaking down, money for the bills, the coursework I'm always trying to complete on time, and everything my father just dumped in my lap vanishes until the only thing I can focus on is how delicious it feels to have his lips coasting over mine.

A low growl rumbles up from within his chest as he angles his head one way and then another before deepening the kiss. It's like I'm being dragged to the bottom of the ocean and can't imagine what it would be like to surface again.

Who needs air to breathe?

Certainly not me.

It's a shock to realize that my arms have twined around his neck and my fingers are tunneling through the thick strands of his short hair. It feels as if I'm clinging to him, hanging on for dear life.

When he licks the inside of my mouth with insistent strokes, I melt against him, needing more. Has anyone ever kissed me quite so thoroughly or with so much authority?

It's a stupid question.

Of course they haven't.

That's all it takes for me to lose track of both time and space. The only thing I'm cognizant of is the firm pressure of his fingers on my jaw, the way his lips are slanted across mine, and the velvety softness of his tongue as it licks and strokes me. It could be minutes or hours that we remain fused together. What I do know is that when we finally break apart, Asher's eyes are heavy-lidded, the glass is fogged up, and we're both breathing hard.

When his tongue darts out to lick at his lower lip, my gaze falls to the movement.

"Mmm, I taste like you."

Those thickly spoken words have another burst of arousal exploding deep in my core. My thoughts are a tangled mess as need throbs insistently through me, sparking sensations to life in places I had no idea existed before this night.

When his hand snakes around the nape of my neck and he drags me closer for a second time, reality crashes around my head and I slap my palms against the steely strength of his chest to keep him at bay.

It takes effort to find my voice. "We probably shouldn't."

His penetrating gaze stays focused on mine. "Why not?"

That's an excellent question.

My brain spins, trying to come up with an answer. "It'll only blur the lines of our friendship."

The thick haze clouding his eyes gradually clears. "Is that what we are? Friends?"

A couple weeks ago, I would have said absolutely not.

Now, I'm not so sure.

"I think so."

Indecision flickers in his eyes before his grip loosens and he backs off, putting some much-needed space between us. The arousal burning in his bright blue eyes is enough to scorch me alive. That's when I realize it wouldn't take much to ignite a fire between us. One that could easily burn out of control.

That's not something I can allow to happen.

My life is complicated enough.

Adding him into the mix would be foolish. And that's the last thing I am. I've made it a point to always think a couple of steps ahead and make smart decisions that propel me forward. Asher will only mess with my head and bog me down. Even if he doesn't mean to, that's exactly what will occur.

I refuse to let it happen.

He plows a hand through his hair before glancing at the fogged-up windshield. After a second or two, his gaze slides to mine before locking on it. A potent concoction of relief and disappointment swirls through me now that the desire swimming in his eyes has dissipated.

"I meant what I said earlier," he says, breaking into the tangle of my thoughts. "You can call anytime."

"Thank you." My fingers shake as I grab my backpack from the floor of the vehicle before popping open the passenger door. Once my feet hit the pavement, I suck a deep breath of chilly night air into my lungs and hope it's enough to clear my head. Since I'm unsure when we'll meet up again, I say, "Talk soon."

"You can bet on it."

The unexpected promise filling his voice has my eyes widening before darting to his. That's when I realize that whatever has been set in motion tonight isn't over.

Not by a long shot.

16

ASHER

My gaze coasts over the sea of colorfully dressed students packed into the first floor of our house as I bring the green bottle to my lips and take a swig. Almost every girl is wearing a bikini and tiny shorts or a grass skirt. The guys have kept it lowkey with T-shirts and board shorts. Needless to say, everyone who's walked through that door tonight has gotten lei'd.

I've strategically placed myself at the edge of the living room, so I have the perfect view of the entryway. Unfortunately, the particular female I'm searching for continues to remain elusive.

Sure, I could tell myself that I'm not waiting around for Lola, but that would be a lie. I'm desperate for the sight of her. Even though it's been a couple of days, I still can't stop thinking about the kiss we shared in the truck and the way she melted against me, turning unexpectedly warm and pliant in my arms.

Who would have ever believed it was possible for Lola to become so soft and willing?

Not me.

I've been with my fair share of girls over the years, but none of them have ever crawled inside my brain and set up residence. It's a strange feeling to wake up to thoughts of someone and have them pop into your head at random times throughout the day. And then have the same damn thing happen as you slide between the sheets at night.

There have been a handful of times when I pulled out my phone, tempted to shoot her a text. As soon as I realized what I was doing, I carefully slid the cell back into my pocket.

That's not me.

I don't text or call girls.

And I sure as hell don't strike up friendships with them either.

We fu—

I'm jolted from those thoughts when slender fingers trail over my chest and rounded breasts press into my side. I blink back to the present, only to find Mallory smiling up at me. She's wearing a string bikini. My guess is that if she takes one deep breath, her breasts will burst free.

"Hi, Asher. I've missed you." Her lower lip pops out in a pout. "We barely spend time together anymore."

The surge of disappointment that floods through me when I find a different girl from the one I've been thinking about is almost enough to knock me on my ass. Since when is one soft, willing female any different from another?

Instead of scrutinizing the confusing rush of feelings, I lift the bottle to my lips and take another drink. "Yeah, it's been busy."

"I liked it better when I was helping you with homework." She flutters her mascara laden lashes.

Helping?

I snort. "Actually, you were completing my homework for me."

And I was sitting back, doing nothing. Lola's comments from the other night about how easy it's been for me to skate through school without lifting a finger reluctantly circle through my head. A wave of shame crashes over me as I realize just how much I've taken advantage of the system along with the people around me.

Especially girls.

I was just happy it freed up more time to play video games, drink, smoke, and screw around.

Literally.

Her fingers trail up and down my chest, pulling my attention back to her. "What does it matter? It's not like you were actually planning to use your degree." Her voice turns into more of a purr. "You'll be playing in the NFL next year."

So...I don't need an education?

Is that what this chick is trying to tell me?

The sentiment has never bothered me before, but for some reason, it does now.

"What if that doesn't happen?" I've never dared to release those words into the atmosphere. You know what? They're just as scary as I assumed they'd be.

Her brow furrows as she cocks her head. "I don't understand."

I jerk my shoulders, wishing she'd back off and give me a little space. "What if I don't get drafted?"

Laughter tumbles from her lips as she playfully swats at my chest. "That's not going to happen, silly. You'll turn pro and make millions. Everyone says so."

Here's the thing—I'm pretty sure it doesn't matter what *everyone* says.

"Even though it's late in the season, I could still get injured and then all my prospects would be flushed down the shitter. What would I do then?"

Her face scrunches as bewilderment flickers in her eyes. These aren't the kinds of convos we're used to having. Actually, we don't converse much. And certainly not about anything of importance.

"I don't know, but you'd figure something out."

I jerk a brow and take another drink from the bottle clenched in my hand. It doesn't taste nearly as good as it did a few minutes ago. "Would I?"

Without an education to fall back on?

This is the first time I've really allowed myself to think about what would happen if I don't get drafted to a team. Even if I graduate with a Communications degree, without a career in the NFL, a cushy broadcasting position with ESPN isn't going to happen.

What else would I do with that degree?

I'm not gifted when it comes to numbers like my brother. And I don't want to follow my dad into the FBI. All right, that's not necessarily true. It does sound like a cool job, but I've smoked way too much weed to make it through the application process. Trust me, my father has been quick to point that out.

So yeah…

A future without football feels like a scary abyss. One I now feel ill equipped for. And that, unfortunately, is my own doing.

"Of course." Mallory reaches up to stroke my cheek. "I know exactly what'll help take your mind off this and get you back into the party spirit."

Before I can open my mouth, she turns and waves to a girl wearing a matching bikini and tiny shorts that barely cover her ass. The brunette's eyes light up before she hustles over. It's almost like she was waiting for Mallory to give her the bat signal. With a bright smile glued in place, the other girl squeezes in next to her friend.

"You remember Grace. Right?"

Not really.

"Sure."

"We were just talking about how much fun the three of us could have."

I shake my head, uninterested in the direction this conversation has swerved in. It doesn't escape me that if their proposition for a threesome had occurred a couple of weeks ago, I would have happily obliged. Hell, I would have been leading the charge.

Now, it's the last thing on my mind.

What I need to figure out is an extrication plan.

And pronto.

When the front door swings open, I glance away from the girls and spot the one I've spent the last hour waiting for. A mixture of relief and excitement floods through me. Unlike all the other chicks, Lola isn't wearing a bikini or grass skirt. She's dressed in jeans and a sweater.

And I can't take my eyes off her.

"You know what?" I pry Mallory's hands away before carefully forcing her back a step. "A friend just arrived. I'll catch you two later, okay?"

The blonde's mouth falls open. "What? You're leaving? Are you sure?"

"Yup." I couldn't be more certain.

Disappointment fills her eyes as she reaches out and tugs at my lei. "But I thought—"

"Sorry." It takes a couple of seconds to untangle myself from them before cutting a direct path to Lola. There's no need to push and shove my way through the thick crowd—it parts like the Red Sea. A few guys pat me on the shoulder as I pass by, congratulating me on the game we won this afternoon. As much as this is a party to celebrate Demi's birthday, it's also a way to blow off steam after the first playoff game.

Even though I knew Lola wouldn't be in the stands, cheering me— I mean, *us*—on, I couldn't help but scan the crowd, hoping to find her there. Normally, when I'm on the field, I'm laser focused on what needs to be accomplished. I'm able to block out the static from the outside world.

That wasn't the case this afternoon. And it had everything to do with the dark-haired girl who just walked through the door.

As soon as I'm close enough, I say, "Hey."

Her gaze flickers to mine before darting away. "Hi."

I search my brain for something to break the strange tension that has fallen over us but come up empty. When was the last time I had a problem making conversation with a girl?

Usually, they do all the talking and I sit back, drink my beer, and nod every once in a while, so they think I'm paying attention.

Sweat springs to my palms.

What the hell is that about?

I drag a hand across my thigh to wipe off the wetness.

When silence stretches to the point of uncomfortableness, I grab the lei from around my neck and pull it over her head until it settles against her chest.

I clear my throat as her gaze cuts to mine. "You, ah, looked like you needed to get lei'd."

That probably came out wrong.

Instead of taking offense, her lips spring into a slight smile. "Thanks. It's been a while."

My brows rise with interest. "Oh?"

"Yeah…well…you know."

I really don't. But I'd like to.

Before I can fire off any questions on the subject, she holds up a small gift bag. "I brought a present for Demi."

"Then we should find her." It goes without saying that I'll latch onto the flimsiest of excuses to grab hold of her hand and keep her with me. Fingers locked around hers, I drag her through the entryway and into the dining room, where I last saw Demi and Rowan hanging out.

When I don't find them there, we move into the kitchen. The birthday girl and her roommate, Sydney, are at the makeshift bar where there's a wide array of alcoholic beverages for the partygoers. A smile lights up her face as soon as she sees Lola before pulling her in for a hug. I'm forced to release her while they talk. Even though I'm trying my best not to appear stalkerish, my attention stays riveted on Lola the entire time. My heartrate kicks up its tempo when a smile breaks out across her face and a throaty laugh escapes from her.

Is it my imagination, or is she even prettier than the last time I saw her?

What's even more strange is that Lola doesn't do anything to enhance her beauty. She's not wearing hair extensions or fake lashes. There isn't makeup caked on her face or form-fitting outfits clinging to her body.

Her beauty is subtle and natural.

How didn't I notice it before?

I eat at Taco Loco with regularity, and up until our first run-in when she didn't want to seat us or take my order, I don't remember seeing her. Now that she's standing in front of me, I find it impossible to look away.

And no…that's not the alcohol talking. My gaze flickers to the bottle in my hand. I'm still working on my first one. I've been nursing it for the last hour. My brow scrunches. I really don't understand what's going on with me. I'm not drinking like I usually do, and I've just turned down a threesome with two hot chicks.

I blink back to the present when all three girls lift small plastic shot glasses and clink the rims before belting back the liquid. As soon as the alcohol is drained, they scrunch their faces in unison.

"Whose idea was it to do a tequila shot?" Demi asks.

Lola points to Sydney, who shrugs with a grin.

"I'm pretty sure this occasion calls for a second round," the blonde soccer player says.

"Hell, no." Demi shakes her head. "That taste is going to linger in my mouth for a while."

"It's way better than other things that have a tendency to linger," Sydney says with a snort before raising a brow at Lola in challenge. "How about you? One more shot in honor of the birthday girl?"

"Normally, I'm not much of a drinker." She glances at me before adding, "But it's been a rough week."

Sydney flicks a look in my direction. "How about you?"

I shrug. "Sure, why not?"

She pours three shots and distributes them. "Wait! I knew we were missing something." She grabs the saltshaker and a small bowl of cut-up limes.

We each lick a small patch of skin between our thumb and pointer finger before sprinkling salt on it.

Lifting our shots, Sydney says, "To Demi's twenty-second birthday!"

Lola and I echo the sentiment before raising the miniature glasses to our lips and tossing back the liquor.

Well, hell.

The alcohol might be smooth, but it still burns a fiery trail down my throat. As soon as I set the glass on the counter, I glance at Lola, who already has a lime between her teeth. Instead of grabbing my own, I wrap my fingers around her neck and bring her mouth to mine so I can steal the wedge. My lips linger for a few seconds before reluctantly backing away to meet her wide gaze.

When a surprised giggle escapes, she claps a hand over her mouth to keep the sound trapped inside. Her shoulders shake as mine do the same. This Lola is different from the one I've been spending time with. I can't say that I don't like when she unbends just a little and lets her guard down.

Brayden and Rowan make their way into the kitchen before each of them wraps their arms around their respective girlfriends. It's tempting to tug Lola to me, but she's not mine. A little pang of longing flares to life deep within before I stomp it down.

What's weird is that I've never wanted that kind of relationship or been interested in having a girlfriend. I've always enjoyed doing whatever I wanted and not being held accountable to anyone but myself.

Life is just easier that way.

Except...

I don't know.

It feels like something is shifting beneath my feet and I can't stop it from happening. Uncomfortable with the thoughts swirling through my brain, I shove them away and nod toward the dining room, where all the drinking games are set up.

"Any interest in playing beer pong?"

She glances in that direction. I'm expecting a solid no in response. You can imagine my surprise when she says, "Sure."

I grab her hand for the second time this evening as we make our way into the other room and watch the game already in progress. When one team loses, we join in on the action. Crosby and I are on one side of the table while Lola and Brooke stand on the other.

Little does this girl know that I'm a beer pong master. I've spent years cultivating and honing my skills. Ten minutes later and I haven't missed a single shot. Lola pouts as I make her drink another plastic cup of beer. It's kind of adorable. Playful Lola isn't someone I've met before. But she's out tonight, and I'm here for it.

Brooke is laughing and drinking as well. It only takes a few well-placed shots to win us the game. Crosby walks around the table before tugging his girlfriend into his arms and nuzzling the side of her neck.

I almost roll my eyes. These two can't keep their hands off each other.

Am I jealous of what they have?

Hell, no.

All right…maybe a little.

There might be a teeny tiny part of me that wishes I had someone to hold close. And not just for a couple of hours but the long haul. Someone who would be there for me and talk about all the things I keep buried deep inside. My earlier convo with Mallory springs to mind.

What's obvious is that she doesn't give a shit about me. If I sustained a career-ending injury, she'd vanish before I blinked my eyes, moving on to another player whose future in the NFL looked bright and shiny.

That realization leaves a bitter taste in my mouth. I hate to admit it, but most of the girls I hook up with are carbon copies of Mallory. That's always been by design.

It's exactly the way I wanted it.

At least…that used to be the case.

When the music changes and a popular song gets blared through the speakers, a loud cheer goes up and everyone sings along, belting out the lyrics. It's a shock when Lola shimmies her way toward the space that has been carved out for dancing in the other room.

A couple of minutes tick by as I watch her lift her hands and tip her head back, her lithe body swaying to the thumping beat of the music. My cock stiffens as I stare from the edge of the space.

Who knew she could move like that?

When some random dude gets a little too close, putting his hands on her hips and trying to grind on her, I straighten as jealousy rears its ugly head. That's all it takes for me to shove my way through the sea of dancers. It's not like we're together or anything, but I'm not about to let some drunk asshole take advantage of her either.

Once I reach her side, one hard look aimed in the dude's direction is all it takes for him to slink away without so much as a word of protest. I wrap my hands around her waist and tug her close until our bodies are pressed together.

When she lifts her head and meets my gaze, a slow smile curves her lips and my heart stutters in response.

That's never happened before. In all honesty, I'm not sure how I feel about it.

Here's what I know—when I'm with Lola, everything feels different.

I feel different.

And I don't want that to end.

17

LOLA

*A*rgh.

My head.

It's pounding so hard that it feels like it might roll right off my shoulders. Someone needs to make the insistent throbbing stop. I haven't dared to crack open my eyes, and already the bright sunlight hurts them. It's tempting to drag the pillow over my head and go back to sleep for a couple of hours, but I don't have that luxury. Even in my incapacitated state, I remember that I'm working the afternoon shift at the restaurant. With the way I'm feeling, it's going to be grueling.

The thought of serving food all day has my stomach roiling as if I'm standing on the deck of a ship that's being tossed around by the ocean.

Why did I guzzle down so much alcohol last night?

I'm not much of a drinker. And I certainly don't get wasted.

Like, ever.

But…it had been Demi's birthday, and the situation with Tony had been weighing me down, making it impossible to breathe. I'd wanted to turn off my thoughts and escape my life if only for a few blissful hours.

And that's exactly what I did.

Images flicker through my brain like a slow-motion picture show.

There'd been laughter. Enough to make my belly hurt and tears spring to my eyes. When was the last time I laughed that hard?

Or that much?

Probably never.

And then there'd been Asher.

He stayed by my side all night. No matter where I was, he'd been there, which had allowed me to cut loose and simply enjoy myself. That's not something I do on a regular basis or with just anyone. There aren't many people I'm comfortable with or trust. But with him…surprisingly, I am. It doesn't make sense. We haven't known each other very long, but that doesn't change the way I feel.

And then there'd been the dancing…

I shook my booty until it felt like my feet were going to fall off.

Another memory gradually takes shape in my brain.

Kissing.

And lots of it.

Did it go any further than that?

I sift through the memories, but everything remains murky. When nothing more comes to mind, I blow out a slow breath and attempt to pry my eyes open. It feels like they're cemented shut. After a minute or two, my eyelashes finally flutter, and I glance around the space before realizing that nothing looks familiar.

Well, hell.

I steel myself before chancing a look at the other side of the mattress, only to find it empty. A ridiculous amount of relief rushes through me. I'm in no way a detective, but by the state of the rumpled sheets and indent on the neighboring pillow, my guess is that I didn't sleep here alone. I pick up the blankets and peek under them to find that I'm naked from the waist up with only my panties to cover me.

Thank goodness for small miracles.

With a little more care, I glance around the room for a second time. There's a football jersey thrown over the back of a chair shoved up against the desk with a couple Communications books piled on top of it. I have the sneaking suspicion from the clues I've been able to piece together that I crashed in Asher's room. I should probably make a hasty exit before he returns. The last thing we need is any awkward morning-after convos. Especially since I can't remember what exactly happened.

Just as I throw off the thick comforter, the bedroom door opens and Asher strolls in, wearing a black tank top and loose-fitting athletic shorts. Even though my head continues to throb an insistent beat and it feels like my eyes will roll out of my head any given moment, that's not enough to stop my gaze from licking over his biceps.

They're massive. It's not like I haven't caught sight of him in T-shirts, but this is something else altogether. I should definitely look away. Except I can't bring myself to do it.

Even his bulges have bulges.

"Hey, you're up," he says, strolling toward the bed.

There's just a hint of a flush staining his cheeks.

I don't realize he's carrying a small brown paper bag until he sets it on the nightstand and holds out a tall to-go drink container for me to take. As soon as I wrap my fingers around the cup, the scent of freshly roasted coffee permeates the air and hits my nostrils. I can't help but close my eyes and inhale the delectable aroma.

Sweet baby Jesus, that smells amazing. Even hung over, I'll take coffee every single time. If anything has the possibility of jump-starting my brain cells, it's caffeine.

When my eyelashes flutter open again, I find Asher standing next to the bed, wide gaze pinned to my chest. My brow furrows as I glance down to see what's captured his attention.

It takes my sluggish brain a moment to remember that I threw off the blankets. If I was studying his arms as if preparing for a crucial test, he's now examining my breasts with an equal amount of intensity. A little zing of electricity zips through my body as I grab the comforter and tug it upward.

Heat explodes in my cheeks as I glance at him, only to find a grin simmering around the edges of his lips. To cover my embarrassment, I bring the coffee to my mouth and take a tentative sip. The hot liquid slides smoothly down my throat, filling me with warmth. My eyelids drift shut for a second time as I savor the sharp bite of flavor.

Mmm…so good.

"I think I might love you," I say with a contented sigh.

My eyes pop open as I realize what just escaped from my lips. If it's possible, my cheeks grow even hotter until it feels like they're on fire and I'll burst into flames.

"I didn't mean it like that," I whisper in mortification.

His smile grows wider as he winks. "Girls usually say that *after* I've slept with them. Not before."

Of course that would be his response. The funny thing is that he's probably not exaggerating. But still…that comment deserves an eye roll. As soon as I give in to the urge, my gaze gets snagged by the small bag off to the side. I'd been so distracted by the sight of his muscles that I almost forgot about it.

With my cup in hand, I gesture to the nightstand. "Anything interesting in there?"

He shifts his stance before nodding toward it. "Why don't you find out."

Don't mind if I do.

I make sure the sheet and blanket are tucked beneath my arms and covering my breasts as I nip the bag and open the flap before stealing a look inside. What I find is a flakey pastry. The scent of warmed chocolate is all it takes to make my mouth water. Without hesitation, my fingers delve inside to carefully wrap around the croissant. As soon as it's free from the bag, I bring it to my mouth and take a bite.

It's so light and airy that it practically melts on my tongue.

If I thought the coffee was delicious, this is a thousand times better. Focused on my sweet treat, I lean back against the pillows to enjoy the amazing concoction of butter and flaky dough. Almost magically, my belly settles, and my head seems a lot less throbby. Waking up with a hangover sucks, but breakfast in bed has done wonders for it.

Asher disappears into the private bathroom attached to his room. Once he returns, he holds out his hand. "You should take these."

I set the coffee on the nightstand and open my palm. Two white pills get dropped in the center of it.

"You drank quite a bit last night. I gave you a couple of Tylenol and had you drink a glass of water before we went to bed."

I wash the pills down with the coffee and take another bite of the pastry. Melted chocolate oozes from within the center. With a tilt of my head, I refocus my attention on Asher. It's almost shocking that he could be so thoughtful. The more time we spend together, the more his behavior surprises me. It makes me realize how much I judged the guy before actually getting to know him.

"Thanks for everything."

He shrugs as if taking care of me in my inebriated state wasn't a big deal. "No problem."

This time, when his gaze dips to my chest, I don't care that the blankets have fallen to my waist, and he gets an eyeful.

"Why were you up so early?" I ask before taking another bite.

"I wanted to get a run in, and then I grabbed you something to eat. I figured it might help with the hangover."

"No one's ever brought me breakfast in bed." Something softens inside me that he went to all this effort. "I could definitely get used to it."

That comment prods him into movement. When he swallows up the distance that separates us, I raise my chin to hold his steady gaze.

"If you'd like to spend every night in my bed, that can be arranged."

His voice dips, becoming more of a rumble that strums something deep inside me.

Every muscle freezes as the air shifts in the room, becoming more explosive as tension ratchets up. A shiver slides through me as arousal bursts to life deep within my core. That's all it takes for my headache to melt into the background as our gazes stay locked.

In all my twenty-two years, I've never experienced attraction like this. As foolish as it sounds, it makes me curious to explore it further. There's something sexy about being practically naked in Asher's bed as he stares down at me with desire heating his bright blue depths.

My pulse picks up tempo as I remain still, trapped within his gaze.

When his face lowers, I realize he's giving me time to make a decision. I can slap my palms against his chest and shut down what's about to unfold, or I can lose myself in it. Stopping him—or this—is the last thing on my mind. More than anything, I want to feel the firm pressure of his lips roving over mine, dragging me to fathomless depths where thinking becomes an impossibility. That's exactly the kind of drugging effect his kisses are capable of. They make me forget, transporting me to a place where only pleasure exists.

When I tip my face to his, satisfaction floods his expression.

"Are you sure?" he asks.

"Yes." That one syllable comes out surprisingly breathless.

His mouth slants across mine as his hands settle on each side of the headboard, caging me in with all those sculpted muscles. The outside world melts away until it's only the two of us. Just like when we were in his truck, his lips brush across mine. They sweep back and forth until I'm opening, desperate for the feel of his tongue to tangle with my own. He torments me until a groan works its way up from my chest.

"You seem frustrated," he whispers. "Is there a problem?"

"I want you to kiss me properly."

"Properly?" Humor and arousal spark to life in his eyes. "Isn't that what I'm doing?"

"No, you're teasing. There's a difference."

His lips tremble around the corners. "But I like teasing you."

When a growl escapes from me, his tongue delves inside my mouth to play with my own. That's all it takes for every thought to leak out of my ears. He doesn't rush a single second or change the speed of how the moment unfolds. The urge to twine my arms around his neck and pull him close thrums through me, but the croissant and coffee are still in my hands, making that impossible. The way he licks at the inside of my mouth has need exploding within me and dampens my panties.

He pulls back just enough for our gazes to lock. "Is that more like what you had in mind?"

Before I can jumpstart my brain and come up with a response, he snatches the drink from one hand before setting it on the nightstand. Then he grabs the half-eaten pastry and swipes one thick digit through the center of it, coming away with a dollop of chocolate. I stare with interest as he sweeps the same finger across one hard-tipped nipple before repeating the maneuver on the other side.

Air gets clogged in my lungs as he leans down and licks the stiff little bud before sucking it deep inside his mouth. A moan slips free as my back bows in pleasure. My fingers tunnel through his thick blond strands, attempting to lock him in place as sensation explodes throughout my body like a brightly colored firework.

I don't understand what this guy is doing to me. Every time he touches my body, it feels like I'm dangerously close to coming undone. He shreds all my carefully controlled composure. It's strangely addictive. Like walking a tightrope without a net. Any moment, I'll fall, plummeting to my death. And there's nothing I can do to save myself.

Another round of arousal detonates in my core before throbbing an insistent beat until it feels like I'll burst right out of my skin. When I can't take another second, he releases my breast with a soft pop. There isn't a chance for me to suck in a ragged breath before his lips crash onto mine. When his tongue delves inside my mouth for a second time, I open, allowing him entrance. What he's doing feels more like an assult on my senses. And I love it.

By the greedy way he attacks me, it's almost like he's just as turned on as I am.

But how can that be?

My guess is that this is an everyday occurrence for Asher.

Me, on the other hand?

Not so much. The feelings he's managed to rouse are both new and exciting. I want to drown in the sensation he's stoking to life. Before I can fully sink into the kiss, he pulls away and lowers his face to my chest so he can lap at the chocolate still covering my other nipple. Once it's been licked clean, he draws the bud into his mouth. His hand rises until his fingers can tweak and pull at the other one. Bliss reverberates through every fiber of my being, igniting a firestorm in its path. My fingernails rake against his scalp as he plays with both stiff peaks.

"Asher..."

Barely do I recognize the low scrape of my own voice as desire pummels my senses, making me needy for more.

He bites down on the tight bud just enough to send a shockwave of pleasure-infused pain spiraling through my system. When I gasp, he tweaks the other nipple before licking and kissing his way down my ribcage and belly, arriving at the elastic band of my panties. He continues to nip at my flesh with sharp teeth as he glances up at me, capturing my gaze with his heated one.

"Should I stop?"

Stop?

I'll probably self-combust right here in this bed if he pulls away now. I shake my head, desperate for more. Desperate for everything he's willing to give.

"Are you sure, or is that the chocolate croissant talking?"

A pained chuckle slips from my lips. "Probably both."

"Then we shouldn't go any further. The last thing I want is for you to have regrets."

"If you stop, I just might kill you." At least that's the way it feels. I can't imagine this ending. Not now. Not when I'm wound so tight. Not when the slightest touch will send me rocketing into the stratosphere.

"Hmm. That sounds suspiciously like a threat," he says with a low chuckle.

How can he tease me at a time like this?

Instead of waiting for an answer, he drags down the band of my underwear until he can bare the top of my slit. His face lowers until his teeth can sink into the plump flesh.

"Tell me what you want."

I hiss out a shuddering breath at both the sharp bite and the way his warm breath feathers over me. "Take off the panties."

"Then what?"

My tongue darts out to moisten parched lips.

Is he really going to make me say it?

When I remain silent, his voice drops, becoming more of a growl. The sound of it is like the strike of a match, sending a rush of need careening through me.

Heat floods my cheeks as I force out the words. "I want you to lick and kiss me."

"Where, baby girl? Where do you need my tongue?" His blue eyes glow like twin flames, burning with the same intensity that has taken up residence inside me.

Unable to hold his gaze, mine darts away in embarrassment as I gulp. "My pussy."

"Eyes on me," he demands.

My attention snaps back to him. Gone is the chill guy who's always joking around and doesn't seem to care about anything except football. In his place is a man who is able to command my presence and bend me to his will.

As much as I don't understand it, I like it.

Need it.

"Do you want me to lick your pussy until you come?"

The question makes my inner thighs clench. "Yes."

I've never begged for anything in my life. But I can't stop the word from tumbling free. "Please."

Deep satisfaction fills his eyes. "If that's what you want, then that's exactly what I'll give you."

Relief rushes through me, pummeling everything in its path. I'm so turned on that all he has to do is breathe on me and I'll likely shatter into a million jagged pieces.

His thumbs slip beneath the elastic before tugging the material down my hips and thighs. Instead of rushing, he takes his sweet damn time until it feels like I'll self-combust with the arousal crashing through my body.

Is that what he wants?

To bring me to my knees?

The cotton fabric drags across my bare skin, raising goosebumps in its wake as he pulls them free before tossing the slip of fabric over his shoulder. His gaze lifts, taking in every inch of my naked body. If my nipples weren't already stiff little peaks that ache with awareness, they would be after the intense scrutiny. It's as if he's taking a mental snapshot to tuck away for later.

His fingers wrap around one leg, lifting it until he can settle between them. I've always known that Asher was tall and broad, but he looks even more so between my spread thighs.

For a long, tortuous moment, he eats me up with his eyes. My teeth sink into my lower lip to stifle the whimper that is desperate to slip free. No one has ever inspected me with such thoroughness. There's no hiding with the bright sunlight that pours across the queen-sized bed. I can almost feel the heat of it warming my bare flesh.

Or maybe that's his gaze.

When he reaches out, carefully stroking a finger across my slit, I arch beneath the caress.

"You're so fucking pretty."

My breath catches, becoming wedged in the middle of my throat, making it impossible to exhale. No man has ever said that to me. And certainly not about that part of my body. Hot bursts of pleasure explode to life inside me as my legs unconsciously widen.

His gaze flicks to mine as he drags his finger over me for a second time. "You know that, right?"

Unsure how to respond, I shake my head.

"Well, you are. Never doubt it."

Needing to get back on even ground with him, I say, "I suppose you would be a connoisseur on the subject, having seen your fair share of vaginas."

"Does that bother you?"

I draw in a shuddering breath as he strokes me with a featherlight touch until it's impossible to focus on the question.

"You didn't answer." He raises a brow.

I blink and rack my brain. "What?"

A smirk flashes across his face as he continues to batter my senses with his touch. "I asked if my experience bothers you."

I don't know...does it?

Trying to hold onto that thought while so much pleasure is crashing through me is a challenge. "No," I gasp. "Everyone has a past."

"I suppose you're right about that." His finger dances along my slit. "Do you?"

My core throbs with painful awareness as he caresses me with the pad of his finger until I'm shifting restlessly beneath him.

"Of course."

His gaze drops to my pussy before rising to lock on mine again. "Do you enjoy sex?"

I gulp, trying to find the right words to answer that question. "I, ah, guess."

"Interesting answer. Hasn't it always felt pleasurable?"

One thick finger sinks inside my softness until I'm dizzy with the sensation. It's becoming almost too much to wrap my mind around. Any second, I'll burst apart at the seams.

I blink and try to remember what he just asked. "Um, what?"

"You're so damn wet," he growls, dragging the digit from my body and repeating the maneuver. "Hasn't sex always felt good? Didn't the guys you were with make you come?"

That's a hard no. Most of the time, they didn't last long enough for me to even get going.

"It's..." I bite down on my lower lip when his thumb settles over my clit, and he rubs soft little circles against it. "It's been okay."

My voice comes out sounding high pitched and squeaky, even to my own ears. Almost as if I'm barely holding it together, which is precisely the way it feels. The truth is that I'm hanging on by a thread.

He arches a brow, keeping up the steady pressure. "Just okay?"

"Ahhhh..."

"Hmmm. We should rectify that situation." There's a pause as his finger falls into a steady rhythm. "Don't you agree?"

"Yes?" I'm incapable of thinking, only feeling the flood of sensations that rushes through me.

His movements cease. "Is that a question?"

"No," I nearly shout, only wanting him to continue playing with me. It feels much too delicious to stop. Not now. Maybe not ever. Even though I know that sounds crazy, it's the only coherent thought circling through my brain.

"Just making sure."

I almost groan when his thumb returns to my clit and his finger sinks deep inside my pussy. Intensity continues to ratchet up until orgasm feels inevitable. Just as I arch, ready to fall apart, his hand disappears. I don't realize that my eyelids have drifted shut until they fly open in confusion. A protest gathers in my throat before it dies away when his fingers are replaced by the velvety softness of his lips and tongue.

Oh.

My.

God.

A guttural-sounding groan escapes from me as his wide palms settle on my thighs, spreading them farther until he has access to every delicate inch. He laps at my slit before spearing his tongue deep inside. My spine arches one vertebra at a time from the mattress as he repeats the maneuver, driving me higher before circling my clit and sucking it gently into his mouth.

I…

Feel like I'm going to shatter.

There's no other way to describe the onslaught of sensation whipping through me.

My fingers curl into the sheets as everything swirling through my body reaches a fever pitch, and I have no other choice but to scream out my pleasure. His palms press me into the mattress as I lose control. Not once does he let up on his assault. His thumbs settle on my lips, stretching them open as he laps at my shuddering softness until I'm nothing more than a limp mess in the middle of the bed.

Only then does he press a kiss against me. "It's not like I'm looking for a score or anything, but that was better than just okay, right?"

I huff out a laugh. Even though I'm staring up at the ceiling, I feel the penetrating heat of his gaze pinning me in place, making it impossible to escape the intimacy of this moment.

"It was a solid eight."

When my gaze slides to him, I find him watching me through narrowed eyes.

"An eight?"

"I said *solid* eight. Don't forget the solid part."

He snorts and shakes his head. "I don't think so."

My muscles are so loose that it takes effort to rise to my elbows and prop myself up. "You thought it should be higher?"

With a growl, he springs forward, his heavy weight landing on top of me, pinning my naked body in place as he glares.

"All right, fine. It was and eight point five. There," I say with a chuckle, "are you happy?"

"The way I played with your sweet little pussy was a solid ten."

His confidence shouldn't be so sexy, but I can't deny that it is. I've never been with anyone like him.

I lift a brow. "Was it now?"

"Abso-fucking-lutely."

He nips at my lower lip before sucking the fullness into his mouth. His gaze never strays from mine as he releases it. "You taste like chocolate."

"And you taste like pussy," I murmur.

"Now that's a delectable combination. Maybe I'll have to spread chocolate there next time."

"Next time?" My pulse picks up speed at the thought of this happening again.

He smirks. "Did you really think once would be enough for either of us?"

Honestly?

I have no idea what to think. This is new terrain for me. There's a voice in my head screaming that I need to be cautious. When I remain silent, he presses a quick kiss against my lips before rolling off the side of the mattress and rising to his feet. For a long moment, he stares at me sprawled out naked in his bed before grabbing the hem of his muscle shirt and dragging it up his body and over his head.

Air gets wedged in my throat as my gaze licks over every hard plane. Say what you want about him, the man is definitely built. His fingers settle at the elastic band hanging low on his hips before shoving both the shorts and boxers down his legs until he's as naked as I am.

My attention falls to his dick. Even though I tell myself to look away, doing so feels impossible. He's both long and thick.

And hard.

Deliciously so.

He wasn't kidding when he claimed to be hung like a bull. It's one hundred percent true. What would it feel like to be fucked with a cock like that?

Even though I just came minutes ago, desire bursts to life inside me again.

I clear my throat. "What are you doing?"

"Taking a shower. Why?" He smirks as if he can read my thoughts. "What does it look like?"

I really need to stop staring. This is becoming embarrassing. It takes effort to look away from his erection. The smile lifting the edges of his lips tells me that my intense perusal hasn't gone unnoticed.

"Any interest in joining me?"

As tempting as the offer is, I shake my head. I think we've done more than enough this morning to muddy the waters. "I should probably get moving. I have to work at noon."

He stalks closer before leaning down and caging me in with all that brawny strength. I'd be lying if I didn't admit to wanting to turn my head and nip at his bulging bicep.

"Last night was fun," he says.

I find myself nodding in agreement. "It was." Probably the most I've had in a long time.

Arousal leaps into his eyes as his lids lower. "This morning, too."

My mouth turns cottony as his penetrating gaze holds mine. "Yes."

Just when I think he'll kiss me all over again, my phone chimes with an incoming message. My palms flatten against his bare chest before gently pushing him away. What I need is perspective, and that's not possible when he's invading my personal space.

It's only now that I realize just how dangerous this guy is.

Was there really a time when I foolishly thought I was immune to his charm?

Ha!

It's disturbing to realize that I'm just as fallible as the other girls on this campus.

Almost reluctantly, he retreats before straightening to his full height. I roll from the bed and scoop up my discarded clothing. When most of the garments have been collected, I turn away before yanking on my panties, shoving my arms into the straps of my bra, and grabbing my sweater. It takes a few seconds of hunting around to find my jeans. It's like I stripped everything off in a hurry and threw them all over the place. I shake my head as more memories flash through my brain. Even though I had fun, it'll be a long time before I drink that much again.

Once I'm dressed, I grab my small, cross body purse from his desk and dig out my phone. From the corner of my eye, I catch sight of a very naked Asher watching me.

The man is built like a Greek god carved from marble.

He's utter perfection.

After the explosive orgasm this morning, it's easy to understand why girls flock to him in droves. He has serious skills in the bedroom.

All those good vibes buzzing beneath my skin disappear as I open the message from Tony.

A groan slips free as I skim the text.

He takes a step toward me. "Is there a problem?"

"No. Not really," I mutter, raking a hand through my disheveled hair. "Tony has invited me over for dinner on Tuesday." With a glance, I state the obvious. "I don't want to go."

The idea of spending time alone with his family makes my belly pinch with nausea. That's all it takes for my brain to reject the invitation. Asher closes the distance between us before slipping his arms around my body and tugging me close. I have to tilt my chin to meet his gaze.

"Then don't. It's not like you owe them anything."

Air escapes from my lungs like a tire with a slow leak as I admit, "I know, but part of me feels like I should hear them out." Now that I've had a couple days for the situation to roll around in my brain, my stance has softened just a fraction. Not when it comes to Tony, but toward his daughter. I can't imagine what it would be like to deal with this kind of health issue at her age.

Is she scared?

Angry?

Resigned to the circumstances?

Kylie should be focused on school, dating, parties, going out with friends and having fun. Maybe even thinking about what college she wants to attend. Not whether she'll make it through the next couple of years.

"Why? These people aren't a part of your life. And they certainly aren't your family."

My heart clenches because it's the truth. "I know..."

His brows lift. "But?"

"I haven't made a decision yet. I can come up with dozens of reasons to do this and just as many not to."

"Do you really think talking to them will give you clarity?"

I shake my head and whisper, "I don't know."

I really don't.

He presses his lips together before saying, "You can't go there alone. I'll come with you."

Surprise and confusion spiral through me. "Why would you do that?"

His eyes turn serious. Gone is the heat and sexy banter from earlier. "Because we're friends, and right now, that's exactly what you need."

"Are we?" It feels strange to ask that question when he was just between my legs, licking me to orgasm.

"Yup."

When his arms tighten, it only feels natural to lay my cheek against his bare chest. The steady thumping of his heart fills my ears and settles everything rioting dangerously inside me. No one in my life has ever filled me with such a sense of comfort.

How is it possible that this man does?

"Text me the time and I'll swing by your place and pick you up after practice."

"As much as I appreciate the offer, you don't have to do that."

I've become so used to relying on myself that I have no idea what to make of this. The truth of the matter is that I'm afraid to trust him. I'm scared to depend on someone—especially a guy like Asher—only to have him let me down. It's so much safer to keep my walls firmly intact and hold everyone at a distance.

It's the only way not to get hurt.

He pulls away until I'm forced to lift my head from his chest and meet his eyes. A stubborn glint fills them. "I'm coming with. It's a done deal."

When I open my mouth to argue, he smacks a kiss against my lips before sauntering to the bathroom. My attention drops to his backside.

I can't deny that he has a fine one.

"Instead of checking out my ass, maybe you should get moving so you're not late for work."

I snort and force myself to do exactly that. Although…staring at his perfectly sculpted cheeks just might be worth it.

18

ASHER

I pull the Escalade over to the curb in front of Lola's house before cutting the engine and exiting the vehicle. Once on the sidewalk, I head to the front door and ring the bell. My hands slide over my button-down shirt, smoothing away any imaginary wrinkles. Nerves dance beneath the surface of my skin, which is strange. The only time I feel like this is when I step onto the field before a big game.

I'm not given any more time to contemplate the situation before the door swings open and I find a tiny woman standing on the other side of the threshold. The resemblance between her and Lola is uncanny, except that there are more lines bracketing her eyes and mouth.

The corners of her lips slide upward as she takes a quick step in retreat and waves me inside. "Hello. You must be Asher," she says in lightly accented English.

I nod and follow her into the living room. Next to her petite and fragile-looking form, I feel like a giant oaf. Her long, dark hair is pulled into a thick ponytail as she tips her chin upward to hold my gaze.

Even though Lola isn't much taller than her mother, those aren't words I'd use to describe her. In fact, she'd probably kick my ass if I did. Lola is strong willed and determined. I don't think I've ever met another girl who is such a force to be reckoned with. I have a feeling that whatever she sets her mind to, she accomplishes. I've seen first-hand how hard she works.

"I am." I thrust out my hand for her mother to shake. It feels important that I make a good impression. "It's nice to meet you."

"Mariana." She sneaks a peek toward the short hallway and bedroom before leaning closer and dropping her voice. "Thank you for doing this. Lola needs someone to come with her, and obviously it couldn't be me."

"It's not a problem." I shove my hands into the pockets of my khakis. "I'm happy to help."

Anger flashes in her dark eyes as her brow furrows. "I hate that Tony's put her in this kind of position. He hasn't bothered to pick up the phone and call her in years. And now he contacts her for something like this?" She shakes her head. "No."

I blink in surprise, unsure how to respond to the emotion crackling in her voice.

Before I can say anything, Lola chooses that moment to join us.

My gaze settles on her, and the conversation with her mother falls right out of my head. She's wearing a pale pink sweater that hugs her slender curves and dark wash jeans that fit like a glove. Her hair has been left all long and loose to float around her shoulders.

We haven't seen each other since Sunday morning. It's only now that I realize how hungry I've been for the sight of her. My mind tumbles back to the way I played with her naked body—touching her breasts, sucking the hard tips into my mouth, licking her softness, before forcing her to surrender. As I continue staring, her beauty hits me like a punch to the gut.

"You look gorgeous." The compliment escapes before I can stuff it back inside my mouth.

A light blush hits Lola's cheeks as our gazes catch and hold before she glances away.

"Thanks." Her hands drift over her sweater as she shifts her stance.

Her discomfort with the compliment is palpable, and it makes me wonder why more people haven't told her this. It's so tempting to swallow up the distance between us and take her into my arms. I'm starving for the feel of her beneath my hands. When my tongue darts out to lick at my lower lip as if I can still taste her there from the other morning, her gaze drops to the movement.

Is she thinking about it as well?

She clears her throat and rips her attention away before focusing on her mother. "Are you sure you'll be all right?"

Mariana smiles before patting her daughter's arm. "Of course. I'll probably watch a little TV. Maybe read a book. You don't need to worry."

She nods toward the kitchen. "The carne guisada is ready. Just give it a couple minutes to cool."

"I'm not hungry right now. Maybe later."

"You need to eat."

"I know," she says with a wave. "I will. I'm not a child."

Lola bites down on her lower lip, worrying it between her teeth. "If you need anything, just text or call. Okay?"

"I'll be fine." Mariana glances at me from beneath a thick fringe of inky-colored lashes. Even with her dark complexion, a blush stains her cheeks. "You worry too much."

"So you like to tell me," Lola says with a sigh.

As I listen to their conversation, observing their interaction, it hits me that their roles almost seem reversed. Even though we've been spending more time together, she doesn't talk much about her childhood. I know her father bailed when she was a kid and she lived with her mother after that. Only now am I picking up on the fact that there might be other issues at play. It's obvious that there's a lot of love between these two women, but it's equally apparent that Lola has taken on the role of caretaker.

What isn't this girl dealing with?

The strange urge to take care of her thrums through me. Has anyone in her life ever bothered to do that?

There are so many adult responsibilities resting on her slender shoulders. A mountain of them, and all her father has done is sweep into her life and add more.

The older woman wags a finger at her. "I know we talked about it before, but don't let them pressure you into making a decision. Do you understand?"

"Mama," Lola murmurs. "We're just going to hear what they have to say. It's just dinner."

Her mother snorts. "We both know that's a lie."

Lola's shoulders wilt.

After a few more minutes, we make our goodbyes, and she closes the front door behind her before we walk in silence to the truck. There are so many thoughts crashing around inside my brain that they're impossible to keep straight. Questions sit perched on the tip of my tongue, just waiting for the opportunity to burst free. I give her a bit of side-eye, realizing she won't appreciate them.

Once she's inside the vehicle, I round the hood and slide in next to her before starting the engine. She rattles off the address and I tap it into the GPS before pulling away from the curb and onto the street. With a glance at the estimated arrival time, I realize that her father doesn't live far from us.

I rack my brain for something that will smooth over the rising tension, but my mind remains blank. Instead of trying to make small talk, I flip on the radio to fill the silence.

Twenty minutes later, we drive through a neighboring community. The restaurants and stores we pass are more upscale. Quaint lamp posts decked with holiday boughs and strung with colorful lights line the shopping district, giving the place a charming, small-town feel.

The closer we get to our destination, the more she fidgets with the hem of her sweater, twisting the fabric with her fingers. Her anxiety is palpable. Like a living, breathing entity that fills the vehicle. I hate that she's being eaten up inside with nerves. More than that, I hate that the man who was supposed to protect her failed so miserably and is the one putting her through this emotional wringer.

She deserves better.

When I slip my hand over hers, she glances at me. I rip my gaze away from the road to briefly meet hers. In this moment, all I want to do is offer comfort. I'm just not sure how.

"You know that everything is gonna be fine, right?"

She chews her bottom lip as her brows slant together. "Do you really think so?"

"Yup, I do." Because I'll be there, and I'm not going to let anything happen to her.

"I don't know," she whispers. "I hope you're right."

"What don't you know?"

Her normally strong shoulders collapse under the heavy weight of our conversation. "I'm not sure what to tell them. I need more time to think. Even though I haven't made a decision yet, I feel like Mama is right, and that's what they're looking for."

I give her fingers a little squeeze. "It doesn't matter what they want." Not that she needs me to tell her this, but I can't resist adding, "What they're asking for is no small favor. You should take as much time as you need, and if they can't understand that, it's their problem. Not yours."

"I know, but..." Her voice trails off. "It's all I can think about."

"We'll listen to what they have to say and that's it. If the evening goes sideways, we take off. Easy as that."

Another heavy silence falls over us. After a mile or so, she clears her throat. "Thanks for coming with me."

I glance toward the passenger seat and find her staring straight out the windshield.

"You're welcome." There's a beat of silence before I add, "Whatever happens tonight, I'll be there. You're not alone."

As the words escape, I realize I've never meant anything more.

19

LOLA

erves skitter across my flesh as I stare at one ginormous house after another. As we drive further through the fancy neighborhood, searching for Tony's address, they seem to increase in size. A couple seconds later, Asher pulls the truck to the side of the road as we stare at the sprawling stone mansion with white columns flanking the front porch. The roof line is made up of at least five different elevations and peaks, while the lawn is meticulously manicured with sculpted hedgerows running the length of a brick paver walkway.

The house is massive. At least ten thousand square feet.

This is where Tony lives with his family.

Nausea roils in the pit of my gut, threatening to shoot up like a geyser as my mind tumbles back to the few times I swallowed my pride and asked him for money to pay the bills. We're talking heat or electric. The mortgage. Or maybe a couple of bucks for groceries when Mom's check ran out at the end of the month. That question was always quickly followed by an uncomfortable silence before he told me that he was cash strapped.

I can't help but remember how the child support payments stopped the day I turned eighteen. As if I didn't need money to buy food or pay for new clothes once I hit that magic number. It's the reason I started waitressing at my uncle's restaurant when I was barely old enough to get a job. We needed the extra cash I brought in to make ends meet.

Gaping at this gorgeous house that is grand enough to be in a glossy magazine spread—one that could probably fit ten of the tiny two-bedroom ranches I live in—seems more like a cruel joke than anything else. If I needed further proof that my existence means absolutely nothing to my biological father, I have it.

This is the first invitation that has ever been extended. As I continue staring with my face smashed against the window, I realize that would still be the case if they didn't need something from me. I'm forced from those thoughts when Asher lays a hand on my shoulder and gives it a gentle squeeze.

"Are you okay?"

A gurgle of laughter threatens to bubble up and break loose.

No...I'm not.

I'm as far from okay as you can get.

But I can't admit that. For as long as I can remember, I've always pretended to be strong, even when it felt impossible, because there was no other choice in the matter.

"Yes. I just want to get this over with."

When I continue to stare out the window, strong fingers settle under my chin before gently turning my head to meet his gaze.

He searches my eyes for a long, drawn-out moment. "You don't have to lie to me."

My mouth turns cottony as my tongue darts out to moisten my lips. "What would you like me to say?"

"The truth. Just be honest about what you're feeling."

"I want to be anywhere but here," I whisper into the darkness.

"That's understandable." He cocks his head. "You know that we don't have to do this. We can cancel. All you have to do is say the word and we'll get out of here." He nods toward the house. "They can fuck themselves."

A burst of air explodes from my lungs. For some strange reason, the earnest offer settles something deep inside that gives me the strength to carry on.

I straighten my shoulders as if preparing for battle. "No."

"Are you sure?"

"I am." I nibble at my lower lip before adding, "Hopefully, we won't have to stay long."

"It doesn't matter what they want. When you're ready to go, all you have to do is tell me, and I'll make up an excuse. Would it make you feel better to come up with a code word or something? Maybe an eye twitch?"

His left eye spasms, making him look ridiculous.

When a chuckle slips free, my lips bow with a slight smile. "I don't think that's necessary."

"If you say so." One thick finger sweeps across my lower lip. "Did you bring your lipstick?"

My brows pinch as I nod, unsure why he's asking.

"Why don't you get it." His gaze stays pinned to my mouth. "You've chewed yours off."

Instead of questioning the directive, I drop my gaze and fumble around in my purse for the slim tube. Once I've retrieved it, I pull off the cap and raise it to my face. Before I'm able to make contact, his fingers wrap around mine, halting the movement.

"Let me."

My belly hollows out as I give my head a slight shake. "I can do it myself."

Stubborn light fills his eyes. "I know, but I want to do it for you."

It takes effort to swallow past the lump of wet sawdust that has settled in the middle of my throat. This time, it has nothing to do with the impending visit and everything to do with the guy sitting next to me.

When he plucks the tube away, my hand drifts to my lap. His fingers slip under my chin again before angling my face upward. The world around us fades to the background until it only encompasses the two of us.

His brow furrows in concentration as he slides the soft pink stain over the fullness of my lower lip before carefully doing the same to the top. My heart skips a painful beat as I remain still, caught up in this moment. What he's doing feels strangely intimate. Almost more so than when he was between my legs.

And that doesn't make the least bit of sense.

He stares at my mouth for several heartbeats before running the pad of his thumb gently over the edges to wipe away any smudges. "Perfect," he says softly, recapping the tube and handing it back to me.

My fingers tremble as I grab hold of it like it's a lifeline. "Thank you."

"Anytime."

A heavy silence falls over us as we continue to stare. When the tension heightens to unprecedented levels, I clear my throat and rip my gaze away. I have no idea what's happening here.

Whatever it is, I can't deal with it.

Not now.

Not before I head inside to god only knows what.

"Are you ready?" he asks, breaking into the chaotic whirl of my thoughts.

With a nod, my fingers slip around the handle and pop open the door. The fresh air that rushes over my cheeks as I step onto the wide expanse of lawn helps clear my head. I don't get more than a few strides before Asher reaches my side. His larger hand slips around mine as we make our way to the house.

Before I can chicken out and back away from the front porch, he presses the doorbell. A fresh round of nerves detonates at the bottom of my belly as I force myself to stand still instead of running away like every instinct is prodding me to do.

My wide gaze slides to Asher. I have no idea what I'd do if he weren't standing beside me. I've never allowed myself to depend on anyone. What terrifies me most is that I'm unsure if the handsome football player can be trusted. The last thing I want to do is put my faith in someone who is ill equipped to handle it and will only let me down in the end. I'm not one of those *it's better to have loved and lost than never to have loved at all* kinds of people. I'd prefer to skip the heartbreak altogether if possible.

"Thanks."

His lips lift as he winks. "You're welcome."

The door swings open, and I find a pretty blonde woman standing on the other side of the threshold. Her gaze bounces from me to Asher. Surprise morphs across her features before being swiftly masked behind a polite smile. Although, the expression isn't enough to cover the strain flooding her bright green eyes.

"Lola?"

"Yes." With a nod, I thrust out my hand as manners take over. Even though only a couple of seconds have ticked by, there's nothing about this interaction that doesn't feel bizarre.

"It's nice to finally meet you. I'm Charlotte."

Her fingers are cool as she squeezes mine lightly before releasing them. As soon as she does, my arm falls back to my side. I have no idea what to say or do. My mouth feels like it's packed full of cotton as sweat springs to my palms.

Her curious gaze resettles on the man at my side. "I didn't realize you were bringing your boyfriend."

Boyfriend?

Oh, no, no, no.

As I open my mouth to correct her, Asher steps in. "I thought Lola could use some support. I hope that's not a problem."

A mixture of emotions flickers in her eyes. "Of course not." She retreats into the entryway before opening the door wider and ushering us inside. "Please, come in."

As we step into the foyer, I can't stop my gaze from bouncing around the vast double-story space. A fancy chandelier hangs suspended from the ceiling, throwing sparkling light throughout the area. There's an oversized arrangement of colorful fresh flowers in a crystal vase on an antique side table near the door. A cluster of silver-framed photographs surrounds it. I don't give them more than a cursory inspection, knowing I won't find one of myself among them.

If there's a kernel of hurt attempting to bloom within me, I crush it before it can cause further damage.

"I thought we could get to know one another in the living room before dinner," Charlotte says, breaking into the turmoil of my thoughts.

When Asher's hand settles on the small of my back, I say, "Sure."

Is it too late to give him a code word or eye twitch?

It takes effort to force my feet into movement as we cross the entryway with its elegant sweeping staircase before entering a long gallery and then, finally, arriving at another immense room. There are groupings of expensive furniture along with a black baby grand near a wall of floor-to-ceiling windows.

As I take in the luxurious surroundings, all I can think is that the man whose name appears on my birth certificate has been living twenty minutes away in a monstrosity of a house and couldn't be bothered to visit. Or introduce me to his new family. Or help pay tuition for college so I might claw my way to a better life.

Charlotte stretches a slender arm toward a cream-colored sofa. "Why don't you sit. Tony will be out shortly. He's in his office, wrapping up a business call. Can I get you anything to drink?"

As much as I want to shake my head, I say, "A glass of water, please?" We've just arrived, and already my throat is parched.

With a nod, she glances at Asher. "For you as well?"

"That would be great. Thanks."

She spins away, heels clicking against the ocean of hardwood that stretches as far as the eye can see before disappearing at the far end of the room.

Instead of settling on the small couch, Asher reaches out and wraps his fingers around mine. "Breathe."

As soon as he gives the quiet command, I realize that air has become trapped in my lungs, and it escapes from my body in a burst.

"You still okay?"

Even though I jerk my head into a tight nod, I'm a mess of nerves, anger, and disappointment. All three whirl within me, jockeying for top position. Already, I know that coming here was a mistake.

"It's all right if you're not. This is a fucked-up situation." His voice dips. "Hell, I'm just a bystander and it feels like a twenty-car pileup on the highway with multiple fatalities."

That description sums up this mess perfectly.

"I'm really sorry for dragging you into this." He's probably wishing he could ditch me and take off.

"That's not what I meant. I'm just saying it's a lot to deal with, and I wouldn't want you here by yourself."

Before I can respond, echoing footsteps catch my attention, and my head swivels in the direction of the hallway until my gaze lands on Tony. Just like his wife, he glances at me first before his eyes dart to the guy at my side and then back again. As soon as they do, Asher moves closer before slipping an arm around my waist. The knowledge that he's at my side gives me the strength to straighten my shoulders and stand a little taller.

"Hello, Lola." Instead of enveloping me in a hug, he stuffs his hands into the pockets of his dark slacks. "Thanks for accepting our invitation. Sorry I wasn't able to greet you at the door."

As I continue to stare at the man before me, it's difficult to believe there was ever a time when he was a permanent fixture in my life. That I ran to him when I scraped my knee, and he dried my tears. Or even that we share the same DNA. It feels more like I'm talking to a stranger on the street than anything else. Not even a distant, far-flung relative.

"No problem."

The conversation sputters and dies as suffocating tension blankets us. It's like we're all players being forced to act out this bizarre farce. It's a surprise when Tony steps forward and reaches out to shake the younger man's hand.

"Hello, I'm Tony. It's nice to meet you."

"Asher."

He doesn't bother to ask who the guy at my side is or how we know each other, because at the end of the day, he doesn't actually care. I wasn't invited here so we can get to know one another on a deeper level and develop a relationship.

When another handful of seconds slip by, he clears his throat, pointing to the couch. "Why don't you sit. Did Charlotte ask if you wanted anything to drink?"

"Yes, she's getting it now." I shift, uncomfortable in my own skin and feeling out of place.

Just as Asher and I settle on the sofa, his wife returns with a tray of beverages. There's a couple of waters along with a diet soda and an expensive beer. She hands over our bottles before offering the alcoholic beverage to her husband and taking the silver can for herself. They both migrate to the longer couch situated across from us.

Unsure where we go from here, I busy my hands by twisting off the cap and taking a quick swig. My throat is as dry as the Sahara. Somehow, I don't think twelve ounces of water will help solve that issue.

Charlotte's hand flutters over her husband's. "Thank you for agreeing to meet with us." They exchange a meaningful look before she continues. "We're aware this isn't an easy situation." Her voice cracks with emotion as her eyes fill with tears, turning them luminous in the soft lamp light that floods the room. "We've exhausted all other alternatives. Cousins, distant family, donor lists."

My chest tightens with every word that falls from her lips until it feels like a vise is squeezing it. Any moment, it'll explode.

"I haven't made any decisions yet," I blurt.

"Of course." Her tongue darts out to moisten her lips. "As grateful as we are for your consideration in this matter, please keep in mind that time is of the essence."

"Yes," I say with a nod, "Tony mentioned that."

She swipes trembling fingers at a tear that treks down her ashen cheek. "It seems like every day, Kylie's condition worsens. She's on dialysis, but it's not a permanent solution. It could take years, maybe longer, for a kidney to become available. Right now, you're our best bet."

The pressure of her words crushes me to the earth.

It's a relief when Asher says, "Even if Lola decides to get tested, she might not be a match, right?"

Both of their expressions turn solemn as they nod.

"Yes," Charlotte says. "The clinic will take a sample of Lola's blood, along with a tissue typing to verify if her HLA antigens are compatible with Kylie's. There's also testing to make sure Lola is healthy enough for surgery." She glances away before tacking on in a quieter voice, "That's if you decide to go through with the donation."

"And we'd pay for everything," Tony says, drawing my attention back to him. "You wouldn't need to worry about any of the financial burdens associated with the transplant."

And we'd pay for everything.

The ease of which he adds the comment echoes hollowly throughout my head. As much as I try to steel myself against the pain, it still hits me like a punch to the gut.

The knowledge that he's willing to fork over any amount of money when it comes to his daughter with Charlotte hurts. And yet, he couldn't spare a dime when I needed it to survive.

I shift and clench my hands tightly together. "I still need time to think it over."

Her face falls before she rises to her feet. "Maybe it would help to meet Kylie."

No. That'll only make everything more difficult.

Before I can shake my head and nix the idea, she rushes from the living room. Once in the cavernous foyer, she calls out both children's names.

Avoiding eye contact with Tony, my gaze darts around the room before landing on the large family portrait that hangs prominently above the fireplace mantle. The four of them are decked out in formal attire with a gorgeous outdoor landscape in the background. Charlotte and Kylie are wearing matching black velvet dresses while Tony and his son have on charcoal sweaters and fitted black trousers.

Another pang of sadness fills my heart as I think about the framed photographs of Mom and me scattered throughout our tiny ranch. Nothing we have comes close to the grandness of this picture.

It's beautiful.

And, more than likely, *expensive.*

I'm knocked from those thoughts when Charlotte returns with two teenagers in tow. Her smile is forced as she introduces Kylie and then Antonio. Much like their mother, my faux smile is pasted firmly in place. At any moment, it'll shatter.

Or maybe I'll shatter.

This is turning out to be even more emotionally draining than I anticipated.

At first glance, Kylie looks to be the perfect mix of her parents. She's blonde like her mother but has dark eyes that are similar to Tony's.

And mine.

Charlotte lays her palms on Kylie's shoulders as she presses close to the girl.

Antonio, on the other hand, is all his father. Same dark hair, eyes, and slim build.

Even though I knew Tony had two kids, it's a little surreal to sit in the same room as them. When they were born, I wondered if we might have a relationship. As the years went by, those hopes were snuffed out.

The teenage boy gives me a chin lift in greeting before his uninterested gaze flickers to Asher, where it stays locked. It only takes a few seconds for his eyes to widen to the size of saucers.

"Wait...are you Asher Stevens?"

The blonde football player smiles. "Guilty."

Antonio's face lights up as his voice fills with excitement. "Dude! I can't believe you're actually standing here in my house! No one at school is gonna believe this." He rambles off a couple of stats, talking a mile a minute.

His parents and sister turn their attention to the guy sitting beside me with new interest.

"Would you mind signing one of my footballs?" he finally asks, running out of steam.

"Sure, no problem."

He punches his fist in the air before racing from the room and pounding up the staircase to the second floor.

Tony's brows draw together as he tilts his head. "I assume you play football?"

Asher shifts on the sofa, one arm sliding along the back of the cushion until his fingers can strum my shoulder.

"Yes, for the Western Wildcats."

The older man's expression turns thoughtful. "You must be pretty good if Antonio is this excited."

Asher shrugs modestly.

The boy returns with a football and program from one of this season's earlier games for him to sign. And Asher, bless him, does it graciously. Antonio fires off question after question before telling him all about the position he plays on his middle school team. The atmosphere lightens as they discuss Western's season and then Asher's prospects for the draft.

Even though I try not to stare, my attention is continually drawn to Kylie. Charlotte fusses over her, leading the waifish teen to a chair before dashing off to get her something to eat and drink. When our gazes collide, I can't help but notice the fatigue that fills her dark eyes.

It would be impossible to ignore the marked difference between her behavior and that of her younger brother, who is brimming with exuberance and life. Throughout the rest of the evening, Kylie doesn't contribute much to the conversation. A few one-worded responses here and there. There's a solemness to her features that makes her seem older than her sixteen years.

Even though I do everything possible to steel my heart, I can almost feel it cracking wide open and slowly bleeding out.

20

ASHER

s soon as I slide onto the leather seat next to Lola and start up the engine, she bursts into tears. Instead of pulling onto the road and getting the hell out of here, the way every instinct is prodding me to do, I tug her into my arms and hold her tight. She buries her face against the front of my shirt as her shoulders shake. Minutes tick by as she releases all her pent-up emotion.

I don't think I've ever felt more powerless in my life than I do at this moment. All I can do is stroke her hair and murmur that everything will be all right, even though I have no idea if that's true. What I do know is that I'd like to stalk back inside their fancy-ass house and wring both of their necks for putting her through this.

I understand that they're concerned about their daughter and want to do anything they can to help her. There's no way I can begin to imagine what that would be like. But it's apparent from their actions that neither gives a damn about Lola. Tony didn't hug her or even try to strike up a conversation. Would it have really been so difficult to feign a little interest?

Apparently so.

He has no fucking idea how amazing and resilient his daughter is.

And it pisses me off.

When she finally quiets, I lift her face so I can kiss away all the tears that leak from her eyes until none are left.

By the time we said our goodbyes, Lola had relented, agreeing to the tests. I thought she'd wait, taking more time, but I should have realized that meeting Kylie would change everything. Even though she tries to project a tough exterior to the world, I suspect it's covering a soft heart that can be easily damaged. And that only makes me want to protect her more from these people.

"You don't have to go through with the testing. No one would blame you for changing your mind."

She shakes her head before wiping away another tear that slides down her cheek. "How can I do that?"

I glance away as fury whips through me. "They're assholes for putting you in this position. They're not playing fair."

"What's not fair is that Kylie needs a kidney transplant at age sixteen."

I press my lips together. It's almost impossible to argue with that point.

Confusion flickers in her eyes as she jerks her shoulders. "Does it really hurt for me to get tested?"

"I don't know." I really don't. It feels like a simple action that has the potential to open Pandora's Box. I'm afraid of what will happen after she lifts the lid.

"It's always possible that I'm not a match and then there won't be anything further to discuss."

True.

Do you know what will happen then?

Tony and his family will disappear from her life just as abruptly as they forced their way into it.

When the need to touch her pounds through me like a steady drumbeat, I wrap my hand around the nape of her neck and pull her close until my mouth can slide over hers. It's nothing more than a gentle caress.

There is so much emotion crashing around inside me. I want her to understand the depth of it, but that would be impossible, since I'm none too sure about it myself. All I can hope is that it's enough for Lola to realize that I'm here and I'm not going anywhere.

As I reluctantly pull away, my gaze falls to her lips. They're so soft and pliant. It makes me want to dive back in for more, but the desire to get her the hell out of here is stronger. With one last glance, I straighten and start the engine, maneuvering the truck onto the road. The drive back is made in silence, both of us lost in our own private thoughts.

Halfway to her house, she says, "I don't want to go home." Her gaze finds mine in the darkness. "Not yet, anyway."

"Do you have someplace in mind?"

When she remains silent, I say, "You didn't eat much at dinner." Although how could she? The entire visit was stilted and uncomfortable. "Do you want to grab something?"

Her face scrunches before she shakes her head. "No. The thought of food makes me nauseous."

"Okay." I rack my brain for alternatives. A bar seems too crowded. Too noisy. "Want to go back to my house for a little bit?"

"Yeah," she says with a sigh, relaxing against the leather seat.

As odd as it sounds, given her age, I can't help but ask, "Should you let your mom know?"

"Probably. I'll do it now." She slips her phone from her purse before tapping out a quick message.

Even though I'm hesitant to ask too many questions, the words shoot out of my mouth. "Will she be all right?" My gaze darts to hers, locking on it for a heartbeat before returning to the pavement stretched out in front of me.

"She'll be fine." Her voice grows softer. "She isn't responding, which probably means she's already asleep."

At eight o'clock at night?

Seems kind of early.

There's a long stretch of silence before she admits quietly, "Mom has bipolar depression."

I search the far recesses of my brain for an adequate response but come up empty. What do you say to that?

I'm sorry?

That doesn't seem quite right.

"Oh."

Yeah…that reaction falls kind of flat.

"She was diagnosed when I was in high school. Honestly, it was a relief and answered a lot of questions."

"Does she take something for it or talk to a counselor?"

"Yes, on both accounts. She meets with a psychologist on a regular basis and takes medication. The meds can be a fight," she says with a small sigh. "She doesn't like the way they make her feel. Sometimes, she'll stop taking them. And I get it, they can upset her stomach and give her headaches. Days will go by, and she can't get a decent night's sleep. Then, she walks around like a zombie before crashing. The problem is that she can't function without them. Not long term. When it gets bad, she can't get out of bed for days. It's kind of a catch-22."

Well, fuck.

Lola's life couldn't be more different than my own. I have no idea what it would be like to step up and take on the responsibility for the care of your parent. My heart constricts at the idea of her being forced to grow up so fast without anyone but herself to rely on.

Is that part of the reason Tony walked away?

Was it easier than sticking around and dealing with a mental health issue?

My voice drops as all this swirls through my brain. "I'm sorry. I didn't know."

She slants a look in my direction. "Why would you?"

The simple answer is that I wouldn't. Lola is an expert at keeping everything buried deep inside where it can't see the light of day. If I hadn't forced myself into her life, I wouldn't know anything about her. We'd probably still be taking verbal swipes at each other.

"Do you talk to anyone about this stuff? A counselor or maybe a friend? Someone you can vent to?"

She shakes her head before staring out the passenger side window. "Nope. I don't need to. Everything is under control."

Is it?

On the surface, it might appear that way, but now that I understand more of what's going on, how doesn't she feel like she's constantly drowning? It's a lot to deal with. Especially for someone her age.

"You can always talk to me," I offer.

She studies me carefully in the darkness. When she fails to respond, I shift on my seat, wondering what exactly she sees when she looks at me.

The remainder of the drive is made in silence. I'm consumed with thoughts of the girl sitting beside me. She's so much stronger than I imagined and the most determined person I've ever met. If I'm being honest with myself, it makes me ashamed for always taking the easy way out. The path of least resistance, as my parents would call it.

Lola didn't have the same opportunities as I was given. Instead of quitting when shit got tough, she dug deep and took care of what needed to be done, because in the end, there wasn't a choice in the matter.

How can I not respect and admire that?

Once we hit the familiar tree-lined street near campus, I ease the truck over to the side of the road and find a parking place. As we exit the Escalade, I slip my arm around her shoulders, steering her up the front porch stairs and into the house. A burst of laughter and raised voices greet us as we step inside the entryway. There are a dozen people packed into the living room as the pumping beat of music blasts throughout the first floor. A couple of pizza boxes are strewn across the dining room table along with cans of beer.

A couple teammates call out my name in greeting. My gaze scans the room, looking for the people who actually live here, but they're conspicuously absent. It's all a bunch of underclassmen. Two couples are going at it hot and heavy on the couch. One of the girls is straddling a guy's lap. She's wearing nothing more than a lacy bra and jeans. I have a feeling that it's only a matter of time before the rest of her clothing vanishes and these two are putting on a free, X-rated show.

I give Lola a bit of side-eye, worried that this kind of PDA will piss her off, but she doesn't say a word and her expression remains neutral as if their sexcapades haven't registered. I give everyone a chin lift before hustling her through the dining room and swinging a left down the hallway where my room is located.

For the first time, I wish I had a bit more privacy. I've spent the last three and a half years partying my ass off, drinking until I was on the verge of passing out, and smoking bowls. Just generally living my best life until I get drafted to the pros. I never thought there'd come a time when I was over it. It's tempting to kick all their asses to the curb.

Don't these people have homes of their own?

Why the hell are they always hanging out here?

Once I close the bedroom door, the music and noise become muted. Lola walks in before loosening her jacket and throwing it over the desk chair. I hover near the threshold, unsure what to do now that I have her here.

"Do you want something to drink? Maybe a shot?" My brows pinch as I glance around the space. "I've got some weed around here somewhere. Would that help take the edge off?"

She glances at me before shaking her head. "No, I probably shouldn't do any of that if I'm going to get tested."

"Good point," I mutter, feeling like a dumbass. I should have thought about that before offering it up. I shift my weight and rack my brain for something that will lighten the mood and take her mind off the situation.

Before I can come up with any alternatives, her fingers settle at the hem of her sweater, tugging it silently up her chest and over her head. She drops the pale pink material to the carpet before toeing off her shoes and then socks. My mouth dries as she flicks open the button of her jeans and lowers the zipper, shoving the thick denim down her hips and thighs until she's standing in front of me in nothing more than a plain bra and panties.

Ripping my gaze away from her feels impossible. "What are you doing?"

She tilts her head. "Isn't it obvious?"

"With you?" I force out a harsh laugh. "No, nothing is obvious."

This girl constantly keeps me on my toes. That's when I realize just how much I like it. The challenge of trying to figure her out. Nothing has been easy, which only makes the small victories even sweeter.

She takes a purposeful step in my direction. "I want you to fuck me."

Her blunt words have my throat closing up.

"I want you to make me forget everything that's going on. Just for a couple of hours." There's a pause as she tilts her head. "Can you do that?"

Well, hell.

I wasn't expecting this.

Even more than that, I'm afraid of taking a misstep with this girl. Something that will push her further away when all I want to do is tug her closer. With anyone else, I'd already be stripping off my clothes and sinking deep inside the heat of her body.

But Lola is different. It's for that reason, I need to be careful. Not only with her, but with whatever is unfolding between us.

"Is that really what you want?" I study her expression, trying to get a read on her thoughts.

Her gaze stays pinned to mine as she lifts her chin. "I think we both know it's what I need."

Unable to stay away another second, I eat up the distance that separates us. "Are you sure? I don't want you to regret this." There's no way I could stand for that to happen. Not now. Not when I want her this much.

She sucks in a steady breath before releasing it. "I won't."

"How can you be so certain?"

"Because I've wanted it—*you*—for a while."

When we're no more than a foot apart, I reach out and cup both her cheeks before tilting her face upward so that she has no other choice but to meet my searching gaze. This girl is so fucking beautiful. I have no idea why it took me so long to see it.

I'm only thankful that I have.

My gaze drops to the plushness of her mouth as my thumb drifts across her lower lip. It's another reminder that the tough exterior she arms herself with is nothing more than a paper-thin façade.

When she reaches behind her and unsnaps the bra, the stretchy material springs apart before the straps slink down her arms, revealing the taut peaks of her breasts. All I can think about is what it felt like to draw her pert nipples between my lips the other morning.

That's all it takes for my erection to throb to life.

As much as I want to spread her out across the mattress and sink deep inside her heat, I rein in my need. This isn't about me. It's about Lola, and I want to make it the best experience I can. She needs to forget, and I'm going to damn well make sure that happens. When I'm done with her, she'll have a hard time remembering her own name.

My hands drift from her face before settling on the fullness of her breasts. They're not huge by any means, but they're not small, either. They're the perfect handful, with delectable little nipples that beg to be played with.

I've never had a specific type when it comes to females. I like them all. I've been with girls who are athletic and toned and ones with curves that go on for miles. As long as they're game for anything and enjoy having a bit of fun between the sheets, that's all that matters.

But Lola?

She's perfect in every way.

I take my time, palming her breasts until her eyelids fall to half-mast. I love how responsive she is to my touch. It only stokes the flames of my desire and heats me up even more than I already am.

I pinch and tweak the hard buds before squeezing all that softness until a whimper escapes from her. Only then do I run my hands down her ribcage to the gentle flare of her hips. My fingers slip beneath the elastic band of her panties before shimmying them downward until the scrap of cotton puddles around her feet and she's completely bared to my sight.

When I step closer, she retreats. I force her backward until her calves hit the mattress and she tumbles onto the bed. She bounces once or twice before propping herself up on her elbows. With her dark hair falling in waves around her shoulders, I can't help but stare at the erotic picture she makes.

"You really are beautiful."

Surprise flickers in her eyes before she shakes her head. "No, I'm not."

"One hundred percent you are." I lean down, caging her in with my arms until I'm close enough for her warm breath to drift across my lips. "And tonight, I'm going to prove just how gorgeous I think you are."

"Promise?" she whispers, tempered hope filling her voice.

"You have my word."

As soon as I press my lips to hers, she opens, hungry for the caress. My tongue slips inside her mouth to dance with her own. It's so easy to lose myself in the taste of her. No other girl has ever driven me this crazy.

There's no way I'll ever get enough. The urge to devour her in one tasty bite thrums through me. I pull back just enough to tug the plumpness of her lower lip with my teeth before releasing it. A groan escapes from her as I lick my way down the narrow column of her throat, grazing the fluttering pulse before continuing my descent.

Along the way, I make sure to adore every inch. From shoulders that hold the weight of the world to her delicate collarbone before arriving at her breasts. I lick at the rounded undersides before drawing one pert nipple into my mouth. When her back bows off the mattress and a throaty sound escapes from her parted lips, I release the tight peak, making sure to give equal attention to the other side. Her fingers tunnel through my hair, raking across my scalp, attempting to draw me closer.

Once the hard tips are rosy from my attention, I sink lower, kissing a hot trail to her navel and then farther south. I nip at the gentle curve of her belly before pulling away to stare down at her.

Fuck, she's so beautiful. Especially when there's desire flooding her dark eyes, giving them a sexy, heavy-lidded quality. What I love even more is that I'm the one who put it there.

No one else.

Only me.

That thought has my cock turning rock hard.

I'm slammed with the realization that all the other girls who have come before her have been nothing more than preparation for Lola. The one who actually matters. It's a scary thought. One I don't allow myself to dwell on. Not in this moment.

"Spread your legs for me, baby girl."

Her sharp white teeth rake over her lower lip as her thighs fall open in silent invitation. My hungry gaze falls to her bare pussy. It was only a couple of days ago that I got my first taste of her, and I've been dying for another ever since.

I drop to my knees before running my hands over the silky skin of her inner thighs and forcing them farther apart. I want her impossibly wide so I can admire every pink inch. My mouth presses against the top of her slit before I pull away, stroking my fingers along her entrance and dipping two thick digits inside her heat. Long minutes pass as I play with her, ramping her up until she's shifting restlessly beneath me. With my hands locked around her inner thighs, my thumbs pull her lips apart. Unable to resist the temptation any longer, I take a long lap of her softness.

A moan escapes from her as I do it a second time and then a third before slowly circling my tongue around her clit and drawing it gently into my mouth. Her body tightens as her breathing picks up speed, becoming more labored.

Just when it seems like she'll crash over the edge, I pull back. Her body twists, arching to get closer as I kiss a trail from her lips to her inner thigh before sinking my teeth into the delicate flesh. She gasps as I lick and nibble my way back to her pussy. Her body is drenched with arousal and all but aching for my touch. Instead of burying my face against her sweet heat, I rise to my feet.

Heavy-lidded eyes crack open as I kick off my Sperrys and strip out of my clothing until I'm just as naked as she is. The heat of her gaze licks over my body as her tongue darts out to moisten her lips.

My hands wrap around her hips before flipping her over onto her belly. She gasps as I crawl onto the bed and straddle her pert little ass.

It's so tempting to sink my teeth into the curved roundness of each side. Instead, I flex so that my hard cock can slide along the cleft separating her cheeks.

I lean forward, pressing a kiss to the side of her face before gathering up the long strands of her hair and draping them on the other side of her head so I have better access to her neck. As my body hovers over hers, I continue to lick and suck, all the while rubbing my dick against her. Arousal leaks from me, smearing along her bared flesh.

She shifts, spreading her legs as far as mine will allow, giving me just enough room to sink between her cheeks until the tip of my cock can nudge her back entrance.

A groan escapes from her as she wriggles against me.

"You like that, baby?"

"I do. It feels so good."

Damn right it does. As much as I'd like to continue playing with her backside, I'll go off like a shot if I keep it up any longer. And that, I refuse to allow.

I nip at the tops of her shoulders before sinking lower, adoring her honeyed flesh with my mouth as I drift down the long line of her spine until I reach the subtle flare of her hips and the rounded curve of her ass. I knead the taut muscles with my hands, massaging them until she relaxes, practically melting into the mattress.

Every so often, I sink my teeth into her cheeks before soothing the abraded flesh with my tongue and lips. Not one delicate inch of her body goes untouched. Only when she's completely relaxed do I flip her over again so she can face me.

"Ready for more?"

"Yes."

A dazed quality fills her eyes as she watches me move around the side of the bed before yanking open the nightstand drawer to grab a condom. I rip open the packet with my teeth before covering my cock in latex. And then I'm back, standing between her sprawled thighs. My fingers strum the soft skin of her calves before locking around them and dragging her to the edge of the bed so I can line my dick up with her entrance. One flex of my hips is all it takes for my tip to slide inside. It's not a lot. Just enough to tease.

Even through the latex, she feels fucking amazing.

Hot.

Soft.

Tight.

I can't imagine what it would feel like to be buried deep inside the warmth of her body. All I want to do is draw out this pleasure for as long as humanly possible.

Her teeth sink into her lower lip as her eyelids flutter open until our gazes can cling. Whatever tentative friendship that has formed between us intensifies in that moment of intimate connection. Instead of backing away from the intensity that surges through me, I find myself moving toward it.

The strange emotions she rouses inside me are new and powerful.

For me, sex has always been a way to release stress and have a few mindless hours of enjoyment. It never went any deeper than shooting my load.

But this…it already feels different.

For the first time in my life, I'm not thinking about me. Or my pleasure. I'm focused on Lola and making sure I meet every one of her needs.

"Asher," she whimpers as I keep my thrusts shallow in an effort to draw out her excitement. What I want most is to blow her world apart at the seams so she can never be put back together again.

"What, baby? You need more?"

"I need all of you." A breathy sigh falls from her lips as she writhes beneath me.

And that's exactly what I'm going to give her.

Every last piece of me.

I pick up my tempo, sliding just a bit farther inside her body. Even though it's taking every bit of my control, I keep the strokes slow and measured so that there's a steady rise in anticipation. My jaw locks, the muscle throbbing in my cheek, as I battle my own instinct to pummel her, burying myself balls deep inside her sweet heat. Never in my life have I experienced something that was both heaven and hell.

But that's exactly what this is.

The sight of her spread wide, pinned to the mattress by my cock, turns me on like nothing else.

Naked and willing.

Practically begging for my dick.

It's a mental snapshot I'll keep tucked away forever.

I continue teasing, drawing out her pleasure until her body is as tight as a bowstring. Until my shaft is completely buried inside her softness. Until her eyes are rolling back in her head and she's whimpering with need.

When my balls draw up against my body, I realize that this is it. I won't last much longer. My fingers loosen from around her thigh so that my thumb can settle over her clit before rubbing soft circles. My teeth are so tightly clenched, it feels like they're in imminent danger of shattering.

That's all it takes for her to fall apart beneath my fingertips. As soon as she cries out my name, I lose it, following her over the precipice. The orgasm that streaks through my body is like nothing I've experienced before. As much as I want to close my eyes and savor the delicious sensation, my gaze stays pinned to hers, needing to see every thought and feeling as it crashes over her features.

Have I ever seen anything as beautiful as Lola when she lets go of the tightly harnessed grip she keeps on her emotions, giving herself over to the pleasure coursing through her?

That's when I realize I need more.

More of *this*.

More of *her*.

21

LOLA

As soon as my eyelids flutter open, I realize that I'm in Asher's bed for the second time in less than a week. Unlike Sunday morning, I turn my head and find him sprawled out beside me, snoring softly. I can't help but take a few moments to soak him in.

The man is certainly a sight to behold.

Even in sleep, he oozes sex, power, and masculinity. I haven't wanted to admit to myself just how attractive he is. I didn't want to have anything in common with the hundreds of girls on this campus who clamor for his attention, trailing after him like lovesick schoolgirls.

It's disconcerting to realize that I'm no different from them.

When exactly did I let down my guard enough for him to sneak past it?

Better question—how do I resurrect it again to keep him out?

When he stirs, I blink back to the present and refocus my attention.

My fingers itch to reach out and tunnel their way through his thick strands. I tighten my hand until the rounded nails sink into my palm in order to resist the temptation.

His eyebrows are a few shades darker and make a striking contrast to the golden blond hair. There's a sweep of thick eyelashes resting against his cheeks. Any female would be jealous of their length and thickness.

As I scrutinize him with more intensity, I notice the slight crook in his nose as if it might have been broken. It's a flaw that should lessen his male beauty, but instead, the imperfection only adds to it. His cheekbones are surprisingly sharp. The guy could probably model if he wanted to. Sadly, I could imagine him on a Time's Square billboard wearing nothing but tight-fitting boxers that show off the goods. My gaze drifts to his mouth before settling on it.

I'll say this…the amount of pleasure those lips are capable of giving is almost impossible to comprehend.

At least to me it is.

Last night was—hands down—the best sex of my life.

Now…is that necessarily saying much?

Probably not. The guys I've been with have been mediocre at best. It was always a crapshoot. Sometimes, I'd orgasm and others, it would remain frustratingly elusive. Most were in a hurry and couldn't control themselves. Or maybe they just didn't care enough to bother.

Asher is the first guy to make me feel like I want to claw my way out of my own skin. Even when he went down on me the other morning, I'd never felt such intensity flood through my body. After that experience, I completely understand why women spread their legs so easily for him.

Who wouldn't want more of that?

Hell, I'd probably be tumbling headfirst into…*something* with him if I didn't know better.

Thank god, I'm smarter than that.

Last night, I did something I normally wouldn't and let go of the tight grip I keep on my emotions, allowing myself to splinter apart. Nine hours later, I've carefully put myself back together again. Dinner with Tony and his family turned out to be a far more emotional affair than I'd prepared myself for.

Because of that, I'd been a total wreck afterward. I don't regret letting my guard down. I released a lot of pent-up stress and I feel better for it.

Looser.

More in control.

But that doesn't necessarily mean I want it to happen again.

Maybe Asher isn't the guy I originally pegged him to be, but he's still a player. As intrigued as I am by the different facets he's revealed, it's still not enough to take a chance and let him in. I've got too much going on in my life to take on another complication. And that's exactly what Asher is—a complication I don't need.

Or want.

Yesterday, he told me everything I'd always secretly yearned to hear.

Do I necessarily believe him when he said that he'd stand by my side and be there for me?

Of course not. Why would he bother?

The one man who should have championed me has been a complete no-show in my life. Why would a guy like Asher Stevens stick around?

The idea is almost laughable.

And it's more than enough to quash the sliver of hope that this was anything more than sex.

Great sex, even.

But still…just two bodies coming together for mutual pleasure.

That thought has me turning away before carefully rolling from the bed. As good as last night was, I need to get the hell out of here before he wakes up and we're forced to engage in an awkward morning-after convo. I'm sure it happens with such frequency that he has a whole scripted spiel he gives the girls who spend the night.

That thought leaves a bitter taste in my mouth.

When he stirs again, I throw a cautious glance over my shoulder and pick up my scattered pieces of clothing before hauling up my underwear and slipping on my bra. Then, I pull on my sweater, yank up my jeans and grab my shoes, jacket, and purse before tiptoeing across the carpet like the place is boobytrapped with explosives.

The hinges creak as I open the door just enough to slip through. If there's a strange mix of emotions bubbling up inside me, I tamp them down and pretend they don't exist. Last night was fun. I'd needed to lose myself in another person and get my mind off the shitshow that is my life, and that's exactly what Asher provided.

Extremely well.

Well enough that I fell into a deep, dreamless sleep for a solid eight hours.

When was the last time that happened?

I don't even remember.

Once in the hallway, my muscles loosen. I pause, shoving my feet into my Chucks and walking into the dining room, which is a mess of bottles and pizza boxes. It smells like a brewery in here.

I stride past the living room, where someone is sacked out on the couch, snoring lightly, before arriving at the entryway of the two-story house. Just as escape is within reach, a loud creak from the staircase breaks the silence and draws my attention. I swing around, only to find Demi making her way down the carpeted stairs. As our gazes collide, her footfalls falter as surprise morphs over her expression. Her appearance is just as disheveled as I imagine mine to be.

She pops a brow as the corners of her lips tremble. "I'm not sure if we're having an awkward moment or not."

With a snort, my shoulders loosen. "Definitely awkward."

For me, not her. She has a boyfriend who lives here, I don't. It doesn't take long for her to figure out who I spent the night with. I can almost see the moment it dawns on her.

"So…you and Asher, huh?"

I shake my head. "No. Absolutely not."

"Really? That's funny, because now that I'm thinking about it, this isn't the first time I've seen you two together."

"He needed help with a class. And now," I shrug, trying to find a way to define our strange relationship, "I guess we've become friends. Sort of."

She cocks her head as interest grows in her eyes. "Is that what the kids are calling it nowadays?"

I grab the handle of the door before yanking it open, only wanting to escape this uncomfortable conversation. "It's super casual."

"If you say so," she sing-songs obnoxiously, walking down the remaining stairs until we're standing side by side.

"I do. Plus, this is Asher Stevens we're talking about. Is he the type of guy to get serious with anyone?"

"Not that I know of."

A ridiculous amount of disappointment floods through me when I realize she isn't going to argue the point.

Trailing me outside to the front porch, she glances up and down the empty street. It's still early and everything is quiet as the sun rises in the eastern sky, painting it with pink and purple hues.

"Where's your car?" She glances at me with curiosity. "Do you need a lift?"

Yeah…I guess I do. I was so intent on escaping the situation and getting some much-needed physical—as well as mental—distance, that I didn't consider how I'd get home.

"If you don't mind driving me, that would be great."

Demi slings an arm around my shoulder. "Girl, I don't mind at all. It'll give me more time to interrogate you about your relationship with Mr. tall, blond, and studly."

I groan. "On second thought, maybe I'll just Uber it."

22

ASHER

I load two burgers and a large fries onto my tray before grabbing an orange Gatorade from the cooler and glancing around the wide-open space. A few girls wave as I catch their gazes. I give them a chin lift in greeting before finding Crosby, Carson, Easton, and Brayden camped out at a table along with a couple of other guys from the team. Sydney, Sasha, and Elle are seated next to their respective boyfriends. A few groupies buzz around the table, looking for vacant laps to settle on.

Over the months, those laps have dwindled. All the guys I hang out with are now involved in committed relationships. They don't look twice at the jersey chasers who attempt to catch their attention.

As soon as that thought pops into my brain, an image of Lola swiftly follows.

I woke up the other day, rolled over, ready to put my morning wood to good use, only to discover that she'd taken off. Nothing deflates an erection quicker than realizing the girl you took to bed the night before couldn't escape from you fast enough. Even though I've tried to shrug it off, it still pricks my pride.

I'm going to be perfectly candid here—normally I have to kick chicks out of my bed after we sleep together. Not a single one has ever run away at the crack of dawn.

Hell, she probably sprinted.

Know what annoys me even more than that?

She's ignoring my texts and calls.

Can you believe that shit?

It's been days since I last saw her. I'm embarrassed to admit that my head is on a constant swivel, searching campus for even a glimpse of her. So far, she's remained elusive. It's like she's deliberately going out of her way to avoid me.

It took a handful of texts before I realized she wasn't going to return my messages. As amazing as the sex had been, I wouldn't have slept with her if I'd known she would ice me out of her life.

And isn't that a kick in the balls.

Trust me, I've considered hauling ass to Taco Loco and demanding answers, but that seems slightly...desperate.

All right, maybe more than slightly.

Fuck...this girl makes me feel like a needy bitch, and I don't like it. Not one damn bit. If she isn't interested, there's not a lot I can do about it.

If I were smart, I'd evict her from my brain. And the best way to do that is to hook up with someone else. There are plenty of girls at Western who are interested in sleeping with yours truly and won't gnaw off their own arm to escape my evil clutches.

I glance at the available females fluttering around our table. We're talking gorgeous girls, wearing lowcut tops that cling to their curves like a second skin.

Unfortunately, none of them are doing anything for me.

There's absolutely no movement south of the border.

It's almost disturbing.

Except...all I have to do is think about Lola spread out on my bed like a goddamn feast and I get a raging boner.

Here's the other issue—it's not just about the sex. I'm genuinely concerned about her. I need to know she's all right. Has she been tested yet? Is her mom okay? Is she getting enough sleep? Or making sure to eat three squares a day? Because sometimes she forgets.

Like, how the hell do you forget something like that?

It's beyond me. If I'm not thinking about football or sex, my mind is on food.

All this churns through my head as I settle at the far end of the table next to Crosby and Brooke. Of course, these two are making googly eyes at each other. Who would have ever believed there was a time in the not-so-distant past when they couldn't stand the sight of one another?

When he snakes his hand around her neck and tugs her close for a kiss, I grumble, "Is it possible for you two to keep your hands to yourselves for five damn minutes? We're all trying to eat here."

Brooke's cheeks go up in flames as a slow smirk settles on Crosby's face.

"Looks like someone's in a shit mood," he says, voice filled with glee.

I shoot him a hard glare. Apparently, we traded dispositions when I wasn't looking. He's always been a surly motherfucker, but his temperament has mellowed since he got together with Brooke.

Ignoring his inquisitive stare, I unwrap my burger before taking a massive bite. As I chew, Demi settles across from me with her tray of healthier options. Rowan follows, dropping down beside her. Wherever Demi goes, Rowan is sure to follow. It was obvious to most of us from day one that our QB had feelings for the head coach's daughter.

Just as I swallow down the masticated meat and bun, Demi asks, "What's up with you and Lola?"

When I pause, a piece of beef gets lodged in my airways. Tears sting my eyes as I cough and splutter before eventually choking it down. "Excuse me?"

She arches a brow. "You heard me. I want to know what's going on with you two."

I pound a fist against my chest before taking a gulp of Gatorade to wash it down.

When I'm finally able to form words, I ask, "What makes you think something's going on?"

Her narrowed gaze pins mine in place until I'm shifting on my chair. Just to be clear, Demi probably weighs half as much as I do. It's not like I'm afraid of her.

Not really.

All right…maybe a little.

When she stares like that, it kind of reminds me of Coach.

And not in a good way.

"Because I have eyes, and I've seen you two together several times."

I shrug, striving for nonchalant when all I want to do is turn the tables and pump her for information. I've never had a girl dominate my thoughts, and I don't know what to make of the situation. Especially when the female in question has gone into avoidance mode and wants nothing to do with me.

"We're friends." For a little bit, I'd thought we were more than that, but now I'm not so sure.

"Interesting. That's exactly what she said."

Well, fuck. That's not the response I was hoping for. Sure, it's the one I gave, but still…

"Then I guess you have your answer." For some reason, that pisses me off even more, because maybe I have mine as well. Only, it's not the one I wanted.

For the first time in my life, I want something more.

It's a relief when Demi drops the conversation and picks up her grilled chicken sandwich before taking a bite.

I'm just about to turn my attention back to the lovebirds at my side, because anything is better than talking about the girl who ditched my ass, when Demi says, "You know that Lola means the world to me, right?"

When my gaze reluctantly locks on her dark one, she continues in a lower voice. "She's been through a lot with her family, and I don't want to see her get hurt."

I straighten in my chair as my brows snap together. "Exactly what are you trying to imply?"

"I'm not trying to imply anything. I'm giving you facts. Lola has a lot going on and doesn't need to get jerked around by some guy."

It takes effort to mask the hurt that flares to life within me. Demi and I have known each other since freshman year and have never had a problem. Hell, I've always tried to look out for her out of respect for Coach. "So now I'm just *some guy?*"

Even though she winces, her chin inches upward. "Come on, Asher. You're not interested in her. Not really."

"And you would know that how?" I shoot back.

Her brows arch as disbelief rings throughout her voice. "Are you really trying to tell me that you want more than a hookup?"

A few heads swivel our way as more people listen to our conversation.

I press my lips together and glare, refusing to answer the question. How the hell did I get sucked into this uncomfortable convo?

As soon as I glance at her boyfriend for help, he holds up his hands and shakes his head.

"Sorry. I'm not getting involved in this one."

"Traitor," I grumble.

His lips quirk as he pulls his girlfriend close before dropping a kiss on the top of her head. "Go easy on him, Dem," he whispers loud enough for me to overhear. "Maybe the resident player has finally found a girl worth changing for."

When I give him the finger, his shoulders shake with silent laughter.

"Look," she says, huffing out a breath, "I'm not trying to get all up in your business—"

"Really? Could have fooled me."

Her eyes narrow. "I'm just protective of my friend. If you know anything about Lola, then you can understand why I would feel that way."

Her eyes bore into me.

Unsure what to say, I plow a hand through my hair. Here's the funny thing—I'm not the one who skipped out after a night of phenomenal sex. I'm also not the one who won't return calls or texts.

It's tempting to admit all that, but I'll be damned if I do. It's not Demi —or anyone else's—business.

I force my muscles to loosen. "Yeah, I get it. Whether you believe me or not, I have no intention of hurting her, okay?"

Confusion flickers across her face, and for a moment, it seems like she might say more before finally nodding. "All right."

The tension simmering in the air dissolves as quickly as it sprung up. I polish off the rest of my burger and fries. Normally, lunch is a twenty-minute break in the day where I can bullshit with my friends, flirt with a couple of girls, and chill out.

That's not the case this afternoon.

Even though I try to shove Demi's comments from my head, along with the girl who wants nothing to do with me, it's impossible. Lola has pitched a tent and is currently camped out there, refusing to budge. I'm knocked from those thoughts when Mallory settles on my lap and tangles her arms around my neck.

"Hey, Asher." She presses closer, wriggling her ass against my junk. "I miss you. Every time I drop by the house, you're gone."

"Sorry, it's been busy." From the corner of my eye, I catch Demi glaring in my direction. I can practically feel the burn of her gaze attempting to singe me alive.

"Dr. Nichols won't even let me sit by you in class," she says with a pout.

Not that I'll admit it to Mallory, but I don't mind that our professor has moved me to the front row. It cuts down on the distractions and forces me to pay attention to the dragon.

I wrap my hands around the blonde's waist before hoisting her off my lap and setting her on her feet.

Then, I pop to mine and grab my tray. "It was great running into you, but I gotta take off."

"What? I just got here," she says, eyes filling with confusion. "I was hoping we could talk."

Yeah…talking is the furthest thing from her mind, and I have zero interest in that. The realization gives me pause. Mallory and I have fooled around dozens of times. She knows how to have fun and keep everything lowkey, which is exactly how I like it. If there's a girl who could take my mind off Lola, it's the curvy blonde with the banging body.

And yet...I don't want her.

I don't want anyone but Lola.

2 3

LOLA

"Are you working tonight?" Mama asks as I grab my purse from the worn seat of the car and wrap my fingers around the door handle.

It's an odd day off for me. "Nope, but I have a ton of homework to catch up on. So, that's the plan."

"And the boy?" Her expression turns playful as she waggles her brows. "Will you be seeing him anytime soon?"

I glance away, breaking eye contact before jerking my shoulders into a shrug. "I'm not sure. We're both really busy with school."

"Hmmm. That's too bad. He's very handsome."

"Yes, he is." What's surprising is that he's turned out to be so much more than that. But still...

I have too much going on to get involved with someone like Asher.

Before she can fire off more questions that I have zero desire to answer, I point to the mechanic's we're parked in front of. "I should probably get moving."

She nods. "All right. *Te amo.*"

I smile as everything loosens within me. Then, I lean over and press a quick kiss to her cheek. "Love you, too."

Sliding from the LaCrosse, I lift my hand in a wave as she pulls out of the parking lot and onto the main road before pushing through the glass door into the reception area. It's a sprawling, one-story building made of cinder blocks in a neighboring suburb, about thirty minutes from the university.

Asher texted earlier this morning, letting me know that my car was all set and could be picked up and offered a ride if I needed one. Even though I didn't necessarily want to reply, it felt rude not to. It's the first time I've responded to one of his messages. He hit me up a handful of times before the texts abruptly stopped.

I've been avoiding him since we slept together. I don't know what it is about the blond football player that has me in such a tangle. He's the last person I expected to burrow under my skin. It's the reason I decided to take a giant step back. Even if he was interested in a friends-with-benefits situation, that wouldn't work. Not with the feelings that have mushroomed up within me. So, cutting off our relationship before anything more could happen was the smartest move to make.

Once at the front desk, I glance around for someone to help me, but I don't see any employees. After a handful of seconds, I gravitate toward an open door that leads to a garage before peeking around the corner and scanning the space. The faint whisps of music play as I spot a green VW Bug parked in one of the bays, a couple of sedans, as well as an SUV hoisted on a lift.

And there, in the back, is my baby.

Just as I step inside the garage, a deep voice says from behind, "Is there something I can help you with?"

I jolt and swing around, only to find a lanky guy wiping his stained fingers on a towel.

"Um, hi. My car was towed here after an accident, and I was told that it's ready to be picked up." With a gulp, I realize I'm babbling. "My name is Lola."

He shifts his stance and tucks the cloth in his back pocket. "The Fusion, right?"

When I nod, he says, "Yup, it's all set. We were just changing the oil and topping off the windshield washer fluid. Follow me."

"Great."

It'll be nice to have my baby back again. She might be old with a ton of miles, but she's mine. I saved up the money I earned from working at the restaurant and bought her after high school graduation. We've been through a lot together. I was kind of afraid the mechanic would take one look at the damage and declare the car not worth fixing.

Thank god that didn't turn out to be the case.

When he steps around me and through the doorway into the garage, I trail after him. Now that I'm standing inside the large space, I hear a couple of guys talking over the alt rock music playing in the background. One's under the hood of a small sedan, and the other has the lower half of his body sticking out from beneath a truck.

"You guys working or bullshitting in here?" the man in charge asks in a raised voice.

The one beneath the vehicle rolls out until he's able to meet our gazes. There's a smudge of something dark on his forehead. When he flashes a smile, I realize just how handsome he is.

Instead of answering the question, he tosses one back. "Isn't it possible to do both?"

"For you two? No way." He glances at his watch. "I promised Mrs. G we'd have everything finished up on her Subaru by three o'clock, so let's make sure it happens."

"You got it, boss." The younger man gives him a salute before rolling back under the vehicle and getting to work.

With that, he turns to me and says, "Why don't we take a look at the repair, and you can make sure everything looks good."

I nod as we cross the wide space before arriving at my silver Ford Fusion. Eyes widening, I walk around to the rear and drop down to inspect the exterior before running my fingers across the paint. If I hadn't seen the damage firsthand, I wouldn't know there'd been an accident.

My gaze flicks to the mechanic, who stands beside me.

"For a rush job, I'm pretty happy with how it turned out," he says.

"Actually, it looks better than when I bought the car."

He nods before leaning against the vehicle and folding his arms across his chest. "Asher asked if we'd take a look just to make sure there weren't any other issues. It's a good thing that we did. The radiator was cracked. Have you noticed that it's been leaking fluid?"

My brows furrow as my mind sifts through the past month or so. Now that he's mentioned it, there have been a few dark spots in the driveway.

"Umm, yeah," I mutter, feeling like an idiot for not realizing something like that could be serious. "I guess so."

"We fixed it and changed out a few spark plugs along with the oil. It should run a hell of a lot better now. Just make sure you stay on top of the maintenance, all right? The oil needs to be changed every three months or three thousand miles, whichever comes first. With some of the newer vehicles, you can wait five or even seven thousand miles," he taps the hood, "but I wouldn't recommend it for this one."

"I'll keep that in mind."

"All right then, let me grab the keys and you can get out of here."

As his footsteps fade, my brain spins, trying to figure out how much all these unexpected expenses will cost. I scraped together three hundred dollars, and there's fifty bucks on my debit card. There's no way it'll be less than that, which means I'll have to use my credit card to pay for the rest. I'm always afraid I won't have enough at the end of the month to pay off the balance. When you can barely afford to cover the cost of the bill, the last thing you need to get slapped with is high interest rates. I'd rather bust my ass waiting tables just so that doesn't happen. Or go without. The problem is that I need my car.

Before he can disappear from sight, I raise my voice and blurt, "How much do I owe you?"

He swings around to meet my gaze. "Nothing."

What?

That can't be right.

"I don't understand." I point to the Fusion. "It sounds like you fixed a number of issues in addition to the body work."

"Yup, but it's already been paid for." He cocks his head. "Asher took care of everything when I spoke to him on the phone."

I blink as my mouth turns cottony, making it difficult to swallow. It takes effort to keep my voice level. "He paid for all the repairs?"

His brow furrows as he continues to eye me curiously. "Yeah, I figured he would let you know."

"He never mentioned it," I say, lips sinking at the corners.

"Huh." If he notices my upset, he doesn't comment on it. "I guess that's something you can take up with him."

"Yeah," I mutter darkly. "I'll be sure to do that."

A few uncomfortable beats pass before he clears his throat and jerks a thumb over his shoulder. "I'll just get those keys for you."

With that, he crosses the space and disappears into the lobby. So many thoughts crash through my head, and none of them are good.

Less than two minutes later, the mechanic is back. "Here you go." The key ring dangles from his forefinger. "You're all set."

As stupid as it sounds, part of me is loath to take them from him. I didn't pay for any of this. And I have the sneaking suspicion this repair is way more expensive than I assumed.

I'm almost afraid to ask, but I have to know.

When I don't immediately reach for the keys, he gives them a shake to get my attention. Reluctantly, I stretch out my hand and take them.

"I'd like to know what the final bill was." As the words escape, my heart picks up speed, jackhammering a painful staccato against my ribcage. Money has always had this kind of effect on me. Especially when we're talking large sums of it.

Before he can say anything, I realize that no matter what the amount is, I'll have to find a way to pay Asher back. I don't want to be indebted to him, and it really pisses me off that he put me in this uncomfortable position.

"In total? For both the collision and mechanical work?"

I steel myself, hoping it's not as much as I suspect. "Yes."

He shifts before casually throwing out a number. "Twenty-five hundred and some change."

Holy shit.

My mouth crashes open as my eyes widen.

That's so much more than I imagined.

Twenty-five hundred dollars.

That number is enough to make me want to vomit. It's almost impossible to fathom having that much money at one time. How am I going to pay him back?

It's a struggle to find my voice. Even though there's only five or six feet that separate us, I don't know if the words are loud enough for him to hear. "He mentioned something about a friends and family discount."

The guy smirks. "Yeah, that *is* the friends and family discount. Otherwise, it would have been almost twice as much. I only charged for parts, not labor. The Stevens are good people. If one of them needs a favor, I'm always happy to help."

The air gets sucked from my lungs, making it difficult to breathe. It's tempting to bend over and brace my hands on my knees. Any moment, I'm going to hyperventilate and pass out.

"And he paid the entire bill?"

"Sure did. You're free and clear."

No...no, I'm not.

Free and clear is the last thing I am.

The backs of my eyelids sting and my nose burns with the building pressure.

"Hey, are you all right?" He points to the general vicinity of my face. "You look a little pale. Want to sit down for a few minutes?"

I blink, trying to regain my bearings. "That's not necessary. I'm fine. Thanks again for everything."

"No problem. If you notice any issues, just let me know and we'll take care of it."

Oh, there are going to be issues all right, but it has nothing to do with this guy. He's an innocent bystander who has been sucked into this shitstorm. It has more to do with a certain blond football player who's about to get his ass chewed out.

2 4

ASHER

*E*verything hurts.

All my muscles are screaming bloody murder as I push open the front door of our house and step inside. After practice wrapped up, I decided to stick around and lift. Even though I spent two hours on the turf, there was still all this restless energy rushing through my veins and no way to expel it. I'd hoped a good pump would do the trick and alleviate the problem.

No such luck.

Instead of clearing my mind like I'd hoped, Lola continues to swirl through my thoughts. I have no idea what I'm going to do about that girl. As tempting as it is to hunt down her ass and force her to have a conversation, I refuse to do that.

When have I ever forced a chick to speak with me?

Normally, I can't get them to stop yapping.

A few guys are already hanging out in the living room, knocking back a couple of drinks, and shooting the shit. For a change, they're the ones who actually live here.

"Hey, want to grab something to eat?" Carson calls out as I stride past. "I'm thinking half a dozen tacos would hit the spot."

Tacos?

No, thanks.

I'll be steering clear of a certain Mexican restaurant until graduation, which sucks, because it's my favorite.

He lifts a brow when I shake my head. "Seriously? Since when are
you a hard no to tacos?"

Since a certain dark-haired waitress with a smart-ass mouth
ruined them for me.

"I've got a ton of homework to plow through. I'm just gonna make
something here."

Carson snorts. "Come on, dude. Since when do you turn down
tacos for homework? A better question would be—when do you actually complete your own assignments?"

I glare before giving him the finger. I've been doing that with more
frequency these days. When a grin breaks out across his face, I stalk to
my bedroom and slam the door closed behind me. I make it two steps
over the threshold before grinding to a halt when I find Lola lounging
on my bed with a scowl.

Even though all I want to do is rush forward and tackle her to the
mattress, I fight the urge, dropping my athletic bag to the carpet
instead.

"What's up." I give her a chin lift, striving for nonchalance.

I've never had a problem talking to girls. Hell, all I have to do is
flash them a smile and most fall onto their backs before spreading
their legs wide.

This one, however, isn't like the others.

And there's something I like about that.

The fire burning in her dark eyes doesn't escape me.

Instead of returning the greeting, she growls, "You lied."

"Is that so?" I yank off my sweatshirt and cross the room, tossing it
over the back of the chair before settling my ass on the corner of the
desk. The tension vibrating through the air continues to heighten as I
fold my arms across my chest. "How exactly did I do that?"

Her attention drops to my arms before she swallows thickly and
raises her gaze to mine again. "You told me the car would only cost a
couple hundred dollars to repair, and it ended up being thousands."

I should have realized she would ask Declan for the total amount instead of just letting it go. This is one girl who wants to take care of everything herself. She'd rather die than allow anyone to help her, even when she's in a pinch.

"He also fixed a couple other things," I tell her.

"Oh, I'm aware." Springing off the bed, she jumps to her feet and advances. "Here's the problem—I didn't ask you to do that!"

"You're right, I made an executive decision because it needed to be done." I push away from the desk and take a step forward before grinding to a halt and holding myself back. "Exactly how long do you think your car would have lasted with a cracked radiator?"

She opens her mouth to no doubt blast me into next week before snapping it shut again and giving her head a quick shake. A few silent seconds tick by before she grudgingly admits, "I don't know."

I inch forward, closing more distance between us. She's so angry that I can practically see smoke billowing off her in waves.

"Well, I do. Did you realize that a car can overheat with a cracked radiator? What if something like that happened when you were coming home from school or the restaurant?" When she stands her ground, I swallow up another couple of feet. "What would you have done then? You'd be stranded. Alone. At night."

Her teeth sink into the plumpness of her lower lip as she glances away. She's so damn stubborn.

So fucking independent.

And it turns me on like nothing else.

Her attention snaps back to me as I take another step. I'm so close that she has to tilt her chin upward to hold my gaze. Some of her fury evaporates, but not all of it.

"You should have been honest from the start. You knew it would be expensive. And you also realized I didn't have the money to pay for it on my own."

She's right about that. But I also knew what would happen if she didn't get her car fixed. It would make her life more difficult, and I didn't want to see that happen. Maybe I took the decision out of her hands, but I did it for all the right reasons. Whether she wants to see that or not.

I cock my head. "What would you have done had I told you the truth?"

The delicate column of her throat constricts as she swallows. "I'm…not sure."

That's a lie, and we both know it. I'm so tired of this girl fighting me at every turn.

"Yes, you do. Now you're the one lying."

Her eyes flare.

When she remains silent, I ask, "Would you have repaired your car if you'd known about the cost?"

In answer, her shoulder slump and she glances away.

But I'll be damned if I let her off that easily. "Well?"

Shame claws at her cheeks. "We both know I wouldn't have been able to afford it." Her voice drops until it sounds as if it's been scraped raw. "I have no idea if the damn thing is worth the money you sank into it."

Even though it's a risk—and I'm probably taking my life into my own hands—I reach out and stroke my thumb along the curve of her jaw. "I don't give a shit about the cost. I care that your car is safe for you to drive. That's all that matters to me."

Her brows pinch together as renewed fire leaps into her eyes. "I don't want your charity or pity, Asher. I don't need it."

"Who said that you did?" Instead of calming her down, everything I do only seems to rile her up more. My fingers continue to stroke over her soft skin. "You're the most independent person I've ever met and more than capable of taking care of yourself. I just helped a little bit. That's it."

Uncertainty flashes across her features as she presses her lips together.

When she remains silent, I ask, "So what the hell is the problem here?"

She tightens her hands into balls before exploding. "Is it so hard for you to understand that I don't want you doing nice things for me?"

Out of everything she could have said, that throws me for a loop. I'm tempted to laugh, but her solemn expression stops me from giving in to the urge.

"Why is that such a crime?"

When she attempts to avoid eye contact, my fingers slip beneath her chin, swiveling her head until she has no other choice but to meet my gaze. I want her attention locked on me.

Always.

"Answer the question. Why is it such a problem if I'm nice to you?"

The tension vibrating between us continues to heighten until it feels like it's enough to choke on.

"Because no one ever has been," she blurts. When my eyes widen, color creeps into her cheeks as she rushes on. "I've gotten this far in life without relying on anyone else for help. I'm not looking to start now."

"Seems like an awfully lonely way to live," I say carefully, fighting to keep my voice neutral. The last thing she wants is my sympathy.

Or—god forbid—pity.

It takes all my self-control not to gather her up into my arms and press her close. The urge to protect this girl pounds through me until it's the only thing I'm cognizant of. I want her to understand that I'm here now and she doesn't have to face these problems alone. I can help shoulder the burden.

"It's all I know," she whispers.

"It doesn't have to be."

Even though moisture pricks her eyes, the tears don't slide down her cheeks. "Everyone I've ever trusted has let me down."

I shift my stance. "Have I done that?"

Instead of giving me an answer, her teeth scrape against her lower lip.

"I won't hurt you, Lola." There's a beat of silence. "You get that, right?"

Her eyes go a little wild as laughter gurgles up from deep within her chest. "No, I don't. Not one damn bit."

Now that I've gotten to know her better, I get why she's so skittish. "Maybe I don't totally understand what's happening here, but I realize that I've never felt this way about anyone else. I like you. More than that, I like the way you make me feel when we're together." *And I think you feel the same.* I search her eyes, hoping to see a hint of softening within them. "Isn't that why you've been avoiding me?"

Almost stubbornly, her chin inches higher. "That's not what I've been doing. I've been busy."

With a smirk, I take another step toward her until I'm able to invade her personal space. "Is that so?"

"Yes. You don't scare me."

"I'm calling bullshit, baby." She's practically shaking in her Chucks.

Her tongue darts out to moisten her lips. "Whether you believe it or not, it's the truth."

My gaze drops to the movement, and a punch of arousal hits me square in the gut. That's all it takes for my cock to stir. I've never wanted anyone the way I do this girl. This growing need I have for her should scare the shit out of me. Strangely enough, it doesn't.

When my chest bumps into her breasts, she attempts to create more space between us by retreating, but she won't get away from me that easily. Not anymore. I stalk her movements until the backs of her knees hit the bed and she tumbles onto the mattress with a gasp.

For a long moment, I loom over her. There's something about the way she stares up at me with those wide, luminous eyes and lips that are slightly parted as the pulse in her throat flutters madly against her flesh. All of it makes my dick rock hard.

The turmoil that flickers across her expressive features is so easy to read. I like Lola best when her mind clicks off and she allows herself to simply feel, living in the present instead of worrying about the future. I don't think she allows herself to do that very often. Her mind is always spinning, constantly worrying about what new calamity is barreling around the corner.

Bending forward, I cage her in so that her spine is pressed against the mattress. My chest pushes into the softness of her breasts as she flattens beneath me. Barely have I touched her and already her breathing has picked up its tempo. When my lips ghost over hers, air catches at the back of her throat.

"Do us both a favor and just admit you like me. It's okay, Lola. I'm the only one who will hear your confession."

She gulps before giving her head a little shake. "No, I don't like you at all."

Her denials are useless. I know exactly how this ends and what I need to do to smash through her defenses, so she'll admit the truth not only to me, but to herself once and for all.

My mouth hovers over hers, barely touching it. When she lifts her chin, attempting to get closer, I draw away. "Not until you tell me the truth."

She huffs out a frustrated breath. "I don't like you."

So fucking stubborn.

"Maybe you don't want to, but you do. There's no way you'd be here otherwise. You knew exactly what would happen when you came to my house and waited for me to show up. I'll bet your pussy got wet just thinking about it."

"No." She shakes her head as her eyes grow desperate. "I was mad—"

"Come on, baby. Admit the truth. You want me just as much as I want you." Fear and panic swim around in her dark depths. It's enough to have guilt slicing through me for continuing to push and prod her into giving me an answer.

Here's the thing—if this relationship is going to progress, I need total honesty between us. She also needs to stop running away and holding me at a distance.

Does this girl think she's the only one who's scared?

Fuck, no. I've never felt this way about anyone else before, and the time we've spent together has only made me realize that. Now, she just needs to accept it as well. Otherwise, neither of us can move forward.

So...if I have to play a little dirty and deny us both what we want, then so be it.

I nip at her lower lip, sucking the plump flesh into my mouth before releasing it. Instead of kissing her the way I want, I slide downward, grazing the sharp curve of her jaw. A smile trembles at the corners of my lips. Does she even realize that she's bearing the delicate column of her throat for me?

I drop kisses along her silky soft skin, sucking and licking as I go. The sooner Lola realizes that she now belongs to me, the easier it'll be for both of us.

My teeth sink into the flesh that flutters madly over her pulse. "Tell me."

A whimper escapes from her.

"Sorry, that's not going to cut it," I growl.

The war I'm waging continues to rage as I arrive at her collarbone and yank the neckline of her shirt down before running my tongue across the exposed flesh until she grows restless beneath me.

"Asher," she groans, voice brimming with need, "we shouldn't…"

"The hell we shouldn't," I mutter, undeterred about my course of action.

Whether she wants to accept it or not, this is happening. There's no turning this bus around.

Not anymore.

One hand snakes down her body until my fingers reach the hem of her shirt before shoving it upward until her simple white bra is bared to my sight. I've been with plenty of chicks who enjoy wearing lacy little underthings that are meant to get a man's blood pumping. That's not the case with this one. It's strictly utilitarian in nature.

Just like Lola.

And yet, for reasons I can't quite pinpoint, this bra turns me on more than any frothy undergarment ever has.

I hover over one breast before biting down on the hard little nipple that pokes through the fabric. A moan falls from her as she arches her back, offering herself up to me. I suck the stiff bud through the fabric into my mouth before giving the same ardent attention to the other.

"We both know what the truth is. Come on, baby girl. All you gotta do is admit it."

"No." She shakes her head, refusing to give up the fight.

Doesn't she realize that the outcome has already been written?

I've never been more convinced of anything in my life as I am about her.

Now, I just need her to tell me she feels it too.

2 5

LOLA

I don't understand what this guy is doing to me.

All right—physically speaking—I get it.

The moment Asher lays hands on my body, I fall to pieces. Even when I'm pissed off and smoke is pouring out of my ears, all he has to do is touch me—even look at me in that heated-up way of his—and all my anger dissipates until I can't remember what I was mad about in the first place. The effortless spell he's able to weave is disturbing on so many levels. If I could snuff it out, I'd do it in a heartbeat.

But that's not possible. Not when his mouth is drifting over me, licking and sucking at my flesh. Or when his calloused hands stroke over my body. He makes me want things I have no business longing for.

Doesn't he realize that I have a plan?

One I've followed since high school…and he's attempting to derail it. The most frightening part is that there are times when it's tempting to give in and wave the white flag. To do the unthinkable and take a chance on this brawny football player who has coasted through life without so much as a hiccup.

How crazy would that be?

And how insane does that make me for even considering it?

I mean, come on…this is Asher Stevens we're talking about. His name and monogamy are not exactly synonymous. To my knowledge, he's never even been in a committed relationship.

Oh my god.

Who said anything about this being a relationship?

Committed or otherwise.

It's official—I've lost my mind. That's the only reasonable explanation for this lapse in judgment.

I blink back to the present when his teeth bite down on my nipple. There's a flash of pain before pleasure crashes over me like a wave, threatening to suck me under. I'll drown if I'm not careful. That's what this man does to me.

"You like that, baby girl? Does it force you out of your head and into the moment?"

Fear spirals through me that he can read me so easily. If I wasn't pinned to the mattress, I'd probably race from the room like my ass was on fire.

Thankfully, a response isn't required as his lips trek further down my chest before arriving at my belly. I draw in a deep breath, trying to clear my muddled head. Instead, it remains fuzzy. Almost as if he's able to stop the neurons in my brain from firing.

"Look at me, Lola."

I don't realize my eyelids have feathered shut until he growls out the demand. That's all it takes for them to fly open and lock on his.

"I get that you're scared. If I'm being perfectly honest, so am I—but I won't hurt you. I promise."

His words are like a punch to the gut. They steal my breath away like a thief in the night.

"How can you say that?" I whisper. "You have no idea what will happen in the future."

His blue eyes grow so serious that looking away from the sincerity shining from them becomes impossible. "Because I've never wanted to take more care with anyone in my life than I do with you."

No matter how I try to hold strong, those words are my undoing. The impenetrable walls I've fought to keep firmly intact come tumbling down, leaving me vulnerable and exposed in a way I've never been.

As difficult as it is to push out a response, I find myself saying, "All right." I might be giving in of my own free will, but that doesn't stop the icy-cold tendrils of panic and fear from rushing through my veins.

He stares as if he didn't hear me correctly. "All right?"

With a nod, my teeth scrape across my lower lip. I can only pray that I won't regret this impulsive decision in the not-so-distant future. I don't understand how this can end any other way than badly.

Our gazes stay locked as he crawls up my body until his mouth is perfectly aligned with my own.

"Do you believe me when I say that I won't hurt you?"

The question echoes throughout my head.

"I want to," I tell him truthfully.

"I guess that's good enough for now. It'll just take time to prove that I'm a man of my word. I won't ever lie to you. Do you understand me?" He presses a kiss against my lips. "And just so you know, I've never made that kind of promise to anyone. You're the first. The only."

When something warm blooms to life inside me, my initial instinct is to stomp it out. As tempting as it is to believe him, I refuse to get my hopes up.

"You're doing it again." When my brows furrow, he murmurs, "Thinking too much. We need to do something about that."

And then he's moving down my body, kissing and nipping before reaching my bare belly. His gaze stays pinned to mine as he flicks open the button and drags down the zipper. The metal teeth grind, shattering the silence of the room. My excitement grows, ratcheting up with every inhalation. I can't help but tremble beneath him, impatient for his touch. He shoves the denim down my legs until I'm free of the thick material. His attention shifts to my core as I twist beneath him. No one has ever made me feel so restless.

Or achy.

As if there's a fire blazing deep inside. One that will burn out of control and scorch me alive. Not once did it occur to me that sensations like these actually existed. I always chalked it up to the make-believe stuff that filled romance novels and movies. To think that Asher Stevens is the only man capable of rousing this kind of intensity blows my mind.

When he presses a kiss against my panty-covered core, it takes every bit of self-control to bite back the sharp moan that sits perched on the tip of my tongue. He'll unravel me if I allow him to, and I'm not sure I'm ready for that just yet.

"You had to realize that one time was never going to be enough for either of us."

He's right...I did. It's the reason I disappeared. Had it solely been amazing sex, it would've been far easier to keep an emotional distance and enjoy everything he was offering. A much-needed break from reality. But that's not what happened. Instead, an emotional connection was forged. One I have no idea how to sever.

"Answer me."

I hiss out a breath when his teeth sink into the plump flesh above my slit, and a potent concoction of pleasure-infused pain reverberates throughout my entire being until it echoes in the tips of my fingers and toes.

"Yes," I gasp.

His thumbs hook into the elastic band of my panties before dragging them down until the top of my pussy is bared. His heated gaze licks over me before he presses a kiss against my naked flesh.

"Good girl. Now we're getting somewhere." He flicks his gaze to mine, spearing me with a hot look. "Is this what it'll be like between us? Me forcing every little acknowledgement from you?"

He lowers his mouth until his tongue can swipe over me. When he repeats the maneuver, I can't stop the moan from slipping free.

"Because that's exactly what I'll do. Every damn time, if that's what it takes. I let you run from me once and I'm not gonna allow it to happen again. Understand?"

I have no idea why a small, defiant part of me wants to fight him. Maybe I need to push him into proving that he's serious and the promises he's making aren't empty ones.

A challenging light fills his eyes when I remain silent.

"Have it your way," he growls.

When he rises from the bed, the warmth of his body disappears, and I shiver at the loss. His fingers wrap around the slim band at my hips before ripping them down my legs. The renting of fabric is the only sound that can be heard over our labored breathing. Once the panties have been torn away, he moves between my legs, widening them until he's able to fit.

I hate the thrill of excitement that rushes through my veins as he presses my thighs impossibly wide until he can see every pink inch. His gaze drops to my core and heat gathers in my cheeks as he studies me.

My heart pounds a painful staccato as the burn of his gaze licks over my body. I can't help but squirm as another burst of need explodes inside me. His fingers bite into my flesh, holding me in place. The grip isn't painful, more like a constant reminder of his dominating presence. Deep down, I know if I told Asher to stop or back off, he'd do it in a heartbeat.

The problem is that's not what I want.

What I want is his forcefulness.

There's something strangely freeing about being at his mercy and giving in to the rush of sensations that crashes over me like a tidal wave. It forces me to forget about everything else going on in my life and focus solely on him. On the pleasure coursing through me.

And for that, I'm grateful.

Just when it seems like I'll self-combust from the intensity of his scrutiny, he takes a long, leisurely lap of my core. The firm pressure of his tongue leaves me arching, silently seeking out more. It's only when I'm writhing beneath him that he circles my clit with the tip of his tongue.

That's all it takes for me to go from zero to sixty in two seconds flat, and then I'm hovering at the edge of oblivion. One little nudge and I'll dive headfirst off the precipice.

I want so badly for him to send me spiraling.

Instead of giving me the relief I seek, he pulls back and nips at the soft flesh of my inner thighs with sharp teeth. All that sensation swirling through me collapses in on itself, leaving me to feel frustrated, achy, and on edge. A puff of air bursts from my lips.

"Asher…" Even though I try to keep my voice level, it's riddled with pleading notes that embarrass the hell out of me. I hate asking for anything, and that's exactly what he's forcing me to do.

Beg for every little touch.

Every caress.

Just so I understand who is in charge and calling the shots.

"What, baby girl? What do you want?"

"I want you to…"

"Tell me."

"I want you to kiss me."

He presses his lips against my pussy but doesn't take it any further. "There. Like that?"

I groan. My body feels like it's on fire, a raging inferno that he's carefully stoking to life. And because of that, he's the only one capable of dousing the flames.

"No."

"No?" He presses his mouth to my clit. "What about this?"

I raise my hips in silent invitation as need thrums through me.

"Admit you feel something for me."

One thick finger sinks inside my heat. I can't help but clench my inner muscles around him as he slowly withdraws the digit. The pleasure spinning through me is nothing short of delicious. And I want more.

So much more.

"Give me an answer, Lola."

I…

He drives inside me again before falling into a steady rhythm, pumping in and out until it feels like I'll splinter apart. His lips hover over the little bud until his warm breath can drift over me. I struggle beneath him, unable to hold myself still. When his tongue darts out to swipe over my delicate flesh, a whimper escapes.

His touch is agonizing. There and gone before I can fully sink into the pleasure of it.

"Tell me the truth. I need to hear it from you."

When his tongue rasps over me again in tandem with the steady slide of his finger, the words pour from me in a torrent. I couldn't keep them trapped inside even if I wanted to. It needs to be purged from my system once and for all.

"Yes! All right? As much as I don't want to feel something for you, I do! That's why I stopped returning your calls and texts. I was hoping a little distance would help me realize that you don't mean anything to me, but it's not true. I want you, Asher. And I want this—whatever the hell *this* is."

With a growl, he attacks my flesh. A scream tears from my lips as he slips two fingers deep inside me. Both his teeth and mouth go to work on my clit. That's all it takes for me to explode against him.

My body goes whipcord tight as I scream out my orgasm. He doesn't let up on the firm pressure until every drop has been wrung from my over-sensitized body. Until I'm nothing more than a limp mess, staring sightlessly at the ceiling.

Only then does he raise his head. "There's no more running and hiding. You're mine now. You belong to me."

I suck in a shuddering breath as his words crash over me. The finality of them should light a fire under my ass. Instead, they do the opposite. An odd amount of peace suffuses my entire being. It doesn't make sense. But then again, nothing with Asher does.

He rises from between my legs until he's able to loom over me. His fingers slide around my ribcage before settling on the clasp of my bra. A second later, the stretchy material springs apart and he tugs it from my body, dropping it to the floor. A shiver slides through me as I realize he's still dressed in both his shirt and shorts.

His gaze rakes over me before flicking back to mine.

"This is exactly how I like you, Lola. Naked, soft, and vulnerable."

Even though I just came, arousal bursts to life in my core.

When one large palm settles over my breast, I arch into his touch. He squeezes the plump flesh before his thumb and forefinger tighten around the taut peak. A moan slips free as he tweaks the sensitive bud before pulling at it until another round of explosions detonates inside me.

"Am I hurting you?"

I shake my head. It's a curious concoction of pleasure and pain, but ultimately, the way he's touching me feels good.

Better than that, if I'm being truthful.

"Turn over."

The gruffly uttered words don't immediately penetrate the thick haze clouding my brain. When I continue to stare, he wraps his hands around my hips before flipping me onto my belly. I don't have a chance to catch my breath before he drags me to the edge of the bed and pulls my ass high in the air.

A groan rumbles up from deep in his chest as his rough fingers drift over my flank before spreading my cheeks. "Fuck, you're gorgeous."

My teeth sink into my lower lip as I squeeze my eyes shut. All it would take is one simple word and he would back off, but I can't seem to summon the directive. Even more telling—I don't want to. No man has ever toyed with my body like this or coaxed these kinds of responses from me.

How could I possibly ask him to stop now?

"Is this all for me?"

I've spent my entire life being strong and in control, never allowing myself a single moment of weakness or my guard to falter. Even though I want to do that with Asher, I find it difficult to give in completely. To hand myself over for his safekeeping without him proving first that he can be trusted. A silent war erupts inside my brain. It doesn't take long to lose myself in the turmoil of those thoughts.

It's only when a hard smack lands on my ass that I jolt, a gasp escaping from me, as a fusion of shock, pleasure, and discomfort explodes in my core.

"You didn't answer the question," he growls before enunciating more carefully, *"Is all this for me?"*

My eyes widen as he drags a finger along the cleft between my cheeks before his large palm settles over my pussy, squeezing it possessively with a tight grip.

"Yes," I whisper. Barely has he touched me and another orgasm is already gathering strength like a storm. My head spins as sensation swamps my system, making it impossible to think straight. I have no idea what this man is doing to me.

His fingers dig into my flesh before disappearing, and then he smacks the other side of my ass. His warm breath wafts over the nape of my neck. "Here's what you need to understand—I know exactly what you need, and when you finally bend, I'll give it to you."

Emotion that had long been dormant breaks free and rises within me, swirling like a tempest until it becomes painful. Almost as if it's trying to claw its way out.

He grips my cheeks in his hands, massaging them, tugging and pulling. I no longer care if he's staring at the most vulnerable part of me. The way he's handling my body feels much too good to protest.

"Don't move." That order is accompanied by another smack.

The reverberations of it echo throughout me, flooding my core with more arousal. I don't understand how something that should be humiliating and painful has the opposite effect.

My cheek is pressed against the mattress, facing the opposite direction. All of my senses are heightened as I listen intently to what he's doing. The drawer of his nightstand is yanked open before there's a tearing sound.

A condom.

I'm grateful that at least one of us is cognizant enough to think about protection, because it certainly isn't me.

And that's a first.

The last thing I want or need is to end up pregnant. That would ruin all my plans, and I can't afford for that to happen. Not when I'm so close to digging my way out of the hole I've spent my life in.

The cool air of his room swirls around my damp flesh, making me even more aware of my vulnerable state. As tempting as it is to cover myself, I remain still. I don't understand my desire to follow Asher's directive, but I find myself unwilling to do otherwise. The fact that one of his teammates or friends could barge into his room at any given moment only heightens the arousal rampaging through my system.

Did he lock the door when he came in earlier?

I rack my brain but can't remember.

Before I can give voice to the question, he's back, positioning himself behind me. Anticipation clogs my throat, making it impossible to breathe. His hands settle on my hips before moving to the base of my spine and stroking upward to my neck before trailing down again.

"I know what you need, Lola. Even if you don't understand it yourself."

A sliver of fear slides through me. That's exactly what I'm afraid of.

"Here, in the privacy of this room, you can relinquish control and give it over to me for safekeeping. The weight of the world doesn't always have to rest on your shoulders."

I squeeze my eyes tightly shut.

Does he have any idea what he's asking?

Even if it's exactly what I want?

Or—like he claims—what I need.

That takes trust.

His hands caress the length of my back until my muscles loosen, the thick tension and confusion leaking from me one tendon at a time, until I'm lulled into a state of relaxation.

"I don't know any other way," I whisper, surprised when the words escape from my mouth.

"I realize that."

"I'm scared," I force myself to admit, feeling even more vulnerable.

The firm pressure continues to glide over me until my eyelids grow heavy and droop, and I can't help but relish the feel of his strong hands.

"I get it." He only ceases the tender ministrations long enough to press a kiss against one shoulder blade. "You like this, don't you?"

It's not really a question. More a statement of fact.

"I do."

"Then let me do this for you. Let me be there for you."

My lids crack open just a bit. "I don't want to be disappointed or hurt."

"You won't be."

So badly do I want to believe him.

Believe *in* him.

When the head of his cock nudges my entrance, I push against him, only wanting to feel his rigid length buried deep inside me. After the time he's spent rousing my body to a fever pitch, I almost expect him to slam into me before pounding me senseless. And part of me wants that. It would be so much easier than dwelling on the promises he's made.

Instead, he gradually slides inside my body until he's buried to the hilt. Once there, he holds perfectly still. He doesn't withdraw, not right away. There's something powerful about the feel of his muscular body fitted tightly against me. The dominance of his position and the submissiveness of mine.

Allowing him to lead so I can follow.

As those thoughts flood my brain, I realize how much I like it. How much easier it is to simply be and have the decisions taken out of my hands.

He's right.

Not only do I want it, I need it.

I'm forced to the present when he gathers up the long strands of my hair and wraps them around his hand. He pulls on the length until it becomes necessary for me to tilt my head. The pressure remains firm but not painful. The feel of him holding me like this sends an arrow of lust straight to my core before exploding upon impact.

"Am I hurting you?"

It's tempting to shake my head, but I can't without inflicting pain onto myself. "No."

"Do you want me to let go?" His voice grows taut, filling with tension as if he's walking a tightrope.

Is that what I do to him?

Is that what *this* does to him?

It's a heady sensation.

"No."

"Good, because I like looking at you like this. On all fours, bent over with your ass in the air, your hair gripped tightly in my hand while I feed your needy pussy with my cock."

Oh god.

Those words.

They echo hollowly in my head and turn me on even more. Only then does he withdraw before thrusting deep inside and filling me to the brim.

It feels amazing.

So fucking amazing.

The sensation on my scalp is a relentless pressure as his other hand curls into my hip, keeping me flush with his body. As unlikely as our friendship is, we somehow fit together perfectly. Two pieces of a different puzzle. It doesn't make a damn bit of sense, and quite honestly, I'm tired of trying to find fault with it.

I can't do it any longer.

Pleasure mounts, gradually building as he maintains a steady rhythm. It's the tight hold on his self-control that allows me to surrender and give myself over to him the way he's patiently urged. My muscles slacken as the internal protests chirping in the back of my brain are finally silenced.

"That's it," he grunts. "Let me do this for you."

When his grip on my hair increases, I find myself arching, tipping my head farther as his thrusts intensify until he's able to hit a place deep inside. The steady tempo is like the rocking of the ocean, lulling me into a strange, contented state.

"Such a good girl."

The praise has my pussy contracting, flooding with heat.

"You like that, don't you?" he says knowingly.

Before I can summon a response, his fingers loosen from my hip, and he smacks my ass. The sharp sound resonates throughout the room.

"Yes," I bite out, surprised by the swat, but loving it at the same time.

His pace increases as his hand snakes around my hip before finding my clit.

"I want you to come for me," he orders, applying more pressure to that tiny bundle of nerves as his thrusts reach a crescendo. *"Now."*

And just like that, I fall apart on command. Stars explode behind my eyelids as an orgasm rips through my body. Asher groans, and the deep scrape of his voice only amplifies my pleasure. My pussy clenches around him, milking the last of his release before he collapses on top of me. A few harsh breaths later, he loosens the grip on my hair and presses a kiss against my shoulder as his cock softens. And still, he doesn't move. We stay fused together in the most primal and intimate way imaginable.

Everything that just happened, the way I willingly gave myself over, crashes through my head and my muscles stiffen.

When his teeth sink into my flesh, I yelp.

"Stop it."

My eyes widen. "Stop what?"

"Thinking. There's no going back. Only forward."

"I—"

He pulls away enough to smack my ass with the flat of his palm. "Don't lie to me. Not when I'm buried deep inside your body." He gives me another swat in the same place. It's not enough to cause pain or damage, only to capture my attention. "Do you understand?"

I nibble at my lower lip, unsure how to respond.

"Lola," he growls. "I'll spank you all damn night if that's what it takes to get it through your thick skull."

"Okay," I whisper.

"Okay, what?"

"I won't lie to you."

"And?" He stretches out the word.

My muscles loosen as I capitulate. "I won't fight this."

He rubs the abraded area. "Good girl."

A feeling of loss floods me as he pulls out and pads into the bathroom. I remain still, only turning my head enough to watch him. A few seconds tick by before he walks back out and beelines for me. That's when I realize I'm still kneeling on the bed with my ass in the air. As I jolt, attempting to scramble away, one large palm settles on my lower back to pin me in place as something warm and damp is pressed against my exposed core.

I gasp as a strange pleasure floods through me.

"I can clean myself off," I whisper, embarrassment stinging my cheeks.

"I'm aware of that, but I want to do it for you."

The tension gripping my muscles, locking them in place, gradually dissipates as he presses the heated cloth against my pussy before stroking it over my flesh and wiping away my arousal. The more he rubs, the more turned on I get, which is ridiculous. The man just gave me two amazing orgasms, I should be completely sated.

And yet…

I shake away those thoughts.

"I love that you're so fucking sexual," he rasps.

Yeah…that's the funny thing. I've never been that way until now.

Until him.

26

LOLA

I glance at Asher, who is camped out at a small table at the back of the restaurant, studying and plowing his way through some homework. His AirPods are shoved in his ears to drown out the noisy chatter surrounding him.

Every once in a while, he'll look up and our gazes will catch. Electricity will sizzle through my veins before settling deep in my core like a heavy weight. I have to clench my thighs to styme the arousal that crashes through my body each time it happens.

True story—I'm twenty-two years old and this is the first time I've been caught up in someone. It's as scary as it is exhilarating. Kind of like swinging on a trapeze without a net.

"I see lover boy is here again," Carmen says, sidling up beside me when I wasn't looking. "We're gonna start charging him rent."

I startle, knocked from my thoughts, which is probably for the best. This guy is consuming way too much of my energy. What I've discovered about Asher is that he has more depth and intelligence than he allows people to see. I'm not sure what the reason is for that. We're still learning each other.

Exploring…

I clear my throat and straighten my shoulders. This isn't the time or place to dwell on that. Plus, the last thing I need is to get all hot and bothered. Especially when there's nothing that can be done about it. "I'm tutoring him."

"Uh-huh. Sure."

My cousin knows me well enough and isn't buying that lame-ass excuse for a minute.

"What *exactly* are you tutoring him in?" She waggles her brows suggestively. "That's what I'd like to know."

"Please…" I grumble, embarrassed by this line of questioning. I've never been one to kiss and tell. My philosophy is that private matters should stay private. Carmen doesn't subscribe to the same opinion. I've been treated to descriptions that go into way too much graphic detail.

Things that can never be unheard again.

Her eyes widen as she straightens. "Holy shit, you're blushing!"

She crows this loud enough for her brother, Mateo, to turn and stare. When he hikes a brow, more heat fills my face. Instead of tag teaming me, which they've been known to do on more than one occasion, he thankfully walks away with a pan full of dirty dishes.

I glance around, hoping no one else is paying attention to our convo before grumbling, "I am not."

"Yes, you are. Your cheeks are totally red." With a shake of her head, she plants her hands on curvy hips. "I never thought I'd see the day you caught feelings for some hot jock."

"I haven't caught feelings," I lie. Even though I've admitted as much to myself, that doesn't mean I'm willing to talk about it with my cousin. Not yet, anyway.

We're just so…different. Is it even possible for a relationship to work between us?

I'm serious minded, and he's the furthest thing from it.

You have to drag me to a party, and he's the life of it.

I'm low profile, and he's anything but. Even here at the restaurant, people stop by his table, wanting to talk football. He's always gracious about indulging them.

Humble.

That's one word I never thought I'd associate with the guy. The other day, José brought in a football for him to sign and Asher did it without question before bullshitting with him for another ten minutes, agreeing to meet with his kid in a week or so.

My heart turns unexpectedly gooey just thinking about it.

Our lives, our personalities…we're night and day.

And yet…

I like him.

I like spending time with him.

The more that happens, the greedier I am to be with him. I wish it were possible to close out the rest of the world so it was just the two of us. He's the only person capable of making me forget everything that normally eats away at my brain.

I still as those thoughts circle through my head. If I hadn't realized how deep I was in with this guy, I certainly do now.

"Yes, you have. It's written all over your face." She angles her head and narrows her eyes. "You're falling for him."

When I unconsciously raise my hand to my cheek, she bursts out laughing.

"What am I going to do," I whisper, panic flooding my voice as I drop the charade. "I don't want to like him. He's just…*too much*."

She glances at Asher and studies him, as if assessing that comment along with the situation. "Damn right he is. Savor it. Savor everything you can with that guy, because I bet he's hot AF in the bedroom."

I press my lips together, refusing to comment.

When I remain silent, she chuckles. "You deserve to have fun. Maybe no one's ever told you this before, but there's nothing wrong with loosening up and enjoying life, even if it's just a little bit."

Enjoy life?

Ha!

When have I ever been able to do that?

The answer is never. There's always been too many balls I'm attempting to juggle or too many fires I'm trying to put out. It's exhausting. Much too exhausting to focus on fun.

What scares me most is not being able to stop myself from falling for him even more than I already have. Because in the end, he'll walk away and move onto the next girl, and I'll be stuck, wishing we were still together.

That's never happened before. Guys come and go from my life, dropping in for a few brief moments before leaving again. None have ever made a lasting impression.

I didn't allow them to.

It never bothered me when they vanished. I've always had too much going on to get overly involved. When you're treading water, just hoping to make it through another day without drowning, a relationship is the last thing on your mind and a luxury you can't afford.

It's a relief when a customer makes eye contact with Carmen, and she takes off across the dining room. Shoving Asher from my thoughts, I stop by a few tables and make sure everyone has what they need before reluctantly gravitating to him to check his progress.

Well…that's what I tell myself, anyway.

As soon as he glances up and our gazes collide, energy crackles in the air. It feels like a living, breathing entity swirling through the atmosphere.

My mind empties as we continue to stare. Unsure what to say or do, I point to the book and attempt to gather my scattered thoughts. "How's it going?"

Instead of answering, he nabs my fingers and tows me to him. When I'm close enough, his hand slips around the nape of my neck before pulling my face down until his lips can coast over mine.

Just as I lose myself in the caress, someone clears their throat from nearby. Startled, I jump away, only to find my cousin with a shit-eating grin on her face as she saunters past with a platter of food held in one hand. Even though she doesn't laugh, I can practically hear the husky sound ringing unwantedly in my ears.

Heat fills my cheeks as I settle across from him and try to refocus my attention. His books are spread out across the table along with his laptop.

I blink and try not to stare at his lips as memories of how he used them on me the other night flit through my head. "Getting much work done?"

"Yeah," he says with a nod. "I've plowed my way through one assignment and I'm just about to start a paper for my other Comms class."

"I have a couple minutes if you want me to glance at it."

He taps the keyboard a few times before swiveling the computer in my direction. I pull it closer and scan the document, correcting a few minor grammatical errors before returning the device.

"It looks good."

His lips lift into a slow smile before he glances at his phone. "You're done in an hour, right?"

"Yup."

Heat fills his eyes as the lids fall to half-mast. "Good. Looking forward to having you all to myself again."

The air once again turns charged as our gazes cling. Liquid heat gathers in my core before I quickly stomp it out. "I, ah, should go."

"All right." His attention flickers to the books. "I'll just be here, working diligently."

I nod before rising to my feet and taking off through the dining room as my pulse thrums a steady beat. I don't think I'll ever get used to the way he makes me feel.

"I just seated some customers for you," Carmen says as we pass by one another.

My gaze travels around the open space before landing on a group of four college-aged guys. I stop and fill up glasses of water on my way over to the table. After setting them down, I give them my spiel.

"Hello, I'm Lola. Welcome to Taco Loco. Do you need more time to look over the menu?" I meet their gazes one at a time. I've been waitressing long enough to know when a group is going to be a problem, and that's not the vibe I get from this one. There's nothing worse than a table full of assholes.

One of the dark-haired guys flashes me a grin. "You go to Western, right?"

I nod, all the while keeping a friendly smile on my face. "Yup."

"I think we're in the same International Marketing section."

I tilt my head and study him more closely. The class he's talking about has thirty students in it. Instead of admitting that I don't recognize him, I say with a bright smile, "Oh, right. Sure."

"Professor Connelly is so freaking boring. Half the time I just want to take a nap."

"Really? I like him. He's my academic advisor. The guy really knows what he's talking about. This is the third course I've taken with him."

He shrugs. "Maybe I'll sit next to you from now on and you can help me stay awake."

Like I want to babysit this guy?

Umm…no thanks.

When I give him a tight smile in response, just wanting to get this conversation back on track and take their orders, he says, "I was kind of wondering…"

His voice trails off when heavy hands settle on my shoulders.

The guy's eyes widen before he audibly swallows. "Hey, Asher. How you doing?"

"I'm good." He doesn't bother to volley the question back as he draws me closer to his body. "I see you've met my girl."

The dark-haired guy's gaze flickers to me before bouncing back to Asher. "Umm, yeah." That's all it takes for awkwardness to descend. "Sorry, man. I didn't know she was with you."

"Well, now you do," he says easily. The steely strength that has crept into his voice doesn't go unnoticed by anyone.

"Yup," he mutters, picking up his menu and pretending to peruse it as his friends do the same. Even though the restaurant is filled with chatter and music, it's quiet enough at the table to hear a pin drop.

I bite down on my inner cheek to keep a straight face and not smile. There's a tiny part of me that feels like I should be irritated with Asher for coming over and marking his territory. Especially while I'm at work. Unfortunately, I'd be lying through my teeth if I didn't admit that a bigger part is flooded with pleasure.

It's almost like he can read my thoughts as he pulls me close enough to whisper, "You're mine, and I want everyone to know it."

Before I can respond, he presses a kiss against the side of my face and disappears as quietly as he interrupted.

I clear my throat before asking cheerfully, "So, who's ready to order?"

27

ASHER

With my backpack slung over my shoulder, I wait for Lola near the hostess stand. I'm impatient to hustle her sweet ass out of here so I can finally get my hands on her. I've been fighting the urge since I walked into the restaurant earlier. Especially when that bonehead thought he could pick her up.

Even from across the room, I could tell what was going on. Hot sparks of jealousy had erupted inside me. It's not something that's ever happened before. No girl has ever made me feel possessive. In fact, it's always been the opposite. If they were off flirting with another guy, then they weren't solely focused on me. The last thing I wanted was for one of them to think we had something more meaningful than it was.

I couldn't feel more different about Lola.

I blink out of those thoughts when movement catches the corner of my eye and excitement stirs inside me, thinking that she's finally mine for the rest of the night. My head swivels and I'm just about to take a step in her direction when I realize that it's not the dark-haired beauty, but her cousin instead. She's leaning against one of the pillars with her arms crossed over her chest.

Once our gazes lock, they remain fastened. After a long stretch of silence ticks by, she arches a sculpted brow. If she thinks her open examination will be enough to make me squirm, she couldn't be more wrong. I'm used to people staring. And pointing. Not to mention, talking loudly enough for me to overhear their conversation.

"You and Lola, huh?"

I shrug and try to keep my stance relaxed. "Yup."

Even though I've met her mother and father—if that's what you want to call him—and that went well enough, her cousin looks like she'd be more than happy to drag me into a small room and grill me using questionable tactics.

But here's the thing—I can't blame her for being protective. If I had a sister, I wouldn't want her getting tangled up with a guy like me either.

After another minute of intense scrutiny, she pushes away from the pillar and strolls closer. "I'd like to know what your intentions are."

My intentions?

Umm...

"We're just—you know—hanging out and having fun," I mutter.

Her expression darkens. "So, you're just in this for a good time? Is that what you're telling me?"

A good time?

Is this girl serious?

Fighting Lola tooth and nail to even get this far has been the exact opposite of fun. It's been a lot of fucking hard work. Totally worth it in the end, but still work.

"I had to practically force your cousin into admitting that she was interested in seeing me."

That brings a reluctant smile to her lips. "Sounds about right."

My attention drifts to Lola, who's busy counting out her tips near the back. "She's not an easy nut to crack."

She follows my gaze until it lands on her cousin. The small smile fades from her face. "Nope, she's not. If you actually get to know her, you might discover the reasons for that."

I shift my weight and cross my arms against my chest. "If you're alluding to the situation with her father, then yeah—I'm aware of it."

Her gaze sharpens on me as surprise laces her voice. "She told you about that?"

I jerk my head. "Met him, too." I glance at Lola again, wanting to make sure she hasn't snuck up on me. "From what I could tell, he's a real piece of work."

"That's one way of putting it." A heavy silence follows that comment. "Then you can understand why I wouldn't want to see her get jerked around. She's been through enough with her family. If you're just here because you're looking for a little flavor to spice up your life, you should make yourself scarce before it goes any further."

I straighten to my full height and glare. "That's not what this is."

"You sure about that?"

"Yeah," I bite out, "I am." I've never been more certain about anything in my life.

"She doesn't open up and share herself with many people. If she's let her guard down, then you better realize how special that is and treat her right. Don't inflict more damage."

My brows lower. "What makes you think I'd do that?"

She pops a shoulder. "No reason. I'm just giving you a friendly warning."

There's absolutely nothing friendly about the steely look in her eyes. Is this pint-sized chick seriously trying to threaten me?

"Hey, I'm all set. Are you ready to get out of here?" Lola asks, interrupting our tense conversation.

I keep my gaze locked on her cousin. "Yup."

Lola shifts, throwing a glance at the other girl as if only now sensing that all might not be right between us. Her smile slowly falls away. "What are you guys talking about?"

"Nothing," we both say at the same time. Although, my tone is more clipped and hers is silky as if we've been shooting the shit, just getting to know one another.

"Huh." Her brows inch up her forehead. "Now why don't I believe either one of you?"

Before Lola can fire off any more questions, Carmen says, "It was great meeting you, but I need to get back to work." With a bright smile, she pulls Lola in for a quick hug. "See you tomorrow?"

"Where else would I be?"

With that, she takes off, sauntering into the dining room without a backward glance. I stare after her, trying to figure out if I read too much into the conversation before my gaze slides to Lola.

A suspicious light fills her narrowed eyes. "All right, now that she's gone, tell me what Carmen really said."

"Nothing," I say with a forced shrug. "It was just a little chit chat." Maybe she didn't threaten bodily injury, but the promise was there in her eyes.

When she gives me a dubious look, I clear my throat and change the subject. "Want to get moving?"

It takes a few seconds for her muscles to loosen as a smile curves her lips. "More than ready."

I throw an arm around her shoulders before hauling her close as we push out into the frigid air. When the wind whips over us, she tugs her jacket more tightly around her as we walk to the Escalade. Once we're both inside, I start up the engine and allow it to idle for a few minutes before shifting into drive and pulling out of the parking lot.

As I turn onto the street, an earlier convo with my brother pops into my head. Nerves spring to life in the pit of my gut as I try to keep my voice casual. "I'm meeting up with Jack for breakfast on Wednesday. Any interest in coming with?"

Her gaze flickers to mine in the darkness. There's a moment of hesitation before she says, "Do you really want me to?"

"Yeah, of course. I wouldn't have asked otherwise." Even though I'm trying not to make it sound like this is a big deal, it kind of is.

Her teeth rake over her lower lip as a handful of silent seconds tick by.

Just when I'm about to downplay the invitation, she says, "Okay."

Tension leaks from my muscles as a ridiculous amount of relief floods through me. A small smile curves my lips. "Cool." The next question is out of my mouth before I can rein it back in. "You gonna spend the night at my place?"

Now that I've had her in my bed on a regular basis, it's difficult to imagine sleeping without her. Which is…yeah, I'm not going to lie, it's a bit strange. Girls have warmed my bed before and it's not like I have any hard and fast rules when it comes to the female species, but even I realize that once you allow someone to get comfortable in your space, it isn't long before expectations follow.

Like a toothbrush and a box of tampons in the bathroom.

Maybe a small drawer of personal belongings and a few items of clothing.

And then, before you know it, you're sucked into a full-blown relationship. I've avoided those in the past like a nasty STI, making sure to steer clear of chicks who give off any *I'm looking for a boyfriend* vibes.

"I should probably go home and check in with my mom. Make sure everything's okay."

That's not the answer I was hoping for. "We could always swing by your place before heading to mine."

God…could I sound any more desperate?

"I think it's better if I just stay at my house tonight." Her gaze flickers to mine. "Is that cool?"

I shift on the leather seat and tamp down my disappointment. "Yeah, of course. No problem."

Silence descends before she breaks it. "Tony sent over the donor information." There's a pause. "I set up an evaluation for Thursday, and I'll probably be there for about eight hours."

Holy shit.

I'd assumed there would be blood work before moving forward with any further testing. Apparently, that's not the case.

I rip my gaze from the ribbon of road stretched out in front of me to scrutinize her expression. What I've learned about Lola is that she has a damn good poker face and likes to keep everything close to her chest. She's not one to give away her feelings. While most girls want to talk something to death, she'll barely mention it in passing.

I reach out and wrap my fingers around hers, wanting to offer as much support as I can. Even if it's just being there with her, holding her close, and telling her that everything will be all right.

"Are you having second thoughts?"

She keeps her gaze focused straight ahead. "No, it's just testing. I haven't committed to anything more than that."

"Why does it take so long?" Eight hours. That's all damn day.

"From what I understand, there's a ton of things that need to be done." Her teeth rake her lower lip. "Bloodwork, urine analysis, a physical examination, chest X-ray, and EKG." Lola shakes her head as if she's having a hard time wrapping her mind around all of it. "I wrote it down when I spoke with the coordinator to set up the appointment."

"And all of that will take eight hours?"

When she releases a steady puff of air, I squeeze her fingers, wanting her to concentrate on me and not everything churning in her head.

"No. After that, there are consults with a social worker, kidney specialist, and transplant surgeon. Maybe even a nutritionist. Honestly, I can't remember."

"Wow. That's a lot," I murmur. "I'll come with if you want."

She shakes her head. "That's not necessary. I can do it myself."

Always so damn reluctant to accept help or even support. It's like she's an island unto herself.

"What I should have said is that I'll be coming with you."

She glances at me with wide eyes. "But—"

I shake my head as my expression hardens. "There are no buts. We'll go together and I'll stay with you the entire time."

Even though I turn back to the road before taking a left onto the street that leads to her house, I'm aware of her gaze fastened on me. I can almost hear the questions and indecision whipping through her brain.

Once I pull into the short drive, I park the truck and swivel toward her. "I'm coming with you on Thursday. End of story. Got it?"

For a moment, it seems like she might argue, and I prepare myself for battle. This isn't one she's going to win.

When I raise my brows in challenge, she huffs out a breath. "Fine."

"What time is the appointment?"

"Nine. At the transplant center near the hospital."

"Then we'll leave at eight thirty. That should give us plenty of time to get there and check in."

"What about your classes and practice? Can you really afford to miss them?"

I wave away her concerns. "I'll email my professors and talk to Coach. It won't be a problem."

Even though Lola doesn't necessarily like me telling her what to do, it would be impossible to miss the relief that floods into her eyes.

When she glances away, staring into the darkness, I reach out and slip my fingers beneath her chin before turning it until she can meet my searching gaze. "When I told you I wouldn't hurt you, I meant it. Haven't I earned even a little bit of your trust yet?"

Her tongue darts out to moisten her lips as confusion flickers across her expression. "I wish it were that simple."

"It could be, if you'd lower your guard just enough to let me in."

Before she can respond, my hand drifts from her chin, strumming along her cheek, to the nape of her neck before dragging her forward until my mouth can stroke over hers. As her lips part, my tongue slips inside to mingle with her own. I don't think I've ever enjoyed kissing another girl this much. There's something about her sweet taste that leaves me hungry for more.

A few seconds of contact and I'm ready to devour her in one tasty gulp. Arousal rushes through my veins and my cock stirs with interest. It's so tempting to take this further, but I refuse to do that. Not while we're parked outside her house.

An internal battle wages within me, and it takes every ounce of self-control to pull away. Especially when I see the way her eyelids have fallen to half-mast and how her lips are swollen from my kisses. I have to stifle the groan that rumbles up from my chest along with the need that demands I yank her back into my arms where she belongs.

"You better go," I growl, only wanting to lay my hands and lips back on her. I want to sink into the welcoming heat of her body, fucking her until she has no other choice but to admit that she belongs with me.

To me.

Her tongue darts out to moisten her lips. "I could stay for a few more minutes."

When I cup the side of her face with my palm, she presses closer.

"First off, what I want to do won't take a couple of minutes. And second, the last thing either one of us needs is a ticket for indecent exposure."

And third—although I keep it to myself—I don't want anyone catching a glimpse of Lola when I'm pleasuring her. Whether she's fully wrapped her head around it or not, she belongs to me. I might have shared girls in the past, but it'll be over my dead fucking body that happens with her.

28

LOLA

"Are you sure I should come with?" I ask, still lounging on his bed. Amusingly enough, I didn't think there was anything that could take my mind off the appointment that's set up for tomorrow, but I was wrong.

Asher glances at me from the steam-filled bathroom as he dries off.

Even though I've seen him naked numerous times, I'm still transfixed by the sight of him straight out of the shower.

"Yeah, why not?"

I refocus my attention on his face and shrug. "I don't know. Maybe you want to spend time alone with your brother."

He runs the towel over his arms and chest before lifting a leg to the toilet seat and running it over his thickly muscled—

"You keep looking at me like that and I can guarantee we won't make it to breakfast." Heat flashes in his eyes. "Actually, I'll be eating breakfast. Again."

Would that be such a bad thing?

Probably not.

Even though we had sex before he jumped in the shower, arousal bursts to life in my core. Never in my life have I felt this insatiable. It's like I'm addicted to the man.

"Sorry," I mutter, dropping my gaze as heat slams into my cheeks.

"Hey."

When I glance up to meet his eyes, he says, "Don't ever apologize for wanting me. I fucking love it." There's a pause. "Now, get your ass dressed. We're supposed to meet up with him in twenty minutes."

Even though Asher has met my mom, this feels like a big deal. One I'm not sure I'm ready for. It's a little surprising that he is. Sometimes it feels like this relationship is moving at the speed of light. With those thoughts swirling through my head, I rise from the bed and grab my panties, bra, jeans, and T-shirt. I might not be looking at him, but I can feel his heated gaze licking over my naked body.

"Hmmm. Maybe I should cancel," he says, voice turning low, strumming something deep within me, "and we can just hang here for a couple hours before class."

I yank on the shirt before smoothing it out. It would seem like a subject change is necessary, otherwise he's right—we won't make it to the restaurant. "When was the last time you saw your brother?"

Now that he's dried off, he hangs up the towel and saunters into the bedroom, yanking open the top drawer of his dresser and grabbing a pair of black boxer briefs from inside. My gaze unconsciously falls to his cock. Even in repose, it's thick and long.

When he chuckles, I gulp and force my gaze away.

"About a month ago. I stopped by the house and grabbed dinner."

"It's just you two, right? Are you close?" I settle on the bed and gather the long strands of my hair into a ponytail. Technically, Kylie and Antonio are my half-siblings, but I don't consider them family since our relationship is nonexistent. Growing up was lonely, and I always secretly longed for a sister or brother.

He shrugs. "Yeah, it's just us, and I guess we're close."

I guess?

Before I can fire off any more questions, he pulls on a T-shirt and jeans, stuffs his feet in Sperrys, and runs his fingers through his hair before grabbing his keys. "All set."

I blink, disappointed that he's already clothed. There's nothing more that I love than watching him. Especially when he's preoccupied and isn't paying attention to my perusal. Then, I can eat him up with my eyes as much as I want.

When he stretches out his hand, I grab hold of it before we walk out of his room and then the house. His Escalade is parked down the street. Once we reach it, he clicks the locks, and we slide inside. The restaurant we're meeting his brother at is only a five-minute drive from campus. There's barely enough time for nerves to bubble up inside me.

I give Asher a bit of side-eye as I nibble my lower lip.

Before I can ask for the umpteenth time if he's absolutely sure about introducing us, he lays his hand over mine and squeezes. "You're making a bigger deal out of this than necessary. It's just my brother. You'll like him." His lips tremble around the corners before he adds, "He's type A, just like you."

It takes a moment to decide if I should take offense to that comment.

"How many girls have you introduced to your family?"

His gaze flicks to mine before locking on it. "You're the first."

Even though I kind of expected the answer, it still makes my heart constrict. "And he knows you're bringing me?"

"Yup. Can't wait to meet you."

I narrow my eyes. "He actually said that?"

"Sure did."

I draw in a deep breath and try to relax against the leather seat. Just when everything within me calms, he swings into the parking lot of the Sunrise Café. It's a popular place that serves breakfast all day long.

After he cuts the engine, we exit the vehicle and meet near the hood. With a reassuring smile, he grabs my hand as we head to the entrance of the restaurant. There's a burst of noisy chatter as we walk inside and stop by the hostess station instead of seating ourselves.

Asher tells the girl standing behind the podium that we have a reservation under Stevens. That's all it takes for recognition to light up her eyes. It's tempting to roll mine. It seems like everywhere we go, people instantly recognize him. She fires off a few questions before asking to snap a selfie. With an apologetic look aimed in my direction, he takes the photo.

"This is exactly why I hate going out in public with this guy."

I startle at the deep voice near my ear and swing around, only to find a tall, handsome man with dark blond hair and blue eyes. He looks so much like Asher that the resemblance is uncanny.

When I remain silent, he flashes a bright white smile before thrusting out his hand. "Jack Stevens. Nice to meet you."

I clear my throat as his fingers slip around mine. "Lola."

"Yup, I figured." His gaze bounces to his brother, who is attempting to untangle himself from the hostess. Before he can do that, a handful of people wander over, asking to take more pictures. "Do you think we should seat ourselves and hope that he can join us at some point?"

Even though it sounds like he's joking, I get the strange feeling he's not. It takes a moment to find my voice. "I'm sure they'll finish up in a minute."

He jerks his head toward the growing group that surrounds Asher. "If you want to get in the photos, go for it."

Umm…no thanks.

Why would he even ask that?

I shake my head. "Nope. I'm good."

Jack stuffs his hands into the pockets of his khakis as he studies me with more care. "It was a surprise when Ash mentioned that he was seeing someone. Guess there really is a first time for everything. How long has it been?"

The comment gives me pause. Is it my imagination, or is this guy being a jerk?

"A couple weeks."

"Wow. That's practically an eternity for him. He's more of a one-night stand kind of guy, if you catch my drift."

Nope. It isn't my imagination at all. Asher's brother is a massive jerk.

"So, how did you crazy kids meet?" Before I can answer, his lips quirk as he says, "Wait a minute, let me guess—you hooked up at a party."

My spine stiffens as a chill enters my voice. "Actually, he asked me to tutor him, and then we started spending more time together."

"And you still decided to date him after that?" With a snort, he shakes his head. The smile stays firmly plastered across his handsome face, which I'm now tempted to punch. "You must be a real glutton for punishment."

My mouth tumbles open. For a second or two, I'm stunned into silence. I was wrong about him being a jerk, he's an asshole.

A raging one at that.

I straighten my shoulders and snap, "Yeah, I did. The more I've gotten to know him, the more I actually like spending time with him."

He nods, glancing at his brother for a moment. "What's not to like? Asher has always been the life of the party."

Anger bursts inside me as my voice hardens. "Actually, he's a lot more than that. And it's a little surprising that you, as his brother, don't realize it."

He blinks in surprise before shifting his stance. "I think you're taking what I'm saying the wrong way. I love the guy—"

"Do you?" As soon as the words escape from my lips, I want to snatch them out of the air and shove them back inside. Except...part of me doesn't. As much as I was hoping Jack would like me, he's a total dick. Maybe he thinks he's being funny by making snide comments about his brother, but I'm not amused. It pisses me off.

Thankfully, the hostess breaks away from the small group before grabbing three menus from the thick stack on the counter. "Your table is all set. If you're ready, I can seat you now."

Relief flashes across Asher's face as he wraps his arm around my waist before whispering in my ear, "Sorry about that."

His brother trails after the waitress without waiting for us.

"It wasn't a problem." It takes effort to keep the anger from seeping into my voice.

"I saw you talking with Jack. Everything go all right?"

My teeth rake across my lower lip with indecision. There's a voice inside my head prodding me to keep this convo to myself. The last thing I want is to cause problems with his family.

"Lola?"

"Yeah, it's fine." Even though I'm trying to put on a good face, I hear the tremble that fills my voice.

He picks up on it as well.

Instead of following the hostess through the dining area like his brother, Asher grinds to a halt. With my hand locked in his, I don't have any other choice but to do the same. "Is there a problem?"

"I wouldn't necessarily call it that."

His brows furrow as he carefully searches my gaze. "Then what is it?"

"I don't know." I jerk my shoulders before glancing at Jack, who is now seated at the table and talking with the hostess. By the way she's smiling at him, it's obvious they're flirting. "He just said some things…"

"Like what?"

I fidget, growing uncomfortable beneath his relentless stare. "Just that you like to party and…"

"And what?" he asks softly, expression sobering.

When I remain silent, understanding flickers in his eyes. "That I'm some kind of dumbass, right?"

"Not exactly." But yeah, pretty much.

Hurt flashes across his face before being quickly hidden behind a mask of indifference. Or maybe it's acceptance. I'm not sure. "Yeah, well…Jack has always been the brainiac of the family. The guy is super smart."

Maybe he is, but he's also a major dick. "So what?"

He shifts his stance before glancing away. His voice dips, becoming low. "My parents are impressed by academic achievements, not athletic ones. And Jack is just like them. You could say that I've always been the odd man out."

My heart constricts, imagining what it must have been like for him to grow up in this family. Never feeling like you were accepted or what you excelled at was important. And here I'd thought Asher lived a charmed life without incident. Maybe I was wrong. Maybe he has scars just like the rest of us. He just chooses not to show them.

"You're just as smart as they are," I say fiercely.

A slight smile tugs at the corners of his lips before he shakes his head. "No, I'm not. They've all made sure I realize how lucky I am to be a gifted athlete, or I'd be up shit creek without a paddle."

Oh my god...is that really what they've been telling him all these years? Feeding his insecurities of not being good enough?

Smart enough?

What's more upsetting is that he believes it.

Sorrow wells inside me. It's almost a surprise to realize that the backs of my eyes are burning. Asher is so much more than they give him credit for, and only now do I realize that he's more than even he believes. All I want to do is gather him up into my arms and soothe the hurt that must live inside him.

"That's not true. You're so much more than a talented football player. We've been working together long enough that I can see how intelligent you are." I rise on the tips of my toes until my mouth can brush across his. "And don't you dare let anyone ever tell you differently."

He wraps his arms around my body before tugging me close. "As long as you think so, that's all that matters."

29

LOLA

"Hey, you doing all right?"

I glance at the concern marring Asher's face before dropping my gaze to our loosely clasped hands. As much as I like the feel of his warmth wrapped around me, I'm still not completely used to it.

He's so easy and free with his affection.

And possessive.

It probably shouldn't be such a turn on, but I can't deny that it is.

When I remain silent, his fingers tighten. "Lola?"

I blink and meet his gaze. "Sorry." It takes effort to shake those thoughts away and refocus on the question. "Yeah, I'm fine. This isn't a big deal." That's been the mantra playing on repeat inside my head for the past couple of days.

I blow out a steady stream of air, needing to focus on this process one step at a time. If I don't, I'll freak out. Even though I told him he didn't need to accompany me, I couldn't be more grateful for his presence. Mom certainly wasn't going to do it. She's pissed that I'm even going through with the testing.

Asher holds open the glass door as we head inside the transplant center and check in at the front desk. After receiving visitor stickers,

225

we're directed to a bank of elevators to take to the second floor, where we'll meet with the coordinator who will walk us through the process.

In the quiet of the corridor, my Chucks squeak against the linoleum floor. With my hand tightly clenched in his, he reaches out to stab the button. Once the doors open, we step inside the elevator and wait for the car to rise to the second floor. My chest continues to tighten as a burst of nerves scampers down my spine when the door slides open, and we step into the hallway.

He meets my gaze, scouring it as if trying to pick through my private thoughts. "It's not too late to change your mind," he says softly. "No one would blame you for not going through with this."

It takes effort to gulp down my nerves as I straighten my shoulders. "I won't change my mind. I just want to get it over with."

There's no way I could live with myself if I didn't at least get tested.

"Okay." He tugs on my fingers, pulling me to him before wrapping his arms around my body and holding me close. It's all I can do to stop myself from melting into his warm embrace. There is so much comforting strength to be found in his arms. More than I ever imagined possible. In that moment, I realize how much I need it. Maybe I've become a master at projecting outward strength, but that doesn't necessarily mean I don't need someone to lean on every once in a while.

How is it possible that Asher has stepped up and become that person?

He drops a kiss on the top of my head before setting me free. A few minutes later, we find the office. I get one step over the threshold before stumbling to a halt when I find Tony, Charlotte, and Kylie already settled in the waiting room.

I wasn't expecting to see them today.

Especially here.

Tony rises from his chair. "Kylie had an appointment this morning, so we thought we'd stick around for yours."

Asher's hands settle on my shoulders, the firm pressure an instant reminder that I'm not alone. He's here, standing beside me. And that makes all the difference in the world.

I rack my brain for something to say but come up empty. What I refuse to do is pretend that we're one big, happy family. This man might have been present at the time of procreation, and stuck around until I was six years old, but then he disappeared from my life, leaving me to fend for myself with a mother who could barely take care of herself most days.

Honestly, it's a wonder I don't have daddy issues.

I give Asher a bit of side-eye as the other night crashes through my head. The way he took control, commanded me to let go, and then spanked my ass.

Huh. Maybe I spoke too soon.

I shake the errant thought away and point to the front desk. "I should probably check in."

It's a relief to turn my back to them as I give the receptionist my name and she hands over a ream of paperwork. Once it's been completed, I turn in the clipboard and take a seat next to Asher. From beneath the thick fringe of my lashes, I can't help but study Kylie.

She looks tired. Pale. There are dark smudges under her eyes and her body seems too thin. I didn't get a chance to meet her before the diagnosis, so I'm unsure how drastic a change there has been in her appearance.

What I can say is that she doesn't look like a normal, healthy sixteen-year-old. My mind tumbles back to the dinner at their house. The difference in energy levels from her younger brother had been significant. I can't imagine being her age and facing this kind of medical crisis.

Tony sits next to her while her mother flanks the other side, petting her hair. They couldn't hover over her anymore if they tried.

A long stretch of uncomfortable minutes slide by before Charlotte meets my gaze. "You must be excited for the fall semester to end."

It doesn't escape me that this is the kind of polite, surface-level conversation strangers engage in. No matter what blood ties I have to this family, that's exactly what we are.

Strangers.

"Yes," I say with a nod. "Just a couple weeks to go."

"I suppose if this works out, you'll be able to recover from the surgery during the break before school starts up again."

That realization is like a punch to the gut and brings the situation into sharper focus. I'm trying to take everything one step at a time and not get too far ahead of myself.

I shift on my chair. "Yeah, I guess so."

Asher slips his hand around mine. When he gives my fingers a gentle squeeze, I yank my gaze from hers and glance at him. His quiet strength feels like a lifeline, and it hits me that I could easily drown without him here. He gives me a slight smile, one that's meant to reassure. Strangely enough, that's exactly what it does.

I'm saved from further conversation with Tony and his wife when an older woman emerges from behind a closed door with a warm smile.

"Lola?"

As I pop to my feet, everyone besides Kylie does the same.

Tony clears his throat. "We were hoping to sit in on the appointment with you."

My gaze flickers to Asher in uncertainty as the muscles in my belly contract. I'd much prefer they didn't, but I find myself unable to give voice to that response. "Sure, no problem."

The woman holds open the door before herding the five of us into a small room down the hall. Charlotte directs Kylie to one of two chairs before settling next to her and slipping an arm around her thin shoulders. When she presses a kiss against her cheek, I glance away. Much like in the waiting room, Tony stands sentinel on the other side of his daughter, almost as if she's in need of protecting.

Once the woman closes the door, she looks over the group before meeting my gaze. "Hello, Lola. It's nice to meet you. My name is Sue, and I'll be walking you through what to expect today. The evaluation process consists of three parts. The first entails medical tests, where you'll have a physical exam. We'll take a health history, blood and urine test, chest X-ray, a 3D reconstruction CT/CAT scan, a MRCP of your abdomen, and an EKG which takes a snapshot of your heart."

When I release a steady breath, she smiles. "I know it sounds like a lot, but the tests aren't invasive. The second part consists of meeting with the living donor team. This will be your assigned social worker, kidney specialist, surgeon, dietician, transplant nurse coordinator, and an independent living donor advocate. The goal here is to make sure you have all the necessary information to make an educated decision."

My head swims from information overload. As much as I tried to prepare myself by researching the surgery, it's still overwhelming.

"Then, lastly, there will be an educational component to the program. We'll talk you through the process and what each stage looks like, the risks that are involved, donation options, the surgical procedure, pain management, and aftercare." She glances at Kylie. "From my understanding, your sister will be the recipient of your direct donation."

It's on the tip of my tongue to correct her. Instead, I remain silent. Surprisingly, no one else pipes up either.

"It's completely normal to feel overwhelmed," Sue says softly. "Do you have any questions that I can answer before we get started?"

Tony clears his throat, drawing everyone's attention. "If Lola turns out to be a match, how soon can we schedule the surgery?"

I stiffen, wishing more than ever the trio had stayed in the waiting room. Or better yet, returned home after Kylie's appointment. The only thing they're doing is setting my nerves on edge. It doesn't feel like I can open up and talk honestly with Tony and Charlotte listening to every concern or question that comes out of my mouth.

"That depends. It'll be important for Lola to take some time and think about her decision. This surgery isn't something to be taken lightly. After today, she'll have a better sense of the process and be more informed."

"Of course, we understand that. The problem is we don't have time to waste." He squeezes Kylie's shoulder before giving her an encouraging smile.

Sue's warm expression never falters. "I think at this point, it would probably be best if you take Kylie home. Once the team has gathered all the pertinent information, they'll meet to discuss whether Lola is a good candidate for donation." Her gaze touches on me again. "If it turns out that she is, Lola will need to make that decision, and from there, it could take a few weeks. Maybe less, depending on surgeon schedules."

"Oh." Tony frowns before glancing at his daughter. "I'm sure Charlotte can take Kylie home and I—"

The older woman shakes her head before turning her attention to Asher. "Were you planning on staying here, young man?"

"Yup," he says with a nod, "I'll be with her all day."

With a warm but determined smile, she turns back to the couple. "I think your daughter is in good hands."

Tension gathers in the crowded room until it's thick enough to cut with a knife.

It's a relief that Sue has kindly told them to go home. The last thing I need is for the three of them to shadow my every movement throughout the day, waiting impatiently for the results. I get it— they're pinning all their hopes on me to save their daughter, but having them here, staring at me like I'm nothing more than a potential organ, isn't helping matters.

Charlotte and Kylie reluctantly rise to their feet before Sue escorts all three from the room. As soon as she closes the door, I wilt in relief. One stride is all it takes for Asher to close the distance between us and take me in his arms before crushing me against his chest.

"That was a lot of information to take in. Are you still good?" He presses his lips to the top of my head.

"Yeah. I'm just glad they're gone." I don't understand why every-thing feels so much better when I'm cocooned in his strong embrace.

"I know." There's a pause. "I've said it before, and I'll say it again— you can change your mind at any time. You don't have to go through with this."

I bury my face against the warmth of his sweatshirt. "At the very least, I'm going to complete the testing. One step at a time," I remind, unwilling to look any further into the future until we have more information.

"Just remember that you don't owe Tony or his family anything. Hell, we both know it's the other way around."

That might be true, but my heart still goes out to Kylie. It's the only reason I'm sitting in this office, contemplating this procedure. It has nothing to do with Tony whatsoever.

We break apart when there's a soft knock on the door and Sue pokes her head in. "They're ready for you, Lola."

I draw in a deep breath, holding it captive in my lungs before gradually releasing it with a nod. Asher slips my hand into his and squeezes it tightly. No matter what happens today, this man is here for me and that's more than I can say for anyone else.

3 0

LOLA

"I'm ready for a break," Asher says with a stretch, his thickly corded arms reaching for the ceiling as we study in the library on one of my rare nights off from the restaurant. "How about you?"

My attention gets snagged by the movement as I watch the play of sinewy muscle. Holy hell, the man has the best arms. All that tightly harnessed pow—

"Lola?"

My gaze reluctantly snaps to his face and the smirk now lifting his lips. "Hmmm?"

"See something you like, baby girl?"

Heat floods my cheeks as arousal bursts to life in my core.

Ugh. He's so damn smug.

I'm not saying that he doesn't have a right to be…

But still.

It hasn't taken him long to figure out that I go a little stupid when I see the bulging muscles of his biceps.

I shift on the chair and clench my thighs, trying to stymie the arousal flooding through me. Asher has spent the last two hours studying for a test in Comms. It's the last one before the final at the

232

end of the semester. It's important that he does well.

"Nope, not at all," I lie, attempting to play it cool.

He pops a brow. "You sure about that?"

"Yup."

"So…this doesn't do anything for you?" He brings his arms down, flexing them until all the muscles tighten and swell.

My mouth turns cottony as a straight shot of need explodes in my core. "No. Is it supposed to?"

His eyes narrow. "Methinks you're lying, woman."

I shake my head as my gaze stays focused on his arms. "Sorry, I'm just not that interested."

He lays both palms on the table before rising from his chair.

I blink as a thrill shoots through me. "What are you doing?"

"Proving that you're a liar," he growls.

Before I can respond, he stalks around the rectangular table and wraps his hands around my ribcage, hauling me up from my chair. After he settles on it, I find myself perched on his lap.

"You need to keep working. We shouldn't take a break just yet."

"Why not?" His fingers tighten around me, locking me in place.

Just as my mouth ghosts over his, my phone buzzes, startling both of us.

"Don't pick it up," he groans. "Let it go to voicemail."

I glance at the screen but don't recognize the number. A wave of anxiety crashes over me, dousing the arousal that had flared to life so unexpectedly.

"Who is it?"

"I don't know," I whisper, meeting his gaze.

When my mouth dries for a second time, it's for entirely different reasons. I've been an anxious ball of tightly wound nerves waiting for the results of my tests and the committee's decision.

During the eight hours we spent at the transplant center, I met with a social worker and living donation advocate, both of whom walked me through the process, wanting to make sure I understood all the pros and cons of my decision. When I first arrived at the center that day, I'd planned to keep all the details of the situation to myself, but in the end, I decided to open up and share the specifics.

"I should really answer it," I whisper, barely able to force the words from stiff lips.

His arms band around my body, holding tight as if it's possible to anchor me to him. "If it's important, they'll leave a message."

"I know." But still…

Tony has called every day since the testing was completed, asking if I've heard any news. Each time, he reminds me that decisions need to be made quickly as if I'm the one delaying the process. Even though I feel bad, I've stopped answering when his number pops up.

A pit the size of Texas takes up residence at the bottom of my belly as I straighten my shoulders. It's never been my style to run and hide from reality. And I'm not going to start now. Decision made, I grab the cell before I can chicken out and slide the green button across the screen before holding the slim device to my ear.

"Hello?" It takes effort to keep my voice strong and steady.

"Hi, this is Sue calling from Regency Transplant Center. Is this Lola I'm speaking with?"

I draw in a deep breath before forcing it out again, hoping to calm all the nerves that have burst to life inside me. "It is."

My gaze locks on Asher. His expression fills with tension as the corners of his lips sink. It's such an odd look on him. He's usually so easy going and laidback, always smiling or laughing. And I realize that's how I like him best. Most of the time, his good mood is infectious and lightens my own. It's one of the reasons I gravitate to him like a flower seeking out the sun.

I blink back to the conversation when she says, "I wanted to let you know that the team met this afternoon and looked over all the results. Everyone you spoke with had input into whether you'll be a candidate for the transplant procedure. The medical tests are, of course, important but they're not the only deciding factor."

Air becomes trapped in my throat as everything in me stills.

"After careful consideration, the team decided you were a match for Kylie, and if you'd like to move forward with the donation, we'll proceed with the next steps." The breath held hostage in my lungs escapes in a rush. "What's important now is that you take as much time as you need to make a decision. You met with Andrea, our independent living donor advocate, and she's available to answer any further questions you might have. Any and all concerns you discuss with her will remain strictly confidential. Do you understand?"

"Yes."

"Excellent. I'll touch base with you in a few days, all right?" There's a pause. "Just remember that no one is going to rush this process."

Even though she can't see me, I jerk my head into a nod. "Okay."

"Are there any questions I can answer for you?"

"No, not at the moment. I'm still processing everything from the other day."

"That's understandable. It's a great deal of information to take in. Please feel free to call or schedule an appointment if that would be helpful. The team is always available to discuss any questions or concerns that might arise."

"Thank you." Throughout this process, Sue has been wonderful. Everyone I met and spoke with has been great. Knowledgeable. Comforting. If I decide to go through with the transplant, I'll be in skilled hands.

Hitting the end button, I stare blindly at the phone as everything whips through my head. Even though I feel shitty for thinking it, a tiny part of me was hoping I wouldn't be a match. Then, the decision would be taken out of my hands. But that hasn't turned out to be the case.

I'm probably Kylie's best bet when it comes to receiving a donor kidney. No matter how scared or nervous I am about the surgery, I don't think I can snatch this opportunity away from her.

"Lola, baby?" His fingers gently caress my cheek. "I heard the entire conversation. Are you all right?"

My gaze lifts, locking on his. There's so much concern swimming around in his blue depths.

I force my lips into a thin smile. "I'm fine. Just trying to get my head straight now that we have an answer."

"I also heard her say that you need to take a couple of days to think everything over. You should probably get in contact with the living donor person—"

"Andrea," I cut in quietly.

"Right, Andrea. You should probably reach out tomorrow. Maybe set up an appointment."

"Yeah, I could do that."

A few moments of silence tick by.

"But you're not going to, are you?" His voice turns gruff. "Because you've already made up your mind."

As our gazes cling in the quietness of the library, I realize he's right. I've made my decision. What makes no sense is that he can read me so easily. That he knows what I'm thinking almost before I do.

"I think so. I'm leaning toward the surgery."

His arms tighten, pulling me closer until I'm almost flattened against the steely strength of his chest. Instead of feeling suffocated by the crushing pressure, his presence only makes me feel more secure in my decision.

"You need to listen to them," he says harshly. "They're the experts. If they're telling you to take a few days to think through this decision, then that's what you should do."

I pull away enough to meet his gaze. "Everyone is telling me I have a choice in the matter, but that's not the way it feels. I'm Kylie's best shot at having a normal life." I shake my head. "How can I deny her that opportunity?"

"And what about you?"

"Me?" I blink. "What do you mean?"

"They talked to you about the short- and long-term risk factors. Have you really thought about the ramifications of giving up one of your kidneys?"

My muscles stiffen. "Of course."

How could I not?

It's all I've been able to dwell on. When I should be studying, I'm zoning out, thinking about the future. I lie awake at night with all this churning in my head. The only time I'm able to forget is when I'm with Asher.

"What if you develop a disease like diabetes or high blood pressure and it affects the functioning of your only kidney?" When I remain silent, he continues. "Do you realize there's a natural decline in kidney function as you get older? Or that an increased amount of protein can spill into your blood because you only have one kidney functioning in place of two? Or how about the possibility of nerve damage from the surgery? Have you considered any of that?"

My heartbeat picks up tempo, pounding harshly under my breast as everything inside me stills. "You remember all that from the meeting?"

There was so much information thrown at us throughout the day that it's all a giant slush pile in my brain. Vaguely do I recall what he just mentioned.

"No. I decided to do some research on my own in order to better understand the process and risks."

Wait a minute...Asher Stevens has been on a fact-finding mission? *For me?*

Thick emotion gathers in my throat, making it impossible to swallow.

Instead of focusing on the meaning behind his actions, I whisper, "Why are you bringing all that up?"

He gives me a penetrating look. One that would make a lesser person squirm. "Isn't that obvious? I'm concerned about you. I want to make sure you've thought through the consequences of this donation. From what I've seen, no one is putting your interests first. Certainly not the people who should be."

I have to blink away the moisture that pricks the backs of my eyes.

Sometimes, I don't understand what this guy is doing to me. He's unraveling me in the best—or worst—way possible. I'm just not sure which one it is.

When was the last time someone was concerned about me? Or focused solely on my wellbeing?

As much as I love my mother, she's the one who requires support and needs to be tended to. Ever since Tony walked out of our lives, our relationship has been flipped around, and it's exhausting.

What would it be like to have parents who put me first?

It's not a question I like to think about. What I've learned is that hoping and wishing life would have dealt me a different hand doesn't change what is. It just burns energy that could be directed elsewhere.

As I stare at Asher, it hits me that he wasn't blowing smoke up my ass. His actions actually match his words. He promised to be here for me, and that's exactly what he's doing. My heart seizes, spasming painfully in my chest as thick emotion gathers in my throat. Even though I don't want it to, the realization chips insistently at my crumbling walls.

I press my lips to his before whispering, "Thank you."

"For what?"

"Just being you. And you're right, I'll take some time to think it over."

It's on the tip of my tongue to say more, to tell him everything—just how much I'm falling for him and how terrified that makes me—but in the end, I remain silent, afraid of saying too much.

Afraid of being hurt.

ASHER

With our hands clasped together, we stroll through the grocery store. I'm going to be perfectly honest, I've never been much of a shopper. That's exactly what Instacart and Door Dash is for. You order food online and bags magically appear on the front porch.

Best invention ever.

Or I'll grab something out.

Hello, Taco Loco. Where have you been all my life?

But tonight, I told Lola that I'd whip up dinner for her and her mother. Trust me, it's not going to be anything fancy. Just spaghetti and garlic bread.

I should be able to handle that.

Open a jar. Throw some noodles in a pot. Toss the frozen garlic bread into the oven.

And voilà—dinner is served.

Lola has a lot on her plate right now.

What am I saying?

That girl's plate is always overflowing. How she's gotten this far without self-combusting, I have no idea. She deserves all the best things in life, and I want to be the one who gives them to her. Every time I do something unexpected, surprise fills her expression. It's quickly followed by a thousand questions that churn silently in her dark depths.

I hate it.

Hate that the people in her life have let her down so completely that me doing something small and seemingly insignificant gives her so much joy. It makes me want to tug her into my arms and hold onto her with all my might.

All right, so maybe that's exactly what I end up doing.

No matter how much I have of her, it's never enough.

I want more.

I want everything.

There's been a few times when she's muttered that she doesn't understand what I'm doing to her. The funny thing is that I get where she's coming from. I feel different when I'm with her. I'm not the same guy I was just a short month ago. I've spent the last twenty-two years fairly content with who I was. But that's no longer enough.

I want to be better.

Lola needs someone.

Someone who will look out for her best interests and protect her. Maybe I haven't voiced my concerns because ultimately, this surgery is her decision and I want to support her no matter what, but it fucking terrifies me. I've only just found this girl.

I don't want to lose her.

We stroll through the produce aisle before grabbing a pint of strawberries. If I have my way, we'll be doing something interesting with these tonight. That reminds me, whipped cream should be added to the shopping list we put together. I want to do something that will take her mind off this decision. Even if it's for a few short hours.

We also grab a Caesar salad kit that includes everything in one handy dandy bag. How's that for easy?

It's practically foolproof.

Then, we meander up the world foods aisle and stop in front of an endless array of pastas.

Ridiculous.

"Why are there so many choices?" I point to the shelves. "And look at all the different shapes."

Lola flashes me an easy smile before pulling a long blue box from the shelf. "I usually buy thin spaghetti noodles."

Does it really matter?

Noodles are noodles.

"And what about the sauce?" Because there are just as many options as the pasta.

She peers closely at the middle shelf before picking out a bottle. "This one is good."

As she sets the glass jar in the basket hanging from the crook of my arm, I tug on her fingers and pull her close, needing to feel her soft lips against mine. It's getting increasingly more difficult to keep my hands off her.

Just as she sinks into the caress, someone clears their throat from behind us. Lola startles before drawing away in embarrassment. There's already a blush tingeing her cheeks. I, on the other hand, don't give a rat's ass who sees us.

Walk on by, asshole. No need to disturb.

Lola stiffens as I glance at the couple now standing a few feet away.

Tony and Charlotte.

Of all the rotten luck to run into them here.

We haven't seen them since the day of the testing. He's texted and called Lola a dozen times, wanting to know about the results. When he wouldn't stop bombarding her, she told him that when a decision had been made, she'd be in touch. By his snappish response, he hadn't been happy.

If they didn't have a cartful of groceries, I'd think they were stalking her.

Charlotte's lips lift into a tight smile. There's even more strain filling her face than the last time we were together. "Hello, Lola." Her gaze flickers to mine before darting back to the girl at my side. "How have you been?"

"Good. And you?" Lola winces, and I can tell she wishes she could snatch the question out of the air.

Pain leaks from the older woman's bruised eyes as her smile wobbles. "We're holding in there the best we can." There's a pause before she adds lightly, "Just waiting to hear from you."

When Lola inches closer, I wrap my arm around her shoulders and pull her to me. I hate that I feel the need to protect her from these people who should have embraced her into their family years ago.

"Have you made a decision yet?" Tony blurts, drawing our attention.

There's no greeting from him. It's just right down to the point.

Hurt flashes across Lola's expression before being quickly masked. She'd rather rip out her own fingernails than allow Tony or his wife to glimpse an ounce of her pain. Their careless treatment ignites my temper, sending it skyrocketing into the stratosphere. The only reason they're bothering with her is because she has the best chance of helping their daughter.

I've never had much of a temper. During a game, I'll happily crack a few skulls together to make sure we pull off a win. Other than that, I've never given a shit about anything or anyone enough to dredge up that kind of intense emotion. My feelings for Lola are proving to be different at every turn.

Her muscles stiffen. "No, not yet."

It's tempting to rub soft circles along her back just so she remembers that I'm here.

Charlotte reaches out, grabbing hold of her husband's hand. When he glances at her, she gives him a barely perceptible head shake. He smashes his lips together in response.

"If you have any questions regarding the donation process, we'd be happy to sit down and discuss them with you." Her gaze flickers to mine almost as an afterthought. "And, of course, your friend."

"Asher," Lola says. "His name is Asher."

From the corner of my eye, I watch as her hands tighten until the knuckles turn bone white.

"Right. Sorry," the older woman says in a rush. "Asher. He's more than welcome to join us."

"That's not necessary. I've spent a lot of time talking everything out with the advocate. I just need a few more days and then I'll have an answer for you."

Irritation flickers across Tony's face.

So help me god, if he opens his yap again, I'll go off like a shot.

"That's understandable," Charlotte says, voice becoming strained around the edges.

Unable to take another moment of their callousness, I say, "Hey, babe, we need to get moving. Why don't you grab the garlic bread and parmesan cheese?"

Surprise fills Lola's eyes as she meets my gaze and searches it. "Right now?"

"Yup."

Silent understanding passes between us as her teeth sink into her lower lip.

"Go on," I say softly before unwinding my arm and giving her a little push toward the end of the aisle. "I won't be long. Promise."

"Are you sure?"

"Positive."

Our gazes stay fastened for a couple of heartbeats before she reluctantly walks away. When she finally reaches the endcap, she sends another glance over her shoulder before disappearing around the corner. Only then do I swing back to Tony and Charlotte.

I can't even bring myself to call this man her father. It's exactly like she claimed—he's nothing more than a sperm donor. It's funny, when she originally made the comment, I'd thought she was being harsh. Maybe even a little dramatic. Unfortunately, I now see it's the truth.

"I hope you both realize that Lola doesn't owe you a damn thing."

Charlotte's mouth falls into a small O of shock as Tony gnashes his teeth. It's obvious from the way he straightens that he wants to argue, but we both know he doesn't have a leg to stand on.

When they remain silent, my voice grows louder. It's so fucking tempting to blast them into next week. "You should be thankful that she hasn't given you a flat-out denial. All either of you has done is hound her for an answer. When that didn't work, you laid on the guilt." There's a pause as I search both their expressions. "Except, Kylie isn't really her sister, now is she? How could they be siblings when you've done everything in your power to keep Lola out of your lives and away from the two people she could have had a relationship with? If you didn't need something, you wouldn't be giving her the time of day. Don't think for a second that she doesn't understand that."

Charlotte's face turns ashen as she whispers, "That's not true."

Her husband glares but remains impassive.

"Sure, it is. Don't lie to yourself or me. And especially not to Lola."

It takes every ounce of self-control not to grab Tony by the shirt-front and wring his damn neck. I'm so fucking close to losing it.

"Just so you know, I don't think Lola missed out on a damn thing by your absence in her life, but the same can't be said for you." My gaze flickers to his wife. "You have no idea what an incredible person she is." I jerk my thumb in the direction where Lola last stood before disappearing from sight. "That girl is fucking amazing. I'm lucky she let me in, because she doesn't do that with many people. And you're part of the reason. I hope you realize she deserves way better than you."

Now that I've finished my tirade, a heavy silence falls over our small group.

Charlotte's tongue darts out to moisten her lips. "We just always thought it would be less confusing—"

Revulsion burns my insides as I wave away her lame explanation. "Save it, lady. That's horseshit, and we all know it. You didn't want to be bothered with her. My guess is that you didn't want a kid from your husband's past tarnishing the picture-perfect life you were trying so damn hard to create." I glare at her and then Tony. "You both make me sick."

When they remain silent, I realize I've hit the nail on the head. I didn't think it was possible for me to feel any more disgusted.

"When Lola makes a decision, she'll inform the transplant center and they'll let you know. Don't call her again."

"How dare you!" Tony growls, face turning a mottled purple hue.

I take a step toward him before stopping myself. The last thing I want to do is stress Lola out more than she already is by getting into an altercation with her—

Whoever the fuck this guy is to her.

"I'm serious. Don't bother her again," I snap before swinging away and stalking down the aisle.

I'm so angry that I'm practically vibrating with it.

How dare I?

How fucking dare he!

They can both go to hell, as far as I'm concerned.

As I turn the corner, I come to an abrupt halt when I find Lola standing there with wide eyes and tears staining her ashen cheeks.

Aw, fuck. It was never my intention to hurt her. I didn't want her to hear any of that.

My shoulders slump as guilt bubbles up inside me. She's probably going to be pissed. "I'm—"

Before I can force out an apology, she hurls her body into my arms.

"I can't believe you said all that," she whispers, thick emotion clogging her throat. "Thank you."

She clings to me as if she'll never let go. And in that moment of intense connection, I realize I don't want her to.

LOLA

An hour later and I'm still shellshocked from the run-in at the grocery store. My gaze stays pinned to Asher as I sit at the table and watch him putter around the small kitchen as he prepares dinner.

Every time I pipe up, offering a helpful hint, he shoots an exasperated look my way. So, I've decided to keep my mouth closed for the time being and enjoy a man doing something nice for me. Because, at the end of the day, that's exactly what his intentions are. And I couldn't be more grateful.

Or feel luckier.

I grab my glass of ice water and take a sip. My gaze resettles on Asher as he dumps a box of noodles into a boiling pot. It takes effort to stop myself from commenting that half the box would have been more than enough for the three of us. His brows draw together as he stares at the directions before swinging toward the microwave and pressing a few buttons to set the timer.

Good lord, could this guy be any sexier?

What is it about a man moving around a kitchen, preparing food as you sit and watch?

While filling a large stainless-steel pot with water, he casually mentioned that he's never cooked a meal in his life.

Not once.

And here he is, carving out time in his busy schedule to do it for me. That's all it took for my heart to melt into a little puddle of goo. Although, if I'm being perfectly honest, I'm pretty sure my heart was already gooey from what he said to Tony and Charlotte. Maybe I shouldn't have stuck around and listened, but I was afraid he was going to get into it with Tony. I didn't want that to happen. Especially if it ended up causing problems for him with school or football.

Just so you know, I don't think Lola missed out on anything by your absence in her life, but the same can't be said for you. You have no idea what an incredible person she is. That girl is fucking amazing. I'm lucky she let me in, because she doesn't do that with many people. And you're part of the reason. I hope you realize that she deserves way better than you.

Tears sprung to my eyes as my heart nearly beat out of my chest. No matter how long I live, I won't ever forget that moment. Or the way he sounded as the words tripped off his tongue.

So yeah…my head is still spinning, and I'm not sure when it'll stop.

Fifteen minutes later, the noodles have been strained, the garlic bread is out of the oven, and the salad has been divided into three bowls with croutons and dressing. Even though he told me not to, I set the table.

It's the very least I could do.

Mama is sitting across from Asher as she picks up her fork. "This looks wonderful. *Gracias.*"

Having a man come to our house and cook for us is a new experience, and I can tell Mama is even more in awe of Asher than the first time they met. Trust me, his good looks and charm totally bowled her over. She didn't stop talking about him for days.

"You're welcome. It wasn't that difficult," he says modestly, flashing a smile. "I might actually try making this for the guys."

Mama hasn't always been the best judge of character when it comes to men. All the ones she's brought home have been losers.

Either they didn't have jobs, or they were just plain assholes. It was always a relief when they decided to take off. There were a few who had me locking my door at night and forcing myself to stay awake until I couldn't keep my eyelids open any longer.

But her assessment of Asher is spot on. He's turned out to be a good one.

"Thanks for this," I whisper, overwhelmed with emotion for the second time today. I've always been able to keep my feelings tamped down inside where they couldn't see the light of day. Getting through life is just easier that way.

That's not possible with him.

His lips quirk as he winks.

My belly spasms with everything that churns within me, almost making it impossible to enjoy this meal. Asher, on the other hand, bulldozes his way through his spaghetti before helping himself to seconds. And then thirds. The guy certainly has one hell of an appetite. The funny thing is that he's so lean and cut. I have no idea where he puts it.

After Mama finishes, she disappears back to her room, telling me that she's going to spend a little time searching online for a job. The new medication she's on took a couple weeks to work, but it seems to be making a difference. Her moods are more stable, she's getting out of bed in the mornings, and she's even leaving the house during the day.

She's also talking to another guy online. A little part of me groaned when she told me about him the other day. I can only hope this relationship doesn't end like the last one. I don't want to see all her steady progress blown to shit.

Once we're alone, Asher pops to his feet and grabs his plate.

I take it from his hand before dumping it in the sink to wash. "I've got it. Why don't you sit and relax? You made dinner; I'll clean up."

When I return to the table to grab more dishes, he nabs my fingers and slowly draws me to him. A second later, I find myself situated on his lap. It's become one of my favorite places.

"The whole point of this evening was to take care of you."

"And you did," I say, pressing a kiss against his mouth. "No one has ever cooked dinner for me, and I'm really appreciative." I glance toward the small hallway. "I think Mama enjoyed it, too."

His lips lift into a wider smile. "I'm glad I could be your first."

He has…for so many things. That's the moment I realize I'm truly falling in love with this guy. It feels like a swan dive into the deep end of the pool. There's no longer a way to yank myself back from the precipice. I'm in way too deep.

The silent acknowledgment is as thrilling as it is terrifying. I've always been so careful to protect myself from getting hurt. And yet, Asher managed to slip past all my ninja-like defenses. He was an unlikely hero, and because of that, I didn't take him seriously. By the time I realized the error of my ways, it was too late.

"Me, too." I clear my throat along with all those thoughts. For now, I need to keep it to myself. "Do you want to stay here tonight?"

His brows shoot up as he searches my eyes. "Are you sure that's cool with your mom?"

"It'll be fine." I give him a knowing look. "We'll just have to be quiet."

A slow grin spreads across his face. "Hmmm. That sounds like a challenge."

"Definitely not," I say with a chuckle.

"Are you sure?" He cocks his head. "It's awfully tempting to see if I can make you scream louder than the last time."

That's all it takes for the delicious things he did to me the other night to crash through my brain. The man certainly is…talented.

And mine.

That's not something I ever thought I'd say.

Warmth spreads through my chest before settling in my core like a heavy stone.

Instead of responding, I nip at his bottom lip. He groans, tightening his hold on my hips.

"Let me clean up the kitchen and then maybe I'll be the one to make *you* scream."

"Like a little girl?"

Laughter gurgles up in my throat. "Possibly."

A smirk curls around the edges of his lips as I rise to my feet. He swats my ass as I gather up the rest of the plates and drop them off in the sink. I have no idea why it should heat me up, but there's no denying the effect it has on me.

Every.

Single.

Time.

Fifteen minutes later, the leftover food has been placed in containers to be stored in the fridge and the dishes have been washed. Asher insisted on drying, and I have to admit that there's something nice about standing beside him, doing domestic chores. It's almost enough to have my mind wandering to the future and what it could look like. That's not something I've ever allowed myself to do.

Once the kitchen has been tidied, I grab his hand and tow him to my bedroom before closing the door and leaning against the hollow wood. It's not that I think Mom will have a problem with him staying over, but it feels awkward. Maybe I act like the parent more often than not, but she's technically my mother. And no matter how many bills I've taken care of with my paycheck, it's still her house.

"Now that you've got me here, what are you going to do with me?" His voice deepens as heat dances like blue flames in his eyes.

Good question.

Not to mention an interesting one.

When we have sex, Asher is always the aggressor and takes control of the situation.

Of me.

And I love it.

It took a bit of mental adjustment to admit that he's right. I enjoy surrendering to him. I can't imagine feeling comfortable or safe enough to do that with anyone else. It's nice to let go and allow someone else to take control every once in a while.

But not always.

Maybe it's time to turn the tables and take back some of the power.

Decision made, I shove away from the door and close the distance that separates us until I can reach out and stroke my hands over his T-shirt-clad chest. The sheer amount of power and strength he keeps tightly harnessed within him is impressive.

Tilting my head, I glance up from beneath the dark fringe of my lashes. "Hmmm. I'm not sure."

One hand glides across his ribcage to his belly before drifting past the button of his jeans to his cock. He groans when my fingers tighten around the hard length. Just as he flexes his hips—pushing farther into my palm—I release him, sliding upward until they settle on the button of his fly and flick it open before dragging down the zipper. My hand delves into his boxer briefs and wraps around his erection. I remember that night in the restaurant when he cornered me, whispering in my ear that girls liked him because he was hung like a bull.

He wasn't exaggerating.

The man is huge.

He also claimed it was because he knew how to eat pussy.

Just another thing he wasn't lying about.

Not only is he able to bring me quickly to orgasm, but they're strong enough to whip through my body like a force of nature. They leave me breathless and drained, wondering what the hell just happened.

"Mmm." The sound that vibrates from his chest is deep and growly and turns me on like nothing else.

The need to touch more of him thrums through me. I slip my hand from the cottony material, grabbing the waistband of his jeans and underwear before shoving them down lean hips and muscular thighs until his dick springs free.

I take a few moments to appreciate the fact that Asher manscapes. The root of his cock and balls are clean shaven, and I have to admit that it looks so much better this way. I reach out and cup the soft weight of his sac in my palm, squeezing gently.

My gaze flicks upward before I slip my hand free and sink to my knees.

"Lola, baby," he groans, "you don't have to do that."

I tilt my head until our gazes can lock. "I want to."

That's not something I ever thought would come out of my mouth. I've gone down on guys before, but it's always felt like an unspoken expectation. This couldn't be more different. I'm on my knees because that's where I want to be, not because someone is making me feel like it's necessary.

Asher has done nothing but take care of me these past couple of weeks, showing me so much pleasure and giving me exactly what I didn't realize I needed. Not once has he demanded anything in return.

Our gazes cling as I lean forward and kiss the tip of his erection before nuzzling it. He's hard as steel and yet so soft. I run the tip of my tongue from the bulbous head, down the length of his shaft, to the root before drifting lower to circle one ball and then the other.

Another deep, guttural sound explodes from him as he gently brushes the hair away from my eyes before tunneling his fingers through the thick strands. There's a possessive edge to his touch as if he needs to lay claim to me the same way I do to him.

"I fucking love seeing you on your knees."

Strangely enough, I like it, too. There's something about having to tilt my head to meet his heavy-lidded gaze that is beyond sexy. It has need throbbing to life in my core.

Once my tongue dances over every inch of his balls, I lick my way back up his cock before sucking the tip into my mouth. His fingers tighten around my skull as his eyelids droop.

"God, that feels so damn good."

Each time I slide along his hard length, I take him deeper until he's able to nudge the back of my throat. Another groan rumbles up from within his chest as I keep up a steady rhythm. My hand slides from his thickly muscled thigh to his backside so I can cup one taut cheek and press him closer as the other rises to massage his sac.

"*Fuuuuck.*"

He tilts his pelvis and pushes forward. When my mouth turns voracious, his body stiffens before he attempts to shove me away.

Instead of allowing that to happen, I keep my gaze trained on him and continue sucking his dick.

"Really, baby. It's not necessary," he mutters, jaw clenched. His voice is so tightly strung that it sounds as if it could shatter into a million jagged pieces.

When his balls draw up against his body, and his muscles tense, I know he's seconds away from finding his release.

"Lola," he growls as the first drops of cum splash against the back of my throat before I swallow them down greedily. His fingers sink into my scalp, holding me close as he orgasms. It's only when he softens that I set him free.

As soon as I do, he reaches down, slipping his arms around my upper body and hauling me to my feet. The moment his mouth fastens on mine, I open so his tongue can delve inside to tangle with my own.

After a few seconds that have me turning breathless, he draws away. "I don't think there's anything sexier than the taste of me on your lips."

He swings toward the twin bed before setting me in the middle of it. Straightening to his full height, he grips the hem of his T-shirt and whips it over his head before tossing it to the carpet. His jeans and boxer briefs follow suit, getting shoved down powerful thighs. He pulls off both shoes and socks until he's naked. I can't help but eat him up with my eyes, enjoying the sight of him.

Asher is physically imposing and so damn beautiful. All those chiseled muscles honed from years of playing football and lifting weights. Some girls might go weak in the knees for a hard chest, six-pack, or nice ass.

My downfall is bulging biceps.

Everything about Asher is sharply defined. Especially his arms. What I love most is the feel of them wrapped tightly around me. When he's holding me close, I feel protected and safe. I'm not used to that kind of physical security and can't help but revel in it.

As I continue to stare, lost in the sight of him, his cock thickens again, turning hard.

I raise a brow and meet his gaze. "Kind of insatiable, aren't you?"

"When it comes to you? Damn right I am."

The way those words rumble from his chest sends a flurry of excitement spiraling through me.

When my fingers drift to the hem of my shirt, ready to remove it, he shakes his head. "The pleasure of stripping you bare is mine. Don't take that away from me."

Another thrill shoots through me as my arms drift to my sides.

His lips curve upward. "Such a good girl."

That comment has desire exploding in my core and dampening my panties. My mouth turns cottony as he closes the distance and grips the edge of my shirt before lifting it, baring more of my body to his sight. There's nothing rushed about the movements. It's as if we have all the time in the world to explore one another. Once the top has been tossed to the floor, my bra comes next. The latch is unfastened until the cups can fall away from my breasts.

He groans at the sight of my nipples before reaching out and tweaking one little bud until it stiffens and then doing the same to the other. I can't help but arch into his touch, loving the way he makes me feel.

His fingers drift from my breasts to the button of my jeans before flicking it open and slowly dragging down the zipper. It's tempting to knock his hands away so I can tear the denim off in one hasty movement. Instead, I sit back and force myself to suck in a deep breath before slowly exhaling, allowing him to do it because it gives him pleasure. After the thick material is shed, my panties are all that keep me from being as naked as he is.

"You're so fucking beautiful, sitting there nicely, waiting patiently for me to fuck you."

A whimper escapes as I shift restlessly. I just want the underwear to disappear so he can climb between my thighs and sink deep inside my body. I've been thinking about him all day, and I'm eager for his cock to fill me up and make me forget everything outside these four walls.

When my fingers hover over the elastic band, he gives his head a little shake.

"Don't you dare." His brow quirks as heat fills his eyes. "Unless you're looking to get spanked."

Another burst of arousal detonates in my core.

His lips lift as he nods toward the wall I share with my mother. "Unfortunately, I can't guarantee you won't scream when my palm makes contact with your sweet little ass. So…we'll have to wait on that."

My teeth scrape across my lower lip as disappointment swirls through me.

"Tomorrow," he growls. "I promise. Now, let's get you out of those panties before they're totally soaked."

I groan as heat fills my cheeks.

He draws closer until he can press his mouth against mine. "Don't be embarrassed, baby. I love that you're so horny for me."

Before I can fully sink into the caress, he pulls back. His fingers settle at the band before ripping the cotton fabric away. I can't help but shiver beneath his steely gaze as it licks over my length. It doesn't take long for me to grow restless under the intense scrutiny.

"How much do you want me, baby girl?"

Instead of answering, I allow my legs to fall open until I'm spread wide.

His eyes grow hotter as his voice dips. "That much, huh?"

"Yes."

"Mmmm. You're so fucking pretty. All soft and pink. You make my mouth water with the need to taste you."

"Please, Asher." I've never been one to beg. Especially a man. But I will for him. I'll crawl on my hands and knees if that's what it takes.

This is exactly what he reduces me to.

I don't give a fuck if that makes me weak. All I care about is the way it feels when he touches me with his fingers, mouth, and cock.

"Tell me what you want."

"You," I whisper. "I want *you*."

My heart leaps, thumping harder, faster, when he shackles his fingers around my ankles and drags me to the edge of the bed until we're perfectly aligned. He leans over, caging me in with his powerful body. One hand is placed on each side of my head as his face hovers over mine. Back and forth his lips strum until I want to scream with the intensity building within.

"Stop teasing."

"Why?" His mouth curves. "I like driving you crazy. Know what I love even more?"

He doesn't give me a chance to respond.

"Bringing you to your knees and making you beg. There's nothing better than that," he growls, continuing to torment me. "I never thought there'd come a day when you'd plead for my dick to fill that sweet pussy of yours and yet, here we are. You belong to me, and my cock is the only one you'll get."

His words crash over me like a tidal wave, threatening to drag me to the very depths of the ocean. They fill me with so much excitement that it's almost impossible to fathom. Especially when he toys with me like this.

When I remain silent, lost in an endless sea of sensation, he nips at my lower lip. "Right?"

There's a momentary burst of pain before pleasure rushes in, drowning out all other sensation.

"Tell me," he growls. "Tell me you belong to me."

"I do." It's only when the answer escapes that I realize it's the truth.

I belong to Asher Stevens. I have no idea when it happened, but there's no denying that it has.

"Just like you belong to me," I tell him.

The expression on his face turns fierce. "Damn right I do."

Joy explodes inside me as his lips crash onto mine and his tongue invades my mouth. Just as I give myself over to the kiss, he draws away. Air bursts from my lungs as he sinks lower, nibbling at my jawline.

Everywhere he touches, my flesh burns as if it's on fire. I bare my throat as he moves steadily along the narrow column before licking my pulse, bathing it with moisture. At this very moment, it feels as if it's beating solely for him.

He drops kisses along my collarbone before continuing his downward descent until reaching the rounded curve of my breasts. He nuzzles the softness before drawing one pebbled nipple into his mouth. The tug of his lips sends a burning arrow of need straight to my core. When I can't stand another moment of the intensity, he releases the bud before giving the same attention to the other one. My back bows, craving more of the addictive feelings that rush through my veins.

My fingers tunnel through his thick blond strands, sinking into his scalp, attempting to hold him in place. Instead of lingering, he nips at the sensitive peak. When I gasp, he sets me free, dragging his tongue over my ribcage and belly before using his hands to spread my legs wide, forcing my knees to the mattress until I'm completely exposed. Instead of delving straight in, he presses his mouth to my inner thighs before nibbling at the flesh.

"Asher," I whimper. How did he turn this around on me so fast? As swiftly as the question flickers through my brain, it evaporates.

"What?" he asks, giving the same treatment to the other side.

"You're teasing again."

"Am I?"

His gaze latches onto mine from between my thighs as his fingers bite into the delicate skin of my legs, locking them in place when I squirm beneath him.

"Yes."

"And you don't like it?"

My breath catches as his teeth sink into me.

"I do."

"Then what's the problem?"

"I want you inside me." More like I need him inside me, filling me to the brim, making the world around us fall away.

My teeth rake across my lower lip as he kisses his way to my center. Anticipation builds, swirling in my lower belly as my breath becomes wedged in my throat. When his mouth finally settles over me, it feels like it's only a matter of time before I burst out of my skin. He licks from the bottom of my slit to the top before circling my clit with the tip of his tongue. When I arch—needing more—the soft touch disappears.

Just as I'm about to protest, the tips of his fingers swat my clit and pleasure explodes inside me like a firework. His gaze stays locked on mine as I gasp. He does it a second time before leaning closer and feasting upon me.

The fire rampaging in my core explodes as he laps at my shuddering softness, thrusting his tongue deep inside my body. My hips roll against him as everything continues to reach a frenzy. Right before I spiral out of control, he pulls back. His fingers spread my lips, exposing my clit before his warm breath drifts over me again as his tongue circles the delicate bud. I'm so dizzy with pleasure that it's entirely possible I'll lose my mind.

The velvety softness vanishes for a second time as he gives my clit another sharp slap. I cry out as my pussy throbs with pleasure-infused-pain. I'm so close to coming that hot tears prick my eyes and sobs gather in my throat.

Instead of pushing me over the edge, Asher rises to his feet and grabs his jeans from the floor. A condom is pulled from his pocket. Not more than a second later, there's a tear and he's covering himself with latex. Barely am I able to suck in a shaky breath before he's driving deep inside me, burying himself to the hilt.

That's all it takes for an orgasm to explode throughout my body and rock me to the core. With his hands wrapped around my thighs, he pulls out just enough to drive back inside. My inner muscles clench his hard length, milking his release. A deep growl vibrates within his chest as he loses control.

It's so tempting to scream this house down with all the pleasure that rushes through me, but I can't. Not with Mama in the other room. Instead, I press a hand to my lips to keep the sound trapped inside as his rough grunts mingle with my own and we both come undone.

For the first time in my life, I wish there wasn't a condom to separate us from each other. I want to feel everything about this moment. I want to feel the hot spray of his cum as it paints the inside of my womb.

More than anything, I want to belong to Asher in a way I've never belonged to another man before.

33

ASHER

With my tray in hand, I snag a table at the Union. It's finals week, and thanks to Lola cracking the whip, helping me to get ready for my exams, I actually feel prepared. Trust me, I'm just as shocked by this turn of events as anyone else. I've never studied so much or so hard in my life. I'm willing to bet that if you added up all the time I've spent on homework at Western, it wouldn't amount to what I've done this past month.

How's that for crazy?

And do you know where all that hard work has gotten me?

An A, two Bs, and two Cs. One of those Cs just so happens to be in the dragon's course. Shove that up your ass, Professor Nichols. When she asked me to stay after class this morning, I thought for sure I'd failed the latest quiz.

Turns out I'd passed.

With flying colors, thank you very much.

This calls for a celebration, and I know exactly how I'm going to do that.

More like *who* I'm going to do it with.

My gaze scans the crowd for Lola's dark head. It takes several passes before I catch sight of her walking toward me with a tray in hand. As soon as our gazes collide, a zip of energy sizzles through my veins. Even after all this time, I'm still not used to the feelings she rouses inside me or the way my body reacts to her. Every muscle becomes whipcord tight as my heart skips a painful beat before pounding harshly into overdrive.

Know what I like best?

That she sees me for the guy buried beneath all the hype. Lola doesn't give a shit if I'll turn pro in a couple of months. She doesn't care if I sign a multimillion-dollar contract. She's not a groupie impressed with my celebrity. Honestly, I think she'd prefer if we could go out to eat or to the store without people stopping me, wanting an autograph, or talking football.

The fame and notoriety doesn't mean jack shit to her.

The closer she gets, winding through the sea of students, the more intense my need becomes. I've always been a touchy-feely kind of guy, but this...

It's on an entirely different level. I have a hard time keeping my hands to myself when she's in the vicinity.

"Hi," she says, setting her tray on the table across from mine. "Have you been waiting long?" She unwinds a knitted scarf from around her neck before unbuttoning her jacket.

I glance at the scarf, wondering how she'd look with it tied around her wrists, her arms hoisted above her head so she can't escape my touch. The thought of her stretched out naked on my bed is enough to give me wood.

I clear my throat along with those thoughts. "Nope. Just got here."

Unable to rein in my desire another second, I nab her cold fingers and tow her to me. With her body pressed against mine, she twines her arms around my neck before lifting onto the tips of her toes.

"I missed you," I growl between kisses, my erection becoming insistent.

I'd like nothing more than to take her back to my place and have my wicked way with her, but I know she has a final later this after-noon and needs to study. The last thing I want to do is get in the way of her nailing this exam. I want to be just as good for her as she is for me.

"Missed you, too."

Just as she draws away, some fucker passing by shouts, "Hey, Stevens, get a room!"

It's on the tip of my tongue to yell back that I'd love too, but I have serious doubts it would go over well. The last thing I want to do is piss off my girl.

Yeah, you heard me right. Maybe we haven't made it official, but for all intents and purposes, Lola Diaz is my girl. It's been buzzing around in the back of my brain for the past week. With everything going on, I haven't wanted to broach the subject. She's under enough stress and doesn't need anything else adding to it.

I'm waiting for the perfect time to spring it on her. Maybe after finals are wrapped up, we can take a breather and have a convo about our relationship.

Heat gathers in her cheeks as she steps away and settles on the other side of the table. I follow suit. Although, I would much rather eat my lunch with her sitting on my lap.

As I pick up my burger and take a bite, she says, "I decided to schedule the surgery."

I blink before carefully setting the sandwich back in its basket. "Are you sure?"

Uncertainty flickers across her expression as she presses her lips together. "I've thought about it so much this past week that it's almost impossible to focus on anything else. As nervous as I am about going through with it, I just can't say no." Her voice dips, becoming lower. "How could I live with myself if I didn't help her?" She slowly shakes her head. "It's a guilt I would always carry with me."

Deep down, I knew this would be her answer.

I roll my neck from side to side to alleviate the growing tension. "Have you thought about—"

"All the risks involved?" She reaches across the table and lays her hand over my larger one. "Yes, I have. Like I said, it's been difficult to think about anything else. I even jotted down a pro and con list." She glances away. "No matter how many cons there are, it's impossible to equate them to saving someone's life."

"Is your mom still against it?" It feels like a shitty card to pull, but I do it anyway.

"Yes, but she'll get over it." She releases a slow breath. "I think that has more to do with her feelings for Tony than anything else."

I slip my hand from beneath hers until I can cover her warm flesh and squeeze tight. "They don't deserve you."

"What Kylie deserves is a shot at a normal life, and I'm her best bet at achieving it."

I huff out a breath. It's hard to argue with that kind of logic, but that doesn't mean I like it. "When are you going to call the transplant center and tell them your decision?"

Her teeth sink into her lower lip before she admits, "I already did."

"Are you serious?" My brows slam together as the corners of my lips sink. "When?"

"A few hours ago."

Everything in me stills. "Why the hell didn't you tell me?"

Her gaze drops to her untouched tray of food. "Truthfully?"

"Yeah, I want the fucking truth," I growl.

She sucks in a deep breath before slowly forcing it out again. "I was afraid you'd try to talk me out of it."

Damn straight I would have.

When I remain silent, her voice drops. "Please, Asher...say something."

It takes effort to shove down the mix of emotions that pounds through me. The last thing this girl needs to deal with on top of everything else is me being butthurt. I have to get over myself and give her what she needs most—my support.

"Okay."

She blinks, as if she didn't hear me correctly. "You're...not angry?"

"No. And you're right. If you'd told me beforehand, I would have tried to talk you out of this decision." Since we haven't opened up and shared our feelings, I say carefully, "I don't want to see anything happen to you."

I lift her fingers to my mouth before brushing a soft kiss against her knuckles.

Maybe I've been too chickenshit to say the actual words out loud, but that doesn't mean I haven't tried to show her how I feel through my actions. I've never taken more care with another human being then I have with Lola.

Her shoulders loosen as relief floods her expression. "Thanks for being so understanding."

It's only now as her body wilts that I realize how much tension had been radiating off her. It makes me feel like a real piece of shit. Here she is, thanking me for not being pissed off when she's doing something so selfless.

"When's the surgery?"

"January ninth." She picks up her fork and spears a piece of chicken and lettuce with the tines before popping it into her mouth.

"The ninth?"

With a nod, she continues to chew. After swallowing, she adds, "That's the earliest date the surgeon had available."

I drag a hand through my hair as that new bit of information circles through my brain. "That's the same date as the championship in California."

"Oh." With a frown, she drops the fork to her bowl. "Sorry, I must have forgotten."

Fuck.

Now what am I going to do?

How can I take off and leave her here?

Sure, Mariana will be with her...

But her mom can't always be counted on.

What if something happens and I'm halfway across the country? There's no way in hell I'll be able to concentrate on the game. My mind will be solely focused on her. I need to know Lola's getting the best care possible.

"Everything will be fine," she says quickly, attempting to downplay the situation. "I'll be in the hospital for a couple of days. And the surgery is done laparoscopically, it's not really that big of a deal."

My gaze sharpens. How the fuck can she even say that?

"Everything will be fine *if* the surgery goes well and there aren't complications."

She shifts and says quietly, "There won't be any issues."

Even though I'm trying to remain calm, my voice turns sharp. "Oh? Do you have a crystal ball I don't know about?"

If that were the case, she would've seen me coming from a mile away and run for her fucking life.

"Of course not. But I'm healthy and—"

"That doesn't mean something can't go wrong."

"Maybe," she concedes. "But it does lower the chances."

This girl…

She'll drive me batshit crazy.

And I love her for it.

Fuck.

Did I just think that?

Yup, I did.

I love Lola.

That's all it takes for me to realize what needs to be done. "I'll tell Coach that I won't be playing in the game."

Her eyes widen as she straightens on her chair like someone just rammed a two-by-four up her ass. "You can't do that."

"Sure, I can," I say calmly. "I can do whatever the fuck I want."

"No, you have to go. I don't understand exactly how the draft works, but I realize it's important that you play in this game." Her dark eyes plead with mine. "You've worked so hard to get where you are, and it's your last college game. You *have to* go, Asher."

I fold my arms across my chest, prepared to dig in if it becomes necessary. "Do you really think I'm going to travel out of state if you're having major surgery?" Slowly, I shake my head. "No way." Lola's not the only one who can make a decision without input.

"What about your agent? Or your family?" she whispers in a last-ditch effort to sway me. "Won't they be upset?"

To say that Greg Abbot, my sports agent, will be displeased with the news is a major understatement.

But…you know what?

Tough shit.

And my family?

They don't give a damn. Other than my brother, no one else is going to show up for the game. Mom and Dad are still in the Netherlands and won't be flying home until graduation in May. Then, they'll be off again.

"Don't worry, everyone will be cool with it."

She scrapes her teeth across her lower lip. "Please, Asher. You're making too big of a deal about this."

My arms drop to my sides as I lean forward. "And you're not making a big enough deal out of it."

A heavy silence falls over us as we continue to stare.

"Hey, this place is packed. Glad you found a table."

I rip my gaze away from her, only to find Crosby standing next to us with a loaded-down tray. Normally, I'm happy to see my friends. Especially since they've all gotten wifed up and aren't around as much as they used to be.

But at the moment?

I'd much rather be alone with Lola.

Crosby drops down beside me and the rest follow suit. Brooke, Carson, Elle, Sasha, and Easton fill the empty chairs at the long stretch of table. The quiet is broken by boisterous chatter and laughter. If anyone notices the thick tension hanging in the air, they don't comment on it. Lola's brow furrows as she stares at her barely touched chicken salad.

Demi, Rowan, Brayden, and Sydney pull chairs up to the already crowded table, squeezing in beside us. Even though I would have rather finished our conversation, that's no longer an option. Not with all these people surrounding us. It's probably for the best if we table this discussion for the time being. Although, I'm not sure what good it will do. There's no way I'll change her mind about the surgery, just like she isn't going to change mine about the game.

The only thing left to do is talk to Coach.

And hope he understands.

3 4

———

LOLA

A sigh falls from my lips as I hold his blue gaze in the darkness. There's just enough silvery moonlight slanting in through the unadorned window for me to see the intensity that fills his expression.

Has anyone ever looked at me like this?

Like he can see straight down to my soul?

Asher is the only man who has ever stared at me with so much pent-up emotion or made me feel like I've been shoved off a cliff and am in freefall. Whatever this is between us, I never saw it coming.

My mind tumbles back to the day he walked into Taco Loco with a blonde tucked under each arm and a handful of teammates like he owned the joint. His easy demeanor—as if he were used to taking his fame, the female fan club clinging to him, and good looks in stride. Everything about the guy had rankled me. The strange urge to knock him down a peg or two had thrummed through my veins until the challenge was impossible to ignore.

That one run-in was all it took for something unexpected to snap and sizzle in the air between us. It was easy enough to tamp down until we started spending time together. That's when everything changed, and I got to know him on a deeper, more personal level. It didn't take long for all my preconceived notions to fly out the window as we built a friendship.

I'm forced from those thoughts when his thick length slides inside my body. Unlike the previous times we've had sex, there's a tenderness to his movements. As if he's making a concerted effort to slow everything down and take care with me. The strange thing is that it's exactly what I need. It's baffling how this man can understand what I crave on a deep level when I don't have a firm grasp on it myself.

But he does.

And he gives it to me every single time.

With every thrust of his body, mine dances closer to the precipice. Not once does he increase the tempo or lose control. Each movement is measured and precise, almost as if it were designed to draw out as much pleasure as possible until I beg him to make me come.

His gaze stays locked on mine as a muscle tics in his shadowed jaw.

Just when I can't take another moment of this sweet torture, he growls, "I want you to come now."

The command sends me careening over the edge and into oblivion. But I'm not alone in that. Asher is right there beside me. The low chanting of my name only catapults me further into the stratosphere.

As I float back to earth, he buries his face against the hollow of my neck. His warm breath feathers over my delicate flesh as I pull him closer, never wanting to let go.

"I love you," he whispers, barely loud enough for me to hear.

It takes effort to pry my eyes open as I stare at the ceiling and hold onto him for dear life. The sentiment sits perched on the tip of my tongue, ready to be echoed back, but I can't force it out.

After a few silent moments, he lifts his face to stare down at me as his gaze searches mine in the velvety darkness that fills the room. His brows tug together as he presses his lips gently to the corner of one eye and then to the other.

"Don't cry."

Only then do I realize that tears sting my eyes. So few people have said those three precious words to me. Coming from Asher, they mean absolutely everything.

He lowers his face to mine and kisses away all the wetness before pulling out of my body and rolling from the bed. He makes quick work of discarding the condom before padding into the attached bathroom. A moment later, he returns with a warm washcloth.

It stirs memories of the first time we slept together and how surprised and embarrassed I'd been when he placed the soft, cottony material between my legs to clean me off. Now, I find the action oddly comforting. Sweet, even.

My heart clenches as he presses the warm fabric to my pussy before carefully wiping away my arousal. Once finished, he returns to the bathroom and discards the towel before sliding back into bed. Gathering me into his arms, he holds me close.

"I meant what I said," he whispers against my ear. "That wasn't just the orgasm talking."

Even though he's trying to make light of his declaration, I can't bring myself to laugh. My life is far from perfect, but with Asher, it feels surprisingly close to it. This man makes me happy.

Happier than I ever dreamed I could be.

No one has ever managed to rouse these kinds of tender feelings. It's like I blinked, and he became my everything. He's been so gentle, taking such care with me, and I want to do the same for him. It's important that I put his needs above my own. Which is exactly why I can't allow him to miss the championship game. I won't let him sacrifice something so important. Something that has far-reaching consequences and the potential to impact his future.

No matter what I have to do to make it happen, Asher will be at that game.

35

ASHER

With a flick of my fingers, I unsnap the chin strap and pull off the helmet before shaking out my damp hair. It might be freeze-your-ass-off-cold outside, but the stadium is heated. Even though there are two weeks before the final game, Coach is still working us over and riding our asses, making sure the team is prepared. Six days a week, we're on the field, running routes, going over plays, and watching game film.

"Dude, that's so uncalled for."

I glance at Crosby and Easton as we fall into line on the way to the locker room. That's the moment it hits me that I'll miss playing ball with these guys. We won the final playoff game last week, guaranteeing our spot in the championship.

Something sharp twists in the pit of my gut at the realization that I won't be going to California. I've stepped foot on the field with my teammates for the last time. After spending the past four seasons with these men, the Western Wildcats have become my family. Maybe we don't always see eye to eye, but we look out for each other. It's impossible to imagine developing the same kinds of relationships with future teammates. Rowan, Brayden, Easton, Carson, Crosby, and I all came in at the same time. We clicked on the field and got close fast.

270

Even I understand how rare that kind of friendship is.

Rowan jogs toward our trio before slowing his pace once he reaches my side.

When I give him a chin lift in greeting, he says, "Coach told me you're bailing on the championship game."

Fuck.

This isn't a topic I wanted to discuss with them. At least, not yet. I was planning on saying something when we got a little closer to the big day. Like, right before the bus pulled out of the athletic center parking lot.

Crosby snorts. "Get the hell out of here, Michaels. Of course Stevens will be there."

When I remain silent, Crosby knocks into my shoulder with his own. "Right, dumbass?"

I glare at him as everyone turns their attention to me.

When I remain silent, the blond QB says, "He wasn't playing around, was he?"

"Have you ever known Coach Richards to joke when we're this deep into the season?" Easton asks.

"Nope," Rowan admits. "So, what's going on? I can't imagine a reason you'd miss this game."

That's the funny thing—if you'd asked me two months ago, I would have said that nothing could keep me from playing in the last game of my college career. Now, everything has changed. It doesn't feel as important as it once did.

When I sat down with Coach the other day, he initially tried to talk me out of my decision. It didn't take long for him to realize that nothing was going to sway me. He went silent for about ten seconds before leaning forward in his chair and steepling his hands together. He told me that I might have come into his program almost four years ago as a boy, but I was leaving it a man old enough to make his own choices in life. With nothing else left to say, we rose to our feet and shook hands before I walked out of his office with a mixture of relief and sadness filling my heart.

When Crosby shoves into me for the second time, I bare my teeth.

His upper lip curls. "You gonna give us an answer or what?"

So far, I've been pretty lowkey about my relationship.

"Lola has a surgery scheduled for the same day as the game." I meet each of their gazes in turn, wanting them to understand how serious this is without me having to put it into words. "I don't feel right about traveling out of state and leaving her here alone."

A heavy silence falls over the group as they digest that information.

"Well, shit. Is she all right?" Crosby asks, expression sobering as concern weaves its way through his voice.

"Yeah, she's fine. She's donating a kidney to her half-sister."

"Wow," Easton says. "I had no idea."

"I didn't realize you two had grown so close," Crosby says.

I give him a bit of side-eye. "Well, we have."

Rowan nods before clapping me on the shoulder. He's always been the quietest and most levelheaded one of the bunch. He's the one our teammates seek out when they want solid advice. "If that's what you need to do, then you have our support."

Air escapes from my lungs in a rush. "Thanks, man. I appreciate it."

I hate that I'm letting down my teammates when they need me most, but it doesn't feel like I have a choice in the matter. It's a relief that they understand. And if they don't, Rowan will knock their heads together until they do.

"You'll be missed," Crosby grumbles from beside me.

"Thanks, but I don't think you guys will have any trouble holding your own. This is what we've been working toward all year. Hell, all four of them."

"You're an integral part of this team," Rowan says solemnly. "Don't fool yourself into believing otherwise."

Thick emotion gathers in my throat, making it impossible to keep my voice level. But I'll be damned if I embarrass myself in front of them. It's a relief when we walk through the tunnel and into the locker room.

What I need right now is to shake off the melancholy that has fallen over me. And the perfect way to do that is by spending a little quality time with my girl. Now that finals are over, we're supposed to go out and celebrate that I've passed all my classes.

I'll never have to see Dr. Nichols again.

Thank fuck.

After showering, I wrap a towel around my waist and beeline for my locker. I'm impatient to get the hell out of here. All I want to do is wrap my arms around Lola and hold her tight. I have no idea why everything feels better when she's tucked against me, but there's no denying that it does.

I yank on my sweatpants and T-shirt before grabbing my black Wildcats football sweatshirt from my locker. Once my athletic duffel is in hand, I pull out my phone, ready to fire off a text.

Except there's already one waiting for me.

Sorry. Have to cancel our plans. Called in to work.

My eyes narrow as I silently contemplate the message.

Normally, I wouldn't think anything of it. Lola picks up shifts at the restaurant whenever she can. I fucking hate that she has to work so hard just to keep her head above water. I try to pay for as much as I can when we're together, but she doesn't like it. And she refuses to accept money when I offer it. I don't think I've ever met anyone as fiercely independent or proud as she is.

It's just another quality I love about her.

Here's where it gets tricky—I dropped the I-love-you bomb five days ago, and she's been acting weird ever since. There have been several times when we've been together, and I've caught her zoning out with a small frown on her face.

With the upcoming surgery, I know she's got a lot on her mind. I've tried not to read too much into the change in her behavior or take the distance she's trying to put between us personally. But in the back of my head, I'm worried she's pulling away. This is the third time she's bailed on me. And she barely calls or texts. I'm always the one chasing her ass down.

It's not that I have a problem doing it, but every time she breaks our plans or doesn't call me back, the pit sitting at the bottom of my gut multiplies in size, becoming impossible to ignore.

As much as I don't want to believe there's an issue in our relationship, what other choice do I have?

36

LOLA

Carmen nods toward the entrance of the restaurant. "Looks like lover boy dropped by for a visit."

My head whips toward the hostess stand before landing on Asher. A serious expression mars his face as he loiters at the entrance of the dining room, scanning the area. The second our gazes collide, I feel the spark of electricity straight down to my toes. Even though it shouldn't surprise me that he showed up here unannounced…it does.

One hand drifts to my lower belly, pressing on it, as if that will be enough to settle the nerves dancing inside. I've been dragging my feet, putting off the inevitable, but I can't do it any longer.

"Will you cover my tables for a couple of minutes?" I ask.

"Hmmm…that doesn't bode well for your boy toy, now does it?"

If it were possible to rip my attention away from him, I'd shoot her a scowl. Now that he's found me, he cuts a direct path to us. I have to crane my neck to hold his steady gaze as he grinds to a halt a few feet away. We haven't spoken a word to each other, and already there are silent questions swimming around in his blue depths. I straighten my shoulders, steeling myself for the inevitable.

"Hey." Instead of tugging me into his arms like he normally would, he shoves his hands into the pocket of his hoodie. "I know you're working, but do you have time to talk? I can wait around until you have a break."

My gaze flickers to my cousin. Even though she never gave me an answer, I say, "No, Carmen will cover for me. Let's go in the backroom where it's quiet."

Tension vibrates from him in heavy waves as he jerks his head into a nod. "Okay. Lead the way."

Everything feels so different between us, and I hate it. More than that, I hate what I'm about to do.

My shoes feel like they're filled with cement as we cut through the crowded dining area to the hallway in the back where the employee breakroom is located. Every step I take makes my heart twist with more agony.

It's a relief when I push open the door and find the space empty. Once Asher crosses over the threshold, my fingers tremble as I close the door, ensuring we have a bit of privacy.

Now that we're alone and all the noise from the restaurant has faded, a heavy silence falls over us. Unsure how to begin this conversation, I wring my hands together in order to resist reaching out and drawing him close.

He clears his throat and shifts his stance. "Sorry about ambushing you at work."

There is so much confusion written across his expression. I know he doesn't understand why I've pulled back. All I want to do is smooth the lines away and make everything better.

"No, it's fine," I force myself to say. "I'm glad you stopped by."

"Really?" He pops a brow. "Because it feels like you've been avoiding me."

Air gets wedged in my throat, making it impossible to breathe. I wasn't expecting him to get straight to the point. While Asher seems laid back and chill, what I've discovered is that he's not that way about everything.

Certainly not with the things that matter. My heart constricts with the silent acknowledgment that I've become important to him.

I hate myself for the pain I'm about to inflict, but I don't see any other way around it. I've tried a dozen times to talk him out of skipping the game. And moving the surgery to a later date isn't possible. Kylie needs the transplant now.

The last time I broached the subject, he shut me down by stripping off his clothes. All the man has to do is peel off his shirt and I go a little stupid. There's nothing better than the sight of his jeans or sweatpants hanging low on his lean hips.

Sweet baby Jesus…the V that disappears beneath the material is enough to make my mouth turn cottony.

Every.

Damn.

Time.

So…maybe having this conversation in the breakroom at Taco Loco is for the best. He can't distract me by shedding his clothes and kissing me senseless.

When I remain silent, hurt seeps into his eyes. "Not even going to deny it, huh?"

As much as I tried to mentally prepare myself, his pain hits me like a punch to the gut. I glance away, hoping it'll be easier to force out the words if I'm not holding his gaze.

"I'm sorry. I—"

Abrupt movement catches the corner of my eye and my head whips in that direction just in time to see him eat up the distance between us with a few long-legged strides.

I throw up both hands to ward him off. "Please, Asher. Don't make this any harder than it has to be."

"Wait a minute…" His tongue darts out to moisten his lips as his voice fills with confusion. "Are you breaking up with me?"

Oh god.

Shock fills his eyes.

"I'm sorry," I whisper, unsure what else to say.

He shakes his head before plowing a hand through his thick blond strands, making them stand on end. "I don't understand what's going on here." There's a pause, and I can almost see the wheels in his brain turning. "Are you pushing me away because I told you I loved you? It was never my intention to scare you."

I clear my throat and force out the lie I've been rehearsing in my head for days. "I think our relationship is moving too fast. With everything that's going on, I just need to take a step back and focus on myself for a while."

He tilts his head as if assessing my words for the truth. "But this isn't a breather, is it?" An uncomfortable beat of silence follows that question. It's like a knife to the heart. "You're breaking up with me."

No.

No.

No.

Even though everything within me is shriveling up and dying, I stand tall, because there's nothing else I can do but see this through to the bitter end. "I think that would be for the best. It'll be a while before I'm up for anything. So, you know..." My voice trails off awkwardly.

"Do you really think that's what I care about? That I'll get bored because we can't go out or hit all the parties?" The scowl he sends me is ferocious. "Is that really the bullshit excuse you're gonna give me?"

I couldn't feel more like an asshole if I tried.

When I glance away, he snaps, "The least you can do is hold my gaze while you break my fucking heart."

Thick emotion wells in my throat, making it impossible to breathe. I lock my knees so that I won't crumple to the floor. "I can't worry about someone else when I need to take care of myself. That's all I'm trying to say."

"Did I ever ask you to worry about me?"

Each grounded-out word falls from his lips like a bomb. I feel the impact of every single one deep in my soul. How is it possible for this to be so much more agonizing than I anticipated? I'm doing everything in my power to hold back the moisture that threatens to gather in my eyes.

"Did I?"

My teeth rake across my lower lip until pain throbs to life.

"All I want is for you to be honest with me."

When he bursts into movement, I brace myself, knowing that there's no way to stop him from laying his hands on my body. And I can't deny that part of me wants to be hauled into his arms and held one last time before I cut him loose.

Barely am I able to suck in a breath before he reaches out and locks his fingers around my upper arms. And then I'm dragged to him, enveloped in his strength. Giving in to my need, I bury my face against his chest as the steady thumping of his heart fills my ears and the woodsy scent of his cologne cocoons me in familiarity. The importance of singeing this moment into my brain pounds through me as a heaviness settles in my soul at the knowledge that I will never meet another man who understands my needs as well as this one.

It takes effort to choke back the sob rising in my throat. I have to end this before I break down and change my mind. "I wish everything could be different." That, at least, is the unvarnished truth. "But I need to be on my own right now."

His muscles stiffen. "That's it? We're just…over?"

I can't believe I'm doing this.

Just opening my hand and letting him go.

"I'm—"

"Don't say it," he growls. "Don't you dare apologize again."

His arms tighten, pressing me so close that it feels like my ribs will shatter into a million pieces the same way my heart is.

And yet, I don't want him to release me.

Not ever.

I remind myself that this is the right decision. I won't jeopardize his future. He's been working toward a career in the NFL his entire life. Since he first picked up a football at age four and tossed it around with his brother in the backyard. Even if he refuses to admit the truth, skipping this game will put all that in danger.

His lips brush against the top of my head before his arms disappear as he retreats until we're no longer touching.

"I can't force you to feel something you don't."

The anguish that vibrates through his voice is palpable, and it takes everything I have inside not to throw myself at him and beg his forgiveness. Maybe I haven't been forthright about my feelings, but I love him. Instead of admitting the truth, I keep it locked deep inside where it can't cause damage.

He clears his throat and drops his gaze as if he's unable to bear the sight of me. "I'll let you get back to work."

Incapable of summoning my voice, I jerk my head into a tight nod as he strides to the exit. It takes every bit of self-control to keep my arms pressed to my sides so I won't reach for him.

Once at the door, he grabs the handle and yanks it open. Air gets clogged in my throat when he hesitates over the threshold. The second or two that passes only heightens the poignancy of this moment.

"I've never told another girl that I loved them. The way I care about you...I don't know if it's possible to feel that way about anyone else." There's a pause. "I think you might have ruined me."

I press my lips together to stop myself from crying out.

Asher might not realize it, but he's ruined me as well.

Thick emotion bubbles up in my throat as hot tears sting my eyes.

When I remain silent, he quietly closes the door behind him, leaving me to pick up the pieces of my shattered heart.

3 7

ASHER

I lift the beer to my lips and take a long swallow, downing nearly all the contents. Like the others I've previously sucked down, it does nothing to dull the pain. If I'm being perfectly honest, I didn't really think it would. But it was worth a shot, right?

Even though I'm twenty-two years old, I've never given love much thought.

Why would I?

Ever since I was a freshman in high school, I've had girls tripping over themselves to please me. What would be the point of tying myself down to just one when variety is the spice of life?

Kind of ironic that I ended up falling for the one girl who broke my heart.

Whoever said that love hurts was abso-fucking-lutely right. It's the most painful thing I've ever experienced. And I've been laid out flat plenty of times on the football field. Here's the funny thing—not only does my heart ache, but everything else as well. My very fucking soul throbs with pain. It's like a virus has infected my body and there's no cure. At least, none I know of.

It sucks.

Serious question—why would someone willingly put themselves through this kind of agony?

It's not worth it. Anyone going out and actively trying to fall in love is a real dumbass. Or maybe I'm the dumbass. Obviously, what I had to offer wasn't good enough or she wouldn't have been so quick to cut me loose.

Maybe *I'm* just not enough.

I drag a hand over my face as these thoughts churn through my brain.

It's been a little over a week since I tracked her down at Taco Loco. All I can say is thank fuck the semester is over. I've been having a tough enough time dragging my ass out of bed each morning. Somehow, I need to find a way to pull it together before the spring semester starts.

"Hi, Asher."

I glance up from the bottle I've been contemplating, only to find Mallory standing next to me with a fresh beer in hand.

When I remain silent, she holds it out as an offering. "I thought you might want another one."

Well…if she's going to insist, who am I to argue?

I pluck the bottle from her fingers before bringing it to my lips and sucking down half of it.

Nope. Still doesn't dull the pain.

"Thanks," I mumble.

"You look like you could use a friend."

Not really. I'd much prefer to wallow by myself. Even in this depressed state, I realize I'm not fit company.

I lift my shoulders, hoping the gesture will suffice.

"Great," she says, dropping down next to me and cuddling against my side. A couple of seconds tick by before her fingers begin to wander along my chest. "I heard about your breakup. I'm really sorry."

Less than twenty-four hours after Lola curb-stomped my heart, news was buzzing around campus and my phone was blowing up with girls wanting to come over and console me. A few even dropped off baked goods.

I'm knocked from those thoughts when the front door opens and Audrey steps inside the entryway. She glances around before spotting me on the couch with Mallory.

"Hi," she says with a wave before lifting the large square tin in her other hand. "I baked some brownies. I thought it might cheer you up."

"Thanks," I grunt. "Appreciate it."

"You can take them on the bus with you. Doesn't it leave tomorrow morning?"

"Yup." I'm trying to gear myself up for the game, but it's impossible to work up any real enthusiasm. My mind keeps circling back to Lola and the surgery. Even though we're not together, I'm concerned that something will go wrong, and I won't be there with her.

"A bunch of us are caravanning to California. We'll all be there to cheer you on! And then party afterward," she adds with a giggle.

The thought of getting on a bus and playing in a game is exhausting. Honestly, I just want these girls to leave me alone. I don't need them hanging on me, texting night and day, or bringing me food. All I want to do is sulk by myself.

Taking my one-worded responses as an invitation, she beelines for the couch before setting the tin on the coffee table and curling up on the other side of me.

Once she's burrowed beneath my arm and laid her head against my chest, she sighs. "I've really missed this."

"Me, too," Mallory says happily as if all is now right in the world.

I don't bother adding to the convo, since it's apparent my opinion doesn't matter.

When their hands begin to wander, I realize that I need to extricate myself from the situation sooner rather than later. It's just too weird having someone other than Lola in my arms. I think everyone just expected that I'd snap back to my old self. But how can I do that when she's renting space in my head and nothing I do permanently evicts her?

I've picked up the phone dozens of times, ready to fire off a text, begging her to reconsider her decision. The only thing holding me back is that I don't want to come off as pathetic. Am I guilty of driving to Taco Loco and sitting in the parking lot like a stalker, all the while attempting to work up the courage to walk inside and talk to her?

Yup.

Several times.

Instead of making even more of an ass of myself, I drove home and smoked a bowl.

It didn't help.

What I've gradually come to realize is that nothing makes it better. Nothing dulls the pain that throbs insistently through me like a living, breathing entity. Nothing purges the memories that play through my brain on a constant loop.

I guess this is one of those shitty situations you hear about where only time can heal all wounds…blah, blah, blah.

"You seem so sad," Mallory says, wriggling close enough for me to feel her nipple poking through the thin shirt she's wearing. Her voice turns husky. "Are you sure there's nothing we can do to turn your frown upside down?"

"You know that we're up for anything, right?" Audrey's purple-lacquered talons trail up and down my thigh. Each pass brings her dangerously closer to my crotch. "You know what they say—teamwork makes the dream work."

A couple months ago, a collaborative effort by these two gorgeous girls would have been more than enough to get my cock's attention. I would have been springing up from the couch and leading them to my bedroom for a couple hours of fun between the sheets.

Now, however?

Absolutely nothing stirs south of the border.

There's not even a twinge.

It's almost disconcerting.

I clear my throat. "As much as I appreciate the offer, I'm not interested."

They both still.

"You're not…*interested?*" Mallory echoes, disbelief ringing out in her tone.

I lift the bottle to my lips and swallow down the rest of the alcohol. "Nope."

"But—"

"Sorry, ladies. There's something I need to take care of."

They stare with wide eyes as I rise to my feet and walk out of the living room.

"We'll be here if you change your mind," Audrey calls after my retreating form.

"All right," I shoot back on the way to the kitchen to grab a water. It's just easier to hang out in my room by myself.

Once the plastic bottle is in hand, I swing around, ready to head to the hallway when Rowan walks in with his arm slung around Demi's shoulders. The pair grinds to a halt when they catch sight of me.

I hate the longing that floods through my system before I swiftly tamp it down.

Some people are just cut out for coupledom.

I—unfortunately—am not one of them.

That pitiful thought has me dragging a hand over my face. Clearly, holing up in my room until I can snap out of this funk is the right decision all the way around.

"Hey, Asher," Demi says softly, drawing my attention. "You doing all right?"

Am I doing all right?

Am I doing all right?

Does it really look like I'm *doing all right*?

Hell, no…I'm not all right. Most of the time, it doesn't feel like I'll ever be *all right* again. I can literally feel myself sliding deeper into a pit of despair, and there's not a damn thing I can do about it.

Alcohol doesn't help.

Sleeping doesn't help.

Music doesn't help.

Lifting doesn't help.

Weed doesn't help.

Nothing fucking helps.

"Yeah, I'm great," I force myself to say. "Why wouldn't I be?"

The dark-haired soccer player gives her boyfriend a bit of side-eye. The dubious expression on her face only has me digging in deeper. Like I need Demi thinking that some pint-sized chick with a prickly disposition is the one who finally did me in?

No thanks.

When she continues to stare, I add belligerently, "Don't I look fan-fucking-tastic?"

"Not really."

My shoulders collapse under those two words. Demi's never been one to hold back with the truth or beat around the bush. In a way, she reminds me of Coach. It's always been one of the qualities I liked about her.

At the moment, though?

Not so much.

It would be nice if they'd both do me a solid and pretend everything is hunky-dory. Is that too much to ask?

"I'm sorry about Lola," she says. "You seemed happy."

That comment is like a burning arrow slicing right through the heart of me. Air rushes from my lungs in a painful burst. It's almost impressive that I'm able to continue standing upright.

It takes effort to keep all the anguish that is nearly eating me alive from flashing across my face as I force my shoulders into a shrug. "Yeah well…shit happens."

Her gaze sharpens as she tilts her head. "Is that how you really feel about the situation? Because it kind of seemed like you liked her."

I press my lips together, refusing to give her the response she's looking for.

What the hell does this girl want me to do? Slit my wrists open and bleed all over the place? Would that make her happy?

"You know, it's all right to be sad. You don't have to pretend that your relationship with her didn't matter."

Fuck.

Doesn't Demi realize that I'm tired of being steeped in sadness?

I don't want to spend every waking minute of the day thinking about the girl who dumped my ass. The very same one who didn't care about me as much as I did about her. I just need to keep everything moving, because if I do that, maybe it'll be possible to outrun the pain. And then, when I finally come to a standstill, it won't hurt so much.

The pitying stares aimed in my direction only piss me off more.

"Who says I'm pretending?" I grumble, ready to end this conversation before it can spiral any further out of control.

"I do." There's a pause before she adds, "Have you considered that maybe you need to fight for her?"

Seriously? Does this girl think I'm a complete dumbass?

Of course I've considered that. I've been so damn close to marching into Taco Loco or showing up at her front door and begging to have one more conversation. But what good will it do?

She doesn't want me.

Rowan clears his throat. "Demi, maybe—"

"No." With a shake of her head, she glances at her boyfriend. "What he needs is a swift kick in the ass. I'm tired of watching him mope around here." She flings one arm in my direction. "In all the years we've known each other, I've never seen him give a crap about anyone. If he cares so much about her, then he needs to fight for her." There's a pause. "You know what else? I've never seen Lola happier. I don't understand why it all went south, but there has to be a reason she pushed you away. Instead of crying into your beer, figure it out."

I blink as some of the mental fog dissipates and a kernel of hope rises within me. I can't help but cling to one thing she said as if it's a lifeline. "You've really never seen her happier?"

Demi shakes her head. "No, I haven't. No matter what happened, you were good for her."

My heart swells with thick emotion. "She was good for me, too."

"I know. That's why I don't want to see it end like this."

"Me, neither."

"Then do something about it," she encourages with a smile. "Don't wait until it's too late and the moment passes you by."

She's right.

About everything.

Lola and I were good for each other. I don't understand why she broke up with me, but I'm going to damn well find out.

38

LOLA

The sun is just peeking over the horizon as I walk through the front doors of the transplant center with a small duffel bag slung over my shoulder and check in at the front desk. I was so ramped up about the surgery last night that I barely slept a wink.

The one person capable of calming my nerves is the very same one I pushed away. As tempting as it had been to call Asher, I resisted the urge. He needs to focus on himself and his future. Everything he's worked so hard for is riding on this game. The school had a big send-off in the parking lot of the athletic center the other day. There was no way in hell I was going, but it was all over social media.

As painful as it's been to set him free, it was the right choice to make. I can see that, even if he can't. What would have really happened between us anyway?

In a couple of months, he'll get drafted to a professional football team and move on with his life, probably halfway across the country. And I'll be here. Stuck in this town, looking for a job that's close to Mama because I can't leave her here on her own.

Who would take care of her when life goes off the rails and she sinks into another depression? Who would make sure she takes her meds?

As much as I wish it weren't the case, she needs me.

Mama was supposed to be here this morning, but she suffered a setback when she met a guy online who strung her along for a couple of weeks before disappearing from her life. The backslide is disappointing, but I can't say I'm totally shocked by it.

Or that I'm here by myself.

This is the way things go for me. It's better to accept reality for what it is than constantly wish it could be different. Carmen agreed to stop by the house before and after her shift to check on Mama. It's one less thing to worry about.

After stopping at reception, I head to the bank of elevators and hit the third floor where the surgery center is located. My fingers tremble as I push the button and wait for the car to arrive. Once it does, I step inside the small space. Just as the doors are about to slide shut, a large hand reaches in to stop it. The metal bounces open, revealing the man standing on the other side of the threshold.

I blink, unable to believe he's actually here. "Asher?"

One side of his mouth quirks as he steps inside, forcing me to back up until my spine hits the wall. "Hey."

I can only stare with wide eyes as the doors close, trapping us in the space together. My heart slams against my ribcage. There are so many questions buzzing around inside my brain that it takes a few seconds to find my voice. When I do, it comes out sounding like a croak. As if I haven't used it in years. "I don't understand. What are you doing here?"

"Did you really think I was just going to walk away?"

I shake my head to clear it, but it's like I'm in a fog. "You're supposed to be in California. The game is tonight."

"As long as everything goes well with your surgery, I'll fly out early this afternoon and be there in plenty of time."

"But—"

He shakes his head. "There's nothing for you to worry about. I've taken care of everything."

My teeth pin my lower lip to stop it from trembling with all the emotion welling up inside me. Any moment it'll burst free, and I'll come undone.

Before anything else can be said, his hand snakes out to nab my fingers before he draws me to him. As soon as my breasts press against the solid strength of his chest, his arms band around me, locking me in place.

It's only when the woodsy scent of his aftershave surrounds me, cocooning me in familiarity, that I can finally suck a full breath of air into my lungs again. The entire time without him, I've been gasping and choking, just trying to draw in enough oxygen to fill my lungs. Now that I'm wrapped up in his strong embrace, everything in my life once again feels right. Unable to hold back, my arms slip around his ribcage and squeeze tight. I don't ever want to let go.

"I can't believe you're here," I whisper.

"There was no way in hell I was getting on that bus," he growls in my ear. "You should know me well enough by now to realize that was never going to happen." There's a pause as his voice dips. "Even if you did dump my ass."

I lift my chin until my gaze can lock on his. "I didn't want you to sacrifice something you've spent your entire life working toward. Not for me."

"That wasn't your decision to make, it was mine. And just so you know—you're worth it." He searches my eyes. "Do you understand that? *You're worth it, Lola.* I promised you that I'd be here, and I refuse to go back on my word."

It takes everything inside me to blink back the wetness that floods my eyes. I've spent so much time tamping down my emotions, just trying to get through the grind, and make it to the next day. But Asher...

He makes me feel things.

And want things I never allowed myself to dream about.

With him, it seems possible to have everything I spent my entire life secretly longing for.

And he's here, even after I pushed him away and inflicted pain.

"Maybe you don't love me, but we're still friends. And friends are there for each other no matter what. I'll always be here for you."

A single tear treks down my cheek.

How did I ever believe the right decision was to break up with him?

"But that's the thing—I do love you, Asher."

Instead of responding, his mouth crashes onto mine. When his tongue sweeps across the seam of my lips, I immediately open until we can fuse together, and I'm crushed against all that solid strength.

I have no idea how much time ticks by before he pulls away just enough to say, "I love you, too. More than I ever thought possible. And I'm not going to let you go. Do you understand me? Not ever."

"Yes." I want that as much as he does. The weeks without him were terrible. There were so many times when I wanted to reach out and beg his forgiveness, but I wasn't willing to jeopardize his future.

As the doors slide open on the third floor, he glances into the hallway. "Are you sure about going through with this? No matter what your decision, I'll support you."

I nod. All the nerves dancing in the pit of my belly gradually dissipate. Not completely, but enough for me to realize that I'll be able to get through this. Especially now that he's here.

"All right," he says, holding me close, "let's get this over with."

He snatches the bag from my hand before snaking his other arm around my body and leading me down the hall.

For the first time in my life, it truly feels like I have someone to lean on. A partner. And nothing has ever felt better.

39

ASHER

ola's hand is clasped tightly in mine as I stare down at her. A heartrate monitor is attached to her and steady beeping from the machine fills the silence of the small recovery room. They wheeled her out of surgery more than an hour ago, and she's been in and out of sleep ever since. Every so often, her eyelashes will flutter, and she'll glance around in confusion, asking where she is before drifting back into slumber.

Thankfully, everything went smoothly. The surgeon stopped by about thirty minutes ago to check on her and said the procedure couldn't have gone better. As long as she follows the aftercare instructions, there's no reason she shouldn't make a speedy recovery.

I might have appeared cool, calm, and collected in Lola's presence, but as soon as the nurse called her name, taking her back to prepare for the surgery, I was a nervous wreck. I spent the entire three and a half hours it took in the operating room pacing back and forth. The woman behind the desk kept staring at me before shaking her head and pointing to one of the chairs.

Did I just so happen to tell the staff that we were engaged in order to get updates and then go back and sit with her after she'd been wheeled to the recovery room?

You bet your ass I did.

There was no way in hell they were keeping me away. I told Lola that I would be with her through every step of the process, and that's exactly what I'm going to do.

I straighten on the chair as my heartbeat picks up its tempo when she opens her eyes again and stares groggily at me.

"Hey," I say softly, pressing closer, "how are you feeling? Need anything for the pain?" The nurse is one call away, and I'll press that damn button all day long if that's what it takes.

She blinks before shaking her head as her tongue darts out to moisten her lips. "No, I'm okay. Can't feel much of anything at the moment. I just want something to drink. I'm really thirsty."

I nod and pick up the small Styrofoam cup filled with apple juice and hold the paper straw to her lips. She takes a long pull from it before huffing out a breath and relaxing against the pillows.

"Thank you."

"No problem, baby." There's a beat of silence. "I'm not sure how much you remember, because you've been in and out of it for a while. The doctor checked on you and said everything went really well, and now you've got a badass scar to show everyone how cool you are."

Her lips quirk. "Awesome. Can't wait to see it. Has there been any word on Kylie?"

"Yup," I say with a nod. "She's fine and was just wheeled into recovery. So far, everything looks good with the kidney."

"That's a relief," she says with a small sigh, closing her eyes for a moment.

"I know." Unable to resist, I lean forward and brush my lips against her forehead. I'm glad the surgery is over, and everything went well. "I love you."

"Love you, too." Her eyelids spring open as her brows draw together. "Wait a minute...why are you still here? Don't you have to leave?"

I glance at my sports watch. "I need to be at the airport by one o'clock and it's only eleven. I have plenty of time to hang out with you."

"I don't want you to miss your plane or the game. You need to be on the field, impressing the hell out of everyone."

I lift her fingers to my lips and drop a kiss on her knuckles. "I don't give a shit about any of that. As long as I impress you, that's all that matters."

"You do."

"Then I'm good."

"Did I thank you for sticking around and not listening to me when I broke up with you?"

I tilt my head and pretend to ponder the question for a couple seconds. "Nope, don't think so."

One side of her mouth hitches. "Thanks. I'm glad you're here. I couldn't have gotten through this without you."

"There's nowhere else I'd rather be." I lean closer before whispering, "And when you're better, I'm going to spank your ass for dumping me."

Her eyes spark with humor. "Promise?"

"Abso-fucking-lutely."

A smile curves her lips. "Good. I look forward to it."

4 0

LOLA

Two months have passed since the surgery, and I've made a full recovery. Asher was right—now I have a cool, three-inch scar below my bellybutton to show off. There was pain the first week or two, and then I was able to wean myself off the meds just in time for the start of second semester.

Asher flew out the afternoon of the surgery and was back in time to pick me up from the transplant center and take me home two days later. He practically moved in with us to help take care of me. I told him that he didn't have to do it, but he insisted. Mama didn't seem to mind at all. He scheduled a meal delivery service and has been trying his hand at easy recipes he finds on the internet. The man has become the casserole king. We've had chicken divine, tuna casserole, enchilada casserole, and something with chicken, wild rice, and bacon lining the bottom of the dish.

It was delicious.

I'm not going to lie—I enjoy sitting at the table and watching him cook. What is it about a man puttering around in the kitchen that is so damn sexy?

Asher Stevens has turned out to be the whole package. It's impossible not to fall a little more in love with him each day. At first, the

296

intensity of my feelings scared the crap out of me. But I've managed to push the fear aside and just go with it. How could I not take a chance when he's gone above and beyond to prove how much I mean to him?

For the first week, he slept on the couch in the living room and would peek in on me periodically throughout the night. After a trip to the doctor to check how my incision was healing, he moved into my room. The twin bed is a tight squeeze, but I wouldn't have it any other way. I love falling asleep with my head resting on his chest and his arms banded securely around me.

My eyes catch Asher's blue ones as he returns from the kitchen with two bottles of water before handing one over. Believe it or not, he stopped drinking and smoking pot. Even though I never said a word about it, I'm secretly glad. When I asked why he decided to quit, he told me that he wants to focus on being healthy and getting into the best shape he can for the draft and what will hopefully follow.

The man already had the physique of a god. Now, he's even leaner and harder.

More droolworthy.

Which means I'm giving girls the evil eye everywhere we go.

Once he's close enough, he leans in and presses a kiss against my mouth.

His lips linger over mine before nipping at my lower one and whispering, "I love you, baby."

Just like always, my heart melts at the murmured words. Asher is so open with his affection. He's not afraid to tell or show me exactly how he feels.

"I love you, too." And I do. More than I thought possible. This man is turning out to be my everything. It's not something I could have imagined months ago, given the way I felt about him. But there's no way I'd change a single second of our story.

Tonight, there's a small get together at the football house to celebrate the team winning the championship game and bringing home another trophy. Everyone at the university went crazy, and there was a week-long celebration.

These guys have worked so hard to make this season successful.

For those who are graduating or entering the draft, their college football careers are now over. The player selection meeting takes place at the end of April. Hopes and dreams will either be made or crushed. Even though I think Asher has a good chance of getting picked up by an NFL team, nothing is written in stone until his name is called out on national TV.

This particular party is a smaller, more intimate one. It's just for the guys who live at the house and their girlfriends. A few other close friends have also been invited.

Demi is here with Rowan. Those two are ridiculously cute together. Apparently, everyone was aware of the fact that he had a crush on her. With the exception of Demi, of course. She spent years trying to keep him at a distance, but in the end, it was impossible to do.

And then there's Sydney and Brayden. She's probably the only girl on campus who didn't swoon at the dark-haired football player's feet. Brayden had a reputation as a playboy and Sydney didn't want anything to do with him. Turns out, they were perfect for each other.

From what I've learned, Sasha and Easton have been best friends since they were in diapers. I'm not sure who decided they wanted more or if it was a mutual decision on their part, but they're adorable together. They know each other so well and can finish each other's sentences.

Now that Asher and I have been together for a couple of months, I've also gotten to know Elle and Carson. Elle is Brayden's younger sister and a theater major with dreams of starring on Broadway. Carson has been Brayden's best friend since elementary school, so the three of them have known each other a long time. I'm not sure when they got together, because apparently there was some sneaking around going on. All I know is that Brayden wasn't happy about their relationship when he found out about it, but he seems to have mellowed.

And lastly, there's Crosby and Brooke. It's funny, because they seem like opposites in every way. I've caught sight of Crosby on campus, and he's always struck me as dark and moody. Add the lip ring into the mix and the girls at Western go wild for him.

With the exception of Brooke. She hated Crosby with the passion of a thousand burning suns. After she broke up with his roommate, Andrew, they somehow became friends. And then more. They're really good together. She has the power to smooth out all his hard edges.

Since Demi and I went to the same high school and played soccer together, we've known each other for more than a decade. Now that I've been dating Asher for a while, I've gotten to know all the other girls and consider them my friends. They've turned out to be ones I can rely on and are there for me when I need them.

I never realized how lonely my existence was until the blond football player forced his way into my life. Not in a million years would I have thought we had anything in common or could even strike up a friendship. And yet, we've turned out to be so much more.

I have no idea what will happen in the future, but we've spent a lot of time talking about it. For me, there's only Asher, and I think he feels the same. In fact, I know he does. At every turn, he continues to prove how much he loves me. I couldn't have asked for a better man. Maybe I didn't need him to sweep into my life and rescue me, but I'm so glad he did.

"What are you thinking about?" he asks, breaking into the whirl of my thoughts.

I flash a smile before shrugging. "Not much. Just all the things I'm going to do when I finally get you alone tonight."

Heat sparks to life in his blue eyes, turning them a darker shade. "Oh yeah? Care to share?"

"Nope." I shake my head. "There's nothing I love more than teasing him. "It's a secret. You'll just have to wait and see."

He glances at his watch. "So…ten more minutes and we can get the hell out of here, right?"

Laughter gurgles up in my throat. "I was thinking more like an hour. It is, after all, a party to celebrate your success."

"You know what I think? That you're trying to kill me," he grumbles, pretending to pout.

"Maybe." My smile broadens.

Kill him?

No way. I love him too much for that.

But tease and torment him?

Abso-fucking-lutely.

EPILOGUE

ASHER

 *wo years later...*

THE CLOSER I get to our apartment, the more I have to force down my growing erection. Ever since rolling out of bed this morning, I've had Lola on my brain, and I can't wait to get my hands on her. No matter how many times I have that girl, it's never enough.

I always want more.

Actually, I want everything.

Am I slightly obsessed with my fiancée?

Yup. And I'll make no apologies for it, either.

After being together for two years, I can't imagine a life without her filling it. She makes everything worthwhile. The man I am now at twenty-four is lightyears away from the one I was at twenty-one. When I look back, I almost don't recognize that person.

In hindsight, I was a bonehead. Other than my attention being focused on football, I was directionless. I played a lot of video games, smoked a shit ton of pot, drank an equal amount of beer, and screwed around with groupies. None of them ever made a lasting impression or meant anything to me. It was just a way to burn time. I coasted through both high school and college, never bothering to apply myself.

Sometimes, I look back and wonder what the hell Lola saw in me. Why would she even give a guy like me the time of day?

Then, I remember how I forced my way into her life and struck a deal she couldn't refuse. That's when everything changed. I got a glimpse into her life and saw just how hard she busted her ass, trying to hold everything together. All that responsibility heaped on her slender shoulders made me want to step up and be someone worthy of her.

Without Lola standing by my side, believing in me, I wouldn't be the man I am today. For her, I want to be the very best version of myself.

And you know what? I think I am. I like the person I've gradually evolved into.

As soon as I shove open the door to our apartment and step over the threshold, female laughter greets my ears.

That's when I remember Lola is having a pizza and movie night with Kylie.

Yup…you heard that correctly. Ever since the surgery, the two girls have become surprisingly close. I'd read about the possibility of that happening when I researched the procedure. For obvious reasons, I didn't expect it to occur with these two.

It all started with a simple text. Kylie reached out, thanking her for the kidney and checking in to make sure everything was all right. After a month of messaging back and forth, they decided to meet for lunch and a friendship sprung up from there.

Occasionally, we'll get together with Kylie's family, but Lola's relationship with Tony and Charlotte is still strained. I don't see that changing anytime soon. But Lola hasn't let that stop her from developing more of one with Kylie and Antonio. Before we moved, we'd pick them up and take them mini golfing or to the movies. No matter what happens with Tony, I'm glad Lola has been able to connect with her half-siblings. It's been good for all three of them.

April of senior year, I was drafted to Nashville in the first round. We spent a few weeks apartment hunting and then moved before training camp started in July. Since Lola didn't want to leave her mother alone, we found an apartment within walking distance from ours. The change has been good for Mariana. For the most part, she's been stable, holding down a job and receiving the mental health care she needs to be independent and flourish. There are still ups and downs, but there are more ups than downs. And that's been nice to see.

Kylie flew out to visit us several times during her senior year of high school and fell in love with the city. We took her on a few college visits, and she decided to attend Tennessee State University. This is her freshman year, and she's living in the dorms. Although, you wouldn't know it by how often she's here. Lola decorated a bedroom for her to stay in when she visits.

Which I'm totally cool with.

Except when I want my girl all to myself.

Like right now.

I walk into the living room and find them sitting on the floor with an open box of pizza and a ton of bridal magazines spread out around them. I proposed six months ago, and they've been busy planning not only the wedding but the bachelorette party. There's been a lot of talk about party buses that cruise around the city, going from one bar to another. Kylie might not be twenty-one, but she's the one spearheading this night out with Demi, Sydney, Sasha, Elle, Brooke and Carmen.

Just to be clear…there's no way in hell I'm allowing that to happen. Nashville is worse than Vegas. I'm trying to cajole Kylie into planning a combined bachelor/bachelorette party, but so far, that's been a no-go. I'll be stepping up my game with bribery.

They both glance up from the glossy pages they're pouring over.

"Hey," Lola says with an easy smile.

If I've transformed over the previous two years, so has she. Lola is so much more open with a sunnier disposition. She's quick to laughter and smiles. I guess that's what happens when you don't have the weight of the world resting on your shoulders.

"Hey, yourself."

"How was practice, babe?" she asks.

The endearment has everything inside me softening. It's not like I haven't heard it trip off her tongue a thousand times before, but still...

I love it.

Love that I'm her man.

And she's my woman.

My plans for the evening might have been placed on the back-burner, but the need to lay my hands on her has only intensified. Once I've swallowed up the distance between us, she tilts her face upward until my mouth can sweep across hers.

"It was good," I murmur. "Missed you today." My gaze flicks to Kylie. "Kinda forgot you were having a girls' night."

The way her lips curve against mine tells me that she knows exactly why I'm making the comment. It's just another thing I love about her. She gets me. Most of the time, she knows what I'm thinking before I do.

My voice drops, becoming husky. "I can't wait to get you alone."

"Just in case you're wondering," Kylie says loudly, "I can totally hear you."

"How much longer is the kid going to be here?" I grumble, shooting her a frown.

Unaffected by my question or disposition, Kylie grins. She's become so much more vibrant since the transplant and it's nice to see.

"Didn't your wife-to-be mention that I'm spending the weekend?" She gives me a look full of innocence before cocking her head and fluttering her lashes.

What?

With narrowed eyes, I glance at Lola for confirmation. When she nods, pressing her lips together to keep them from trembling, I groan.

"We have a lot of wedding planning to do," Lola says with a chuckle. "Decisions need to be made."

"Especially for the bachelorette party," Kylie adds with a smirk.

"We're having a combined shindig, remember, kid?"

"Nope." She shakes her head. "Don't think so." There's a pause. "Unless, of course, you'll let me borrow your brand-new ride to take back to campus for the week."

"The Lambo?" I ask, voice rising. "Are you out of your damn mind?"

She lifts her shoulders. "Just checking."

"That's a hard no."

"Did I mention the cowboy strip club I found? They wear boots, a big ole hat and a banana hammock."

With a growl, I bare my teeth.

Lola pops to her feet before wrapping her arms around me. When I continue to glare at Kylie, she nips at my chin until my gaze swings to her. There's a shit ton of laughter dancing in her dark eyes. "You know she's just teasing, right? I've already agreed to the combined party."

My muscles loosen as I jerk a brow. "Promise?"

"Yup." She rises onto the tips of her toes and presses her lips to mine. "You're the only stripping cowboy I want to see."

"Can I just wear my Stetson and shitkickers?"

"Now there's an image I won't be able to get out of my head," she says with a chuckle.

"Save a horse and ride a cowboy, am I right?"

Lola bursts out laughing before pressing her lips to mine.

"So…what time is the kid gonna hit the sheets so I can have you all to myself?"

"I can still hear you," Kylie singsongs from the floor where she's leafing through a magazine.

"I don't care," I say in the same high-pitched tone.

In fact…

Lola gasps when I sweep her into my arms and stalk toward the hallway where our bedroom is located.

"Hey, where are you going?" Kylie calls after us.

"Mommy and Daddy need a little alone time. You'll have to occupy yourself for about twenty minutes."

I kick the door to our room closed with my foot before she can respond.

Lola arches a brow when I grin. "Mommy and Daddy, huh?"

"Sure, at some point in the not-so-distant future." I jerk my head toward the living room. "We'll practice by taking care of the kid. Lord knows she's here often enough."

Her expression grows serious. "You don't mind, do you?"

"Of course not. Especially if it makes you happy."

Her lips drift across mine. "I love you, Asher Stevens."

"I love you, too, soon-to-be Mrs. Stevens."

She pulls away just enough to search my eyes. "What if I want to keep my last name?"

I shrug. "Then I guess I'll be banging Lola Diaz for the rest of my life."

She smirks. "I guess you will."

With that decided, I carry her to the bed and make sweet love to my soon-to-be-wife.

And yeah…it lasts a little longer than twenty minutes, but who's counting?

Want to read more of Lola & Asher? Signup for my newsletter and receive an exclusion bonus epilogue for free!
Do it here -) Get your FREE copy of Campus Legend Bonus Epilogue (bookfunnel.com)

Coming Soon!

Prince of Hawthorne Prep (Austin's Story) 11/08/22
https://books2read.com/princeofhawthorneprep

Western Wildcats Hockey (Ryder's Story) 07/11/23
https://books2read.com/westernwildcats

KING OF HAWTHORNE PREP

SUMMER

My gaze wanders over the water as white-capped waves roll rhythmically toward the sandy shore. When the wind picks up, a warm breeze rustles through my hair, and I tip my face toward the sun before stretching.

Could life get any better than this?

Doubtful.

A family friend was kind enough to let us borrow their beach house in Door County for the week. Mom and Dad surprised us with the impromptu vacation a few days before we were supposed to leave.

The house we're staying at isn't like one of the newly renovated million-dollar monstrosities that flank us with their gargantuan square footage, swanky pools, and perfectly groomed lawns. But it's steps from the beach and has breathtaking views of Lake Michigan. At just fifteen hundred square feet, this house has three cramped bedrooms, an outdated kitchen, and a ton of seashell décor. Even so, there's something charming about it.

Sweat beads my forehead as I haul myself from the chair I'm sprawled on and saunter to the water's edge. It might look as inviting as the Caribbean cast in varying shades of cerulean and turquoise, but it doesn't feel like it. Especially when my skin has been crispifying for hours beneath the sweltering sun.

A breath hisses from my lips as the frigid liquid rushes past my ankles. The first couple of steps are the worst. As soon as numbness sets in, it gets better. Braving the water, I continue forward as the waves swirl around my calves. I do a little dance, bouncing up and down on my toes, trying to get used to the cold as it sinks into my bones.

I force myself to move deeper until the water reaches my hips.

It's now or never.

With that brief pep talk, I suck in a breath and dive beneath a wave as it peaks and curls. Water rushes around me, instantly chilling my overheated flesh. After a moment, I break through to the surface and expel the lungful of air from my body.

It's easier to submerge myself the second time as I dive to the bottom before trailing my fingers through the fine-grained sand in search of clamshells. When my lungs burn, I pop up again before floating on the surface so the sun can warm my skin. With my eyes closed, I stretch my hands and legs, allowing the waves to rock my body. My mind drifts as the rhythmic motion lulls me to a contented place. Every once in a while, I lift my head and search for our little blue one-story cottage to make sure I haven't drifted to far down the shore.

My plan is to make the most of our little beach vaca before returning to Chicago next weekend. There's so much that needs to be accomplished before senior year begins in the fall.

A couple of months ago, I registered for an introductory astronomy class at a local university about thirty minutes from the house. Next on the agenda are campus visits. I've scheduled tours for the University of Chicago, Northwestern, and the University of Michigan in Ann Arbor. My three dream schools have impressive astronomy programs. To round out the summer, I've snagged a volunteer position at the Adler Planetarium. I'm scheduled to start next Monday at nine o'clock sharp.

Long after my fingers turn pruney, I drag myself from the water.

As I trudge toward shore, a bleached clamshell glints in the sunlight from the bottom and catches my attention. Stilling my movements, I bend over to inspect it. A wave crashes over me, stirring up the sand and covering the shell. Once the debris settles, I turn, brushing my fingers across the bottom until they land on it again.

"Nice view."

I yelp and swing around, straightening to my full height only to come face-to-face with the most gorgeous boy I've ever seen. My breath gets lodged at the back of my throat as his mahogany-colored eyes pierce mine with unwavering intensity. Rooted in place, it's all I can do to take in the thick slashes of his eyebrows before my gaze slides to the slant of high cheekbones, and then on to a perfect cupid's bow of a mouth.

Damn.

He's seriously hot.

Like...*way out of my league* hot.

My heart riots painfully against my chest as I continue to stare. His brows rise as humor sparks to life in his eyes.

Is he waiting for a response?

Did he ask a question, and I wasn't paying attention? I hit the mental rewind button and quickly sift through our limited conversation.

Nice view.

Nice view?

Wasn't I bent over at the time with my ass in the air?

Heat slams into my cheeks with the force of a tsunami. That's *exactly* the pose I'd been striking. When he said *nice view*, he'd been commenting on my behind. The very same behind barely covered by a thin strip of fabric because the beach has been fairly empty since we arrived on Saturday. This guy is one of the few people I've seen.

"Ummm, thanks," I force myself to respond.

His lips slide into a smirk as if I've amused him.

I need to pull it together before I humiliate myself any further. Although, let's be honest, that ship has already set sail. Right now, I'm operating strictly in damage control mode.

Is it possible that he hasn't noticed my awkwardness?

Any chance of clinging to that unlikely prospect is blown out of the water when he tilts his head. "Did you just thank me for admiring your ass?"

All right, so he noticed.

The heat radiating from my face intensifies a few hundred degrees until self-combustion seems likely. Not to mention, welcome.

"Yeah," I mumble, attempting to rip my gaze from his, but that proves to be impossible. It's as if I've become ensnared by the dark depths assessing me in such a forthright manner. "Apparently I did."

The sound of his deep chuckle reverberates throughout my entire body before darting straight to my—

"I'm Kingsley." He steps forward, closing some of the distance between us. His proximity makes my heart pound faster. "And you are?"

Humiliated?

Embarrassed?

Mortified?

It's a dealer's choice.

"Summer," I mutter instead. When you daydream about talking with a really hot guy, this isn't exactly how you picture it playing out.

Relief rushes from my lungs when his gaze flicks from me to the house I'm standing in front of. There's something powerful about his stare, leaving me to feel as if he's able to pick through all my private thoughts, and it's a disconcerting sensation. I want to run and hide, but my feet refuse to move. I'm frozen in place.

He points at the house on the dunes. "Is that yours?"

"Yes." I clear my throat along with those disconcerting thoughts. "We're renting for the week."

He nods as his attention returns to me where it stays put. That same feeling of nervousness fills me. "Who knows, maybe I'll see you around, Summer."

A wave of heat wafts over me at the sound of my name sliding from his lips. I tamp down the response and shrug, trying to play it cool even though it's much too late for that.

"Yeah, maybe."

He flashes a wide grin as if not fooled by my nonchalance before taking off at a brisk pace down the beach.

Now that his attention is no longer focused on me, I'm free to look my fill as all those well-honed muscles shift and bunch as he jogs away. We're talking broad shoulders with a broad, muscular back that tapers into a trim waist. Loose black athletic shorts cover his trunk and thighs. My gaze drops, wanting to commit every detail to memory. Damn, even his calves are well-defined.

There's no way a guy built like that is in high school. He's definitely in college. I'd like to know what university he attends so I can submit an application. As his figure grows smaller in the distance, I realize I don't even care if they offer astronomy as a major.

I chuckle and shake my head at the thought of planning my future around a boy I spoke with for all of two minutes.

Never.

Going.

To.

Happen.

I have plans. Lots of them. And I would never derail a single one for a guy.

No matter how good-looking he is.

Once the boy fades from sight, I blink out of my thoughts and head back to the house. In all likelihood, I'll never see him again.

Want to read more of Summer and Kingsley's story?
You can check it out here -)
https://books2read.com/u/4A7K8p

KING OF CAMPUS

IVY

Ladies, and a few guys as well, ;) keep those Roan King sightings pouring in. Especially the ones of him at football practice. Hot, sweaty, with an extra shot of gorgeous is exactly how I take my Roan King. Don't mind me while I type away with one hand... KingOfCampus.com

"*H*oney," I holler at the top of my lungs before kicking the door shut, "*I'mmmm home!*"

Those words are met with a loud shriek as Lexie flies around the corner before hurtling her small curvy body at me. I'm given roughly two seconds to drop my bags in anticipation of impact. She's lucky I have fairly decent—

The breath gets knocked out of me as we both go crashing to the floor.

Apparently, reflexes are no match when that much force and weight are careening toward you at the speed of light. Physics, I'm guessing, is exactly how I end up sprawled on my back with my best friend and roommate spread out on top of me in our brand-spanking-new apartment. There's a completely manic light filling her big brown eyes. Matching the look, I can't help but beam up at her because it is so freaking good to see her gorgeous face.

It's been precisely fifteen months since we've been in the same room together. Actually, it's been fifteen months since we've been on the same continent. I spent my sophomore year of college studying abroad in Paris.

Needless to say, it was as amazing and spectacular as you'd imagine it would be. Even thinking about it leaves me with a tiny pang of nostalgia for the life I'd left behind.

"Damn, now that's hot! Can I snap a shot for my wallpaper?"

We turn to stare at the tall, good looking male grinning…or maybe the correct term would be—*leering* down at us. His eyes slide oh-so-slowly over our entwined bodies as if he's trying to singe this moment into his memory for all eternity. But it's not in a pervy way…what the heck am I saying? Of course, it's in a pervy way. Which is precisely when I realize that my dear friend, Lexie, seems to be missing the lower half of her outfit.

Yep…she's only wearing panties.

She smothers a giggle before clearing her throat. Rather impressively, her voice whips out in a perfect imitation of a mother scolding her three-year-old toddler. "You damn well better not snap a picture or you won't be seeing this ass for a very long time." To emphasize this point, she gives it a little shake and her boyfriend groans in response.

"Please?" There's a whole lot of whine filling his deep masculine voice. Which is kind of hilarious because he's well over six feet tall and is seriously broad in the chest and shoulders. This one is definitely all man. Lexie, of course, filled me in via Facetime on the football playing boyfriend she acquired about seven months ago. Needless to say, she wasn't exaggerating.

He's pretty damn hot.

If you're into big and muscly.

Which I'm not going to lie… I am.

"The mental snapshot you're burning into your brain will have to suffice."

Folding his muscular arms in front of an equally solid looking chest, he grumbles under his breath, "You always have to be such a hard ass."

Lexie gives me a little wink. "You wouldn't have it any other way, babe."

"True," he sighs in agreement, "very true."

Since Lexie isn't showing any indication of removing herself from my person anytime soon, I'm forced to point out the obvious. "You might want to get off me before your boyfriend has an embarrassing moment in his shorts."

I'm joking, of course.

Sort of.

"You don't have to get off on my account," he quickly chimes in as he continues to ogle us.

Lexie rolls her eyes at me.

"Have I mentioned just how hot you look in that thong?" His voice sounds all heated up and I'm seriously considering shoving Lexie off me before something unfortunate, not to mention awkward, happens and I'm no longer able to look this dude in the eyes again.

"Jeez, Lex, did you have to molest me while only wearing a thong?" No wonder her boyfriend is all but sporting a woody over there.

"Be happy you didn't arrive ten minutes later, I wouldn't be wearing anything at all."

I shake my head to loosen that mental image from my brain. "That wasn't something I needed to know."

Continuing to grin, Lexie smacks my lips with a big wet sloppy kiss. "Goddamn but I missed you, Ivy." Then she does her damnedest to squeeze the very life out of me before rolling gracefully to her side.

"I'm glad to be back, too." As the words automatically spill from my mouth, I realize that I don't necessarily mean them. There's a large part of me that wishes I were still living my life in Paris. With an ocean between me and my dad, I didn't have to dwell on him and the new family he created for himself so quickly after Mom died.

Dad's life carried on while mine fell apart. Even though it's been five years since she died, the ache still feels painfully tender.

Returning to Barnett means that I no longer have an excuse not to visit them.

Shaking those thoughts away, I realize I'm still sprawled on the carpeted floor. I blink my eyes a few times as a handsome face peers down at me before crinkling into a large friendly smile. I don't bother hoisting myself up just yet. Instead, I say in my most formal tone, "Mr. Sullivan, I presume."

His grin intensifies, making him appear even more striking than I'd originally thought. Lexie had gushed about how gorgeous her new guy was. And it's not like I didn't believe her, but it's obvious she wasn't exaggerating.

Like at all.

Because Dylan Sullivan is seriously hot.

Golden blond hair, deep brown eyes, sculpted jaw, and athletic body.

According to Lexie, he treats her like a total princess. Which is exactly how it should be. Lexie deserves someone who appreciates how smart, loyal, and gorgeous she is. She's a damn good friend and I'm lucky to have her in my life.

"The one and only," he beams in response, throwing a flirty wink in for good measure.

Oh, this guy is totally dangerous.

Could they be more perfectly suited to one another?

I absolutely love it.

"Umm, isn't your father Dylan Sullivan the first?"

He shrugs his broad shoulders. Self admittedly, I'm kind of a shoulder and arm girl myself. And Dylan Sullivan certainly has nicely chiseled ones.

"Shhh, you're ruining the moment, babe."

That being said, Dylan offers me a hand, which I grab hold of, before being hauled off the floor and set back onto my sandaled feet. I dust my backside off before my gaze slides to Lexie. The unexpected glassy sheen of tears shining in her big brown eyes has my own widening in confusion.

"Lex, why are you—"

I don't get a chance to wrap my lips around the last word before she's hurtling herself in my direction. Her arms slip around my body before tugging me close.

"I missed you, Ivy-girl," she whispers fiercely against my ear, "so damn much! Fifteen months is a long time to stay away. Don't ever leave me like that again."

I'm not normally an emotional person, but her heartfelt words have me choking up and I squeeze her to me.

She pulls back to search my eyes before admitting quietly, "I was afraid you might decide to stay over there."

That just goes to show you how well Lexie knows me. What I don't mention is that I tried my damnedest to make that happen. To finish out college, find a permanent place to live, a dance gig, all so I could postpone coming home indefinitely. Being back here, even though this is a new apartment, still reminds me that my mom is dead, and my dad has moved on and I no longer have a home to return to.

Not one that feels like home used to feel.

"I'm just so glad you're finally back."

"Me, too," I whisper as hot licks of emotion prick the back of my eyes. I hug her tightly one last time before releasing her.

Lexie and I have been best friends since fourth grade when her family moved in down the block from mine. We made it through middle and high school with our friendship intact and decided to apply at some of the same colleges so we could room together. Luckily, Barnett was on both of our short lists. It has a highly regarded fashion design program for Lexie and a kickass dance program for me.

There's absolutely no one in this world I can count on like Lexie Abbott. I'm actually a little ashamed of myself for failing to remember that. In trying to escape all the painful memories, I forgot about the good stuff, too.

Lexie backs up until she's standing directly in front of Dylan. As soon as she's close enough, he wraps those huge arms around her before pulling her flush against the front of his body. Looking ridiculously contented, he settles his chin on top of her head like he's done it a hundred times before.

Like it's the most natural thing in the world.

I can't help but feel thrilled that Lexie has found someone who appreciates the amazing woman she's grown into.

Unwilling to get anymore sappy than I already have, I shake my head. "Do you two come with barf bags? I've only been here for ten minutes and you're already making me sick to my stomach."

They both flash big cheesy grins at me. I want to roll my eyes before sticking my finger down my throat like I'm going to puke. "I suppose you're going to be practically living here with us?" Yep, I can already see how this will go. Dylan will be our unofficial apartment mascot.

With big innocent eyes, she says, "Didn't I mention that Dylan lives in the apartment next to us with two guys from the football team?"

"Nope," I shake my head, "you definitely did not mention that. I guess that makes things convenient."

"Totally convenient," Dylan adds with a sly grin aimed in my direction.

This time, I actually roll my eyes. "So which room is mine?"

In her exuberance, Lexie all but jumps out of Dylan's arms before leading me down a short hallway. As I trail after her, I'm reminded that she's only wearing a thong.

I mean, sure, she has a great ass but still...

"Er, maybe you should put your shorts back on before you give me the grand tour." Out of the corner of my eye, I see Dylan open his mouth. My narrowed gaze slices to his. "Don't even say it," I warn.

Biting her lip, Lexie stifles another laugh before dashing into her bedroom. In twenty seconds flat she rejoins us sporting tiny white shorts. Then she leads the way into a sunny little room before doing her best auto show model imitation as she gestures with wide sweeping movements to all the wonderful amenities my room has to offer.

She points toward the two large windows lining the wall. "Look at all the gorgeous sunlight that pours in!" Then she throws open the bi-fold closet doors. "And a humongous closet for all the clothes you brought back from Paris." Her arms drop to her sides as she swivels toward me. Her auto show model imitation is forgotten in lieu of possible new stylish European clothing. "You *did* bring me back some clothes, right?"

For a moment, my eyes travel around the room, taking everything in. It's not huge by any means but after living in Paris, it sure feels like it is. I'm used to about a third of the space. So this feels pretty damn luxurious. I can't imagine what I'm going to do with all this space to myself. Then my eyes fall to the double sized mattress shoved up against the far wall and my heart actually swells with unfettered joy.

Oh my god, it's so big! I've been sleeping on a twin bed for the last fifteen months. I literally can't wait to spread out on that huge mattress. Maybe roll around a bit. Make some snow angels...minus the snow. Already I'm looking forward to hitting the sheets tonight.

I spent a little more than eight hours on a plane with a two-hour layover in Amsterdam. And France is six hours ahead of us. So, I'd like nothing more than to fall into bed for a nice long nap.

When I don't respond, a thread of worry weaves its way through her voice. "Ivy?" Her concerned tone snaps me right out of my thoughts.

"Of course I did," I say. "There's a short, thigh length pleated skirt, two hand woven scarves, one cashmere sweater, a gorgeous black knit top and these creamy trouser pants that your ass will thank me for."

If watching Lexie sprawled out on top of me, wearing nothing more than a lacy little thong and a tank top is Dylan's idea of a wet dream, hearing about all the beautiful clothes I brought back from Paris is hers. We're talking flushed cheeks and dilated eyes.

And yes, it's entirely possible Lexie could have an embarrassing moment in her shorts. Although I hope not.

"Oh, I can't wait to see them," she squeals in delight, practically jumping up and down with unbridled enthusiasm.

Fashion design is Lexie's life. She was a budding fashionista way back in middle school before I ever cared about what top went with what bottoms. Thank goodness for Lexie or I probably would have been much more of a walking fashion disaster than I was.

I scraped together enough money and perused a few vintage boutiques to find unique pieces I knew she wouldn't be able to get here in the States. I hope she loves them half as much as I think she will.

"What about some hot French lingerie?" her boyfriend asks.

Since Dylan is standing directly behind Lexie, she doesn't bother turning around to admonish him. Instead, she rams her elbow into his gut. He grunts in response. If she hadn't done it, I probably would have.

"Just stand there and look pretty," she mutters under her breath.

My lips twitch because he is definitely pretty.

Lexie gives me a little wink as if she can read my mind. "Don't let his good looks fool you, he's smart, too."

Of course he is.

Because gorgeous and smart are exactly the kind of guys Lexie attracts. While I, on the other hand, had the sad misfortune to fall for a hot athletic jerk who assured me he was going to remain faithful to his study-abroad-girlfriend when in actuality, he started hooking up with other girls as soon as above-mentioned-girlfriend was out of the country.

I've had the last fourteen and a half months to get over Finn McKenzie. And I have. I am totally over him. Unfortunately, he's been calling and texting almost relentlessly for the last week, which means he's been occupying my thoughts way more than I'd like.

Perhaps I should say he's been *trying* to call and text. I haven't bothered to pick up his calls or respond to his rather lengthy and apologetic text messages. I mean, can you seriously believe that? The guy has some nerve reaching out to me after what he did. Is he so delusional as to think we're going to pick up where we left off now that I'm back at Barnett?

Apparently, he is.

We'd been together for about six months before I left for Europe. And yes, I knew having a long-distance relationship would be difficult, but I was willing to give it a shot. I'd grown to like Finn. I hadn't been gone more than two weeks when Lexie Facetimed me about what Finn had been busy doing...which had been, in case you're wondering, other girls.

And that, my friends, had been the end of that.

Lexie's advice was to forget about my cheating asshole of an ex by hooking up with a bunch of hot French guys.

I hooked up with two semi-hot French dudes and buried myself in dance which was the reason I'd been accepted to study at the Conservatoire de Paris in the first place. After a few months, my heartache lessened. I stopped thinking about Finn, my dad, his new wife, their kids, and I concentrated on soaking up everything I possibly could.

It took some time to adjust but after two months, I found myself with an amazing new life in a city renowned for its art and culture. There was no way I was going to allow anything to ruin this once in a lifetime opportunity. Right around the year mark, I stopped thinking about Lexie and returning to Barnett University and started wondering if maybe I could live here for the rest of my life.

Or, at the very least, the next few years.

When I mentioned this possibility to my dad, he made it perfectly clear that he would not be footing the bill for a life in Paris and said, in no uncertain terms, he wanted me back at Barnett come August. Undeterred by his directive, or perhaps because of it, I'd searched for enough scholarship and grant money to pay for me to continue studying in Paris. Needless to say, I hadn't been able to pull it off which is exactly why I was back at Barnett for my junior year.

"So, do you like it?"

My eyes swing back to Lexie who is standing there with all this hopeful expectation lighting up her face. A tiny smile tugs at the corners of my lips because it really is good to see her after all this time apart. "It's absolutely perfect."

Looking very much like the best friend I left behind fifteen months ago, a huge grin spills across her beautiful face before she hurtles herself at me for a third time.

Want to read more of Roan & Ivy's story?
You can check it out here -)
https://books2read.com/u/bPX7WY

ABOUT THE AUTHOR

Jennifer Sucevic is a USA Today bestselling author who has published twenty-two New Adult novels. Her work has been translated into German, Dutch, and Italian. Jen has a bachelor's degree in History and a master's degree in Educational Psychology. Both are from the University of Wisconsin-Milwaukee. She started out her career as a high school counselor. She currently lives in the Midwest with her husband and four kids.

If you would like to receive regular updates regarding new releases, please subscribe to her newsletter here-
Jennifer Sucevic Newsletter (subscribepage.com)

Or contact Jen through email, at her website, or on Facebook.
sucevicjennifer@gmail.com
Want to join her reader group? Do it here -)
J Sucevic's Book Boyfriends | Facebook

Social media links-
https://www.tiktok.com/@jennifersucevicauthor
www.jennifersucevic.com
https://www.instagram.com/jennifersucevicauthor
https://www.facebook.com/jennifer.sucevic
Amazon.com: Jennifer Sucevic: Books, Biography, Blog, Audiobooks, Kindle
Jennifer Sucevic Books - BookBub

www.ingramcontent.com/pod-product-compliance
Lightning Source LLC
Chambersburg PA
CBHW051121190726
48290CB00006B/1625